When Mankind=Unkind

I was halfway through the stables when I found myself staring at four guys who didn't look very friendly. Morley's advice to watch my back was sinking in. Or maybe I was just in a bad mood. Or maybe I was just impatient. I didn't ask what anybody wanted—I spun.

My oak headknocker dropped the guy behind me without a sound. I turned, dropped, and gave the next guy a love tap in the knee just as he was getting a fist wound up. The two left standing, seeing their comrades go down, grabbed a pitchfork and a shovel. Now, a pitchfork and shovel are unpleasant, but neither was specifically designed to hurt people.

My stick, on the other hand, has no other reason for existing.

I charged.

Glen Cook

FADED STEEL HEAT

A Garrett Files Novel

A ROC BOOK

ROC
Published by New American Library, a division of
Penguin Putnam Inc., 375 Hudson Street,
New York, New York 10014, U.S.A.
Penguin Books Ltd, 27 Wrights Lane, London W8 5TZ, England
Penguin Books Australia Ltd, Ringwood, Victoria, Australia
Penguin Books Canada Ltd, 10 Alcorn Avenue,
Toronto, Ontario, Canada M4V 3B2
Penguin Books (N.Z.) Ltd, 182–190 Wairau Road, Auckland 10, New Zealand

Penguin Books Ltd, Registered Offices: Harmondsworth, Middlesex, England

First published by Roc, an imprint of New American Library,
a division of Penguin Putnam Inc.

First Printing, June 1999
10 9 8 7 6 5 4 3 2 1

For all the wonderful people of
the Baltimore SF Society
but especially
for
Sue Who
& her
Little New Who

1

It ought to start with a girl. The best ones always do. She ought to be kick the lid off your coffin gorgeous. She ought to be in hot water right up to her cute little . . . ears. She shouldn't quite know why, or maybe she just won't say why the guys with the bent noses are after her. She ought to have eyes full of mischief and not be afraid to get mischievous with the right guy.

That's the way it ought to be. But this time it started with *three* darling gremlins, any one of whom could sprain a set of male eyeballs at thirty paces.

Oh. I'm Garrett, aka Mr. Right. Although a jealous acquaintance might lie about it, I'm six feet two inches of handsome ex-Marine. Yeah, sure my face has a few nicks and dings but those just add character. They let the frantic cutie in the deep gravy know she's found a stand-up guy. Or maybe, a guy too dim not to lead with his chops.

Dean, my cook and housekeeper and Door-Answerer General and (a legend in his own mind) majordomo, was out. I had to answer the tap-tap-tapping myself. It was noon. I'd been enjoying my first cup of tea. I was still a little tousled, wearing my charming rogue look. I had treated myself to a late nap in celebration of having survived an infestation of Great Old Ones, olden gods more like world-devouring termites than the woosie celestial accountants populating today's Dream Quarter.

What the heck. Real women like their fellows a little rough around the edges.

I put a bloodshot peeper to the peephole. The day looked better right away. "Eureka!" My stoop was overrun with lovelies cooked up from all the right ingredients. Youth. Beauty. Curve and flow and swoop to make drooling geometricians opt for a very specialized area of study. And right behind them hulked several ugly thugs who provided the element of menace.

I flung the door wide. "How lucky can one guy get?"

The blond was Alyx Weider. She gawked like she'd just seen something pop up out of its grave. She was five feet four and sleek as a mink but nature hadn't shorted her on the extras. "Garrett? Is that you?" Like I was wearing a disguise.

"You grew up." She definitely grew up.

The redhead said, "Stop drooling, Garrett." That was Tinnie Tate, professional redhead. And she took her calling seriously. My semi ex-girlfriend. "You'll get the floor all nasty. Dean will make you mop."

This was the first time Tinnie had spoken to me in months. Right away she had to start in on chores.

"You look lovely this morning, darling. Come in. Come in." I eyed the third woman, the brunette. She had done herself a cruel disservice by falling in with Tinnie and Alyx. She wore plain clothing and had taken no special care with her grooming. Tinnie and Alyx made her seem mousy. But only at first glimpse. The sharp eye could tell she was the most gorgeous of the three. I have an eye like a razor.

I didn't recognize her.

Tinnie said, "You're really working at the bachelor business, aren't you?"

"Huh?" Usually I'm armed with a rapier wit—well, actually, a gladius sort of wit—but when Tinnie comes around my brain curdles.

"You look like death on a stick, Garrett. Slightly warmed over." Tinnie has a way with words. Like the guy at the end of the chute at the slaughterhouse has a way with tools.

"That's my honey," I told the crowd. I backed into the house. "Ain't she precious?"

"You got a honey, Garrett, I don't think her name is Tinnie Tate. Unless there's more than one of us."

"Awk!" I said, stricken. "Impossible! You're unique."

"Did you break a leg? Or forget the way to my house? Or forget how to write?"

She had me. The slickest stoat that ever slank couldn't have weaseled out of this one. I'd done one of those things guys do, that they don't know they're doing when they do them and still don't know what they did after they're done, then I'd had the brass-bottomed gall not to rush right over with a public apology. Lately, I have begun to suspect that standing on principle is a strategic error of the first water.

"I think you didn't come here to bicker in front of your friends." I showed her a lot of shiny teeth.

She showed me a scowl that told me, once again, I had everything all wrong but she was going to let it slide for the moment.

This visit was no surprise except in its timing. The ladies had been around to see me before, while I was otherwise preoccupied saving the world. Alyx's daddy had problems. She thought I could unravel them.

Tinnie knows the hours I keep. Bless her sadistic little heart.

Old Man Weider owns the biggest brewery empire in TunFaire. That's because the clever rascal brews the best brew. The first time he hired me I saved him from an inside theft ring that was devouring his business like a raging cancer. He's had me on retainer ever since. He wants me to work for him full-time. I'm not interested in a real job. When you're your own boss you don't have to please anybody but yourself. Though that arrangement doesn't leave much room to pass the blame.

In exchange for my retainer I make frequent surprise visits to the brewery. Random appearances make it difficult for organized villainy to take root again.

In the old days Alyx was a scrawny kid barely threatening to become a heartbreaker. Her older sister, Kittyjo, was a lot more interesting.

Time trudges on. Sometimes it plays a pretty melody.

I tried again. "Let's not argue, Tinnie. I can't possibly win."

"If you know that how come . . ."

"I didn't say you were right." Damn! I knew I'd blown it before I finished saying it.

"Garrett! I . . ."

2

"Quiver me heart!" a voice squawked. "Feast yer glims, mates! It must be heaven! Where do we start?"

"Is that the infamous parrot?" the new girl asked. Alyx and Tinnie glowered into the small front room. They put enough kick into it to freeze water and crack glass. The room opens off the hall to the right just inside the front door. I hadn't remembered to close up before admitting the ladies.

"That's Mr. Big, yes. Trash beak champion of the universe. Ignore him. Otherwise, he'll get excited."

"Excited?"

"He's restraining himself right now."

Tinnie observed, "Garrett calls him the Goddamn Parrot."

How did she know that? The feathered mosquito didn't arrive till after her famous parting tizzy.

Of course. Her effort to twist my mind around till the last sensejuice leaked out didn't mean that she didn't see Dean. And Dean thinks Tinnie is the next best thing to immortality. He's her enthusiastic mole in the garden of my life.

I said, "I'd call him kitty food if I could wring his neck without offending the guy who gave him to me." Someday I'll get even with Morley. But it's going to be tough.

"He's kind of neat," Alyx decided, changing her mind on the fly. "But I wouldn't take him to visit my Aunt Claire."

"Come here, Sugar," the bird squawked. "Awk! Check them hooters! I am in love."

I muttered, "The only goddamn bird in the world with a vocabulary and he uses it up being obnoxious."

"Before you pop trying to find a safe way to ask," Tinnie told me, her finest taunting smile prancing across her lovely lips while she leaned against me and looked up with total green-eyed innocence, "this is Nicks. Giorgi Nicks for Nicholas."

"Hi, Gorgeous Nicks for Nicholas." Whoops! That slip earned me a pinch.

The Goddamn Parrot sang the praises of Alyx Weider in language that would embarrass stevedores. But it was hard to fault his eye.

Tinnie kept looking up and pinching, the devil in her eyes. "Guess what, lover? She's taken."

"Lucky guy. Mr. Big will be devastated." That foul-beaked jungle buzzard had spied Nicks now. Nicks winked at me. She had an incredible smile and eyes as blue as a cloudless sky.

She said, "I'm only engaged, Garrett. I'm not dead."

Alyx whistled. "Nicks!" Tinnie laughed but her eyes narrowed wickedly.

This looked like a good time to run down the street and see if Dean needed help with the groceries.

Nicks said, "Whoops! That didn't come out right. Are you the Garrett Tinnie brags about all the time?"

"Last time I checked that was still the name. I'm not sure about the brag part."

That earned me a fingernail in the ribs from the nearest beautiful redhead, who observed, "It's going to be mud if you're not careful."

"Just don't put me in the middle of anything, darling."

Alyx said, "Nicks is just being Nicks. She can't help it."

I said, "Huh?"

"Nicks flirts. She's been doing it since we were seven. She can't help it. She doesn't mean it. She doesn't realize she's sending come-on signals. Nicks, for heaven's sake. You can get in real trouble out here in the world."

Alyx was right. There's always trouble if a woman shows she's willing when she's not.

I asked, "Did I miss something? Did you spend your whole life in a harem, Nicks?" That isn't a Karentine thing but the rich do have strange ways. Alyx had been incredibly sheltered as a child.

"Practically." The Goddamn Parrot flapped over, settled on her wrist like a falcon in a clown suit. "My father has strong ideas about saving me from the world. The Weiders and a few other families are the only people I've ever met. Till recently."

Alyx said, "She's staying with us, now. Daddy isn't the big ogre he used to be."

He never was with his baby. Alyx always got anything she wanted with just a cute pout.

Nicks used a finger to stroke the top of the jungle chicken's head. The little monster went along enthusiastically. He tilted his head back so she could get a finger under his chin. I'd never seen him take to anyone so wholeheartedly.

I looked to Alyx. I didn't get anything. What was she doing out of the family fortress herself? Old Man Weider must be losing his grip.

Hell, I knew that already. Didn't I? Wasn't that why the toothsome threesome had come? If Max was on top of everything he wouldn't need help and his baby wouldn't be out looking for it.

I shrugged. "I'll find out what I need to know as we go. Let's visit His Nibs, get comfortable, and talk about it."

Tinnie stepped back. She glared at me. "Shouldn't you get dressed first?"

My gal Tinnie, always looking out for my best interest. "Not a bad idea, sweetheart," though I was perfectly happy dressed the way I was. So what if I was a little rumpled? That was part of my rough charm. "Be right back, my lovelies. If you want tea or anything, you'll have to help yourselves. Dean's out shopping. Tinnie, you know where everything is."

Sneaky Garrett. He will get fresh tea brewed by the very viragos who think they've got him in a clean pin.

I trotted upstairs before Tinnie caught on.

3

I descended the stairway wearing my clotheshorse best only to discover skinny old Dean newly returned. He wrinkled his bony nose, shook his bony head, proceeded into the kitchen. Alyx's blue eyes twinkled. "You don't waste much time picking out your clothes, do you?"

Tinnie was in the kitchen. Dean brightened right up. "Miss Tate! This is a pleasant surprise. May I observe that you are looking particularly lovely today?"

"Mr. Creech! You rogue. Of course you may. Somebody ought to notice. Let me help you with that."

I leaned into the kitchen. Damn! The old boy was being victimized by a hugging redhead.

Life ain't fair. Not even a little. Me she pokes and pinches.

A crackling sense of amused anticipation grew around me. Somehow the ladies had both wakened my partner and put him in a good mood. That filled me with foreboding. Eclipses and planetary conjunctions are less common than the Dead Man awakening in a good mood when the house is infested with females.

I took a deep breath.

Here we went again.

I led the ladies into the Dead Man's room, which takes up most of the left-side ground floor of my house, excepting the pantries off the kitchen.

The cuties made themselves right at home. Without asking they dragged chairs out of my office, which is an ambitious closet across the hall from the Dead Man's room. Tinnie perched on the guest's chair. Nicks claimed the comfortable one that belongs behind my desk. I would cherish the warmth forever. Meantime, Alyx decorated the chair I usually use when I'm in with the Dead Man. The Goddamn Parrot still perched on Nicks' hand, nibbling bits of something she offered him. He cooed like a goddamned turtledove.

You might reserve that admiration for Miss Tate. If you were a gentleman. That was my partner, shoving unwanted advice directly into my head.

"But I'm not. She's told me so lots of times." I glared. Alyx and Nicks smiled as though enjoying a private joke. Maybe Old Bones had shared his remarks with the three heartstoppers, not just me.

Perhaps I blushed, slightly. Tinnie sure grinned.

The Dead Man resides in a huge wooden chair at the heart of the biggest room in the house. Usually the room isn't lighted. In his present state he doesn't need light. But the ladies did and had brought lamps in from other rooms.

They shouldn't have bothered.

The Dead Man isn't pretty. That's partly because he isn't really a man. He hails from a rare species called Loghyr who resemble humans only vaguely. He goes four hundred plus pounds, though the vermin keep nibbling off bits so he's probably dropped a few. He's uglier than your sister's last husband and has a snoot like an elephant. It hangs about fourteen inches long. I've never seen a live Loghyr so don't know how they use that.

He was called the Dead Man when I met him, ages ago. One of those clever street names, picked up on account of he has been dead for four hundred years. Somebody stuck a knife in him way back when, probably while he was taking one of his six-month siestas. He's never bothered to explain.

But he is Loghyr and Loghyr do nothing hastily. They especially don't get into a rush about giving up the ghost. I hear four hundred years is far from a record stall.

Nobody knows much about the Loghyr. The Dead Man will babble on for weeks without dropping a hint himself.

I leaned against a set of shelves loaded with souvenirs from old cases and knickknacks the Dead Man likes to grab with a thought and send swooping around if he feels that will rattle a visitor already distressed by his less than appetizing appearance.

Could you not have selected clothing less threadbare? In business it is important to present a businesslike appearance.

Him too? Steel yourself, Garrett. It's teak on Tommy Tucker time with you in the coveted role of Tommy in the brown-bottomed slit trench. "That's how we'll justify my fee."

Fee?

"Money? Gold and silver and copper. That stuff we use to buy beans for me and Dean and keep the leaky roof from leaking on your head? You recall your days in that ruin on Wizard's Reach? With the roof half-gone and the snow blowing in?"

The women looked at me weirdly. Which meant that they were getting only my half of the conversation. But their imaginations were perking.

Of course. You must maintain a businesslike approach—if not a businesslike appearance. But, perhaps, you have overlooked the fact that we have a retainer arrangement with Mr. Weider and are, therefore, expected to provide our services against fees already paid.

"You got a point." The Weider retainer had seen me through numerous dry spells. "Hey, Alyx. Before we worry about anything else, are you here for your dad or you?"

"I'm not sure. He didn't send me but he asked Manvil if they should think about calling you in. This thing will affect the brewery. He might've sent me if it ever occurred to him that a daughter could do something productive. I think he hasn't sent for you just because he's embarrassed to admit that he can't handle everything himself. He's still hoping he can get by without you but I think it's been too late for that for days."

I didn't have a clue what it was all about yet. I glanced at Nicks.

Alyx told me, "Nicks is in it because my brother is in it and they're engaged and she's worried."

What a cruel world it is where a beauty like Nicks wastes herself on a creature like Ty Weider. Though Nicks did not appear excited by her impending nuptials.

She is not. But she does not have the heart to disappoint two sets of parents who have had this alliance planned for twenty years. She has found ways to delay it several times. Now her time has run out.

"And Tinnie?"

"She's my friend, Garrett. She's just here to lend emotional support."

A wise man would not now insist on subjecting all things to a rigorous scrutiny, Garrett.

I have lived with His Nibs so long that even his obscurantisms and obfuscations have begun to make sense. This time he was hanging a codicil on the rule about not looking too closely at politics, sausage manufacture, or the teeth of gift horses. Tinnie was here. I should enjoy that, not go picking the scabs off sores.

"All right. I still don't have a clue. Start at the beginning and tell me everything, Alyx. Even if it doesn't seem important."

"Okay. It's The Call."

I sighed.

It would be.

Already I knew I wasn't going to like any of this.

4

I asked, "What are they doing? Strong-arm stuff? Extortion?"

"Tinnie says you call it protection."

I glanced at the professional redhead, so silent of late. At the moment she wasn't into her favorite role deeply. "They tried it with my uncle, too." She smiled nastily.

I worked for Willard Tate once. He was a tough old buzzard with a herd of relatives willing to do whatever he told them. He wouldn't be threatened. "He sent them packing?"

Tinnie grinned. "You know Uncle Willard. Of course he did. Dared them to come back, too."

"That might not have been too bright. Some human rights gangs are pretty wicked. Alyx. No. Both of you. Was it The Call specifically?"

The Call—as in "call to arms"—is Marengo North English's gang and is the biggest, loudest, best financed, and most vigorously political of the war veterans' groups. The Call includes a lot of wealthy, powerful men unhappy with the direction Karenta is drifting. As far as I knew The Call only raised funds by donation. But they might extend their reach if rowdier, more radical groups began to attract more recruits.

North English has a big ego and a personal agenda that's never been clear.

Alyx said, "Yeah. No. I don't know. They talked to Ty. He claimed he knew some of them. He said they told him Weider's has to contribute five percent of gross receipts to the cause. And we'll have to get rid of any employees who aren't human."

Ty is Alyx's brother. One of three, all older than she is. Two of those three didn't make it back from the Cantard in one piece. The other one didn't make it back at all. I don't like Ty Weider, though for no concrete reason. Maybe it's his relentless bitterness. Though he has a right to be bitter. He gave up a leg for Karenta. The kingdom hasn't given him much in return.

Ty is not unique. Far from it. Just look down any street. But he belongs to a family with wealth and influence. "Why would they take a run at Ty instead of your dad?"

"Daddy doesn't spend much time with the business anymore. Momma is lots sicker. He stays with her. He only goes to the brewery maybe every other day and then mostly he only stays for a little while, talking to people he's known a long time."

"So Ty is more likely to bump into the public." I glanced at the Dead Man. Was he mining the unspoken side of this? He didn't send me a clue. That suggested Alyx was being as forthright as she knew how.

"Yes. But Mr. Heldermach and Mr. Klees are still in charge."

"Of course." Because Ty Weider is no brewmaster and not much of an executive. Because nobody at the brewery likes Ty. Because Heldermach and Klees are more than Weider employees. They are more nearly junior partners. Their investment in the brewery is skill and knowledge. Both operated their own breweries before consolidating with Weider.

The Weider empire isn't just the big brewery downtown, it's a combine of smaller places scattered throughout the city. Most were struggling when Weider took over and rooted out the inefficiencies and bad brewing policies that kept them from prospering.

The best brewmasters and best recipes stayed on.

"Mr. Heldermach and Mr. Klees were there when The Call talked to Ty."

"They were?" I glanced at the Dead Man. He did not contradict Alyx.

Surprise, surprise. The moment she'd mentioned Ty as interlocuter I set a new conclusion-jumping distance record, figuring Ty for trying to scam his own dad.

I'm convinced Ty was at least marginally involved in the skimming operation whose breakup endeared me to Old Man Weider back when. That involved barrels of beer vanishing into thin air and becoming pure profit for those enterprising characters who used that method to reduce overhead in the tavern business. I spent months posing as a worker to unearth what I had. I never nailed Ty. What evidence I did find was all circumstantial and could have been explained away as easily by stupidity and gullibility as by evil intent. I never mentioned him to his father—which, maybe, was one of the services Weider had expected.

Whatever Ty's role, I closed the brewery's bleeding belly wound without any scandal. And I've kept the stitches from tearing loose again. For which the old man has been more than necessarily grateful. He's kept me on that retainer ever since and even sends the occasional lonely keg of Reserve Dark over to spend the holidays.

Though the Dead Man would have explored any thoughts in the area already, I asked, "What do you think about Ty, Alex?"

"I try to make allowances. We all do. Because of his leg." She wouldn't look me in the eye.

"But?"

"Hmmm?"

"I hear a but. A reservation?"

Alyx glanced at Nicks. She looked like she thought she had said too much already. I glared at the Dead Man.

Bingo! *She is concerned about Miss Nicholas' feelings, Garrett.*

"Huh? Why?" I blurted.

The Dead Man seemed amused. He is whenever I stick my foot into my mouth, though I hadn't gotten a good taste of dirty old leather yet here.

Miss Weider conceals a considerable affection for her brother although she does understand why others find him unlikable. She has an even stronger regard for Miss Nicholas. They have been friends from childhood. Miss Weider will not knowingly cause her pain.

For her part, Miss Nicholas does not care to hear evil of her fiancé because she plans to accept this marriage despite having no desire to do so. She will not disappoint the expectations of so many. She consoles herself with the certain knowledge that Ty Weider, although no Prince Charming, stands to be one of the richest men in

*TunFaire. And the wait may not be protracted if there is substance
to the cluster of fears infesting Miss Weider's head.*

I glanced at Nicks, remembered Ty. Money sure can get the
blood moving, too.

Tinnie seemed to be getting sour. I was too introspective to suit
her today. That was a problem most days as far as she was concerned. "All right, Alyx," I said. "The Call made a threat. They
don't have a history of that but there is a first time for every extor-
tionist. What do you want me to do about it?"

"I want you to stop them but I don't think you could do that by
yourself, so I don't really know."

"I can be pretty persuasive." Usually with Morley Dotes and
Saucerhead Tharpe helping me drive my points home.

Alyx didn't hear me. She was too busy talking. "I guess if there's
anything I really need it's for you to watch out for Dad. He was
pretty blunt in public when he heard about the demands. Somebody might want to make him an example."

Exactly.

Tinnie said, "The men who came to our compound did claim to
be from The Call." The Tate clan manufactures footwear. They got
rich making combat boots during the war. "But I don't think they
really were. They were too nervous."

The Dead Man sent, *I have compared the recollections of Miss
Weider and Miss Tate and must submit the possibility that we have
afoot several bold operators moving in where they believe they can
score quickly by exploiting fear and hatred.*

There's nothing so holy some scroat won't try to turn a few
marks on it. "Somebody's trying to scam the rich? They'll have to
stay way ahead of Marengo North English, then."

And I kept right on having trouble getting my mind around the
notion that a honey like Nicks would even talk to Ty Weider.
Maybe I'd just always caught Ty at bad times. Maybe he wasn't as
hopeless as I thought.

5

"Have you done anything?" I asked Alyx. "Besides coming back here till you caught up with me? Did you talk it over with your dad? Or Ty? Or Manvil? Have they done anything?"

"I didn't discuss it with them. Daddy would say it wasn't proper for a lady to take an interest. But if I went to anybody, he'd want me to go to you. Ty, though, will get mad when he finds out. He doesn't want outsiders around. He's argued with Dad about you."

Big surprise. But Ty's likes and dislikes never were high on my list of concerns. "Think he'd cut off my supply of dark?"

Nobody got it. Not even the Dead Man, apparently. So much for a new career in comedy.

Ladies, you must excuse Garrett. The presence of so much loveliness in such tight quarters has disoriented him completely.

Sarky bastard.

Nicks jumped at the Dead Man's first touch but settled down quickly. She had been forewarned.

Tinnie and Alyx showed the nonchalance of old hands.

His Nibs continued, *And I cannot say I blame him this once. I am overwhelmed myself. And I was dead ages before any of you were born.*

What a sweet-talker. "Thank you, Old Bones. Maybe if I shut my eyes and pretend I'm not a robust, hearty, virile young man whose special lady has shunned him mercilessly . . ."

You might consider supplying shovels, high-top boots, and nose plugs, Garrett.

"How sharper than a serpent's tooth. My eyes are sealed. My breathing is almost normal."

Nicks asked, "Is he always like this, Tinnie?"

"He's pretty tame right now. Wait till he wakes up."

"Not a tooth, teeth," I grumbled. "Alyx. Did your dad take this seriously?"

"He's worried. He's been asking our employees what they think about The Call. He's decided we won't hire anybody but veterans."

He never had. But that wouldn't satisfy The Call. Although most human males are veterans not all veterans are human. And Weider never made a distinction. He wouldn't now. He protects his employees like a she-wolf protects her young. Most give him complete loyalty in return. Me, I even drink his beer.

But there are always a rotten few who slip through any screen, or who are brought in by a big wormy apple already loafing in the barrel.

The ladies babbled on but I got nothing out of them. I turned to the Dead Man. He sent: *They are frightened. Time is passing. Nothing has been done to disarm or appease The Call. Apparently there is a deadline unknown even to Miss Alyx.*

Miss Alyx now, huh? I watched the Goddamn Parrot nibble out of Nicks' fingers. "You want that critter, Nicks? Take him. Call him my wedding present."

Alyx broke into laughter.

So maybe I'm not a complete bust as a comic. But it would help to know why they laugh.

"Sorry," Alyx said. "But I had this picture of Mr. Big kibbitzing Ty and Nicks on their wedding night."

That would be something. Unless they tied the bird into a gunnysack and hung the sack out a window. I glanced at Nicks.

She wasn't smiling.

She looked like a young lady who didn't believe in her future at all.

I couldn't disagree with her. But I had that deep prejudice against Ty Weider.

She is an excellent actress, Garrett. Perhaps inside as well as out. Perhaps able to fool even herself. Even I see something different each time I look at her. I have to remind myself to recognize the surface.

"Interesting."

Save your interest for Miss Tate.

"That was my plan."

Stick to it. This matter will become complicated enough without adding the machinations of women scorned. He does not have a high estimation of the fairer species.

Tinnie, I noted, seemed to be daydreaming. Which meant she was communing with the Dead Man. He can do that. He has several distinct minds and can go several directions at once.

I asked Alyx, "Could there be trouble on the shop floor?"

"There's always sympathy for The Call, anywhere you go."

"I doubt they cheer The Call much in Ogre Town or Dwarf Fort or the elven neighborhoods. I haven't seen many ratmen or pixies carrying banners in The Call's parades."

"Well, they wouldn't, would they?"

Maybe there was some rightsist sympathy right there.

From the sounds of it somebody nonhuman was being real unsympathetic to human rights out front right now. The neighborhood attracts more than its share of political debates.

"Alyx. The guys who brought you. They going to hang around?" Some situations can't be managed with cute and beautiful, a wiggle and a giggle.

"They went to lunch. They're supposed to wait out front afterward."

"Good. It's starting to sound excitable out there." The Dead Man evidently wasn't interested in what was going on. He didn't bother to report.

"We could stay till it quiets down." Alyx winked.

"I couldn't stand the heat. I'm about to melt down into a puddle of tallow now."

Garrett.

"Garrett!"

"Ah, Tinnie me love. My hottest of flames. You're awake after all."

Tinnie gave Alyx a look of exasperation. How was she going to get me trained if even her friends encouraged my delinquencies?

Nicks stayed out of it. She concentrated on the Goddamn Parrot.

Except that when I glanced at her she winked, too.

Help.

They do it just to watch you crackle and fry like bacon left too long in too hot a pan.

6

The ladies departed, headed not for the brewery but Tinnie's family compound. The Tates had to be hurting. The recent outbreak of peace had to be terrible for business.

That's the trouble when some darn war goes on too long. Life begins to revolve around it. We live and die by it at home as much as do the soldiers on the battlefields. Now that the fighting is over, except for mopping-up exercises against the last of Glory Mooncalled's raggedy-ass republican partisans, regiments are demobilizing as fast as the navy can haul them home.

These days many jobs belong to nonhumans because we humans went off to war and only a fraction returned. Today's soldiers come home to find there's nothing to come home to.

The door closed behind those three luscious behinds. I returned to the Dead Man's room and settled into my own chair. The seat was still warm. A clash of perfumes hung in the air. I asked, "What's your boy Glory Mooncalled up to?"

Years ago Mooncalled entered the war as a mercenary captain on the Venageti side. Though a successful campaigner, he failed to have been born into the ruling clique of sorcerers and nobles and so was treated badly. He resented that so much he changed sides. He spent the next decade embarrassing and picking off the men who had injured his pride.

His treatment by Karenta's overlords was not much better. He got paid on time but received few honors, however dramatic his victories. He defected again. This time he collected the tribes of the Cantard under the banner of a republic that rejected both Karentine and Venageti territorial claims. He provided spankings to armies from both kingdoms.

But fate wasn't kind. Karenta got some breaks. The Venageti collapsed. Karentine forces began exterminating the republicans.

The peoples of the Cantard immediately began migrating into Karenta, and especially to TunFaire, where their presence only adds to the social stress. Something I stumbled over during a recent case made me suspect that Mooncalled himself was now in TunFaire.

The Dead Man seemed disgruntled. *In all likelihood he is fomenting disorder under the illusion that his past popularity still assures him support amongst the lower classes.*

"You seem disappointed."

Perhaps heroes are best kept at arm's length. Up close their flaws are too easily seen.

The Goddamn Parrot had taken station on his shoulder. Nicks' fault. She'd put him there. I hadn't been able to talk her into taking the flashy little vulture with her.

The bird started to relieve himself.

He ended in a tangle amongst the mementos on the Dead Man's knickknack shelves. He was so startled he could hardly squawk in parrotese. He got his feet under him, shook his head, took a tentative step, fell off the shelf, and smacked into the floor.

If that thing fails to survive please extend my deepest condolences to Mr. Dotes.

"Wow! What a great idea! Why didn't I think of it before? I'm slow but I'm brilliant. I'll tear him apart in here and blame it all on you. I'll have Morley come over, see all the feathers and parrot shit, he'll just shake his head and forget it. He won't go getting into a feud with you."

Very creative. Try it and I will hang you by your bootlaces from the rooftree. That bird is far too valuable even to joke about.

"Valuable? You can't even eat those damned things unless you're so hungry you already ate up all the snakes and buzzards and crows."

I mean valuable as a communications tool.

"Not to me."

Silence!

"I was only going to—"

We are about to have company. Strangers. Receive them in your office. They do not need to be made aware of my existence.

Dean beat me to the front door but got a silent warning from the Dead Man. He peeped through the peephole, backed off frowning.

"What's wrong?"

"I don't like the looks of those two." He retreated to the Dead Man's room. The Goddamn Parrot flapped into the hall when he opened the door. It landed on my shoulder. "Argh!" I started to swat him. Dean came out of the Dead Man's room, lugging the chairs back to my office.

Easy on the bird, Garrett. Dean, when you finish, shut the door to this room. Do not open it again while those people are in this house.

"Put a kettle on, too. For hospitality's sake."

Dean gave me the look that asked what I thought he should do in his spare time.

The pounding resumed. It had started polite. Now it seemed impatient. I used the peephole myself. "Do I really need to talk to these guys?" The two men on the stoop looked just like the guy Dean wanted me to be when I grew up.

It might be of value. Or instructive.

"To who?"

That would be whom, *Garrett.*

"I'm beginning to get it already," I grumbled, starting in on Dean's battery of latches. He was done moving furniture.

The Dead Man would stir the sludge inside their pretty gourds, ever so discreetly, while I sat through some kind of sales pitch.

Those two were selling something. They were so squeaky-clean and well groomed that I feared their scam would be religion. I'd have trouble staying polite if they were godshouters. I've suffered an overdose of religion lately.

I changed my mind as soon as the door opened, before anybody cracked a word. The erect postures and humorless mouths said they were selling a true belief that had nothing to do with pie in the sky by and by.

Both were five feet six and unreasonably handsome. One had blond hair and blue eyes. I wish I could report that the other had blue hair and blond eyes but he didn't. He was a pretty hunk of brown hair and blue eyes. Neither had visible scars or tattoos.

Clerks, instinct told me.

"Mr. Garrett?" the blond asked. He had perfect teeth. How often do you see good teeth? Never. Even Tinnie has an incisor that laps its neighbor.

"Guilty. Maybe. Depends on what you want."

Nobody smiled. The brunette said, "A friend gave us your name. Said you would be a good man to see. Said as you were a bona fide war hero."

"I could throw bricks with my eyes closed and hit a bona fide war hero eight tries out of ten. Anybody who made it home is a hero. Which Free Company are you guys with?" They wore clothing as though they were headed for the parade ground. Like appearance wasn't just part of being a soldier, it was the whole thing.

Clerks.

Do not antagonize them simply for the sake of deflating their pomposity, Garrett.

I need a new partner. This one knows me too well.

They seemed surprised. "How did you? . . ."

"I'm a trained detective." Self-educated. From a very short syllabus.

"It's obvious?" The brunette almost whined. These would be guys whose self-image included no whinery but who would whine a lot and call it something else. In their own minds they were big hairy-assed he-men.

Clerks.

"When you're headed wherever you go when you leave, compare yourselves to everybody else. To human male people, anyway." That might have the unfortunate side effect of encouraging their feelings of superiority, but they *might* see what I meant. "You can't be a secret agent if you're wearing a sign."

They exchanged baffled looks. They were lost. Pretty but not bright. The blond asked, "May we come in?"

"By all means." I stepped aside. "We can talk in my office. Second door to your left."

Be hospitable, Garrett.

"Either one of you guys want a parrot?"

Garrett!

Both men had wrinkled their noses when first they saw me and my bird. Everybody was a clothes critic nowadays. Why? I was decent. I was even clean. These guys looked around like they expected the place to be a dump. They seemed pleasantly disappointed that it wasn't.

Dean does good work.

We trooped into the closet I call an office. I told them, "My man Dean will bring tea in a minute."

They eyed me uncertainly. How could I know?

My office is less ordered than the hallway. I don't let Dean loose in there. And behind my desk hangs a painting that Dean hates.

At first you just see a pretty woman running from a brooding darkness. But as you stare at the painting more and more of that darkness reaches out to you. The artist who created it had been possessed by a talent so fierce that it amounted to sorcery. It drove him mad. He put everything into this painting, including his insanity. It was personal. At one time it told a whole story and indicted a villain. It doesn't have a tenth its original charge now but still retains an immense impact. It exudes terror.

"That's Eleanor," I said. "She died before I was born but she helped me crack a case." She did a lot more.

The portrait once belonged to the man who murdered Eleanor. He's dead now, too. He doesn't need the painting anymore. I do. Eleanor makes a better sounding board than Dean, the Dead Man, or the Goddamn Parrot. She's seldom judgmental and she never gives me any lip.

Blondie said, "We understand you're often involved in unusual affairs."

"I'm a lightning rod for weird stuff. Thanks, Dean." The big tray carried the right number of cups, cookies and muffins, and a steaming pot of tea. The boys exchanged glances, nervous under Eleanor's piercing gaze and Dean's stern disapproval.

Dean left. I poured and asked, "What can I do for you guys? Really."

They exchanged glances again.

"Look, boys, I'm working hard here." The Goddamn Parrot squawked in my ear. "If you just need a place to get in out of the rain I recommend Mrs. Cardonlos' rooming house up the street. On the other . . ."

"Awk! Queen bitch! Queen bitch!"

"It's not raining." Literal-minded clerks.

"Stow it, bird," I growled at the Goddamn Parrot.

My visitors exchanged looks again.

This could go on all day.

7

The blond said, "I apologize, Mr. Garrett. We were cautioned that we might find you unconventional and should try to become comfortable with that before proceeding."

"Puny penis!" the parrot squawked.

I snarled, "You're going into the sack again, you animated feather duster."

The brunette smiled insincerely. "Is that ventriloquism? When I was little I had an uncle who could—"

"Why does everybody ask that? No. This devil-spawn of a seven-color jungle pigeon does it all on his own. He's got a vocabulary bigger than yours or mine and every word is foul. Fowl. Maybe there was sorcery done him sometime. I don't know. He was a gift. I can't seem to get rid of him."

"Pencil dick."

Now nobody was smiling. Again I thought about choking the Dead Man, only what good would that do? Strengthen my grip?

The blond said, "My name is Carter Stockwell."

So we were going to do business after all. "I'm not surprised. And you?"

"Trace Wendover."

"Of course. Hello, Carter and Trace. Sure you don't want a talking parrot? Cheap? Make a great holiday gift for the kids."

Garrett, once again I must caution you against antagonizing these men.

"No? All right. I made my sales pitch. Your loss. You guys make yours. Or go away."

"We were told you might be ill-mannered." That was the darker one. Trace.

Carter said, "Our mission is to interest you in contributing to our cause."

"Right now I've got about six copper sceats to clink together. The only cause I'm going to contribute to is the Garrett household supper fund."

"We don't want money. Please. Give us a chance to talk."

"You've been here ten minutes. You haven't said anything yet."

"You're right. We are Free Company men. Black Dragon Valsung." Carter watched for my reaction.

"What's that?" I asked.

Trace countered, "You don't know the Dragons?"

"Sorry." Heeding the Dead Man's advice I forebore remarks that might betray my feelings about those quasi-military gangs called Free Companies. There are so many of them that not having heard of a particular one was no big deal.

"Our leader is Colonel Valsung. Norton Valsung." I got intent looks from both pretty boys.

I shrugged. "Doesn't ring a bell, guys. He must have been army."

Carter began to puff up. He'd caught the slight. Trace, though, was made of sterner stuff. "Yes, Mr. Garrett. Colonel Valsung was army. He commanded the Black Dragon Brigade." Trace tossed him a warning look but he continued, "You would be impressed if you were to review his record."

No doubt. War does tend to expose men for what they really are. "Wouldn't be a relative, would he?"

"My uncle."

"The ventriloquist? I recall several colonels who were masters at putting words into other people's mouths."

"No, Mr. Garrett. Not that uncle."

"We're getting somewhere now. We have a colonel who isn't a ventriloquist. What does your uncle the nonventriloquist want with me?"

"Your peculiar combination of talents and expertise, both from your service and your career since."

I didn't get it. "You need a Force Recon guy with experience

ducking vampires and sorcerers and tracking wayward wives to
help you beat up old dwarves and crippled ratmen?"

Garrett!

Both of my visitors turned red. But Carter was out in front because he'd gotten a head start. Trace said, "Mr. Garrett, we do not
roam the streets assaulting people. We are a veterans' mutual assistance brotherhood, not a street gang."

"The other day a veteran, who'd done five five-year hitches,
three in the Cantard, was almost beaten to death right outside. He'd
won eight decorations, including the Imperial Star with Swords
and Oak Leaves. In one battle he lost half of his left arm and most
of that side of his face in a blast from a witch ward. He's in the
Bledsoe now. He probably won't get out alive. Those butchers
won't pay any attention to him. He doesn't have any money. Go
down there and mutually assist him. His name is Brate Trueblood."

"But the Bledsoe is a charity hospital, isn't it?"

"You didn't grow up in TunFaire, did you? In this town charity
is available only to those who can pay for it."

"No. That's ugly." Trace seemed genuinely touched. Carter obviously didn't care but was cooling down. "That's exactly why we
have to band together."

"But there's a problem, Trace. Brate was a real hero and as good
a soldier as ever soldiered. Unfortunately, he made one really
huge, stupid mistake."

My visitors looked at me expectantly.

Garrett, please! Stop now. The Dead Man seemed almost to despair.

"He was so stupid he picked an ogre for one of his grandparents."

It took them a while to catch on. I watched their eyes narrow and
go shifty as they figured it out. Carter was slowest but he was the
first to stand up. He told me, "You have the wrong idea." And,
"Trace, we're wasting our time here."

"You're not wasting your time, Carter," I said. "I just want you
to understand that nothing is black-and-white." I tried to hold
Trace's eye. He seemed to be mulling my parable. "What did you
guys do down there? You were clerks, right? Your uncle got you
some safe assignment, right? Trace? Carter? You had an angel,
too? So who do you suppose did more to defend and preserve the
Karentine Crown? You guys or my ugly quadroon?"

Carter said, "You really don't know what's happening, do you?"
And that actually seemed to please him.

I left my chair, moved to the office doorway. "You aren't wasting your time, guys. I'm right behind you. I just need to know how to reconcile the Brate Truebloods."

Trace started to say something. Carter squeezed his arm.

In moments those earnest young men were back in the street. Carter, I was convinced, would ignore my story, which was true only in a moral sense anyway. There really is a Brate Trueblood but he was just a small hero and the thugs who jumped him didn't put him in the hospital. Ogre blood made him hard to hurt. But these two creeps did want Brate in the Bledsoe. Or worse.

I might have done the devil's work with Trace, though. He looked like a young man who might, on occasion, actually have a thought.

I whistled as I bolted the door, blissful in my ignorance.

8

That was not one of your more salubrious performances, Garrett. That flake of moral hubris may come back to haunt you.

"Come on! They're jerks. Especially the blond one."

Their minds did not reflect the prejudice you expect. But such jerks are quite common today. They are aggrieved. They need targets for their frustration. Those two seemed to be fundamentally good men. . . . Yet—

"Yet? What?"

They had no depth. Even a mind as dim as Saucerhead Tharpe's has its deeps.

"No kidding? They're a couple of pretty boys who never worked a day—"

Not shallow, Garrett. Not that way. Just all surface. Inside. Humans are filled with turmoil. Continuous dark currents collide and roil down deep where you do not see them and do not know them. Always. Even in Mr. Tharpe or Miss Winger. But those two had nothing beneath the fanatic surface. And that fanaticism was not as narrow and blind as is common. They grasped your Trueblood parable. They seemed unable to deal with it only because doing so would not have been in character.

Well, he'd lost me. Except for the part about being all surface.

"That don't surprise me. I know those guys. I've seen a lot of them. They just give up everything and let somebody else do their thinking. Life is easier that way."

Perhaps. But I have a strong intuition that we would have been better served had you held them here whilst I milked them rather than driving them away.

"Milked them? I didn't hear a moo from either one."

Intentional obtuseness seldom finds a complimentary acute observation. You should have probed them for information. You should have held them while I wormed in under their surfaces. He refused to let me exasperate him more than I had already. *Their particular Free Company may finance itself by extorting funds in the name of The Call. But we are in no position to winkle that out now. Are we?*

I hate it when he's right. And he was right. I let my emotions take over. I hadn't thought of those two in relation to the Weider problem. Yet they could have had that in mind. One of their cronies might have noticed the girls coming to my place.

Your problem far too often, Garrett.

"Huh?"

You do not think. You emote. You act on that emotion in preference to reason. However, there was nothing in their minds to tie them in to the Weider matter. Which, of course, is no guarantee that those who sent them are equally innocent.

"Aha! They knew about you."

Those two did not. They knew nothing about you, either, except what they had been told. I believe you muffed this one, Garrett.

I don't know about that. They probably wanted me to work. But I sighed. He really was right. And I definitely hate that. I hear about it forever. "I think I'll just go over to the brewery and—"

Yes. You should do that. But not right away. Go later. After the night crew comes in. They will be the younger men who have the Cantard more freshly in mind. If there are human rights activists there, they are most likely to be found among the younger workers.

What could I say? When he's right he's right. And he has been right a little too often lately. "All right. What're you going to suggest instead?" There would be something.

See Captain Block. Ask him about The Call. Let fall some gentle intimation of the threat to Mr. Weider.

Captain Westman Block runs the Guard, TunFaire's half-ass police force. The Guard is lame but more effective than the predecessor from which it evolved, the Watch, which existed primarily to absorb bribes to stay out of the way. The Watch still exists but only as a fire brigade.

The reason the Guard works is a little guy who is part dwarf, a touch of several other things, and maybe an eighth human. His name is Relway. He's the ugliest man I've ever met. He's obsessed with law and order. His conversations all revolve around his New Order, by which he means the absolute rule of law. When I met him, on a rainy night not that long ago, he was a volunteer "auxilliary" helping Block's tiny serious-crimes section of the Watch. I said something unpleasant to Relway that night. He assured me that I ought to be less unpleasant because he was going to be an important fellow before long.

His powers of prophecy were excellent.

Prince Rupert created the Guard and installed Westman Block as its chief. Then Block sanctioned Relway. And Relway immediately put together a powerful and nasty secret police force consisting of people who thought his way. Offenders have been known to just vanish once they attract the notice of Relway's section.

Probably no more than a thousand people know the section exists. He doesn't blow his own horn. And I'd bet there aren't more than a dozen people who can identify Relway by sight.

I'm one of them. Sometimes that makes me nervous.

That all rips through my mind whenever anyone mentions Block. I get the exact feeling Relway wants everybody to feel—that somebody is watching.

Old Man Weider is one of TunFaire's leading subjects. He's a commoner but is rich and powerful and influential. He has friends in high places who are real friends simply because he is the kind of man he is. Block would take an extra step to protect him.

Relway, being what he is, might take a few steps more if The Call was involved.

"Maybe that's all I really need to do. Get the Guard on the case. Block has more resources."

There is more going on.

"Why am I not surprised to hear that?"

Because you are, at last, becoming somewhat adept at reading people—though not yet at a conscious level. At that same shadow level both Miss Weider and Miss Nicholas fear that Ty Weider was not the recipient of the threat but its source.

"I don't like the guy but I could be wrong about him. Nicks thinks he's got something going."

Miss Nicholas is torn in many directions. I feel for that child.

She does indeed think some good things, though. She has known Ty Weider as long as she has known Miss Alyx. She makes allowances because she knew the Ty Weider who existed before the Ty Weider who returned from the Cantard missing a leg. Have lunch, then see Captain Block.

"Yes, Mom."

Dumb move, Garrett.

The Dead Man took the mental muzzle off the Goddamn Parrot. That freaking jungle chicken just stores it up when he's under control. It gushed.

9

Block's headquarters were inside the Al-Khar, TunFaire's city prison. Handy, what with criminals being rounded up in gaggles lately. The place is huge, stark, cold, ugly, and badly in need of maintenance. It's a wonder prisoners don't escape by walking through the walls. Or by powdering the rusty bars in the infrequent windows. Ages ago some Hill family fattened up by cutting corners on construction, particularly in the choice of stone. Instead of a good Karentine limestone, available from quarries within a day's barge travel, somebody had supplied a soft snotty yellow-green stone that sucks up crud from the air, darkens, streaks, then flakes, leaving the exterior acned. The streets alongside the Al-Khar always boast a layer of detritus.

The mortar is in worse shape than the stone. Luckily, the walls are real thick.

I stopped, stunned, when I rounded a corner and saw the prison.

Scaffolding was up. Some tuckpointing was under way. Some chemical cleansing was restoring the youth of the stone.

Even clean that stone was butt-ugly.

How were they financing the face-lift? Till recently TunFaire jailed hardly anybody so no provision had been made to help maintain the seldom-used prison.

They'd had to evict squatters when Block moved in.

Captain Block not only was in, he was willing to see me. Immediately.

"You're a bureaucrat now, Block. Even if you haven't opened your eyes for fifteen years, you're supposed to be too busy to see somebody without an appointment. You'll set a precedent. You really live here? In jail?"

"I'm single. I don't need much room."

He seemed a little sad and a lot weary. He had shown fair political acumen getting the Guard created but, perhaps, didn't have the moral stamina to keep diverting frequent attempts to scuttle the rule of law.

"You look more relaxed these days." Block's quarters definitely didn't match his standing in the community. Neither did his dress. He should have been decked out like an admiral with two hundred years of service, but he just didn't care.

Block told me, "That business with the serial-killer spell that kept recasting itself made the prince love me. I'm almost untouchable. Almost. My cynical side says that's because nobody else wants the job. It certainly is thankless. But business is good. New villains jump up as fast as we harvest the old ones. They're like the dragon's teeth in that old myth. I'm endlessly amazed that so many of them survived the war."

I shrugged. I didn't know the one about the dragon's teeth.

Block is a compact, thin man with short brown hair quickly going gray. He needed a shave. He'd make a fair spy because there was nothing remarkable about him. You wouldn't notice him unless he yelled in your face. When I first met him, at a time when the law was honored more in the taking of bribes than actual enforcement, he'd had a mouth as filthy as the Goddamn Parrot's and all the manners of a starving snake.

I wasn't sure I liked the new, improved, mannered and unantagonistic, *dedicated* Block better than the angry old one.

I told him, "In the old days you never seemed like the dedicated type. You only did what you had to to get by."

A shadow brushed his features. "I got religion, Garrett."

"Huh?"

"I let Relway talk me into putting him on full-time. Big mistake. His conviction infects everybody around him."

"It does." Given his head Relway will exterminate the concept of crime by the end of the year. He's a man with a holy mission. He's scary.

"So what's up? Going to collect favors owed?"

"Not entirely. I want to ask about The Call. And I want to talk about Max Weider. Somebody's trying to squeeze him." I betrayed tradition and fed him all the details.

He was suspicious. "Why tell me?"

I would have been suspicious, too. In the past I'd kept him in the dark on principle.

"My partner insisted. And I owe Weider. It would be handy if somebody official was watching if something happened."

"What could happen?"

"With these rightsists? Anything."

"No shit. You heard about those people burning up on the north side?"

"I heard. I didn't pay attention. I've been busy."

"They're people with no connection to each other, drunks and no-accounts who couldn't make an enemy on a bet. But they've been burning up."

"You're pulling my leg."

"No. It's happened six times. It's got to be sorcery. Relway wants it to connect with the rights business but I don't see it. I can't see some teetotaling sorceress setting drunks on fire, either, though."

"You think it would be a woman?"

"If it was a teetotaller. You know any men dead set against spirits?"

"Only one." And I have to live with him. "So what about it? Is The Call moving into the rackets?"

"I haven't heard that. Jirek!"

The door opened. A creature limped in. He wasn't human. Not much, anyway. There was a little of everything in him but the three main ingredients appeared to be ogre, troll, and ugly. The whole was complicated by birth defects and wounds. Jirek moved sort of sideways, stiffly and bent, like his back hurt all the time.

"Jirek was injured in the ambush at Council Wells."

A veteran, then. Yet not human. Another one of those inconvenient complications I'd pointed out to Carter and Trace. Some of our biggest heroes aren't even human.

"Council Wells. One of our great victories," I observed.

"Do I detect the odor of sarcasm?"

Council Wells was supposed to have been a preliminary peace conference. The Karentine army concealed commando forces in the surrounding desert. Those patriots murdered the Venageti delegates in their sleep.

Another of those little triumphs that, when totalled, helped Karenta win the war.

"Me sarcastic? The gods forfend."

Jirek's great knobbly green mess of a face twisted and wriggled into a grotesque smile. Then he guffawed. His breath could gag a maggot. But he had a sense of humor.

Block told him, "Relway should be in his cell. Tell him I need him."

Jirek told me, "Good joke," then left.

"What was that?" I asked.

"Jirek. A unique." Which was slang for a breed who had extremely complicated antecedents. "He saved my ass a couple times in the Cantard. He was a perfect soldier. Too dumb to question authority. Just did what he was told. And was one bad boy in a fight."

"I just might change my mind about you."

"Don't brag about it. People might wonder why it took so long to rid yourself of the old, clogged one."

"And I thought I was developing a new relationship with the minions of the law."

Relway arrived. A little guy, he sort of oozed into Block's cell, no knock, like a shadow that didn't want to be noticed.

Relway is another unique, a completely improbable mixture. His interior landscape is a strange, strange land, too. He has a chip on his shoulder big enough to provide lumber for four houses. He's so far into law and order that he considers himself above any law that might restrain his efforts to crush crime. Now his auxiliaries and spies and midnight avengers are everywhere. It shouldn't be long till his name becomes one of the most feared in TunFaire.

Relway the man (using "man" generically, to indicate a sentient creature that walks on its hind legs) is almost unknown. I know him only because chance put me in the right place back when.

He nodded. "Garrett. You been keeping well?" His voice was hoarse, cracking, only half there.

"I'm fine. You pick up a cold?"

"The weather's been strange. I hear you might know something about that."

"Me? I was out there freezing my butt off with everybody else." Why relive my misadventures amongst mobs of low-grade, feuding gods?

He gave me that look all lawmen develop. It says not one word dripping from your filthy mouth is true now, nor ever has been. The power had gone to his head, though there was no denying the good being done. He had the bad guys rattled.

"What's that on your shoulder, Garrett?"

Block had done me the courtesy of ignoring that owl in a clown suit. "My lunch. I'll share. Stoke up the fire."

The Goddamn Parrot—or the Dead Man speaking through the buzzard's beak—had to have his word. "Awk! Jerk alert!"

"How do you do that without moving your lips?" Relway asked.

"It's a trick they teach Marines."

Relway asked, "We got something, Wes?"

They were getting cuddly now?

"Maybe. You've been working the rights gangs?"

"Where I can. They're hard to infiltrate. Mostly they form from groups who knew each other in the Cantard."

I still hang out with guys I knew down there. We don't spend good beer-drinking time trying to figure out how to hurt people, though.

Relway continued, "Big mobs like The Call are more vulnerable. Everybody doesn't know everybody. The Call proper is organized like the army. And Marengo North English is building a real private army. Freecorps Theverly, they're calling it."

"Is Colonel Theverly with them?" I was surprised, though I hadn't known Lieutenant Colonel Moches Theverly well enough to make sound assessments of his feelings toward nonhumans. He treated everybody the same in the zone. He was one of few officers who didn't go around with his head firmly inserted in a dark, stinky place.

"A man of conviction, the colonel." Shadows stirred behind Relway's eyes. "You know him?"

"I worked for him in the islands. Briefly. He got hurt and they pulled him out just before the Venageti overran us. The wound cost him a leg if I remember right. He was a good officer."

"That's not why you're here?"

"No. I didn't know about that."

Block asked, "Is The Call moving into the rackets, Deal? As a fund-raising activity?"

Relway frowned. "You have a run-in, Garrett?"

"I have a client. Max Weider. The brewery Weider."

Relway nodded. My relationship with Weider was no secret.

"His daughter Alyx says somebody claiming to be from The Call took a run at her brother Ty. They wanted a piece of the gross. That didn't sound like The Call. But if they need money to conjure up their own army, they might try more creative ways of getting it."

"They might," Relway agreed. "I haven't heard of it being discussed seriously. Yet. On the other hand, they have discussed other areas traditionally associated with the Outfit—where those exploit nonhumans."

"Two birds, one stone?"

"Exactly. The Call's Inner Council put it, 'We deem it fitting that the disease provide the means of sustaining the cure.' "

Interesting. Sounded like he attended Call council meetings himself. "They're pushing Chodo and they're still healthy?" I wouldn't have thought even the most fanatic member of The Call would dare jostle Chodo Contague. Chodo was the king of organized crime. Nobody poached in Chodo's territory. Nobody, that is, who wasn't ready to fight a major war. It's impossible to imagine a deadlier enemy than Chodo Contague.

I knew the real head of the combine more intimately than Relway suspected. Chodo's daughter Belinda is young but so hard she can cut steel.

Relway smiled his nastiest. "That'll be temporary. You know the Contagues. And what they can do."

"O evil day," I said.

"Cute. The short answer is, The Call have shown no interest in extortion. But this could be a test case. If Weider knuckles under and they get the brewery in their pocket, Weider's peers will fall in line."

"I know Max. He won't give in even if it costs ten times as much to fight. Most of the commercial class would agree—even where their political sympathies belong to The Call. They won't want the precedent set. They didn't get rich by being easily intimidated."

Tinnie and Nicks running with Alyx might be as much business as friendship. The Tates were big in shoes. The family Nicholas, in its several branches, were involved in winemaking, coal mining, and inland shipping.

In each case, possibly even including that of the beer baron, I would have been reluctant to listen to a standard appeal. But send a beautiful girl and you can get Garrett's attention every time.

I'm too damned predictable. But they keep on making pretty girls.

The shadows still swirled behind Relway's eyes. And those focused on me while the darkness pranced. "We have a basis for a deal, Garrett," he mused.

"Uh. . . ."

"Apparently you don't approve of my methods. You don't need to and I don't care if you do. You're a textbook case of inflexible goodguyitis." He chuckled at his own neologism. Scary, a Relway

with a sense of humor. Maybe this one was a changeling. "But that
don't mean we can't help each other."

That's why I came back to see Block. "I'm listening."

"Overwhelm me with enthusiasm."

"I'm a regular ball of fire. Everybody says so."

"You'd fit with the rightsists without any effort. You're the kind
of guy they want."

Must be. Else yahoos like Stockwell and Wendover wouldn't
come pounding on my door. "I'd only have to shuck about half my
beliefs."

Relway's grin revealed teeth definitely not human. "You served
with those people. You know how they think. You've heard all their
knee-jerk crap. How hard could it be to parrot it?" His grin got bigger. He stared at Mr. Big. "Put some words in your own mouth."

I grunted, hoped Relway and Block didn't think too much about
the bird. I didn't need them figuring out the fact that the Dead Man
was riding my shoulder by proxy. "I could. But why should I?"
This was starting to sound like work.

"I can't get my people inside. These crackpots are abidingly
paranoid. If a man has even a tenth part nonhuman blood, he's a
breed and part of the problem. Never mind he might have been a
war hero. The spiders spinning the web of hatred are sure hu-
mankind can be redeemed only through the extinction of the rest of
the races. Even to the extreme of hunting down and expunging
every drop of nonhuman blood. Otherwise us uniques might breed
back to original stock."

I guess my mouth was open. Luckily no flies were working the
cell. "That's so damned ridiculous—"

"What does ridiculous have to do with belief? Those people are
out there, Garrett."

I wanted to argue but my last case had involved several religions, each more unlikely than the last.

People will believe anything when they need to believe something. A lot *have* to believe in something bigger than themselves,
whether that is a cause or a god. *What* doesn't necessarily matter as
long as *something* is there.

"I understand."

"You don't have to sign a pact in blood. Just drift farther inside
than you planned, then let me know what you find."

"And what'll you do for me?"

"Keep you posted on what I learn. And protect the Weiders—if it
comes to that."

I owed Old Man Weider a lot. I owed the Tates some, too. "Could you keep an eye on the Tates while you're at it?"

Relway sighed. "I suppose I can do that." He smiled. Pity about those teeth. "You make peace with your friend?"

My life is an entertainment for all TunFaire. Everybody knows every time Tinnie winks at me. "They're special to me."

"You have a deal. Wes, I've got to wander, see what's new on the street." He can do that. Little scruff like him, nobody would believe he's Relway.

"Wait up," I said. "Couple things more. Ever hear of Black Dragon Valsung?"

Relway shrugged, showed me his palms. "Which is what?"

"Supposed to be a new freecorps. Colonel Norton Valsung commanding, lately of the Black Dragon Brigade."

Relway shook his head. Block said, "Never heard of either one."

"Me neither. That's what made me wonder."

"What?" Relway wanted to know.

"Two squeaky-clean clerk types named Carter Stockwell and Trace Wendover came to the house today. Wanted me to join their outfit."

Block and Relway glanced at each other. Block said, "Means nothing to me."

Relway said, "There're always new gangs. I'll keep an ear open."

Block waved. Relway headed for the door. I started to go myself. Block told me, "Hang on, Garrett."

"Uhm?"

"If you do get involved, you be real careful. These people are nasty."

"I've been playing with the bad boys a long time. I don't make mistakes anymore."

"Only takes one, Garrett. Smart guys get dead, too."

"Point taken. Thanks."

"One more thing. Relway gets too focused sometimes. Doesn't think about whatever don't bear on what interests him right now."

"You leading up to something?"

"Yes. His people saw Crask and Sadler yesterday. Remember them? You should. They're back in town and too stupid not to be seen."

"Never heard either one accused of genius." I shivered. Not much scares me but Crask and Sadler are stone-cold professional killers of the worst sort. The sort who want to hurt Mrs. Garrett's only surviving son. They're that lucky kind of professional who get to do work they really enjoy.

Crask and Sadler have a sack full of bones to pick with Mama Garrett's favorite boy. I helped run them out of town. I helped fix them up with a Combine price on their heads.

"I'll watch out."

"Do. Hey! Teach that ugly sack of feathers to scout for you."

"You hear that, bird?"

The Goddamn Parrot kept his beak shut. A remarkable state of affairs.

10

Crask and Sadler. Damn! I thought those double-uglies were out of my life for good.

They tried to take over when Chodo had his stroke—which few people knew about. Most think he's still in charge. They wouldn't if Belinda hadn't outfoxed Crask and Sadler when they made their grab. Them knowing about Chodo, and their deadly enmity, explained Belinda's eagerness to elevate them to the next plane.

Nowadays Chodo is a lump of meat imprisoned in a wheelchair. Belinda has no use for him except to pretend her orders come from him.

Block again told me, "You take care."

"You too." I decided to say it. "I like this Westman Block better than the old one."

That got me a sour look and, "Might be smart not to turn up here again. You go out on the fringe, you'll never know who's watching or what their real loyalties are."

I paused outside the jail, studied the street. At the best of times watching your surroundings closely is wise. Our great city never lacks for characters willing to steal your gold tooth in broad daylight while you're watching.

Nobody was interested in me. I didn't appear threatening, nor weak enough to be an easy victim.

I felt good. I had an accommodation with the law—which would work for me because Max Weider is a municipal treasure.

It was a gorgeous day, a tad warm but with a nice breeze, a few scurrying clouds dancing on a sky so blue it defined the color for all time. It was the kind of day that makes us daytime people feel good. The kind of day when people laugh, visit friends not seen for a while, conceive children. The kind of day when bloodlettings are few and even the scroats take time off to appreciate what a wonderful world it can be. It was the kind of day when Relway's crew might get into mischief because they had too much time on their hands.

I headed east and north. It was time I visited an old friend of my own.

The streets were crowded but the activists were having trouble working up much indignation. If the weather held, the coffinmakers and crematoria would catch up and have to cut pieces.

A centaur clip-clopped past. He wore an old army blanket. I couldn't make out the regimental mark. He couldn't be real bright. If that blanket was loot and not a Crown issue to an auxiliary formation, possession could get him killed.

Some days it could anyway.

He was drunk. He didn't care.

The air above swarmed with pixies and fairies and whatnot, the young ones tormenting the pigeons. That wouldn't earn them any enemies who weren't pigeons themselves.

Birds were out courting, too. I noted a few hawks and peregrines way up high. The little people better stay alert. . . . A dimwit peregrine dived at a pixie girl. It drew a flurry of poisoned darts. The wee folk were using the nice day to educate a new generation of predators.

It's a pity people are stupider than falcons. Otherwise, we could teach them not to prey on their own kind.

On days like this, when everyone comes out to soak up the warm, it seems impossible that so many beings live in this city. But TunFaire is really several cities occupying the same site. There are evening peoples and night peoples and morning peoples who never see one another. It is both an accommodation and a way of life. It used to work.

The tip of a wing whipped across the back of my hair. The Goddamn Parrot was showing off for his plain-feathered cousins. "I know a Yessiley place where they put pigeon in everything they cook. And they don't care if the pigeon is really a pigeon."

"Awk! I want to soar with eagles and am forced—"

"You want me to call one of those hawks down? They'll soar with you."

"Help!"

"Hey, Mister. Does your bird really talk?"

"Hush, Bertie. The man's a ventriloquist." Bertie's mom gave me a look that said I ought to be ashamed, trying to scam people with an innocent bird.

"You're probably right, ma'am. Why don't you take the poor creature and give him a decent home?"

The air crackled around woman and child so swift was their departure.

Nobody wanted poor old lovable Mr. Big.

11

The place has pretensions toward being a class eatery. It doesn't compete for the Yessiley trade. Its fashionable dishes never include anything harder to catch than squash or eggplant. Its name varies with the mood of its owner, Morley Dotes. The Palms is the moniker he's hung on it lately. His target clientele has gone from being blackhearted second-string underworlders foregathering to plot, negotiate, or arrange an expedient truce to upscale subjects foregathering to plot, negotiate, or arrange an expedient truce.

The staff, however, is a constant.

It was an off-peak hour when I invited myself into Morley's place. Diners of any station were conspicuous by their absence. Staff were making preparations for the hour when the crowd would show. Morley's new gimmick was a money cow. The place reeked prosperity.

"Shee-it! I done thunk we was shut of dis perambulatin' sack a horse apples."

"Better watch using words like perambulate, Sarge. You'll throw your tongue out of joint." How long did it take him to latch on to the word's meaning, so he could use it? It was several syllables longer than any in his normal vocabulary.

A voice from the shadowed back growled, "You let dat damned dog in here again, Sarge? I smell doggie do."

"Dat ain't dog shit, Puddle. Dat's Garrett."

"Tossup which is worst."

"Fugginay."

"You guys ought to take your routine on the road." I couldn't see Puddle but he had been struck from the same mold as Sarge. Both are big and fat and sloppy, tattooed and almost as bad as they think they are.

"Fugginay, Garrett. We'd have 'em rollin' in da streets. Be up to our friggin' noses in hot little gels. . . . Nah. I don't tink. I'm gettin' too old for all dat."

"Watcha want, Garrett?" Puddle demanded. "I tink we done you 'bout enough favors for dis week."

"I don't need any favors," I fibbed. "I wanted to let Morley in on some bad news."

Back there in the shadows Puddle must have reported through the speaking tube to Morley's office upstairs. Dotes' voice came from the stair. "What bad news is that, Garrett?"

"Crask and Sadler are back."

Morley didn't say anything for a good ten seconds. Then he asked, "Where did you get that?"

"Can't tell you." Which told him.

"Shee-it!" Sarge observed. "What'd I say? It smells like poop it's proba'ly gonna be poop. He wants sometin' again."

"Fugginay," Puddle replied. "I'm gonna have me a case a da brown-leg trots he comes in here someday an' he don't want nuttin'."

I tried a ferocious scowl on Sarge as I passed him. He grinned amiably. He doesn't scare. "Nice shoulder ornament dere, Garrett. We knew you'd take to da bird eventually."

These people are my friends. Allegedly.

I told Morley, "You know eggplant used to be poisonous?"

"Yes. I keep a few of the undomesticated variety around in case I want to cook up special dishes for people who don't respect our dress code here." He led the way upstairs. "So who's going to hear you now? Block told you about Crask and Sadler?"

"He got it from Relway."

"Oh. In here." Morley ducked across the room he uses for an office, settled into a plush chair behind a big table. He slipped a toothpick into a forest of nasty sharp teeth, looked thoughtful. "Crask and Sadler. Interesting."

12

Morley Dotes is the kind of guy nightmares are made of if you have a daughter. He's so damned handsome it's painful, in an olive, slim, dark-elven fashion. Anything he throws on makes him look like he spent all last week at a tailor's. He can deck himself out in white and prance through a coalyard without getting a spot on himself. I've never seen him sweat. Females of numerous species stop thinking while he's around.

For all his faults he's a good friend. Albeit a friend of the sort who would give you a talking parrot as a gift—and do it in a way that would tie you in knots of obligation that keep you from disposing of said gift in any sensible fashion. Sort of the way an old hag witch might put a curse on you that you can shed only when some other fool volunteers to take it upon himself.

No doubt Morley chuckles himself to sleep every night thinking about me and the Goddamn Parrot.

I said, "Looks like the new scam has the marks rolling in."

"It was the right move at the right time, Garrett. Took a while to convince the neighbors that they would benefit, though."

I could imagine. The area had been known as the Safety Zone till recently. It was neutral ground where gentlemen of unsavory enterprise who were business rivals or outright enemies could sit down with some expectation of personal safety. The Joy House had been the heart of the Zone. Morley made the Zone work and therefore profitable for the whole area.

A shift in market focus certainly would disconcert the neighbors.

"Rich people have the same requirements and vices as poor people," Morley observed. Lamplight sparkled off the points of his unnaturally white teeth. "But they have more money to pay for them. That convinced everyone."

That and, I didn't doubt, the marketing strategems of Sarge and Puddle and their compatriots.

"Uhm. Crask and Sadler."

"Block do any guessing about who brought them in?"

"Nope. I thought Belinda should know they'd been seen." Morley has better contacts in the Outfit.

"If she doesn't know, she'll be grateful for the warning."

I said, "I'd like to break the news personally."

Morley gave me a double dose of the fish-eye. "You sure that would be smart?"

"She used me up and left. No hard feelings from me."

"From you. Belinda Contague is a strange woman, Garrett. Might not be healthy to get within stabbing distance of her."

"We understand each other. But it'll be easier for both of us if I have you contact her."

"I'll pass it on this time, you bullshitter. But you need to find somebody else to run your love notes. I'm out of that life."

Who was bullshitting who? But I didn't ask. Let the man think he can kid a kidder. If he did. It could be a useful lever later.

"What have you been into lately?" Dotes asked. "We haven't had a chance to just sit and talk and find cures for the ills of the world." His notions for the latter involve either forcing everyone to turn vegetarian or necessitate wholesale slaughters. Or both.

I told him about my adventures among the gods. And goddesses. "I thought about getting you together with Magodor. She was your type."

"Uhm?" He looked speculative.

"She had four arms, snakes for hair, green lips, teeth like a cobra. But she was to kill for otherwise."

"Oh, yes. I've dreamed about her for years."

"Elves don't dream."

He shrugged. "What about now?"

"Now?"

"You didn't visit Block to tip a few beers and reminisce about old murders you solved together."

"Sure I did."

"I know you, Garrett. You have a case."

"It isn't really a case. I've got the deal with the brewery. Somebody threatened the old man. Maybe." I sketched the situation.

"You have yourself a situation fraught with peril, Garrett." He smirked.

"Potential violence. Weider won't stand for it. And if The Call tries moving into the rackets—"

"The Call probably wouldn't. But several fringe groups are trying. They don't attract people with money. We'll see some excitement there. I can hear Belinda sharpening her knives. You going inside?"

"Inside?"

"Into the movement. As a spy. You wouldn't have any trouble. You're ethnically pure. You're a war hero." Morley is a war hero himself, in his own mind. He stayed behind and did yeoman service comforting many a soldier's frightened wife. "You're healthy enough to stand on your hind legs. You're unemployed. Makes you the perfect recruit."

"Except for I don't buy the doctrine."

Morley smiled his sharp-toothed finest. "You better not be seen here if you're going inside. You shouldn't even be around the Dead Man."

"Oh." I didn't swear any oaths with Relway, did I? No thumb-cutting and blood-mixing. Obvious as it was I hadn't thought about the fact that infiltrating the rightsists meant my own lifestyle would have to reflect rightsist prejudice.

Adopting a false identity would be too iffy. Too many veterans knew me. One thing you do when you're single and don't work is hang out with people like yourself. I prefer the company of women but there are rare occasions on an almost daily basis when no woman prefers mine. Hard as that is to believe.

"It won't go that far." I hoped. "I'm going to the brewery to poke around. If Ty is trying to scam Pop's cash prematurely, I'll scare him off. If he's playing straight, I'll still get an idea of the real problem. I can't believe any of our racist lunatics have balls big enough to go after Weider."

"You have true believers involved, Garrett. You ought to know reality doesn't faze those people. They're right. That's their armor. That's all they need." Morley sat up straight. He wanted to move on to something else. "Be careful out there, Garrett."

"I'm always careful."

"No, you're not. You're lucky. And luck is a woman. Be careful. You learned from the best. Take my lessons to heart."

"Right." I chuckled. Morley doesn't lack for self-image.

"Tell Puddle to come up. I need him to run a message."

"I don't think he'll do much running." I did as Dotes asked, though.

Morley never said a word about the Goddamn Parrot. Never asked a question. Never even looked at the bird. Never smirked or rubbed it in.

Morley was playing with me again.

I ought to slice the little buzzard into thin strips and slip them to him buried in one of his strange, overly spiced vegetarian platters.

13

I watched Puddle strain his way upstairs. "That man needs to eat more of what he serves," I told Sarge, who isn't a single pound lighter.

"Fugginay. We're all puttin' on da pounds, Garrett," Sarge muttered, polishing a mug. Though they're all thugs, Morley's guys pretend to be waiters and cooks. "Ya tink about it hard when ya ain't eatin' but den ya wander inta a place where dey got da good beer and da great food, ya go bugfuck and don't tink what ya done till ya done et half a cow."

"I know what you mean." Dean was too good a cook.

Couldn't be the beer. Beer is good for you.

"Fugginay. Hey, I got work to do, Garrett."

"Yeah. Later."

"You be careful out dere, pal. Da world's goin' crazy."

That was the nicest thing Sarge ever said to me. I hit the street wondering why.

A bird's wing brushed the back of my head. Again.

My live-in clown was restless. He didn't speak, though. Luckily. Had the Dead Man not been controlling him, he would have screeched about me abusing infants. Or something. There was an unnatural rapport between the Loghyr and the bird. The Dead Man could touch his mind from miles away. Me he can barely reach in the street outside the house.

It's bad enough to have the Dead Man after me constantly at home. Having him use Mr. Big to keep tabs everywhere else had gotten old two minutes after he found out he could do it.

I reminded him, "I'm going to the brewery." Shift change was coming up.

People noticed me talking to the bird. They gave me a more than normal amount of room.

Because the streets are filled with men who talk to ghosts and shadows. For them the Cantard opened doors to realms the rest of us never see.

War may not be Hell itself but it definitely does weaken the barriers between us and the dark regions.

The Goddamn Parrot took wing. He followed me from above.

The Dead Man's control slipped. The jungle vulture squawked insults at passersby. Some hurled sticks or bits of broken brick. The bird mocked them. He fears nothing that goes on two legs.

Hawks are something else.

A pigeon killer of uncertain species arrowed down out of the blue. Mr. Big sensed his peril at the last instant. He dodged. Even so, bright feathers flew but only the parrot's feelings suffered any real injury. He shrieked curses.

I chuckled. "That was close, you little pervert. Maybe next time I'll get lucky."

The little monster returned to my shoulder. He wouldn't leave again. The hawk circled but lost patience quickly. There is no shortage of pigeons in this burg.

"Argh!" I said. "Where's me eye patch, matey?" I took a few crabbed steps, dragging my left foot. Folks didn't appreciate the effort, thought. Almost everybody has a disabled veteran in the family.

14

Stragglers from the early shift still drifted into the street as I reached the brewery. The stench of fermentation drenched the neighborhood. The workers didn't notice. Neither did the residents. Their noses were dead.

Weider's main brewery is a great gothic redbrick monster that looks more like a hospice for werewolves and vampires than the anchor of a vast commercial empire. It has dozens of turrets and towers that have nothing to do with what goes on inside the building. Bats boil out of the towers at dusk.

The monstrosity sprang from Old Man Weider's imagination. A smaller duplicate stands directly across Delor Street, Weider's first effort. He'd meant that to be a brewery but it turned out to be too small. So he remodeled and moved his family in while he built a copy ten times bigger, to which all sorts of additions have attached themselves since.

We TunFairens love our beer.

The brewery don't have a real security team. Senior workers take turns patrolling and watching the entrances. Outside villains don't get in. The workforce protects the place like worker bees protect their hives.

A spry antique named Geral Diar had the duty at the front entrance. "Hey, Gerry," I said as I walked up. "Checking in."

"Garrett?" His eyes aren't the best. And he was surprised to see me. That was a good sign. If nobody expects me, any bad guys will have no time to cover up. "What're you doing here?"

"Snooping. Same as always. The big house says it's time. Been stealing any barrels?"

"You enjoy yourself, young fellow. Somebody should."

"Oh? You're not?"

Diar is one of those guys who can't not talk if anybody stops to listen. "Not much joy around here lately."

"How come?"

"State of the kingdom. Everybody's got a viewpoint and nobody's got a pinch of tolerance for the other guy's."

This might be germane. "Been some political friction here?"

"Oh, no, not around here. Mr. Weider wouldn't put up with that. But it's everywhere else and you got to get through it to get to work. You can't hardly go anywhere without you run into a brawl or demonstration or even an out an' out riot. It's all a them foreigners from the Cantard. They just act like they *want* to cause trouble."

"I know what you mean." I was in my chameleon mode, where I mirror whomever I'm with. That loosens people up. Diar's comment, though, complimented the Dead Man's suspicion that Glory Mooncalled was trying to destabilize Karentine society.

"Gets depressing, Garrett, knowing you have to go out there. Things was better back when all you had to worry about was thieves and strong-arm men."

"I'm sure the King will do something soon." Like the traditional turn-of-the-back till the mob sorted itself out. Not that the royals deign to spend time in TunFaire, where the upper crust bears them far less goodwill than does the factious, fractious rabble.

"Well, you just have yourself a wonderful day, Garrett."

"And you, too, Gerry. You, too."

When you think brewery mostly you picture the finished product: beer, ale, stout, whatever. You don't consider the process. First thing you notice about a brewery is the smell. That isn't the toothsome bouquet of a premium lager, either. It's the stench of vegetable matter rotting. Because that's the process. To get beer you let vats of grain and water and additives like hops rot under the loving guidance of skilled old brewmasters who time each phase to the minute.

There are no youngsters working in the brewhouse. In the Weider scheme even apprenticed sons of the brewmasters start out as rough labor. Weider himself was a teamster before he went to the Cantard and believes that physical labor made him a better man. But when he was young everybody over nine had to work. And jobs were easy to find.

Weider does know every job in the brewery and occasionally works some of them just to keep in touch with a workingman's reality. He expects his senior associates to do the same.

Manvil Gilbey wrestling beer barrels is a hoot. Which might explain why Gilbey isn't entirely fond of me. I've witnessed his efforts and feel comfortable reporting that as a laborer he's pretty lame.

I said hello to the brewmasters on duty. Skibber Kessel returned a sullen greeting. Mr. Klees was too busy to notice a housefly like me. They were dedicated men, disinclined to gossip at the most relaxed times. I supposed they were happy with things the way they were. No brewmaster is shy about raising hell when he's bothered. The finest brewmasters are like great operatic performers.

When I go to the brewery I try to stay unpredictable. The bad boys don't need to catch me in a routine. Sometimes I hang around only half an hour. Other times I just won't go away. I become like some unemployed cousin loafing around the place, though I will help the guys on the docks, loading and unloading. I shoot the bull with the apprentices, shovel with the guys in the grain elevator, just watch the boys in the hops shed. I wander, double-check counts on the incoming barley, rice, and wheat, calculating inflow against recorded output. In all ways I try to be a pain in the ass to would-be crooks.

The brewery's biggest problem always was pilferage. That's been a lot smaller since I came around but, unfortunately, human nature is human nature.

15

I knew some of the teamsters and dock wallopers well enough to drink with so it seemed I ought to start with them. They wouldn't hesitate to talk about conflicts within the workforce.

There are two ways to reach the loading docks—besides going

around to the freight gate. One leads through the caverns beneath the brewery, where the beer is stored. The caverns and the proximity of the river, on which raw materials arrive, are why Weider chose the site.

The caverns are the more difficult route. The other way runs through the stable. That's huge. Few other enterprises require so much hauling capacity.

I chose the caverns. It's almost a religious experience, wandering those cool aisles between tall racks of kegs and barrels.

They work round the clock down there and I always find Mr. Burkel there with his tally sheets. "Mr. Burkel, don't you ever sleep?"

"Garrett! Hello. Of course I do. You're just a lucky man. You get to enjoy my company every time you come around."

"How can I argue with that? How are your numbers running these days?"

"As good as they've ever been. As good as they've ever been."

Which still meant a slight floor loss in favor of the workforce, probably limited to what was consumed on the premises. Which was fine with Old Man Weider.

Mr. Burkel handed me a huge stein. As chance would have it, that stein was filled with beer. "This is a new wheat we've just started shipping." I sipped half a pint.

"And a fine brew it is, Mr. Burkel. It's heavier than the lager but lighter than the dark I usually prefer." I forebore tossing in some wine snob chat. He wouldn't get the joke. "This's why I like Old Man Weider. He's always trying something. Thanks. Maybe I'll come through again on my way out."

"Do. Now answer me something, Garrett. How come you got a stuffed bird on your shoulder? Looks goofy as hell."

"It's not stuffed. It's alive. It's kind of a signature thing. Other guys in my racket all got a gimmick."

"Oh." You'd have thought I was threatening to tell him about my new wall coverings. "Well, you be careful out there, Garrett."

"Likewise, Mr. Burkel."

16

The Weider freight docks are chaos incarnate, yet out of that confusion flows the lifeblood of the tavern industry. From its heart to its nethermost extremities beer is the blood and soul of the metropolis.

The teamsters and dockhands received me with mixed emotions, as always. Some were friendly, or pretended to be. Others scowled. Maybe some of those were involved in the theft ring I rooted out. They might figure I done them wrong because stealing from the boss is a worker's birthright.

Shadows were gathering in the dockyard. Hostlers had begun retiring the incoming teams. After dark only outside haulers would be loaded. This was a time of day the dockworkers liked. They could get lazy.

It was also the time of day when a keg or three could disappear most easily.

I planted the other side of my lap on a returned empty meant to go back to the cooperage yard for repairs. I stayed out of the way, let the noise and chatter wash over me. The Goddamn Parrot muttered but did not lapse into filth. What little I understood sounded like random thoughts from one of the Dead Man's secondary minds. He must be distracted.

I listened. I overheard almost nothing about the political situation and less about what everybody thought I might be after. I didn't mind. I didn't expect anybody to be dumb enough to plot right in front of me, though the criminal class does boast a rich vein of stupidity.

Mostly I watched how guys behaved when they knew I was watching.

Nobody acted guilty.

"Garrett?"

I opened my eyes. I'd been on the brink of falling asleep. The long nights were catching up.

"Gilbey?" Manvil Gilbey masquerades as Old Man Weider's batman but he's no servant. The bond between them goes back to their army days and is unshakable. Nobody can indict its rectitude, either. Gilbey had a wife who died. Weider still has one he wor-

ships. If Max is the brain of the brewing empire, Manvil Gilbey is
its soul and conscience.

"Max requests the honor of your company whenever you can get
over to the house."

Gilbey needed a few quaffs of the product. He's all right once
he's had a few.

"I'll be over before it gets completely dark."

"Good enough." Gilbey turned and marched away.

A driver called Sparky observed, "That's one guy what never
should of got outta the army."

"Always on the parade ground, isn't he?"

"He's all right, you get to know him."

"One of the good people," I agreed.

"He just never learned to take it easy."

"The streets are filled with people like that these days."

"Tell me about it," Sparky grumbled. "When I get off I've been
driving and hossing them barrels for twelve, fourteen hours. All I
want to do is get home and collapse. So what happens every goddamned night? I've got to walk a mile through morons trying to
save the world from the guy next door. And every damned one of
them wants me to join his mob. They get deaf as a cobblestone
when you tell them to just leave you the fuck alone."

Another driver said, "I'm thinking about just camping out here
till this shit blows over. I'm fed up having to duck a fight every
time I go somewhere."

I suggested, "Maybe you could try a different route. Those rights
guys only show up where they think they can start something. I
didn't get any hassles coming down here. I don't get much trouble
at all, really."

"You think walking around with that stick and stuff don't make
a difference? Them assholes ain't ready to work for it yet."

"Yeah, Garrett. Mosta dem fucks be scared shitless of a guy wit'
a eagle on his shoulder."

"Thank you, Zardo. But don't give the buzzard a swelled head."
I tote my headknocker everywhere these days. Times have grown
so interesting that I no longer feel foolish being cautious. "You
want to buy this bird, Zardo? Sparky? I'll cut you a deal. I'll throw
in an eye patch."

"Dat'd just be askin' for trouble. I couldn't fight my way outta a
weddin' reception."

Sparky said, "I spent my five doing the same thing I do here,
Garrett. I never touched a weapon after Basic."

I didn't know Sparky well enough to preach to him so I just shrugged. "Life's never kind to the good-hearted. I had a friend once who recited a poem over and over about how good men die while the wicked prosper. One of the best men I ever knew. What the crocodile didn't eat we buried in a swamp on an island down south."

"I know that pome."

"I'd better head for the big house."

"Sure. Something I wanted to ask you, though."

"Yeah? What?"

"That bird. It's stuffed. Right?"

"You got a bet on? It's alive. It's just doped." On idiocy-suppressing thoughts from the Dead Man. "If I don't dope it, it cusses worse than old Matt Berry. Usually at somebody who could yank off both of my arms with one hand tied behind his back."

"Oh." Sparky seemed disappointed. He must have lost the bet.

17

I dropped off the dock, strolled toward the stables. Going through was the fastest way to the big house.

I was halfway through, stepping carefully, when I found myself at the heart of a sudden triangle of guys who didn't look very friendly.

Morley's oft-given advice was sinking in. Or maybe I was just in a bad mood. Or maybe I was just impatient. I didn't ask what anybody wanted.

I spun. My oak headknocker tapped the temple of the guy moving up behind me. The pound of lead inside the stick's business end added emphasis to my argument. His eyes glazed. He went down without a word.

I continued to turn, dropped, laid my next love tap on the side of the knee of a huge Weider teamster. He was just getting a fist wound up.

His legs folded. I rose past him, tapped him on his bald spot, stepped aside as he sprawled, turned to the last character. "Something on your feeble mind?"

He kept coming even though he had no tools. That didn't seem encouraging. Why the confidence? I feinted a tap at an elbow, buried the tip of my stick in his breadbasket. He whooshed a bushel of bad breath. I whapped the side of his head, then found out why he kept on coming.

A second wave of three materialized. These boys looked like they were accustomed to muscle work. I didn't recognize any of them. On the plus side, none of them were behind me.

While they decided what to do because Plan One had burned up in their fingers I rethumped everybody already down. I didn't want any surprises.

One of the new bunch grabbed a pitchfork. Another collected a shovel. I didn't like the implications.

The Goddamn Parrot, who had elevated himself to a stringer overhead when the excitement started, said, "Awk! Garrett's in deep shit now."

The third man, who seemed to be in charge, hung back to direct traffic. He and his pals all looked up when the bird spoke.

I didn't.

I charged.

A pitchfork is nasty and a shovel unpleasant but neither was designed to hurt people. My stick, though, has no other reason for existing. A feint and a weave gave me a chance to reach in and crunch knuckles on a hand gripping the pitchfork. Shovel man froze momentarily when his too-slow buddy shrieked. I skipped aside and cracked his skull.

I swear, he shimmered. I thought he was going to fade away. I wanted to whimper because I was afraid some gods were after me again.

I whipped back to pitchfork man. He was too slow to be a threat by himself. A moment later he was sinking and I was ready to go after the last man.

The clown shut the stall gate between us, leaned on it, and smiled. "I'm impressed."

"You ought to be. You're about to be flat on your back in the horse fruit yourself. Who are you? Why the hell are you bothering me?"

"Awk," the Goddamn Parrot observed from above.

"I'm nobody special. Just a messenger."

I rolled me eyes. "Corn by the bucketful. Spare me. I don't mind crippling the messenger."

"Not scared?"

"Just quaking in my little shoesies." I banged a toe off the temple of the guy who had tried to fork me. For half a second he shimmered like his buddy had.

"No skin off my nose, you listen or not."

"Want to bet?" I popped my stick against my palm. "Let's see if you shimmer, too."

"Here's the word. We know where you live. Stay away from the Weider brewery."

"A joke, right?" I indicated my collection of unconscious bodies. "I know where I live, too. You guys want, come on over."

For just a second his confidence was shaky. "I'm telling you. Back off. Stay away."

"Says who? You've gotten something turned around inside your head. You and your company-clerk buddies here are going to keep your lardy asses off of Weider property. Next time you trespass you'll get hurt."

The guy smirked. I flicked the tip of my stick at the fingers of his right hand where he gripped the top of the gate. He bit, yanked back. I kicked the gate. He staggered backward. Unfortunately, my balance wasn't perfect either. My follow-through was a plop into not-so-sweet-smelling straw.

The Goddamn Parrot guffawed.

"Your day is coming."

The big guy bounced off a post, got his balance back. He grabbed a handy hay hook, whooshed it back and forth. He wasn't happy anymore. He snarled, "That was a big mistake. Now you got me pissed off. And I don't need you in one piece."

There are people so stupid they just can't imagine somebody hurting them. And some of those are so dim you can't even teach them with pain. This guy looked like one of the latter.

The Goddamn Parrot made a distressed noise.

I dived for my stick. It had gotten away from me when I fell. I slithered over an earlier victim. He groaned when I got him with an elbow.

"What are you men doing there?" That sounded like somebody used to being in charge. I glanced sideways as I got hold of my stick, saw Ty Weider and his wheelchair maybe fifteen feet away, beyond a couple of stalls. With him were his full-time helper Lancelyn Mac and two stable hands.

The big guy looked, too. He dithered a second longer than I did. Without getting up, I swung my stick and got him in the kneecap.

He yowled and raised his leg. I rolled into the one still on the straw.

"Lance. Ike. See what's going on there," Ty ordered.

I got up. "It's me. I was crossing from the dock to the big house when these guys jumped me." I kicked the big man in the side of the head before he got organized. I wasn't fond of anybody right then. I planted a foot on his butt and pushed him into a manure pile.

Lancelyn and Ike joined me. I asked, "You guys recognize any of these thugs?"

Both looked toward Ty for advice. Weider maneuvered his chair through the mess. "Sit them up so I can see their faces."

I lifted guys. So did Ike. Lance didn't want to get anything under his fingernails. He elected himself director of field operations.

I'd always suspected him of being that kind of guy. He was a tall, golden-haired boy with an inflated notion of his own worth. Women of the shallow variety drooled when he walked past. We'd never gotten along but, then, we'd never had to. I didn't hang out with the younger Weiders anymore.

"You play rough, Garrett," Ty said.

"I took them by surprise."

"In more ways than one, I'd guess."

He was right. For sure these guys hadn't been clear on who I was. Otherwise, they would have been better prepared.

Ty said, "Lance, those faces look familiar." He pointed, indicating the men I'd seen before myself. "What're you doing, Garrett?"

"Going through their pockets." I tapped a guy's head to keep him down. "Might find something interesting."

"You saying this wasn't personal? None of these guys have a sister?"

"Some of them probably do. But I don't know them. It didn't get personal till they tried to thump on me. The one I was wrestling when you showed up told me they were supposed to tell me to stay away from the brewery. He was the only one who ever said anything."

"You don't know him?"

"No."

"Neither do I. Lance? No? Ike? Mays? No? Looks like we have a mystery, then."

"This is Votil Hanbe," Ike said, indicating one of the familiar men. "He cleans stables nights. That one works the dock nights. I don't remember his name."

"Kessel," Lancelyn said. "Milo Kessel. Skibber Kessel is his uncle. Mr. Klees hired him. As a favor to Skibber. I was there when they discussed it."

"We can talk to them, then. Don't beat on those two anymore, Garrett. And what should we do with the rest of them?"

"Whatever you do with trespassers."

"Keelhaul 'em," the Goddamn Parrot suggested.

I continued, "Beat them some more and toss them into the canal. Hello."

"What?"

"All of them have one of these armbands tucked away." I lifted one. It was the black and red and blue common to all the human rights groups. This one boasted a black two-headed dragon on a red field as its main device. "I don't recognize this."

Nobody else claimed any knowledge, either. Ty said, "Lance, get them up and get them out of here. Ike, Mays, lend a hand."

I asked, "Is there any reason one of the nut groups would want me to stay away from here? I'm part of the scenery."

"Who knew you were coming?" Right to the point, old Ty.

"Nobody," I fibbed. He should know, though, unless he didn't talk to his intended. Nicks wouldn't be hiding what she and Alyx were doing from her fiancé, even if Alyx wanted. Or would she? "But I've been here long enough for somebody to send out for help. Only, what would political guys be afraid that I'd find?"

"These people are mainly lower-class veterans, Garrett. You need money to become a political force. Did you check to see if someone's been skimming again?"

"I did. I didn't catch any bad smells."

"I'll reexamine the accounts myself. I'll let you know if I find anything. You say my father wanted to see you?"

"Gilbey caught me on the dock. Soon as I finished I headed for the big house."

"Dad's probably grumbling about you taking so long. I'll let you know what these two have to say. If they don't talk, they'll be looking for work."

The unknowns were headed for the street already, partly under their own power. Those boys would have a fine crop of aches and bruises in the morning.

Not me, though. I'd saved myself all that by moving fast and hitting hard, *first*. Just what Morley has been preaching for so long. Pretty soon I'd be leaving them with their throats cut.

Ty muttered, "I'm going to be late again." He worked his chair around until he was right in there with the brewery employees, both of whom were conscious now. "Lance. We'll question Hanbe first. No sense upsetting Skibber Kessel if we don't have to."

The Goddamn Parrot dropped out of the gloom, satisfied that it was safe to show his ugly beak around me again.

Ty started. Then he grinned. "Put one on the other shoulder, too, Garrett. Add a tricorner hat, a bad limp, some facial scars, and an eye patch. You could pass yourself off as Captain Scarlet." He smirked.

The Goddamn Parrot brings out the worst in everybody. Except me.

"I'll just go see your dad now."

"Yo ho ho."

18

Manvil Gilbey was waiting for me. I barely finished cranking the bell handle before he stuck his bleak face outside. I was surprised. A stiffneck named Gerris Genord usually answered the door.

His nose rolled up instantly. "What in the world? . . . Are you aware of the state of your apparel?"

"Plenty. I was headed over here. I got ambushed in the stable. I'll want to talk that over with the boss, too. But first, why don't I go around back, shuck out of all this horse flavoring, and wash down? If you've got somebody who can bring me a towel and something else to wear."

"Thoughtful of you, Garrett. Take care you don't fall afoul of any pigs or cattle on your journey."

"Careful is my new middle name."

The Goddamn Parrot decided that was his cue to laugh. He sounded like a donkey braying.

I strolled around to the tradesman's gate. I waited there for ten minutes. I started talking to myself, or maybe thinking out loud to the Goddamn Parrot. Gilbey himself finally showed up to open the gate and let me into a large paved courtyard that would have been the shipping point had the mansion actually become a brewery.

"You get lost backstairs? Or are you just the only one home who'll risk—"

"I ran into Alyx. I had to discourage her from supervising your ablutions personally."

That might have been interesting. "Must be this glamorous life I lead."

"I wouldn't get too interested in Alyx."

"Me neither. Max is my bread and butter." Oh, did it hurt to say that and actually try to mean it. The more I thought about how wonderfully Alyx had grown up the more—

"And I understand you're taken."

"Awk!" Chuckles in parrotese.

"This bird and me, we're a hot number. Nothing is going to come between us."

"I expect Miss Tate will be devastated."

Manvil is business all the time. He took himself and life and everything else much too seriously. "You should relax, Gilbey. Take a night off. Go out somewhere where nobody knows you, get fucked up and party your ass off."

Gilbey's eyes widened a skillionth of an inch. "Sound advice, no doubt. It's certainly done you well. I'll consider it."

"Go after it the way you did when you were young and in the service."

"I was in the Judge Advocate's office."

"Wouldn't you know." He probably prosecuted guys for smiling on the job.

"I don't recall ever having criticized the way you live your life, Mr. Garrett."

"Ouch!" Despite his obvious disapproval. "Point taken, Mr. Gilbey. And that makes you a treasure. *Everyone* else *is* critical, including my partner, my housekeeper, my girlfriend, my best friend, even this ludicrous buzzard."

The Goddamn Parrot cracked an eyelid and went to all the trouble of interjecting an "Awk" as bitterly cold as any corpse.

For a second I thought Gilbey might crack a smile.

He didn't but I knew how to get to him now. With the unanticipated. With the kind of humor that blindsides you with the unlikely.

"A troll, an ogre, and a barbarian walk into a tavern. The elephant behind the bar says, 'We don't serve—' "

"Mice are never amusing."

"You've heard it." I hadn't finished the setup.

"I hear them all. Kittyjo collects them. The more off-color the better. I have to listen to them. Here we are. I had several buckets of hot water brought around. Use them as you will."

"Can I ask you something, Gilbey?"

He waited, neither offering permission nor denying it.

"You're a right guy. You're Max's pal. His sidekick. But half the time you talk like some kind of butler or something."

"We are what we are, Garrett. You should find soap, towels, and fresh clothing inside. Rinse down the floor when you're done. Courtesy to the next bather. When you're ready, meet us in Max's study."

"Thanks. For everything and whatever."

I stepped into the place he had made available. The floor was zinc. So were the walls. The staff were allowed to bathe there. Horses got scrubbed down there, too.

A selection of clothing, soap, a brush, and three steaming buckets all sat on a bench. A doorway without a door in it opened into a chamber about five feet by nine, also floored and walled with zinc. The floor sloped to a central drain. A bizarre apparatus consisting of a barrel and lead pipes hung overhead. You filled the tank by climbing a ladder in the outer room.

I figured it out because it resembled a contraption we'd built from a hardtack barrel in the islands, using bamboo for pipes.

I scrubbed up as good as I have in years.

The clothes were not the sort you'll usually find on one of Mama Garrett's boys—mainly because Mom and all her boys together couldn't afford them. Nor were they a choice I would've selected, given a choice. They were too dressy, formal, dull, too dark, more suited to the funeral racket. Also, there was a waistcoat. And ruffles. Not a plethora of ruffles. Not ruffles like you see when Morley dresses up. But ruffles.

Ruffles aren't me.

The Goddamn Parrot resumed station on my shoulder. He made no effort to control his snickers.

The clothing smelled like it had been stored. Maybe it had belonged to one of the Weider boys. In happier times. Not Ty, though. He was smaller than me. Probably the only one who hadn't come home. I couldn't remember his name.

The tools were there so I shaved. I don't know why I didn't seize the opportunity to cut the Goddamn Parrot's throat. It was one in a thousand. And nobody was looking.

19

Old Man Weider stands about two hairs over five and a half feet tall but he has a much bigger presence. He's a round-faced, ruddy-skinned guy with close-cropped white hair, most of which has migrated to the sides of his head, I suppose to escape the direct impact of sunshine and rain. His mustache is doing much better, thank you. Maybe it gets more fertilizer. It's a huge gray bush with flecks of yesterday's brown still hanging on stubbornly.

Weider smiles readily but his smiles seldom take up residence in his eyes. It's like he's really glad to see you but the moment you're actually there he starts calculating all the angles.

He grabbed my hand, pumped it. His fingers were plump little sausages. He grinned as he said, "I hear you had an adventure over in my stables." He has remarkably good teeth for his age. "Ty sent Ike Khame over. He told us what happened while you were cleaning up."

"Ah. An adventure. That don't capture it. I was lucky Ty and Lance turned up when they did."

"Why?"

"What?"

"Sorry. Sit down. You look good in those clothes. They were Tad's. I suppose you guessed. Keep them. In fact, Manvil, tell Genord to have Tad's whole wardrobe shipped over to Garrett's place. You don't have any objection, do you?" This was the boss. Chatter chatter, off in seven unpredictable directions.

"No."

"Sit down. Sit down. You want something to drink? We've got beer. Or beer. Or you can have beer." He worked some change on that joke every time I visited. Which wasn't often. Our relationship may be based on absence makes the heart grown fonder. "Why would anyone jump you?"

"Good question. I don't know. Two were your employees. Ty said he'd get an answer. They all carried armbands from some rights gang. Their emblem wasn't one I've ever seen before."

Gilbey brought a schooner of beer, a Weider Dark Reserve with a strong yeast flavor. The very beer the goats in heaven give instead of milk. He said, "It's spooky, seeing you in those clothes."

Weider agreed. "If we got a surgeon to cut that growth off your shoulder, you'd look a lot like Tad." The old pain rose into Weider's eyes. It was the pain we all know because we've all lost somebody to the war. I took a long drink and tried to forget my brother. My father doesn't hurt because I don't remember him.

Weider didn't have that solace. Nor that of beer. He drinks nothing. He stays away because he loves the stuff too much.

Gilbey drew a mug. He would nurse it all evening. "I don't get out much anymore, Garrett," he said as he settled into the chair he always used, not far from Max, where he could scoot over and get into a cutthroat game of dominoes when the mood hit. "I'm out of touch with popular culture. Are stuffed birds some new fad?"

"A present from a friend." I let it go at that.

With my luck the Dead Man was napping and catching nothing through that hideous jungle chicken.

Weider mused, "So Alyx went to you."

I nodded.

"I didn't send her."

"So she said. But she hinted that you wouldn't run me off if I turned up."

"It's good that you came. You've already generated evidence that something is going on. This cancer people call a human rights movement. It *has* penetrated the brewery."

"Alyx said somebody's trying to extort money on behalf of The Call."

Weider seemed surprised. He glanced at Gilbey. "Manvil?"

"News to me." Gilbey sat forward in his chair, alert.

"She said Ty told her. Tinnie and Nicks backed her up. A couple of brewmasters supposedly saw it happen."

"They did? The Call? Nicks?"

"Miss Nicholas. Ty's fiancé. It doesn't sound like The Call's style."

"Absolutely not. Marengo North English has more wealth than any three men deserve."

Interesting. Weider should be North English's equal in that. "I'd gladly relieve the man of some of the responsibility."

Weider chuckled. "No doubt. But his wealth is why The Call is the biggest rights group."

Gilbey amended, "His wealth and his connections. Most of his social peers share his prejudices."

Max said, "I don't. Even though I consider him my friend. He wouldn't try something that underhanded. He'd come ask for support."

I said, "He might have some renegade troops." I'd had an unpleasant encounter with a Call splinter group not that long ago.

"Plausible." Gilbey took my schooner, restored it to a happier estate, then added, "The men in the stable weren't from The Call."

Weider told me, "Ike seemed certain that Ty had made sure of that."

"Oh."

"Tomorrow night I'm hosting a gala where Ty and Giorgi will announce their engagement. Everybody who is anybody will be here. Including Marengo North English and Bondurant Altoona. And you, I hope. Won't you join us?"

"Uh . . . Me? Socializing with socialites?" I've done that, mostly in shady places, street corners, alleyways, taverns where their own kind won't notice them rubbing elbows with a disreputable character like me.

"You'll manage, Garrett. Just bring your manners. Pretend the guests are all beautiful women and you have charm to waste. Get him an invitation, Manvil. You'll come in like any other guest, Garrett. The security people won't know who you are. Not right away."

I must have let another expression get out and go scampering around my face. Maybe I need to hit the Landing and hang out in the gambling dens until I get my betting face back.

"I didn't have you do security because you're only one man, Garrett."

That was hopping on a crippled leg but I ignored it. I accepted a fancy folded paper from Gilbey, asked Weider, "So why did you send Manvil to get me?"

"An impulse. Possibly driven by an unconscious surge of common sense. I wanted to give you that invitation. Because I suddenly realized that by shutting you out I was putting myself entirely in the hands of amateurs and strangers at a time when I was going to have a house full of outsiders, many of whom I couldn't call friends even during a wedding celebration. And I wanted to find out why you suddenly decided to show an interest in the brewery. Just when things are showing signs of getting weird. Call it my old-age paranoia suddenly flaring up."

I looked at Gilbey. Manvil thinks much less of me than Max does. "You approve?"

"I do." But his gout was nipping him, or he was having a problem with gas pains.

"You have other troubles?"

Max said, "I expect to find out for sure tomorrow night. I mean to flush the snakes out of the grass."

There would be a few of those amongst the bourgeois robber moguls likely to be invited to a Weider soiree. Vipers the size of the crocodile killers we used to cut up and feed to the saber-toothed cats in the islands . . .

Gilbey volunteered, "Alyx wanted you invited, too."

The little darling. "Huh?"

"On behalf of Miss Tate. But also because she's wary of snakes herself."

Tinnie seemed to be wriggling her cute little tail right back into the center of my life. And I didn't mind at all. "I'll see if I can't find something to wear."

"Manvil will have Genord make sure Tad's things gets to your house in time. Please avoid the stables until after the affair."

"I think I can resist the urge to visit them."

Grinning, Gilbey suggested, "If you arrive early, you can critique our arrangements and watch the villains—make that guests—arrive."

I pretended to be businesslike. "A reasonable plan, gentlemen."

"Awk! We'll be here."

"We? I'll sell your feathers first, you glorified duster."

Weider chuckled. He said, "At least one of you ought to show up."

"One of us will. Me. The one with half a brain." I got up. I must have moved too fast. The floor got awfully unsteady suddenly.

Couldn't have been that little dribble of beer.

20

"Will you quit stomping around?" The Goddamn Parrot kept getting more and more restless. I hoped that didn't mean he wanted to exploit me the way pigeons traditionally do statues of forgotten generals. I'd seen enough animal by-product for one day.

Weider's personal sitting room was in a corner of the front of his mansion, on what was called the second floor despite being only slightly above street level. The ground on which the mansion stood sloped. In back you could walk straight out but in front you climbed fifteen steps to reach the front door, then descended half a dozen back to street level. So the first floor lies below actual ground level almost everywhere. Only the rear of the house, including the kitchen, family dining room, and back stairs sees daily use. Most of it is reserved for entertainment.

Even the second floor mainly serves business and entertainment purposes. Weider rules his empire from there. The family lives higher still, on the third and fourth floors. Servants who live on the premises do so in nooks and crannies and under the eaves.

I didn't envy them.

I was about to head down the grand staircase to the first floor when a remote scream stopped me. I glanced back. Gilbey stood in the doorway of Weider's study, silhouetted. He shrugged, pointed upward.

I clomped downstairs muttering, "Tom is still with us." I took several deep breaths crossing the pink-marble floor so when I got to the steps I could bound up to the front door with the spring of a misspent youth. The Goddamn Parrot never stopped prancing on my shoulder.

Max had three sons: Tad, Tom, and Ty. Tom and Ty made it back from the Cantard but Tom left his mind and soul behind.

Rich or poor, we have that in common. We've been to the Cantard. And we've lost somebody. And none of us who survived came home unchanged.

But the war is over. Karenta has triumphed. The Cantard's fabulous mines now serve the sorcerers, who are our real masters. Karenta is the most powerful kingdom in the world. We should be proud.

This month, for the first time in three generations, the Crown conscripted no one.

We won. And because we did our world is falling apart.

Boy, am I glad we didn't lose.

It seemed like a mile to the door. My heels clacked hollowly. Their sound echoed off the walls. Preparations were under way for the party but so far only to the extent that the hall had been stripped of clutter like carpets, furniture, portraits of imaginary forbears, old armor, crossed swords and pikes, and most anything that could become a weapon after the weather turned drunken.

There was no one watching the front door. The old man's paranoia couldn't run too deep. I clomped up and let myself out while making a mental note to suggest a less relaxed security posture.

I surveyed the neighborhood from the porch. Daylight was a

ghost of its former gaudy self. "You got to dump, you'd better go do it now, you runt turkey."

The bird squawked, said, "I wanted you outside so I could talk."

The Dead Man. Of course. I knew we were headed this direction as soon as he started insisting that I take the little vulture everywhere. Not only would he use that ugly feather duster to spy on me, he meant to nag me like he was my mother.

I muttered, "Bird, you are doomed! Doomed!"

"What?"

"You've got me talking to myself. What do you want?"

"You need to come home. We have company only you can handle."

"Damn." What did that mean? I didn't ask because he wouldn't tell me. His excuse would be that the bird could talk only so much before he injured his throat, a limitation I've never witnessed when that vulture—or the Dead Man—had something to say that I didn't want to hear. "Want to name names?"

"No. Don't waste time."

I'll strangle them both. It's got to take more effort to deny me than to say a name.

I took the direct route, which turned out to be a poor choice.

Grand Avenue from the Landing south to the Dream Quarter was choked with prohuman demonstrators. They were mostly younger than me. It didn't seem possible that there could be so many, that they could all belong right here instead of scattered amongst a hundred towns and cities and a hundred thousand farms. But, of course, resentment of nonhumans is an ancient exercise. We had great and vicious wars in ages past. And today plenty of men older than me, secure in their trade or employment, are as intolerant as any youngster with no prospects.

I hit Grand where six hundred guys from The Call were marching back and forth practicing their manuals at arms using quarterstaves and wooden swords instead of pikes and sharp steel. Their apparel was moderately uniform. Their shields matched. Most wore light leather helmets. They were true believers in the highest cause and they had faced deadly enemies on the plains of war. This night would turn nasty if some genius on the Hill decided the army should disperse the demonstrators.

Any troops sent in faced demobilization themselves. An interesting complication.

I relaxed, awaited a chance to cross when I wouldn't inconvenience any nut. You don't want to irritate somebody who has several thousand of his best friends handy. Not unless you're armed with the headbone of an ass.

A nice gap opened. Me and fifty other apolitical types decided to go for it.

"Hey! Garrett! Wait up!"

I knew that voice. Unfortunately. "Damn!" Maybe I could out-run her.

21

"Garrett!" That was my pal Winger doing the hollering. Winger is a big old country girl as tall as me, a good-looker, who abandoned her husband and kids to chase her fortune in the city. "Dammit! You stop right there, Garrett!"

"Wait," the Goddamn Parrot squawked in my ear. I stopped. I was well trained. Several people nearby stopped, too, all startled by the bird's having spoken.

A kid asked, "Does your bird really talk, Mister?" She was maybe five with blond hair in ringlets and the biggest innocent blue eyes ever invented. I wanted to make a date for about fifteen years but her dad looked like a guy who thought too much like a father. "Yes, he does. But it's hard to get him started."

"Awk! Pretty baby! Pretty girl!"

"Unless you're someone special."

The bird spotted Winger. "Awk! Holy hooters! Look at them gazoombies!" Nature had been generous to Winger.

I squeezed the bird's beak before he got me assassinated.

"I love you, too, Mr. Big," Winger said, hustling up. She ignored kid and dad completely. The father decided he wanted nothing to do with lowlifes like us. He took off across the street. Winger de-manded, "Where do you think you're going, Garrett?"

"I was seriously contemplating crossing the street while the goofballs don't have it blocked, Hawkeye."

"He was trying to get away from you, genius," said a voice from behind me.

"Saucerhead!" I turned. Saucerhead Tharpe is a mountain of a man whose face has been rearranged several times too often. He grinned down at me. His teeth were stunted, black, and broken.

Between them Saucerhead and Winger have about enough sense to get out of the rain. After a lively debate obese with irrelevance. But you can count on their friendship. Well, all right, you can count on Saucerhead's friendship. Winger's tends to get slippery if money is involved.

"Hello, Winger my love. Hello, Saucerhead. How are you? I'm just fine myself, thank you. Nice to see you. I can't chat right now. I've got to run."

"We'll run with you," Winger told me.

"Why?"

"Because your sidekick isn't athletic enough to do it hisself so he hired us. He figures you might need your diaper changed."

"Yeah," Saucerhead said. "He's got a notion somebody might actually want to hurt you."

"I can't imagine why."

"I can't imagine why, neither, Garrett," Winger grumbled. "I mean, you only trample all over people's feelings—"

"Stuff it, Winger. Last time you had a feeling you beat it to a midwife to find out if it was gas or pregnancy."

Winger grinned.

The man with the cute little girl increased his pace. He ignored her demands to hear the pretty bird talk again.

The Call guys started a chant and cheer combination that was both moving and chilling. Then they started marching in place. Their feet shook the pavement. They had a band, too, we discovered to our dismay.

I never liked military bands. I don't get real excited about patriotic marches, either.

I paid attention and concentrated when I was in the Corps. I got real good at what I did. I became one of the best in a force made up of the elite of the elite. That helped me stay healthy. Never before then, then, or even now, has my soul suffered any compulsion to become an anonymous fraction of a brainless mass that has its thinking done for it by somebody who shouldn't ought to be trusted to water horses.

Another chance to cross presented itself. I stepped out. Winger and Saucerhead stepped with me, one on either side. What was going on in the Dead Man's minds?

Maybe he was finally drifting away for good, tarrying in a paranoid fantasy before letting go?

"This political crap is out of hand," I told Saucerhead.

Tharpe is no thinker. He takes a while to form an opinion so he must have applied some serious mind work to the matter. "I don't get it, Garrett. They're overreacting. It's like they're screaming because TunFaire is full of people who live here."

If Saucerhead has a prejudice, I've never noticed. Of course, he can develop one professionally if the pay is right. He's a bone-breaker by trade, though he needs odd jobs to keep body and soul together.

"The other day you told me these times would be good for you."

"Yeah. But times being good for me don't mean it's right, what's happening. People are going crazy. It's like some mad wizard cast a hate spell so everybody would act twice as stupid as usual."

Saucerhead and Winger searched the shadows as we walked. I kept an eye on the darkness myself. I was edgy. Times had not been easy lately. I thought about penning an autobiography called *Trouble Follows Me* or maybe *Danger Is My Business*.

Nothing happened except that we had to detour one small riot. Straggler rightsists had run into night folks who didn't share their viewpoint. Most of the night crowd aren't human and none have had sensitivity training so they respond to offensive behavior by breaking heads.

I don't know why when you put three drunks together they decide they can conquer the world. If they choose to start with a troll, they get hurt. No matter how much they drink that troll is still impervious to just about everything but lichen infections.

Beer may not be the root cause of social problems at all, despite what the teetotallers claim. Old Man Weider may be producing the cure for our social ills. Suppose we let the morons get tanked and go looking for big trouble? Big trouble can eliminate them. Bingo. No more problem.

You can't convince me that I'm obligated to save you from yourself. If you want to head for hell by way of smoking weed or opium, or by drinking, or by being dim enough to call a giant names to his face, go head. Enjoy the slide. I won't get in your way.

Nope. I won't hand you a bucket of grease, either. You've got to do it on your own.

22

"What's the drill?" I asked as we turned into Macunado east of my place. I spoke for the Goddamn Parrot, in case the Dead Man needed to let me know about any special plans. Saucerhead and Winger thought I was asking them. They were unaware of the special relationship between the character with no mind and the one with way too many.

Winger said, "We walk you to your door and make sure you're safely inside. You pay us."

"Pay you? That's going to come out of the Dead Man's side of the business. I didn't ask for baby-sitters."

His Nibs didn't rise to the bait. He didn't want anybody to know he used the parrot.

Saucerhead said, "Will you look at them kids, Garrett? That's disgusting."

He meant several youths of preconscription age gathered on a street corner. They were baiting a covey of adolescent elf girls who were way out of their own neighborhood, not to mention out after dark. Their fathers would have whipped their bottoms purple had they witnessed what was happening. The boys were uncomplimentary in the extreme, their vocabularies heavily racist—although the clothing they affected was borrowed directly from elven styles. The girls giggled at the boys and dared them to do something. Anything. Because then they would make the boys look as stupid as they were talking.

"You want me to go tell them to mind their manners?" I asked.

"Huh?" Tharpe responded, baffled. "Manners? What're you talking about, Garrett?"

"No. What're *you* talking about? If not their behavior?"

"Their hair, man!" Tharpe eyed me like he wondered if I was going blind. "Look at their hair."

"They've got a lot of it." Most of them had it up and artificially curled and it looked like hell, but so what? It was obvious already that they didn't mind being the butt of mockery.

Saucerhead never outgrew his military haircut. He grumbled, "What kind of parents would let their kids go around looking like that? You want to know why Karenta is going to hell . . ."

I did but I didn't think Saucerhead's theory would hold much water.

Hair had nothing to do with those boys' behavior—though behavior and hair might be two symptoms of the same disease. And the girls bore an equal responsibility. Hardly anybody, human or elven, would argue that there are any women more beautiful or sensual than the elven—and these girls were blessed additionally with the glow of youth. And they flaunted every weapon they had to get those boys to humiliate themselves.

The boys were too naive to realize they were going to lose no matter what they did. That's a hard lesson for even a man of my mature years. I'm past standing on street corners and howling at the unattainable but I suspect no woman ever gets entirely beyond belittling you, however subtly, for finding her attractive.

I was stretching Saucerhead's mind to its limit trying to explain what was going on across the street when Winger opined, "You're really full of shit, Garrett."

"Tell you what, Winger. You tell me about the women you hang out with."

"Huh? What's that got to do with anything?"

"You're going to tell me how women really think. But you hang out with me. You hang out with Saucerhead when he doesn't have a girlfriend tying him down. You hang out in lowlife taverns trying to get into fights with guys who remind you of your husband. You hang out with thieves and thugs and confidence men and none of them are women so I don't think the fact that you squat to pee qualifies you as an expert on female culture as practiced in our great metropolis."

"Shee-it. There you go cutting me down again 'cause I come from the country."

This could go on for hours. Winger always has a comeback, even if it doesn't make much sense. Lucky for me, we came to my house. It was night out and as quiet as it gets in my block but damned if Mrs. Cardonlos wasn't outside watching my place like she expected entertainment of the sort only I can provide.

I studied the area carefully. First I get an armed escort, then I find my neighborhood nemesis on point. "What's happening, Old Bones? How come the wicked witch of Macunado Street is on patrol?"

Saucerhead looked at me like I'd gone goofier than he'd ever expected. "Just thinking out loud," I said. "Priming him."

"Yeah?" Winger said. "Then tell him to read his account book. There's two marks each due here."

"Two marks? Don't be ridiculous."

It is indeed ridiculous, Garrett. The woman has swung into her avaricious mode. And she is testing our ability to communicate, to establish, if she can, our limits. Two pennyweights silver was the agreed upon fee. And that was overly generous. On reflection I believe you ought to convince them to take an equivalent value in copper sceats. The price of silver is depressed. It will stabilize at a higher level once the euphoria of victory is swept away by reality's breeze.

What was he going on about? "Euphoria? You've got to be kidding. You know what's happening in these streets?"

Winger and Saucerhead gaped.

Yes. I do know. Would you say that what is happening involves the sort of people who deal in large quantities of noble metals?

"All right. I understand." Dummy me. I understood, too, that I had given Winger a bucket of information for free.

Please deal with those two quickly. We have company and I am impatient to correct that.

Oh my.

23

Winger wouldn't take copper. She wasn't bright but she was possessed of a certain cunning. If we didn't want to let go of our silver, we must know something.

She respected the Dead Man's brains.

Saucerhead followed her lead though he wasn't sure why. He gave me a black look for trying to pay him in copper. I told him, "Don't spend it all in one place."

"It's already spent, Garrett. I owe Morley."

Imagine that. Tharpe runs a tab at Morley's place. Even now that it's The Palms. How come Morley lets him?

Winger told me, "You need to consult some kind of expert, Garrett."

"Expert?"

"About your habit of talking to birds."

"I could cure it in a minute. Faster, even. Take him home with you. He idolizes you. And he makes more sense than most people do."

Winger responded with a big raspberry. As they walked away Saucerhead tried to convince her that she'd just blown the best offer she'd had all year. Nobody human had shown as much interest.

"You want a knuckle sandwich for supper you just keep on jacking your jaw," Winger growled.

"Where we gonna eat, anyway?"

I shut the door, pleased that we'd gotten by without Winger trying to enlist me in some harebrained scheme for replacing the Crown Jewels with paste. They say you can't pick your relatives but you can pick your friends. I must have some really strange secret urges.

Garrett. Cease dallying.

I entered the Dead Man's room, calling to the kitchen, "Dean, I need you to come bear witness." I knew the signs. I was about to be granted a nose-to-the grindstone lecture by the all-time grandmaster procrastinator and slough-off artist. Trouble was, the only witness who could really indict him would be another Loghyr. "A little chow wouldn't hurt, either." My own particular Loghyr, despite having been dead for ages, has the reputation of being one of the most ambitious of his kind ever.

Some battles you can't win. Wisdom is attained when you start to recognize those beforehand and slink onward in search of ground you do have a chance to hold.

Dean, please bring our guest when you come. And do put together a platter for Garrett, if you will be so kind. He is hungry and becoming cranky.

I was going to get crankier. His attitude earlier and that message told me our guest was female and under forty. Dean has a way with women young enough to be his daughters. They like to hang out in his kitchen. Partly that's because he's safe, partly because he indulges them like they were favorite daughters, partly because he's a nice old guy.

"Is Tinnie here again?"

No. Tell me what happened out there.

"The Goddamn Parrot was on top of me the whole damned time."

The beast is more limited than you believe. The bird is keen of ear but only in a narrow range. And his visual acuity and sense of smell leave much to be desired.

"You ought to find yourself a human tool." But not me.

Perfect idea. Unfortunately, no human has a mind sensitive enough for remote access. No intelligent creature, whatever the species, fits my particulars exactly. There would appear to be a relationship. I must examine that someday.

"Yeah," I muttered, completely confident that I was a failed experiment.

The door swung open. Dean, platter in hand, held it for someone.

Someone stepped inside.

"You?" I was surprised.

"Me," said Belinda Contague. "Your lack of enthusiasm is breaking my heart."

The woman doesn't have one. But I didn't remind her.

She likes black. She positively *loves* black. She wore a black evening cloak over a masculine-cut black suit of very supple leather. She wore black boots with raised heels. A pair of long black-silk gloves were folded over her black-leather belt. When she arrived, I was sure, Dean had taken her black hat and veil and put them in the small front room. She'd painted her nails black and had put something on her lips to darken and gloss them. Then she'd used a face powder to make her skin appear more pallid.

I have seen vampires with more color.

Despite all that, or perhaps because of it, she was incredibly beautiful. More, she exuded something that made it difficult to cling to common sense and the urge to self-preservation. That bizarre look was very erotic.

"You sent a message. I was in town. I had no other demands on my time. I came here. You were out but Dean was kind. As he ever is."

I glared at the Dead Man, thought hard: You should have warned me.

He didn't respond.

Damn, the woman was bold. She knew what the Dead Man was. Nobody with a conscience as black as hers ought to be anywhere near him.

Back in those remote times when the Outfit was in transition, passing into Belinda's regency, we had a brief fling. I might consider myself lucky because I got out alive. Belinda is very strange. And when it comes to hardness she makes her daddy look like a pet bunny.

I gobbled, "I'm sorry. You took me off guard. You're the last person I expected."

Belinda Contague stands five feet six inches. She looks twenty-five, says she's twenty. She lived a rough life before she took over. Lived like she was trying to kill herself. She was in good shape now, as her apparel proclaimed eloquently. Nature blessed her with a shape that would have them kicking the lids off their coffins if she strolled through a mortuary. Her dark eyes fell smack into the center of that semi-mythical "windows of the soul" class. You will discover more warmth and compassion in the stare of a cobra.

I can't imagine what she ever saw in me.

I always knew she would come back to haunt me, though.

"I'm not as bad as you think, Garrett."

Her daddy used to say the same thing. "Huh?"

"My father turned out to be a good friend, didn't he?" She sounded wistful.

I grunted. My relationship with Chodo Contague had been strange, too. I did him a big favor once, accidentally, and forever afterward he felt he owed me. He did me good turns even when I didn't ask. He covered my ass. He tried hard to entangle me in the Outfit's webs so I'd become one of his soldiers. I repaid him by helping take him down.

"Crask and Sadler are back in town." That would take the play out of Belinda.

"You saw them?" She actually became more pale.

"No. I heard it from Relway. Via Captain Block. He traded the information for a favor." She understood that kind of deal.

She didn't question my source. "What favor?"

"It doesn't involve you or yours."

"Relway isn't interested in us?"

"Of course he is. He's interested in everything. But he's a realist. He knows you offer services the public wants, nor are you breaking the law, mostly. Whatever the priests and reformers say. He's really interested in people who hurt people. Or people he thinks threaten society. But he's Relway. He's a slave to his obsessions. He wants to know everything about everything."

Garrett, being able to read your mind and intentions helps but even so what you have just said makes only marginal sense.

I had no trouble understanding me.

Belinda got it, too, though her coal-chip gaze never stopped boring holes through me.

I asked, "Darling, why couldn't you be somebody else?" Nobody grabs the unreasoning side of me like Belinda Contague.

"Sometimes I wish I was somebody else, too, Garrett. But it's too late."

"Do we have to be enemies?"

"Were we ever?"

Yes. Careful, Garrett. "No. But what we are can drive us places where we're out of choices."

"Sufficient to the day the evil thereof."

I gave her a look at my raised eyebrow. That always charms them.

"And don't try that on me, Garrett. You're in my heart. Suppose we just go on the way you did with my father?"

"Your dad thought he owed me." The final account left me way in his debt, though.

"I owe you. In a different way. You're the only guy I know who treats me like a human being. Even when I was completely weird you treated me right."

"That's just me." I glanced at the Dead Man. He was one witness too many.

"Shut up. I'm not proposing. I'm not going to steal you away from the Tate woman." She has more spies than Relway. "But I do have my small claim on you."

Control your breathing, Garrett.

When I was younger the old guys promised me I'd grow out of the heavy breathing. Maybe you have to be dead, though. There's always a Belinda or Tinnie or somebody scrambling my brain.

"If what Relway wants doesn't involve me, what's the secret?"

Good point. Perhaps. "He wants to infiltrate the rights movement. And I'm involved because some rightsist group is trying to extort money from the Weider family."

Belinda became the kingpin completely, a stone killer handicapped only marginally by her sex. "I have rightsist problems, too," she said. "Those people have no respect. They believe they have the right to do whatever they want because their cause is just."

I grunted agreement. That was their thinking exactly.

"I won't let them tread on my toes."

Oh-oh. Somebody else wanted to sign me up.

I am going to take a short nap, Garrett. I expect it will last all night.

What? Now I knew why I hadn't seen Belinda's coach outside. She'd had no plans to leave and His Nibs suddenly was inclined to humor her. Which he had not been only a short while ago. What intriguing thought had he plucked from her spider's nest of a mind?

24

I'm a devil pig, I'm told, because I like women. A lot. Go figure that kind of thinking.

The preference has gotten me into trouble occasionally. With Belinda trouble could get ugly. The spiders in her head spin strangely kinked thoughts. And she had to turn up just when Tinnie's stubbornness had begun to crack.

I heard about it over breakfast, basking in Dean's disapproval. I hated to let him waste all that bile.

"Thanks," I said, accepting the tea. "You'll need to do up the guest bedroom after Belinda gets up."

The old boy had an idea in his head. He wasn't going to let me confuse him.

"You're wasting an ulcer, Dean." Help! I appealed to the Dead Man. Tell him nothing happened.

I was asleep, Garrett. However, if a small prevarication will oil the machinery . . .

Dean made a sound of disgust. He didn't want to believe the Dead Man, either.

Belinda came downstairs. She was in a bitter mood. She didn't like not getting her own way. She glared at Dean. He responded with the indifference of a man so old he has nothing left to fear.

Belinda shrugged. She cared for no man's opinion, which wasn't always wise. Her world was unforgiving and the penalties for failing to observe its rules often lethal. She worried too little about making enemies inside her own circle. She could have worked something out with Crask and Sadler.

Belinda was Chodo Contague's child, both his creation and his doom.

It must have been hell to be his kid. Belinda wouldn't talk about it but there was no doubt that she was bitter.

There are suspicions that Belinda's mother went to her eternal reward early because Chodo disapproved of her infidelity.

That was common rumor before I ever met Belinda. It might have plenty to do with Chodo's condition now.

I feared Belinda's obsessions might compel the Outfit to take her down. But she was quite capable of taking it down with her.

Belinda asked, "Suppose I explain in person?"

"That might get exciting."

"Is the woman irrational, Garrett?"

"Is any woman reasonable after she makes up her mind? Tinnie's not. I can't figure her out. I hardly try anymore. What're you trying to do to me?"

"Nothing anymore, Garrett. It's just business now."

Did I need to concern myself with the hell hath no fury syndrome?

"Don't worry, lover. These crackpots are bad for business. They'll be dealt with. But—"

"Hey! Could that be why Crask and Sadler are back? Because somebody wants their knowledge about you?"

Belinda smiled like a cat contemplating a cornered mouse. "Possibly. I have an idea. Why don't I be your companion tonight? I can see people I'd never run into otherwise."

"I'm dead."

She has put forth an outstanding idea, Garrett. Consider it.

I had a good notion where she came up with it, too. "You consider it, Chuckles. You don't have to get along with Tinnie Tate."

As Miss Contague has suggested, Miss Tate cannot be entirely irrational.

"Then you know a different Miss Tate." He did see more of Tinnie than I did, though. Maybe he knew something. Maybe the leopardess had changed her spots. Maybe she'd traded them in for saber-tooth tiger stripes.

I told Belinda, "Me and the junior partner need to butt heads. He agrees with you."

"Tell him I take back all the wicked things I ever said about him."

"I won't. I'm going to invent new words so I can say more."

25

"What is this?" I demanded as I blew into the Dead Man's room. "Are you determined to get me lynched?"

I reiterate. Miss Tate is not irrational. Enough of that. There are larger issues at hand.

"Larger to who, Old Bones?"

Thousands. Even tens of thousands. Name for me, if you will, just five nonhumans murdered today who considered Miss Tate's potential ill will an eventuality more dire than the catastrophe which actually afflicted them.

"Unfair. Unfair." He was deft at carving holes in the thickest smoke when the mood took him. "None of them knew Tinnie like I—"

Garrett.

"All right. How is taking Belinda along going to be useful?"

We want to situate you so that you become a recognized intermediary between as many interests as possible. So you can dip into the information flows. This will position you to take advantage of anyone wishing to communicate with the Syndicate. Particularly as regards those with little sympathy for The Call and its ilk.

Ilk? What kind of word is ilk? "Relway?"

An excellent example. With Max Weider and his moderate friends, perhaps, as another spoke to that wheel. With effective guidance I can even see you situating yourself on the axis between the radical parties and Glory Mooncalled's people.

Guess who would do the guiding.

He was feeling smug about his genius. His true plan drifted too near the surface of his thoughts. "Hang on there, Old Bones. There ain't no way I can sell me to all those folks as the hero of their prophecies."

You do not have to sell yourself to Mr. Weider or Mr. Relway. You serve their interests already. No effort is needed to bring Miss Contague along, either. She wants to come aboard. That leaves only the rightsists and the rebels. The former are after you already.

Aw, hell. Why not link up with the nonhumans and all those wannabe revolutionaries who have been lying low since the explosion of rightsist terrorism? The rightsists have no use for those guys, either. Rightsists don't like anybody very much.

"Nothing to it, Big Guy. A piece of cake."

The rightsists should be fish in a barrel, to use your vernacular. You are exactly what they want. A certified war hero.

"I'm a war hero who lives with a Loghyr and a psychotic talking bird and my best friend is part elf."

All faults that are correctable. A man can come to the truth late. You can sell the rightsists because they want to be sold. Glory Mooncalled's is the organization I am concerned about cracking.

"Why bother? I don't share your infatuation with Glory Mooncalled."

Truth be told, Garrett, I no longer share that infatuation with my

*younger self. When Mooncalled was a distant gadfly yanking the
beards of the lords and ladies we love to hate it was easy to cheer
him on. But he is among us now and the glimmers of purpose I
catch are depressingly sinister. Perhaps the Mooncalled I treasured perished along with his dream of an independent Cantard.
Or he may have elected to become Karenta's great foe because we
no longer have serious enemies but deserve them.*

"There's that damned word again, Smiley."

Which word?

'We.' I find nonhumans fond of reminding the rest of us that
Karenta is a human construct. They make big shows of negotiating
exemptions from human law and rule.

*Excellent. Maintain that capacity for dredging up irrelevant
sophistries and The Call will clutch you to its bosom. You may be
promoted directly into their Inner Council.*

"I don't want to do this."

*There is little choice, Garrett. These are pivotal times. Everyone
must take a stand before it ends. Who refuses will be devoured because he will be out there alone. But we who recognize the signs
and portents have the opportunity to deflect or defeat the gathering
darkness.*

"I know where I stand, Windy. But I'd rather be noble and hon-
orable and defend true justice and the divine right of Karenta's
kings while I'm sitting in my office with a mug in my hand, chatting with Eleanor."

And you insist that I am lazy.

"Only because you have no more ambition than a bone that's
been buried for twenty years. You don't have to go out there and try
to run between the raindrops, partner."

That is another matter which warrants future discussion.

26

"Right on time," I said when somebody hammered on my door late
in the afternoon.

Belinda said, "My people are expected to be punctual and to do
their jobs well. And they deliver."

"You should take life easier, Belinda. You don't always have to be—"

"I try, Garrett. But some demon keeps pushing me. I can't beat it. And it'll get me killed eventually."

I nodded. That came with the territory. I looked out the peephole. An unfamiliar hulking creature of mixed ancestary shuffled impatiently on my front stoop. "I think I understand. Is this thing somebody you know?"

She leaned past me, so close I had trouble breathing normally. "That's Two Toes Harker. My driver."

"Driver? He looks like he wrestles ogres for a living."

"He looks badder than he is. He doesn't move very well anymore."

Two Toes knocked again. Despite plaster dust falling all over the house Dean didn't come out of the kitchen. He was exasperated with everybody. And for once he did put the blame where it always belongs: squarely on the shoulders of the Dead Man.

"I'll get my shoulder ornament and we'll be set."

"Why? That bird is disgusting."

Finally, somebody who agreed with me.

The Dead Man relaxed his control of the Goddamn Parrot. The little monster barked, "I'm in love! Look at this sweet fluff!"

"I already looked, you deadweight jungle buzzard. And you're right. She looks damned good. But she's a lady. Mind your stinking manners."

"That was really good, Garrett," Belinda told me. "Your lips never moved once."

Argh! But the bird was right. I was right. She *did* look good, if a little too vampiric for current fashion. She'd had people in and out all afternoon, some to elevate her to this supernal state. She didn't want to go unnoticed tonight. Hell, she was going to raise the dead. I thought about wrapping her in a blanket so we wouldn't have crowds chasing us through the streets.

This evening would be easy on my eyeballs. Alyx was sure to give Belinda a run. So would Nicks. And Tinnie would be absolutely killer if she bothered to try. Belinda would be a blood-dark rose in a garden of brilliant whites and yellows and carmines.

"If I was doing the talking this little shit would say things to score points for me, not to get everybody pissed off."

Belinda laughed. Then she demanded, "What?"

"You startled me. You don't laugh very often. You should."

"I can't. Though I do wish I was different."

A shuddering *déjà vu* overcame me. I recalled her father once suggesting that he didn't really want to be a bad guy but he was in a bind where his choices were to be the nastiest bad boy he could or end up grease under some climber's heel. The underworld is strictly survival of the fittest.

The Contagues survive.

I opened the door. Belinda pushed past, murmured something to Two Toes.

Dean bustled out of the kitchen. "Did you remember your key, Mr. Garrett?"

"Yeah. And this door better not be chained when I get back. Got that?"

He had talked me into installing an expensive key lock, supposedly so I wouldn't need help getting in late. But maybe he just wanted to aggravate me.

It used to be cats. He was always adopting strays, apparently because I didn't want them around. I attract enough stray people.

"Absolutely guaranteed, Mr. Garrett."

I looked at him askance. I didn't like his tone. "Thank you, Dean." I shut the door. "Living with him is like being married without any of the perquisites." I waved to Mrs. Cardonlos, who was outside watching again. I wondered if she knew what she was looking for. I wondered what had become of Mr. Cardonlos. I have a suspicion he's alive and well and happy somewhere far from here.

She got an eyeful of Belinda. That one and its sister both liked to popped. I thought her chin would hit her knee.

Now she had something juicy to chew up and pass around. *What do they see in that man?*

Two Toes had left the Contague coach around the corner on Wizard's Reach. As we strolled behind him I noted that he had earned his nickname the hard way. He had a weird, crooked limp.

I gave him a significant glance, then raised my eyebrow to Belinda. She'd relaxed. She understood. "Old family obligation." She made a noise I would have called a giggle had it come from another young lady. "Guess what? He has a twin brother. No-Nose Harker. The Harker boys didn't have much luck in the army."

I gave the automatic response of every guy who ever made it back from a war when most soldiers didn't. "Sure they did. They got out alive."

If you check the men in the street, particularly in the rightsist freecorps, almost every one bears some physical memento. And beyond the outside scars there are still suppurating wounds of mind and soul. And those affect our rulers as well as the least man among us.

You won't find a duke or stormwarden crouching in a filthy alleyway trying to exorcise his memories with wine or weed but up on the Hill, or out in the manors, the great families have locked doors behind which they conceal their own casualties. Like Tom Weider.

You don't hear about that in histories or sagas. They whoop up the glory and forget the horror and pain. The Dead Man assures me that all histories, whether official or oral, bear only coincidental resemblance to actual events—which few principals considered to be history in the making at the time.

27

Belinda said, "You used to be a lighthearted guy, Garrett. A little cynical, yeah, but it's hard not to be cynical nowadays. What happened to the wisecracks?"

"Darling, a wise man once told me each of us is allowed only so many wisecracks. Then life stops. That's how he explained there being so many sour old farts. I've only got one smart-ass crack left. I'm saving it. Which means that for the next four or five hundred years I'm going to be a sour old fart, too."

Her sense of humor was underdeveloped. She didn't get it. Or just didn't appreciate it. "You making fun of me?"

"No. Never. Just ringing changes on something an old-timer did tell me when I was a kid. This guy was so ancient he could remember when Karenta wasn't at war with Venageta."

"A human?"

"Yeah. I said he was old."

Dwarves and elves and some other species hang around as long as the Loghyr, given sufficient good luck. In fact, elves claim to be immortal. But even the Dead Man isn't sure about that. He hasn't been around long enough to see one never get killed.

Stories about elven immortality come from the same myth cycle that tells us that if you con a dwarf into coming out of his mine in the daytime or riddle a troll into staying up past sunrise they'll turn to stone. Word to the wise. Don't bet your life. Don't bet your favorite cockroach. You'll find out what that red stuff is between trolls' toes.

Sure, you don't see many trolls on the daytime streets of Tun-Faire but that's because trolls don't like cities. Things move too fast. But if you insist on looking for trolls, be sure you don't get trampled by all the dwarves trying to separate humans from their money, day or night.

I continued, "This old man was a real storyteller. Tall tales. I wish somebody had written them down. He claimed he was so old because there was one last joke that Death came and told you and he hadn't heard it yet."

"My father used to say that."

"Chodo?"

"Yeah. Really. Maybe he knew the same old man." She became the cold, hard Belinda I'd come to regret.

"Someday you have to tell me what it was like being Chodo's kid."

"What?"

"Most of the time I like you. But whenever you even remotely connect with your father you go all cold and spooky." The coach stopped. I shut my yap, peeked between curtains. "We're here. Without any trouble."

Two Toes dismounted and came to the coach door. "One minute," Belinda told him. "Garrett, sometimes I'm halfway in love with you. Most of the time I'm not. You treat me decent. I like that. But we can't ever go anywhere. I can't always control the part of me that you don't like. If you shoot your mouth off when I'm out of control . . ."

I hadn't thought she could see it herself. As always, Belinda insisted on being a surprise.

Two Toes helped her down. He worshipped the ground she stalked on. And she didn't notice.

One of those sad songs.

Two Toes gave me a look that said I'd better treat her right.

Manvil Gilbey was out with the hirelings making sure no great unwashed types penetrated the perimeter. "Glad you're here, Garrett. I'm getting nervous. They started arriving before we were halfway ready." He checked Belinda. He was impressed. "I am amazed, young woman. What could such a lovely creature possibly see in this battered rogue?"

"Gilbey?" I asked. "Is that really you?"

He winked as he took my invitation. I wondered if they were

keeping count. He said, "We assumed you'd pair off with Miss Tate."

"Life is chock-full of surprises."

"I believe Miss Tate planned along those lines."

I didn't doubt it for a second. "I'm ready for her." Right. "Can we gossip later? I want to check all the arrangements for myself."

"Of course. I just wanted you to realize that the situation could become complex."

He was rubbing me the wrong way and I didn't know why. "Look, this isn't important now." Maybe it was having to face Tinnie. "My partner felt I should bring the lady along. Because of the other guests likely to appear." I didn't dare proclaim my date as being queen of the underworld.

Gilbey was disinclined to quibble. Neither did he satisfy me that he'd made any outstanding effort to protect the Weiders.

I had cause to be touchy. I was descending into a cone of trouble where the secret police, the rightsists, the Outfit, Glory Mooncalled, and maybe even the business community might want to roll rocks down on me.

"Have a wonderful evening, Garrett. Miss, I'm sure the Weider family will be honored that you choose to share their joy."

Manvil could lay it on with a trowel. And Belinda could make a determined holy celibate regret his vows. Gilbey certainly looked like he had suffered a stunning recollection of what women were all about. He had trouble looking at anyone but Belinda for the next several minutes.

28

Inside the doorway stood Gerris Genord. Genord had a voice like a thunderstorm. He refused to let me sneak in unnoticed. He announced, as though the end of the world was imminent and it was critical that everyone knew, "MR. GARRETT AND MISS CONTAGUE." Genord was the Weiders' majordomo. I did not like him. He sneered at me. I did not belong in this society.

I suppose my chances of getting inside unnoticed with Belinda along were as likely as those of the Crown cutting taxes because the war was over.

We were early, though, so only a small horde heard Genord's bellows.

The Goddamn Parrot made his entrance separately, sneakily. Wearing a parrot to a betrothal ball might be considered a lapse of etiquette.

We got down the steps all right but didn't make it twenty feet farther before I got pinned in the cold-eyed crossfire of Tinnie Tate and Alyx Weider. Tinnie was closer. I shifted course. Best get the worst over now.

I ignored Tinnie's expression. "I've got a letter for you from an old gentleman you know better than I do."

The Goddamn Parrot plopped onto my shoulder. So much for good form. He said, "Read it, Pretty Legs. Bust his head later."

Tinnie gaped. I wondered if I shouldn't have read the letter before I let her have it.

Dean transcribed it for the Dead Man—after I promised not to peek. Belinda glowered because I gave it to Tinnie. Tinnie—and Alyx and everyone else with eyes as good as a mole's—eyeballed Belinda in her vampiric heat and wondered. Frumpy Garrett faded from their awareness, though wearing one of Tad's outfits I was as spiffy as I've ever gotten.

Well, I didn't want to be noticed, did I? Not in my line.

Tinnie read. Tinnie gave me the fish-eye. Tinnie cold-eyed Belinda. Tinnie glared at me some more. The Goddamn Parrot cleared his throat. I got his head in a one-hand squeeze before he made things worse. He flapped and squawked but didn't get any rocks dropped on my bean.

Tinnie decided she needed some fresh air. Her stride was efficient. Her feet pounded the floor, eating up ground. Her red hair tossed behind her.

Alyx caught her. They argued instantly.

Belinda stayed close as I moved toward the far end of the hall. The place wasn't crowded yet but was more so than I'd expected. Where I knew names I named them so Belinda would know. Her name began to circulate, too, after somebody realized which Contague she had to be.

"Yonder are the happy couple," I said. "We ought to pay our respects."

"They don't look happy."

I didn't think they did, either. Ty looked like he had a bad case of constipation. Nicks looked like she'd rather be anywhere else.

Ty perked up when he saw Belinda. And how could you blame him? He asked, "And who is your lovely companion, Garrett?" He never was nicer.

His own lovely companion bestowed a truly ugly look upon him. She didn't really want him. He didn't want her. But, boy, he better not even think about being interested in anybody else. And Garrett was a natural-born pig dog for daring to be seen with somebody as exciting as this wannabe vampire woman.

"Belinda Contague. Belinda, this is Ty Weider. Crown prince of the Weider brewing empire."

Ty failed to recognize Belinda as the crown princess of organized crime. But why should he? Her name was not a household word. Even her father was not universally known. "Charmed, Miss Contague. How long have you known this rogue?"

Did they take a vote on what to call me? Maybe I could be a rake next time around.

"Almost forever, Ty. He used to do favors for my father."

I winked at Nicks. She had made the connection. Maybe she and Belinda had met in another context, though Belinda showed no sign of recognizing Nicks.

Nicks said, "I'll bet your father doesn't know you're out with this rake Garrett."

I didn't want to wait long, did I? I ought to get into the sybil racket. How cruel to label a man a garden tool.

I was sure the women had met before.

Belinda smiled wickedly. "Daddy would have a heart attack if he saw us holding hands." She grabbed my right mitt. "I'm still his little girl."

Daddy Contague might render me down for candle tallow if he knew the whole history of our friendship.

Whatever the game, Nicks was ready to play. Belinda pulled me away. She had to control her surroundings completely. I watched Nicks whisper to Ty, mischief in her eye.

She winked again.

These women might put me in more danger than The Call, the Outfit, and Relway put together, just for the long-legged, red-haired, howling wolf sexy fun of it.

The color left Ty's face.

Chodo really did have a bad reputation.

Genord bellowed, "Mr. Marengo North English and Miss Tama Montezuma."

"Whoa!" I barked. "This might be interesting."

"Why?"

"North English claims Montezuma is his niece. I've never seen her but she's supposed to be . . ." Wrong angle. Belinda's face darkened. When would I learn? "Rumor would lead one to suspect that North English regularly violates the rules about consanguinity. Not to mention he maybe cheats on his wife."

"Everybody loves a scandal."

"Don't they? Let's go over there. I've never seen North English up close."

"Why bother? He sounds like your typical sleazy male to me." But she watched the entrance intently. North English would be one connection she wanted to make, sleazy male or otherwise.

"You're too young and too beautiful to be so cynical."

"It's all your fault. You ruined me. You beast."

The newcomers paused to be seen before they descended to the great hall floor.

"Put your eyes back in, Garrett." Tinnie had materialized behind me. "And shut your mouth before swallows nest in it."

I did as I was told. I'm a good soldier, me. But, boy oh boy, that Tama Montezuma was something!

She was as tall as me, narrow of hip. She moved like a panther on the stalk, radiating an overpowering sexual urgency. Her face seemed animated by a secret knowledge, an abiding amusement at the follies of the world—which is, after all, only a dream. Her muscles were as hard as stone. Her walnut-stain skin was without flaw, showing no hint of a wrinkle, and a shocking amount of square footage was available for inspection. It glowed with a satin sheen of health so good it ought to be illegal. Her eyes sparkled with humor and intelligence. Her teeth were almost too perfect and white to be real. She reeked animal magnetism. Somebody—probably her Uncle Marengo—had invested a fortune in her scant but flattering elven fashions.

"Down, Rover," Alyx whispered over my other shoulder. I hadn't heard her sneak up, either. Maybe I *was* a tad distracted.

I grumped, "You guys are wearing that out, you know." Tinnie, especially, had a tendency to push the needling past the playful stage. "I thought you were just going to work it on each other."

"Tsk-tsk. His skin is thinner than I thought, Tinnie."

Lightly, Belinda observed, "I may be leaping to conclusions

here, Garrett, but that woman doesn't look like she could be that man's niece—and not just because he's so pale." North English did look pallid next to Tama Montezuma. "In fact, she doesn't look much like anybody's niece. She looks a lot more like something a dirty old man dreamed up."

She did indeed. Or even some pure-hearted young man. Tama Montezuma had something that would make people suspicious of her even if she was out with her twin brother and wearing full nun's gear. But her being Marengo's niece was not impossible, technically. Dark-skinned adventurers visit TunFaire all the time. A few have stomachs strong enough to stay around.

North English didn't look at Montezuma like she was any relative, though. Guys who hit a number big and win buckets of cash get the look Marengo had. It says, "I do deserve this but I can't believe it's real."

Belinda asked, "Can you introduce me to these people, Garrett?"

"Me? You know I don't run in their circles. Alyx?" Her family did share those circles.

"Daddy invited him, Garrett. He'll remember me only as a little kid. It's been a long time since he was here last. He and Dad argued. Politics."

Tinnie shook her lovely head. "I can't help. I never met the man."

Belinda demanded, "How would you suggest I meet him, then?"

"He's got a hungry eye. Walk up and tell him who you are and say you need to talk. He'll find time."

Tinnie grumbled something inaudible. I bet it had to do with it not being right, women taking advantage of their looks. That from a lady who grabs every possible advantage out of being a gorgeous redhead—at least when guys named Garrett are around.

"Maybe I'll do that."

"He doesn't look preoccupied right now." North English was posturing, peacock proud, basking in male envy, not noticing that no one hurried to get close to him. "And I've got to desert you anyway. It's time for me to look for bad guys."

Belinda touched my hand lightly, the gesture entirely for the benefit of Alyx and Tinnie.

The big cats really try to hook their claws in one another.

Belinda strode away.

Tinnie smoldered. Alyx demanded, "Who is that woman, Garrett? Why did you bring her?"

Tinnie answered for me. "Her name is Belinda Contague, Alyx.

Her father is the number one crime boss in TunFaire. She's here because our friend the Dead Man asked Garrett to bring her."

So that was what was in that letter. But Tinnie still wanted it to
be my fault.

"How long have you known her?" Alyx demanded. "How come
she acts like she owns you?"

"A few months. But I've known her dad a long time. Same as
I've known your dad for a long time. She acts like that because she
knows it'll irritate Tinnie and because she likes to make me
squirm. Just like you."

That was a good shot. But not good enough. They didn't want to
believe it. I reiterated, "I need to wander around now."

"You're really working?" Tinnie asked.

"Yes. Gilbey's no professional and he knows it. That's why I got
an invitation." I started walking.

Both women followed.

"Uh . . . Ladies . . ."

Alyx said, "I can show you around."

Tinnie's expression said she was going to make damned certain
Alyx did nothing of the sort. I sighed. This was a fifteen-year-old's
dream. At my age it was too rife with complications.

I sighed again. "Suppose we stroll around and see how easy it
would be for somebody to get in uninvited."

29

Tinnie and Alyx stuck like my shadow. Once, when we were close
and Alyx was a step ahead, I grabbed Tinnie's hand for a second. I
asked Alyx, "How many people came in to handle the work on
this?"

"What?"

"The extra staff. How many outsiders?"

"A bunch in the kitchen. A bunch to handle the service. Some
musicians. I don't know. Ask Manvil or Gerris. Or Lance."

I guess she noticed me touching Tinnie.

If somebody really wanted to get into the Weider house, coming
now as occasional help would be a good way.

Sometimes you just have intuitions.

Or maybe you see something and don't recognize it consciously but your mind works on it and you come up with an idea that, later, makes it look like you read the future.

I said, "Let's check the kitchen." The largest mass of outsiders ought to be there. The shindig would require tons of special food.

"Stay with me," Alyx said, eager to regain my attention. Maybe she hadn't gotten her full share growing up the youngest of five, with a father dedicated to empire building and a mother who was already dying slowly.

Following Alyx was no chore. The hardest work I did was to pretend I didn't find being a few steps behind a shapely behind all that interesting.

"You're not fooling anybody, Garrett," Tinnie whispered. I glanced back. She had her devil grin on. I like her best when she's in that mood. Unfortunately, Alyx was right there to keep me in trouble.

We entered the kitchen.

Several religions boast hells that are less crowded, cooler, and quieter. The master of ceremonies was a devil woman so large that at first I thought she must be part troll or ogre. But no, she was just large and ferocious and determined that her domain should be an extension of her will. She never shut up. Her voice was a continuously constrained bellow. She was an immigrant with a strange accent. Platoons of cooks and bakers and their assistants, and boys who stoked the stoves and hauled firewood and charcoal and worked bellows and whatnot in a wild rush to achieve the impossible, were all lashed on by her scorn.

Our entry attracted attention instantly. She spun, prepared to repel boarders. She recognized Alyx only after she'd drawn in a bushel of air. "Miss Alyx," she boomed, "you shouldn't be back here now, you. Dey a party tonight, dey are. And you in your finest, you."

"Mr. Garrett needs help finding his way around."

The big woman dropped her chin to her chest. She glared at me from beneath eyebrows like hedges. "Garrett? Be you dat Garrett, you?"

"Which Garrett?" I had no idea who she was but it sounded like the reverse might not be true. She might even harbor some old grudge. "I don't recall our having met."

"You never did, you. I an' I want to know, I, be you de Garrett, he helps de mister sometimes, him? Dis Garrett, was a Marine, him. He saved my Shoeman from de swamp, him. From de debil crocodile."

"Yes. Yes. And I'm not sure. We all pulled each other out of the swamp a few times. I remember a guy named Harman and somebody called Bobby Ducks. Nobody knew why."

"Dat be him, yeah. Dat be my baby, him. He never like his god name, him. Always want it be Bobby, him do."

I vanished into a huge and powerful hug, me. As my last breath fled me I reflected that Bobby Ducks' daddy must have been a real man's man, him.

The big woman turned me loose. I gulped air like a fresh-caught fish. She told us, "But I have a big job to do now, I an' I. An' if'n I an' I turn my back one solitary minute on dese lazy debils—"

I interrupted. "How much outside help came in for tonight? Some of them may be here to hurt the Weiders." I hoped my imagination wasn't running too wild.

She understood immediately. "In de kitchen us added fourteen pairs of hands, us. For de work on de other side of de door, Genord, he hired sixteen men, him."

Gerris Genord. We knew one another only well enough to dislike one another. He was a bigger snob than even Ty Weider could be. He spent his life scandalized because people like me were allowed inside the house. Unless he had orders from Gilbey, he wouldn't work with me at all.

Maybe I could get around him.

Maybe I'd be lucky and not have to do anything.

"Those the only outsiders here?" I asked. "Besides our guests?" I recalled a mention of musicians.

The big woman nodded and turned away, unable to restrain her bellows any longer.

"And who would she be?" I asked Alyx. Earlier contacts with the Weiders hadn't taken me into the kitchen.

"That's Neersa. Neersa Bintor." She pronounced it Nay-Earsah. "She's been in charge down here since before I was born. Even Daddy is afraid to argue with her."

The big woman stopped bellowing, turned back to me. "You, Garrett. Maybe you want to know dis, you. Some of dese hirelings, dey maybe not so trustworthy, dem. Some keep trying to sneak away into de house, dem. Maybe to steal someding, eh? Dey have not get away from Neersa yet but maybe I an' I, maybe not be so hawkeye sometime, maybe."

"Thank you." That was support for my hunch. Wasn't it? I

glanced around. "I'll keep an eye open. None of these people could melt into a crowd." Most looked like the sort who worked only as occasional labor even in a robust job market. Not backbone of de kingdom, dem. "They all accounted for now?"

Neersa allowed as how she believed that was so by way of an imperious nod.

"I'll circulate here for a while, see if I recognize any villains."

Alyx asked, "What should we do?" like she suspected me of first-degree intent to ditch.

"Wait. I won't be long. I promise." The girl had a vulnerable air that made you want to make promises—even if they were promises you couldn't keep.

Maybe she did need Daddy watching out for her.

30

I wasn't long, either. The odors of cooking combined with the smells of too many unwashed bodies crushed into too tight and too hot a space quickly discouraged me. Also, few of these people appeared smart enough or stupid enough to get involved in a plot against the brewery. And if they did get out of the kitchen, my nose would warn me.

If I was a villain who wanted to make an impact, I'd get in with the serving crew. They would be more presentable and more socially adept. And they would be welcome in parts of the house denied the kitchen staff.

I rejoined Alyx and Tinnie. "Too hot in here." I herded them toward the exit. From the corners of my eyes I watched for anyone paying me any special attention. Once we were out I asked, "Either of you notice anybody watching me?"

"I did," Tinnie replied.

"Uhm? And?"

"I mean, I watched you. Close." She winked.

Which irritated Alyx for sure. "How about you, Alyx?"

"She stole my line." She stuck out her tongue, so maybe Tinnie had. "No. Nobody even looked at you. You blended right in. Looked like you belonged there. Even in that outfit."

Belinda had assured me the Tad Weider hand-me-down was perfect for the occasion. "What's wrong with this outfit?"

Tinnie smirked. "We're talking silk purses and sow's ears, Garrett."

"If I wanted verbal abuse, I'd get me a talking parrot." Speaking of whom, he'd disappeared. If there are any gods . . . What I mean is, if there are any *responsible* gods, one or two might make sure the Dead Man didn't fade while the bird was here. I shuddered to think what might happen if that gaudy cowbird became himself.

"He's not here," Tinnie explained. "Somebody has to take up the slack."

"Where're we going?" Alyx asked.

"Around the corner to where the serving folks should be getting ready to—Hello."

"What?"

"I see a familiar face. In fact, I see two." They belonged to Trace Wendover and Carter Stockwell, erstwhile recruiters, all spiffy in servants' livery. The outsiders were all dressed in the same threadbare outfits. The contractor probably rented them, trying to expand his margin.

Trace noticed me an instant after I spotted him. He didn't acknowledge my interest but did drift toward Stockwell. Carter came alert before Trace got close enough to whisper.

"I was right," I mumbled, smug. "There *was* something going on."

"What?" Tinnie asked.

"I see two rightsists who have no business being here." Stockwell and Wendover weren't the sort to be reduced to daywork. Those pretty boys had to come from families of substance.

Alyx asked, "Should I get Manvil?"

"No. You guys just watch out behind me. Oh, hell!"

"What?"

I'd taken my eyes off the boys for a few seconds. "They're gone." But how? There was no exit they could have reached that quickly, nor did the server gang seem diminished. But Stockwell and Wendover weren't among them anymore. "You'd better get Manvil after all." I didn't like the implications of what was happening.

31

Gilbey brought Ty's pal Lancelyn Mac and a brace of hulking, uncomfortably out-of-place dock wallopers. "You got something?" he asked. He was ready for war.

"I spotted two rightsists who definitely don't belong here. They called themselves Carter Stockwell and Trace Wendover when they tried to enlist me yesterday."

"Interesting coincidence."

"Ain't it, though? They came to my house claiming they wanted me to join a freecorps called Black Dragon Valsung."

"Doesn't ring any bells."

"Not for me either. Just now they spotted me the same time I made them. They did a grand disappearing act. I rounded up Mr. Gresser. That's him with the ladies. He says nobody named Stockwell or Wendover belongs to his crew." Gresser was boss of the contract servants.

"They wouldn't use their real names, would they?"

"Only if they're stupid." Entirely possible with TunFaire's bad boys. "Gresser did concede the possibility that he *might* have employed men who answer the descriptions of Trace Wendover and Carter Stockwell. He doesn't seem close to his help."

Gresser was a weasely little functionary type in a state of high agitation. He was a naturally nervous sort terrified that his plans for the evening would collapse and his reputation would follow. All because I insisted on making a fuss about a few of his people.

Gilbey skewered Gresser with a hard stare. "You know *anything* about your people, Gresser?"

I sighed. I hadn't been sure Gilbey would take me seriously. I still wasn't sure *I* ought to take me seriously. I was running on hunch power. Hunches are one of my more sporadic talents.

I listened with one ear while Gresser whined, "There just ain't no way to check them all out. You do the best you can in the time you got. You come up with a job, first you got to get word out that you need people. Then you take the ones you know. Then you look the rest over and pick the ones that seem the soberest and most presentable, that ain't gonna blow their noses on the table linen or grope the female guests. Then, if you got the extra minute, maybe you ask around does anybody know anything down." And so on.

I kept one eye on Tinnie. She was put out about the whole situation. I kept the other on Alyx. For her this had become a great adventure. She remained poised on the verge of bouncing around like an excited kid.

She did bounce nicely, thank you.

With my free ear I eavesdropped on Gresser's grumbling troops. One voice stood out. I whirled. They all stopped talking, startled.

I didn't spot the man but I knew the voice from the brewery stable.

I jumped again as Lancelyn materialized beside me, tense as a hunting dog on point. "You heard that?" Then he relaxed. "Must have been my imagination."

"You thought you heard the big mouth from the stables yesterday?"

"Yes."

"So did I."

"I don't see him."

"And I just saw two guys who aren't there now."

"What's going on?"

"I don't know. But it smells like sorcery." Wouldn't you know, just when I'd started to think it would be straightforward. "And that's an odor I hate. How's Ty holding up?"

"He's in heaven. He's the center of attention. Which is where he always wants to be. Nicks is the one hurting. You're spooky in those clothes. When I came up behind you you were standing exactly like Tad used to."

"Sorry."

"No need. You think we need to do something more to protect the old man?"

"I don't think he should come out at all. What about those guys in the stable?"

"They didn't know anything. They joined a rights group just last week. They were asked to discourage you if you started nosing around. They didn't like bullying one of their own kind but you were always a pain in the ass so they didn't have much of a conscience problem. Until Ty told them this could get them fired."

"Did they cooperate?"

"Of course. They weren't so fanatic they wanted to go job-hunting. But they didn't even know the names of the men they were helping. They never introduced themselves. They just used the right recognition phrases."

"Things are getting absurd," I grumbled.

"People are scared, Garrett. Times are changing. It don't look like they're going to get better. People want to blame somebody. You put thousands of men used to violence into conditions like that and it would be absurd to expect nothing to happen."

He was right.

I spotted a guy who seemed very interested in me. I didn't recognize him. I tried to keep track as he moved around.

Lance asked, "Have you seen Kittyjo?"

"Not for several years." Kittyjo was older than Alyx by a decade. Like Ty, she was always unhappy. Rumor said she'd tried suicide.

Maybe there's one envious devil god determined to punish Max Weider for his success. Great villains steal and murder and torture and pay only if they get gobbled up by even bigger villains. Weider never played it any way but square, his tools intelligence and hard work. So he loses one son, has another driven mad, has a third crippled forever, has a daughter twisted by severe emotional problems, has a beloved wife dying unpleasantly by degrees, seemingly never more than one breath away from the end. And now the man who deserved none of that had poisonous political snakes trying to slither into his life.

Much more and I was going to get mad.

"She came down before you got here. She couldn't wait, she was so excited. She was like a kid on her birthday. It's the first time she's broken through the melancholy in months."

I asked, "Do I sense a more than casual concern?"

Lance showed me a sick smile. "You found out, Garrett. I don't know how it happened. I figured it would be Alyx. I worked hard at being interested in Alyx. Common sense says Alyx should be your choice if you have to fall for one of the Weider girls. She's the only normal one here. Besides the old man."

Me, I'd assumed he had an unhealthy attachment to Ty. Goes to show you. Nobody is what they appear.

I stared at Lance too long. Naturally, when I checked the serving crew I couldn't find my interested man. "We need to pin numbers on these guys."

There was sorcery in the air for sure.

Gilbey bustled up. "I sent word upstairs, Garrett. Max says screw you. He don't care if you've got Venageti rangers on the roof and commandos in the kitchen, we go ahead with the show. He says it's time to earn your keep."

"I hope his arithmetic is better than mine. Because I flat don't like the way things are adding up."

32

An uproar arose in the ballroom. Feminine shrieks preceded bellows of masculine laughter. "Oh-oh." I had a bad feeling but headed that way anyhow.

My bleak premonition was dead on. My partner's control had slipped. The Goddamn Parrot had done something. Women were trying to catch him. Men stood back offering valuable parrot-stalking advice.

It occurred to me that I wouldn't enjoy myself much if that foul-beaked feather duster fled to me for help.

Mom Garrett didn't raise her boy to die for the sins of overtrained pigeons. And nobody out there looked smart enough to believe I wasn't fooling around with some kind of ventrical locationism.

One of these days, Morley Dotes. One of these days.

"Aren't you going to do something?" Alyx asked.

"And admit I know that babbling vulture?"

"But—"

"He wants to run his beak, let him suffer the consequences. Manvil, do we have enough friendlies to watch all of the serving staff?"

Gilbey made a noise like a infant's whimper. He sputtered in frustration. The Weiders wanted to throw the social event of the season. Its legs were wobbling already. Any more security headaches and the thing might collapse. "Can't you just stay in the middle of them?"

"It's a big ballroom and there're eighteen guys."

Gresser had hung on. He protested, "There's sixteen, sir. Sixteen. That was what was contracted." Righteous indignation bubbled off the man. "I won't provide more than my specific commitment."

"I counted eighteen heads, Gresser. Twice. You got many two-headed employees?" The difference might be why Gresser never heard of Trace or Carter, though. "Why don't we take care of this? There're at least two imposters in your crew. Collect them up."

"Oh, gods! This is terrible! I'm ruined! No one will hire me . . ."

"Gresser! Please! We'll lie for you on your wedding night. Just don't hold us up now."

"Yes, sir." Gresser hustled off to assemble his troops.

"Changeable sort," Gilbey observed.

"Where did you find him?"

Gilbey shrugged. "Genord picked him. He's supposed to be good."

"Mr. Gilbey! Mr. Gilbey!" Gresser was back. Lance Mac was right behind him. Lance looked grim. Alyx, who had begun prowling out of boredom, headed our way, too. "Mr. Gilbey!"

"Yes, Mr. Gresser?"

"Mr. Gilbey, it is my sorrowful and shamed duty to admit that this gentleman was correct. There *were* more men here than I hired. They all agree there were more than sixteen. Estimates vary from eighteen to twenty. I can't understand how that happened. I concern myself deeply with the sanctity of my clients' persons and properties. I'm sure there were only sixteen of them when we entered the service gate."

I'll bet. Gresser found himself in sudden deep sludge and wanted his butt covered when the brown stuff flew.

Lance confirmed my suspicions. "A couple of waiters just did a dash into the kitchen. I couldn't find them again when I looked."

Alyx said, "Garrett, I just saw a waiter take off."

"I know. Lance says two of them just headed into the kitchen."

"Not the kitchen. This one grabbed a food tray and went into the ballroom."

"Another one?" I asked. "Or one of the two?"

Gilbey frowned at Gresser. "How many bandits did you bring?" I added my most ferocious glower to Manvil's. Gresser glowered back, sullenly defiant. We weren't going to make this his fault. We enjoyed a veritable glowerfest. Lance added his glower to ours and slid into position behind Gresser.

"I only hire them!" the little man protested. "For big jobs like this sometimes I have to take on people at the last minute that I don't know. I explained that."

I asked, "Anybody think the man is too enthusiastic in his protests?"

"Yeah. Way too. Bet you he never saw any of those men before today." Gilbey acquired a remote look. "Lance, stick close to Ty. Garrett, I'm going to send some men to watch over Max. Check in when you can."

"Will do. Meantime, I'll prowl. Wherever these villains go, they'll stand out."

I was worried. Those guys had to have a definite plan. Stockwell and Wendover didn't look like commando types but didn't have to be. Had I not been here they wouldn't have been found out.

Which was cause for speculation: How much had I been calculated into their plans?

I had to be. First, they tried to enlist me. Then they tried to scare me. Black Dragon Valsung had some strong interest in Weider brewing. I would worry what later. Right now we had baddies in the house, probably not inclined to be good guests.

I glanced around. Lance and Gilbey had left. Alyx and Gresser awaited instructions. "Carry on, Mr. Gresser. Make this the best damn shindig you can. I'll try not to bother you again. And I'll stop thinking bad thoughts about you."

He bowed. Damn, was he eager to please.

"You do realize that nobody is happy with you right now?"

He bobbed his head, stared at the floor.

"Scoot."

Alyx said, "I don't trust that man, Garrett. He's tiny and he's slimy and every time he looks at me I feel like he wants to pull my clothes off."

"Wow! You're as smart as you are cute. Of course he wants to pluck you naked. I'd worry about a guy who didn't give it a thought."

That improved her mood. She began to look at me like she hoped I might indulge in some plucking myself.

I didn't need to open that hogshead of worms. Not tonight.

I quipped, "Maybe he wants to wear your stuff himself. How about you keep an eye on him for me? What happened to Tinnie?" The redhead had become as scarce as Carter and Trace.

"I don't know." She was irked that I would even ask when I was with her and some banter about getting more comfortable was on her own agenda. "She was here a minute ago."

Ah, well. Might be better not to have her underfoot. I said, "I'm going to prowl." Before really big trouble caught up with me right here, right now.

33

I took the main stairs to the second floor. Bad guys headed up wouldn't use an open route, though, so I set course for the back stairs after pausing outside Weider's study door. Nothing loud was happening in there. And there was no one on the floor except the people in that room. I could hear nothing but the musicians tuning up downstairs.

I climbed the service stair cautiously. The way these spooks faded out indicated a fair knowledge of the layout. *That* suggested inside intelligence, which wasn't a thought I cherished.

I had no weapon sharper than my wits, which meant those guys might not have much trouble disarming me. And the ones I'd bested before would be laying for me.

Somebody fooled somebody. Or maybe I fooled myself. I was sure I would run into an ambush getting to the third floor. But nothing happened.

I didn't find anybody on that level, either, though I didn't check one suite. The Old Man's own was sacrosant. Hannah was in there, committed to the long, slow process of dying miserably. Everyone else was downstairs.

A spine-stiffening scream clawed its way downstairs. Tom would not join the festivities, either. But this shriek seemed different. Had the devils in his mind taken concrete form?

I didn't abandon caution. I did feel naked without my head-knocker. But that thing just didn't go with formal attire. I needed a fancy-dress something, maybe a cane, that could be applied to admonitory effect in genteel surroundings. Maybe a sword cane, good for thumping *and* stabbing. Morley carries one of those.

I saw nothing useful around me. The Weider house is sparsely furnished above the second floor. Not even an old mace or morning-star decorated the walls. All the stuff from downstairs was piled at one end of Weider's study now, out of temptation's way.

Another scream. This one spoke of true physical anguish. Were my missing servants torturing Tom? Why bother? Assume somebody had a grudge left over from the Cantard. How could he get any satisfaction out of hurting somebody who didn't know who he was? Tom lived in a world no one else could enter.

Nothing made sense.

That was only because I didn't have enough information. So the Dead Man would remind me. The bad boys wouldn't be confused about what they were trying to do.

I heard a light step on the stair below me, just out of sight around one of the tight turns. Somebody was being sneaky without being good at it. Easy meat—if I could get out of sight.

I sat down and waited.

Alyx appeared on the tight little half-floor landing. She was watching her feet as she moved with exaggerated care. She squealed when she noticed me.

"Got to watch where you're going, darling," I told her. "Which, by the way, would be where?"

"What?"

"Why are you up here?"

"I'm looking for you." She made big eyes. She could do cute and dumb really well. But she couldn't work that one on me, no sir, not even when she leaned forward so the view down her bodice was open all the way to her waist, not much. I was onto her tricks. "I saw you go into the back stairs."

"You're just as dangerous as you think you are, Alyx. Or maybe more so. You get me boiling like an unwatched pot. But we've both got to get along with Tinnie."

Alyx squeezed down beside me. Those stairs were tight. And warm. They were awfully warm.

"Alyx. . . ."

"Don't hurt me now, Garrett."

I clamped my mouth shut. There are times when I can do that. Alyx's tone suggested that this time would be a good one.

34

"Shh!" Alyx rested a warning hand on my knee.

I nodded. I'd heard it. Someone had entered the stairwell above us, carefully, barely making the door whisper. I signed Alyx to stay still. She nodded. I shifted my weight slightly.

They made enough racket up there to let me rise without giving myself away. I helped Alyx rise, too. I pointed downward. "Slow. Careful," I mouthed, not even whispering. Alyx was pale now. This was no game.

Carter didn't see me till it was too late to help himself. He was burdened with the downhill end of a body, backing downward.

"Hey, Carter."

He jumped. At the body's nether end, Trace froze. I popped Stockwell under the ear. He sagged. I thumped him a few more times while Wendover gaped. Somebody still out of sight barked, "What's happening?"

I climbed over Carter. Trace groaned. He was trying to hold all the weight at his end. "It's me again," I told the guy from the stable. "I need to see your invitation."

Wendover went right on trying to keep the body from falling— whether dead or alive I couldn't tell. The guy from the stable came down behind Trace. He was angry. I thought he might jump over Trace to get at me.

He settled for slamming his fist into a wall so hard he dented the plaster. He retreated, whimpering and blowing on his knuckles. Trace finally let go and took off himself. I was almost close enough to grab him. I leapt, got a pinch of his trouser leg. Not smart, Garrett. Even a clerk can hurt you when he's scared. Good old Trace kicked me in the chops. Oh, that hurt! And me with bruises on bruises already, still not recovered from my last adventure.

My eyes watered. Trace seized the day. He undertook the one-man version of the retrograde action the Corps would call an attack to the rear.

I was beginning to think that me and Trace weren't ever going to get to be good buddies.

Somebody grabbed my leg the way I'd grabbed Wendover's. I fell on the body. Lying there, face-to-face with it, I decided that it had to be Tom the Screamer. The face was that of an older, less vigorous Ty Weider.

Was he breathing?

Maybe . . . No time, Garrett. Somebody is trying to pound you.

Actually, the somebody was climbing me like a ladder. Carter wanted to get back up the stair. Bright boy. He only needed to get by Alyx on the downhill side. I sat up so I could pretend to defend myself.

Alyx, who had not listened and gone downstairs, yanked off a shoe and clouted Stockwell alongside the head with its heel. *Thwock!* Carter went down for his second nap.

"Thanks." I wriggled out from under. "Is this Tom? And why didn't you go when I told you?"

"Yeah." She didn't answer my other question. "Garrett, what the hell is happening? Why would anybody want to kidnap Tom?"

"It makes no sense all right. Let's tie this clown up. We'll ask him about it later." I wanted to chase the others.

I'm no math genius. Obviously. There were still two or three of them and one of me and there was sorcery in it. I shouldn't forget that factor.

"Tie him up with what?" Alyx asked. And she had a point. There wasn't one single coil of rope hanging on a convenient hook.

"All right. I'll find something upstairs. Whap him again if he gets frisky." I wasn't feeling charitable toward Mr. Carter Stockwell.

I hit the fourth floor reluctantly. I'd worked out the math part now. It wasn't impossible for a gang of clerks to beat up on a solitary Marine if he'd lost a step since his glory days.

The clerks, however, failed to discern their opportunity with equal clarity. They were in evidence no longer. The fourth floor was as still as a crypt.

This was my first visit in years. The Weider sprats and some senior servants had quarters there, suites for the former and ratholes for the latter. One door stood slightly ajar. I approached carefully. Must be age making me cautious.

I miss the old Morley Dotes. Used to be, whenever I went into something tight, Morley would be right behind me—or even out front if the mood was on him. But he was changing. He might even go legit—really—and slide away from the underworld. He seemed concerned about growing too old to keep up.

Nobody jumped me when I did dash through that doorway. The bad guys were elsewhere, handling their business, snickering because they'd left me coughing in their dust.

This was Tom's room. The furnishings were spare. A selection of restraints were available on pegs beside the doorway should Tom get frisky.

The air was ripe enough to gag me.

Maybe they should try Tom in a different setting. Something pastoral or sylvan. Wondering why I bothered, what with this world being just one endless bleak season milemarked by pain and death, I held my breath and dragged myself out where there was air that was fit to inhale.

I stood gasping in the hallway while my head cleared, amazed that a place could become so infected by its tenant's madness. Or was it the other way around? Had the room created Tom? Could it be that stifling air?

Someone started to step onto the floor from the main stairway, spotted me, ducked back. I caught just a glimpse of red fabric vanishing. I tried to dash over there but a terrible lethargy slowed me. I needed me a double shot of ambition just to keep on breathing.

There was nothing to see when I got there. Of course.

I checked the other rooms and suites, found no one and nothing interesting.

Where was Alyx? I'd expected her to be underfoot again by now, despite my instructions.

35

As the mists of depression dispersed I grew more alarmed. I headed back to the stairwell.

You're seldom disappointed when you always expect the worst but sometimes you're pleasantly surprised.

This wasn't one of the latter occasions.

Alyx was out cold. Somebody had bopped her upside the head and was beating feet down the stairs. Mr. Carter Stockwell was no longer in evidence. Tom Weider was gone. Somebody had started undressing Alyx before I interrupted, not a project any red-blooded Karentine boy would disdain but I wouldn't consider a stairwell the most romantic site. Nor are unconscious lovers much to my liking.

"Wake up, sleepyhead," I said. "Alyx! Snap out of it!" I considered swatting her the way they do in stories. Not a bright idea here. I had plenty of people unhappy with me already.

Alyx tried to sit up. I helped, asked, "What happened?"

"Are you stupid? Somebody slugged me." I could understand her mood. "They came from downstairs. Didn't you hear me yell?"

"No." It was true. I hadn't heard a thing.

"Well, I did yell. Loud as I could. And when I tried to run away I tripped over Tom and got hit before I could get back up." She became aware of the state of her clothing. "What's this? You only need to say when."

"It wasn't me. I like my girls awake."

"I don't know if I should be glad or have my feelings hurt."

"I wouldn't presume to tell you." Women always take me the wrong way. I assume they do it on purpose.

"I'm wide-awake now."

"Sweet as that sounds, there isn't time. There're bad guys in the house. We don't have a clue why. Any idea what happened to Tom?"

"They must've just gone ahead with whatever they were going to do."

"Probably. Come on. Get yourself together. I'm going to go see your father."

"Don't leave me here."

"I don't intend to. That's why I want you looking less frazzled."

"Oh." The merry hoyden reappeared briefly. Fright chased it away again. "What do you think is happening?"

"I can't even guess. I hoped Stockwell would help us out."

"Stockwell?"

"The one who got away. I've run into him before. His name was Carter Stockwell."

"Do I still look like we just crawled out of the hayloft?"

"Not quite."

"Darn." The hoyden was back. "I kind of hoped somebody would think I got lucky."

"Lucky for you now would mean deep slop for me later, girl."

She'd changed a lot in the last few years. "I won't tell if you don't." She was a little bit forward now.

I'll bet, I thought. She seemed like a girl who would want to celebrate her conquests publicly.

36

Despite Alyx's efforts at self-reassembly, she drew a hard look from Belinda after we invited ourselves into Weider's study. Belinda was head to head with Marengo North English when we arrived. Their discussion seemed very amicable. Marengo's niece was not in evidence.

The dark side always did get along well with the business community.

Weider rumbled, "Garrett! Perfect timing! We were just talking about you."

"We've got problems, boss," I said. "They just tried to kidnap Tom."

"They *did*," Alyx reminded me.

"She's right." I told it quickly. Then I asked North English, "You know anything about this Black Dragon freecorps or its commander, Colonel Norton?"

Marengo made an effort to be egalitarian but only because he was a guest where I was held in high regard. I doubt that he would have spoken to me ordinarily. "I've never heard of either one before. But I'm no student of the war. I put it behind me when I came home. Norton and his Black Dragons may have operated without my permission."

You sarky rascal. "They didn't get mine, either, but I wasn't in the army. I didn't spend much time in the Cantard proper. I'm not up on all the unit names."

Weider beamed like a cherub. He was so pleased to see us kids getting along. He told us, "There'll be a bunch of generals in here later, Garrett. I'll ask questions."

I noted, "You don't seem much worried about Tom."

"How likely is it that anybody could carry someone out of here unnoticed tonight?"

"I don't know. They got in. They have a plan. They must have a getaway scoped. All the suicide commandos got used up in the Cantard."

Weider was not alone there with Belinda and North English. Staying quiet but handy were several men from the brewery docks. Weider told them, "You boys spread the word about what you just heard. And tell Gilbey to come up."

"Tell everybody to watch for Kittyjo, too," I told them. "I haven't been able to find her. Max, these people have some kind of sorcery going. If you take your eyes off them even for a second, they disappear."

That angle was scary. It could mean Black Dragon Valsung had dangerous connections on the Hill.

"Weirder and weirder," Weider grumbled. "Why me? I don't know three people in the sorcery racket and none of them by their first names. They wouldn't pussyfoot, either. They'd stomp me like a bug."

Fire danced in the fireplace. Weider went to stare into the flames. He crooked a finger, calling me away from the others. He murmured, "Am I going to get hurt again?" At the moment he seemed lost, storm-tossed, without compass or anchor.

"Not if I can help it," I promised. I gave North English a hard look. He didn't melt. Somebody probably looked at him hard before. He was all tempered up.

Alyx hugged her father. "Don't worry, Daddy. Garrett will take care of everything."

Which Garrett was that? I wondered. This one hadn't shown me a lot so far.

Weider settled into a comfortable chair. He looked befuddled, unable to keep up with events. I didn't blame him, though that was a side of him new to me.

North English said, "I gather you're not in sympathy with the aims of The Call, Mr. Garrett."

That was a leading remark if ever I heard one. "But I *am* in sympathy. Very much so. I just have trouble with some of the individuals involved. Some of your biggest big mouths. Are they really the kind of guys we want telling us how to run our lives? Not to mention that most of them aren't really interested in rights at all. They just think they can grab something for themselves."

North English eyed me warily, as though he'd opened his breadbox and found a snake smiling back. "The most heartfelt cause will accumulate fanatics and exploiters, Mr. Garrett. That's human nature. It's unfortunate but it's difficult to recruit calm, rational activists like yourself."

Now who was shitting who? "Us calm, rational activists should keep the wild-eyed, wooly-haired types under control. They alienate more people than they convert."

North English's eyes narrowed. He didn't like being lectured by one of the unwashed. In his secret heart he approved of The Call's excesses.

It doesn't take long for any of us to weave elaborate webs of justification and self-deception.

I didn't think much of North English but he was Max Weider's friend and Relway did hope I could slide inside the movement. "I suppose I'm still bitter about my run-in with some of your rogue nutcases a while back."

North English's negotiations mask came out. "Yes. I heard about that. We do try to weed that sort out—which is why so many splinter groups form. Those men were weeds already scheduled to be pulled."

I entertained a suspicion that Marengo had misspoken but refrained from making myself less ingratiating than my history and social standing rendered me already. Relway wouldn't do me any favors if I wasn't in a position where I could help him.

"Please excuse me," I said. "I'm just cranky. I've been trying to help Mr. Weider and things haven't gone well."

"I understand. See me when you're in a better mood. The Call is looking for me like you, men who have been south and who have seen the worst and have given their best and have returned to face indifference, ingratitude, or outright disdain. Men who came home to find everything they fought for controlled by creatures who did nothing to defend it. . . . Pardon me. Without my niece to restrain me I tend to rant. Unfortunately, ranting isn't a good way to attract worthwhile new friends, either."

Marengo North English was one of the richest men of Karenta. Wealth is a superb insulator. Why did he find it emotionally fulfilling to involve himself in a working-class movement? Guys at his level didn't come home to find there was no work. They never worked anyway. "Garrett."

"Mr. Weider?"

"Time is passing."

"Yes, sir." That was as close as ever he came to telling me how to do my job.

37

I was lost. I didn't know how to attack the thing. And the complications would increase as more guests arrived. These invaders—if they were around still—could be anybody in a waiter's outfit. And if they had applied half a brain while planning, they would have arranged not to be handicapped by that. The costume was just a way to get past the door.

I had a horrible thought. An awful recollection, really. Carter and Trace had been inside my house, within yards of the Dead Man, but he hadn't caught a whiff of their villainy.

Another horrible thought trotted in right behind the first. It scarred my brain with its little cloven hooves. The boys knew how to get around the Weider house entirely too well.

Alyx followed me. "What're we going to do now?" I stood at the head of the stair that led down to all the excitement.

"Good question. Find yourself a safe place. They might try to grab you or Kittyjo. Or Ty." Ty couldn't run and Lance was no fighter.

"Won't I be safe if I stay with you?"

"The problem is I might not be safe with you."

"Oh, Garrett! You say the sweetest things."

"Let's find Gilbey."

Gilbey was swamped. The mob was arriving faster than the majordomo could holler. Genord would have a sore throat come morning.

"What?" Gilbey demanded, peckish.

"They've grabbed Tom. At least three men were involved, probably four. They used the back stairs. Tom was alive but out cold when I tried to take him back. Also, I can't find Kittyjo."

"I saw her a minute ago, coming down the main stairs. She's hard to miss. She's wearing bright vermillion. Damn. Another one who'll want to see Max privately." He turned to greet a spear shaft of an elderly gent I recognized belatedly as a retired cavalry brigadier. Gilbey continued, "I'll get word to the men watching the doors."

"The old man sent word already."

"Won't hurt them to hear it twice. Keep looking. They can't get out."

"I'm on the job, boss," I muttered. I moved off as Gilbey offered a slight bow to the brigadier. The old soldier's gaze tracked me. Looked like he thought he ought to know me. Maybe he had me confused with somebody else.

Alyx stayed a step behind as I headed for the service area. Gresser pounced on me. "What am I going to do? I no longer have enough men to cover—"

"Misplace some more troops?"

His cheeks reddened. A vein in his temple throbbed. "Your name is Garrett?"

"I haven't had a chance to change it."

"I don't want to apologize for my failings again, Garrett. If you'd like to discuss something positive that might be done, let's do. Recrimination wastes both our time."

"Point taken. Here's the problem. The guys who sneaked in with your crew have grabbed Tom Weider. I don't know why and it doesn't really matter. I have this urge to mess them up, though. Any ideas about how they might get out?"

I didn't expect any help. Cynical in my old age, I figured Gresser was in on it somehow, around the edge.

"They might grab one of the catering vans."

"The which?"

"The specialty baked goods, the pastries and sweetmeats, all come in from outside. The delivery vehicles are in the back court. The kitchen help brings stuff in so we can replace what the guests consume."

"Mr. Gresser, I take back every wicked thought I ever had about you. I'll put in a good word with Mr. Weider."

"That might help. But what can I do about being shorthanded?"

"Have everybody use two hands instead of one? I don't know. It's your area of expertise."

Alyx tugged my sleeve. "Garrett, they might be taking Tom away right now."

I let myself be led away.

Alyx told me, "You looked like you needed rescuing."

"I don't know—"

"Sometimes you just have to be rude."

"My mom insisted on good manners toward everyone."

"This way." Alyx's manners were good only when that wasn't inconvenient.

Her route wasn't very direct. I spied Tinnie in the distance, headed our way. Would Alyx be trying to avoid her? I waved when the blond wouldn't notice. Tinnie waved back. So did a handsome woman much older than me who seemed thrilled because she'd caught the eye of such a good-looking fellow.

Alyx said sometimes you got to be rude to rescue yourself but I can't, especially when I'm near a beautiful woman.

38

"I thought you were worried about Tom." At the moment Alyx just wanted to be friends. *Good* friends, right here, right now. My well-known unshakable resolve was wobbling like gelatin and my capacious capacity for withstanding torture was approaching its limit. If I didn't get out of that unused pantry fast, I was going to become the closest friend Alyx had.

That pantry had missed spring cleaning for years. I started sneezing. Then Alyx started. I staggered into the passageway outside.

Tinnie materialized, coming from the rear of the house, whither we had been headed. "There you are. I was beginning to think you got lost."

"We're looking for Tom," Alyx said from behind me, not the least embarrassed. She was surprisingly presentable considering what she'd been trying to do seconds ago. "Those men took him from his room. Garrett stopped them once but they sneaked up behind us and got Tom away again. Manvil says they couldn't have gotten out of the house yet so we were looking in all the out-of-the-way places, only Mr. Gresser said maybe they could've—"

Tinnie wasn't fooled. Her glance said we were going to talk later. She asked, "Why would they want your brother?"

Alyx shrugged, reverting to the shy, naive child she used to be, pulling it around her like a cloak of invisibility. I wondered if she hadn't been faking when she was younger. Old Man Weider might not be as much in control as he thought.

He for sure fooled himself about Kittyjo, back when. Kittyjo had been more determined than Alyx. And in those days there were fewer interruptions.

I wasn't eager to renew our acquaintance. Kittyjo was a little past neurotic. She was one of those people who hide it well initially.

I said, "Gresser might've been right about the vans. There's so much dust around here we'd know right away if anybody got dragged through."

Alyx snapped, "Somebody is going to explain how come it built up like this, too."

It was a short way to a rear exit. Tinnie had to have come in through it to have approached from the direction she had. "You see anything out there, Red?" I opened the door and leaned outside.

"Exactly what you see right now."

What I saw was two cook's helpers lugging trays. None of the wagons were big enough to require more than one horse. "Let's look them over."

Alyx announced, "I'm not getting horse dukey all over my new shoes."

"Tate's best shoes, too, I would hope." Moments ago she was willing to get anything all over her new dress. I didn't mention it. That would be "different."

Tinnie wondered, "Why don't you go back to the ballroom, Alyx? Ty can't handle it all forever. And Nicks is in no mood to carry him."

Alyx didn't want to entertain. Alyx didn't want to do anything that Alyx didn't want to do. Alyx had to do some growing up yet. But that was something else she wouldn't want to do.

I stepped into the yard while the ladies chatted.

There were five wagons. I dismissed two right away. They couldn't carry anybody away. I considered the others. Maybe one would tell me it was more than it pretended.

They were all seedy. That don't mean much today. You don't see anything new anymore. I can't recall the last time I saw a building under construction. Before I went to war. Maybe when I was a kid.

People fix what they can and make do with the rest.

I checked the dray animals. The great villains of this world, horses, have most humans fooled. The bad guys' animal might be as blackhearted as its masters and give itself away.

One was sound asleep. A second was trying to get there. The beast between those two, though, watched me sidelong from under lowered lashes with way too much malevolent interest. A gelding, it had a notion to get even by avenging its disappointment on me. And, cautious though I am around those monsters, I got a step too close. It snapped at me. I dodged nimbly, suffering only the loss of a few decorative buttons from my left sleeve.

"You're the one," I grumped. "Got to be the one." The beast wore hobbles. That said plenty. Dray animals don't usually need hobbling. Not in the city.

It watched as I moved to check its wagon, showing me big, ugly horse teeth in a huge equine sneer.

"Why not just snooze in the traces like your pals?"

Another horsey sneer, filled with contempt for all old-timers and their slave mentalities.

The wagon's side was made to fold out and lift up. It was secured by a wooden pin on a leather thong. I pulled the pin, grabbed a pair of thoughtfully placed handles, and lifted.

Somebody whacked my bean with a gunnysack full of horseshoes. I fluttered down into the darkness like a spinning maple seed. I don't recall hitting bottom. Or the cobblestones, whichever came first.

39

I groaned and cracked an eyelid. Couldn't be morning already, could it? Damn! Not another hangover. There'd been too many of those lately.

An angel drifted into view. She whispered. I didn't understand but I had some good ideas about what I wanted her to say. I'd take her up on it just as soon as I learned how to breathe again.

I mumbled, "I must've died and gone to heaven." That's the way things went in my mother's religion.

The angel continued talking. I began to catch her words. "Don't feed me any of your mouth manure, Garrett. I've known you too long."

"Oh. It's the other place. I always suspected you demons were gorgeous redheaded wenches. Or maybe the other way around."

"Flattery will get you everywhere, Garrett."

"Promises, promises. What hit me?" I patted the top of my bean. I found no unusual number of soft spots. "Couldn't have been a bird taking target practice." Unless maybe it was *my* bird.

"I don't know. When I finally talked Alyx into letting up on you I came out and found you right there. A man was getting set to hit you again. I yelled. The kitchen help came out so he ran away."

"What about the wagon?"

"Which wagon?"

"The one that was sitting here. I was just going to check it out when that chunk of sky bounced off my noggin." There was no reason she should have noticed that particular wagon. "I think we've got a problem." A big problem, if my fears were on the mark.

I managed a feeble, shuffling jog to the tradesman's gate. I recognized the sleepy guard only by subspecies. Very big, very strong, very stupid. Gate-crashers wouldn't get past him, no sir. "Did a wagon just leave?"

He checked me from beneath brows like overhanging cliffs. I was startled by the fact that they were hairless. "Who're you?" he growled, disgruntled because his nap had been interrupted.

"Name's Garrett. Chief of Security for the Weider breweries." So I exaggerated a little. Couldn't hurt.

It didn't. "Oh. Yeah. I heard about you. Yeah. The Simon the Pieman wagon went out. That's cute, ain't it?"

"What's cute?"

"The name. Like how it rhymes. Kind of cute and catchy, ain't it?"

"Sure. I get you. Nifty. Keen. Next question. How come you let it go? Didn't you hear we had bad guys in the house and we didn't want them to leave?"

"No." The man looked baffled. "I ain't seen nobody but that driver since I come on. The bakers and stuff was already here."

"Oh, hell," I said, without much volume or any real feeling. "All right. But don't let anyone else leave till you hear from me. All right? How many bad guys went out with that wagon?"

"I told you. Just the guy driving." He was beginning to resent my attention.

I grunted. I hadn't thought that all my bad boys would clear off that easily. They had a mission.

I turned to stomp away.

Tinnie caught my arm. She looked up with big fake moon eyes. "You're so forceful, Mr. Garrett." Her pearly whites looked particularly wicked in the torchlight.

"What I am is irritated. I had stitches on my head the other day. I ought to wear an iron hat. Maybe one of those ugly-officer things with the big spike on top. I bet I could get one of those cheap these days."

"They'd just hit you somewhere else. Then you might get hurt."

"You always see the bright side, darling."

"I try. You could find some other way to waste your life. I bet there're all kinds of careers where you don't have to deal with people who try to break your bones."

Oh-oh. "I'd better see the old man again. Tom might've been on that wagon."

Oh, did she give me a scary look. What a lowlife, subject-changing sewer rat that Garrett is!

Some things we'll never resolve.

40

I didn't think before I burst into Weider's study. I'd never encountered any reason to excuse myself around the Weider place before, little time though I spent there.

I plunged into a silence so sudden it was like the stillness after a thunderclap. Numerous pairs of eyes measured me. Marengo North English appeared to be conducting a summit of the chiefs of every nut group in TunFaire. Every rightsist nut group. I didn't see any democrats or round-earthers.

Belinda sat slightly behind North English and to his right, partially shadowed. The flicker of the fire in the fireplace lent her face a diabolic cast. Even that freecorps psycho thug Bondurant Altoona appeared to be intimidated.

Until you experienced it you wouldn't believe that a woman this young and attractive could come across so threatening. But no one in that room doubted her capacity for launching major mayhem.

I glanced around. "Where's Max?" Cool. Like I butted in on these things all the time. "It's critical."

I could manage without him. But his son was in deep sludge. He ought to know. He needed a say.

After a startled moment North English pasted on his paternalistic smile, told me, "Max just stepped out to confer with Manvil. Gentlemen. This is the Garrett fellow Miss Contague recommended. Mr. Garrett, won't you join us now that you're here? I'm sure Max will return directly."

I engaged in a brief internal debate, decided I ought to find out what gave. It was too late to run that wagon down now, anyway. It could be anywhere in any direction.

I moved a couple of steps into the room, studied the men studying me. A prime lot of political blackguards. Not one was in any danger from the nonhuman side of the community. Those who weren't wealthy, like Arnes Mingle and Bondurant Altoona, had large bands of armed rowdies at their beck. Cynical me, I wondered if The Call wasn't just a device meant to separate my nonhuman countrymen from their wealth and community standing.

North English said, "Garrett, these gentlemen and I, though separated by points of doctrine, all reside in the same ideological camp. Inasmuch as we were all here we thought it might be provident to pool our thoughts concerning these puzzles that have arisen."

Why tell me?

"We've discovered that none of us is responsible for the attempts to embarrass the Weiders. Max may not support our views but he's a friend to every man here." Before I could suppress my cynicism and respond, he continued, "Earlier you observed that none of us can be sure we know about everything happening in our organizations. That's true. But we're agreed that none of us would ever turn on Max."

Belinda's nod was barely perceptible. She had witnessed the discussion.

North English forged ahead. "You said the villains responsible call themselves Black Dragon Valsung." That was not a question so I didn't respond. "None of us knows of any such group. Nor of a Colonel Norton. We've agreed to start looking into that immediately. The group could give our movement a bad name."

I kept my expression bland. "They aren't imaginary," I said. "Several are in the house right now. I came to tell Max that they've kidnapped his son Tom."

Murmurs. "Looney" and "mad" stood out. They knew about Tom.

I offered a sketch of my collisions with Carter, Trace, and the guys in the stable. I avoided sounding antipathetic toward rightsist philosophy.

Weider and a bodyguard blew into the room. The sounds of the revels below came with them. The festivities were in full swing.

"Garrett! Damn! There you are! We found Tom."

"How did you know?"

"Alyx. He's all right. He was wandering around in the kitchen, getting in everybody's way."

I frowned, stared at Weider. He was so obviously relieved.

I wasn't. Something wasn't right.

Something hadn't been right from the beginning but I couldn't pin it down. "Are Ty and Kittyjo all right?"

"Ty's still holding court. I haven't seen Kittyjo. She's sneaking around like a commando. Nobody sees her for more than a few seconds at a time."

Why did somebody knock me over the head?

Gilbey pushed through the doorway. He had Tom Weider in tow. Tinnie was a few steps behind them. Gilbey said, "I have him under control now, Max. I'll take him upstairs. Luke will stay with him."

Something odd . . . "When did he change clothes?"

Everyone stared at me. I said, "He was wearing different clothes a little while ago."

For an instant Tom raised his eyes to look at me, something he'd never done before. It was so fleeting I wasn't sure he'd actually done it. Might've been just a twitch.

"You sure?"

"Yes." And Alyx could back me up.

"I'll check it out when we get upstairs," Gilbey said.

I started to leave so I could help him. I was sure the baddies were still around and still had plans. Marengo North English said, "Would you stay with us a moment more, Mr. Garrett?"

How could I resist when he offered the honorific to a man of my low station?

41

I shut the door behind Weider reluctantly. Old Max left me a meaningful look as he departed. I turned to the assembled barons of bugfuckery. They stared like they expected me to begin belching green fire. I stared like I expected them to spout something incredibly bigoted and stupid. Finally, North English said, "Max tells me that you're very good at what you do."

"I try hard, anyway."

"He also insists that you're sympathetic to our goals."

Remotely. "I believe I've mentioned that myself." I inclined my head slightly so I couldn't be convicted when times changed later.

"Then why haven't you joined one of the rights groups?"

"I'm not a joiner. Unless you count the Marine Corps. And I wasn't offered my preference that time. When I do have a choice I make my own. That's why I'm in the racket I'm in. It lets me be my own boss."

"Exactly."

"Huh?" Often I hide my razor wits so guys like North English will underestimate me.

This wasn't one of those times.

"You appear to be the perfect man to winkle out the truth about these Black Dragon people."

Why not? I was working for everybody but the Crown Prince of Venageta already. Maybe I could get in with Black Dragon, convince Carter and Trace that I regretted my past transgressions and they ought to hire me to find out what that guy Garrett was up to. I knew a guy once, Pokey Pigotta, who used so many disguises and aliases that he did get hired to investigate himself.

"Garrett?"

"Uh? Oh. Yeah. Sounds good, we can work out the financial details. I've got some bones to pick with those guys." I caressed the back of my head. I've been getting bopped way too often lately.

"Financial details?"

"Even us idealists don't get much nutritional value out of serving a righteous cause."

North English scowled and muttered. He was a notorious skinflint.

Bondurant Altoona suggested, "Pay the man and get on with it. You pinch sceats till the King squeals but put out his ransom in silver for—"

"You're right, of course!" North English barked, silencing Altoona. "It would be petty of me to quibble over a few coppers." He yanked a purse from inside his waistband, tossed it at me.

I snatched it out of the air deftly. A few coppers, eh? I started to tuck the bag into an inside pocket of my waistcoat.

North English squawked. The Goddamn Parrot would have complimented him on his accent. His companions grinned. It didn't look like he had many close friends among his own kind. He grouched, "I expect you to take only what you need to compensate yourself for your labors."

"A guy's got to try." The grins got bigger when I opened the purse.

My eyes got bigger, too. What I'd assumed to be a rich man's walking-around sack of coppers, which might include a silver piece or two in case he ran into something really exciting, turned out to be all silver salted with a few pieces of gold. Swiftly I calculated ten days' fees and likely expenses, tripled them and applied my special unpleasant crackpot counter-discount. North English didn't see what I took but he danced like a kid with a desperate need to pee. Silver still isn't cheap, despite our triumph in the Cantard.

There were whispers among the others, some intentionally loud.

Bets were laid as to whether or not North English would follow through.

To make sure I added several silver groats in case I ran into some big meal expenses, like, say, with a particular redhead while we were doing research, then passed the bag back. Eyes watched eagerly, hoping North English would open it up and reintroduce himself to all the survivors and mourn the departed.

He resisted temptation. "I'll leave your name with my gateman, Mr. Garrett. He'll have you brought to me immediately if you have anything to report."

Just a glance at the rest of the room told me North English had numerous "friends" perfectly willing to pay nicely for an opportunity to learn what I discovered before I reported it to the man who had hired me.

North English told me, "That should be all for now, Mr. Garrett." Embarrassed, he didn't take time to offer specific instructions. Fine. I like it like that. Means they haven't told me what *not* to do, where *not* to poke.

Excellent.

I backed out of there.

Weider and his bodyguard were waiting. The old man asked, "What're they up to in there?"

"You'd know better than me. They're your friends."

"Only a few. North English and Clive. Faudie and Slink. They asked me to invite the others. They subsidized expenses. They wanted to get all the names in the rights movement together where they wouldn't attract much attention. I get along where I can. It oils the hinges when I want something myself."

"Favor for a favor. I understand."

"Exactly." He nodded toward Tinnie. "I'm all right. We'll all be all right now. You and your friend go have fun."

"Thank you." I headed for Tinnie. But I wasn't about to take time off now.

42

Let me sip a few pints of Weider dark reserve and I turn into a dancing fool. I made all the girls unhappy. I danced with them all. Tinnie got the most attention but simmered when I took a turn with Alyx or Nicks or Kittyjo—once, guardedly. I even spun a couple with the matron who had fallen in lust with me earlier. She told me she was Dame Tinstall. That rang no bells. Dame Tinstall had outstanding legs for a woman of her maturity. She made sure I noticed them, too.

Alyx was less pleased than Tinnie. Nicks was too friendly for a girl getting engaged, though she didn't mention her feelings about that. Kittyjo, who looked like a shopworn version of Alyx, had little to say—good, bad, or indifferent. She did seem willing to let bygones be bygones. And Dame Tinstall left me in no doubt that she wanted to tuck me under her arm and take me home. I didn't ask what her husband would think of her plan.

I took the occasional timeout to nurture my relationship with the boss's product. I'm a very loyal kind of guy.

I wondered what had become of the Goddamn Parrot.

"What's the matter?" Tinnie asked.

"Something's wrong with me. I'm worrying about that damned talking ostrich of mine. Have you seen him?"

"Yes. I wouldn't claim him right now. If I were you." She had her devil smile on.

"How come?"

"He got thrown out of the house. You're lucky nobody remembers who he arrived with."

"I hope the owls get him." He'd asked for it.

The majordomo, Genord, who hadn't had a chance to yell much lately, approached us. He bypassed Alyx and Kittyjo. Alyx appeared incapable of harboring a kind thought about her big sister. Kittyjo, though, seemed only about half-alive and was completely indifferent to Alyx.

The majordomo handed me a folded scrap of paper. It had been used and reused. "A gentleman sent this in," he husked. "He said it was important."

Tinnie scowled, sensing more trouble. I feared she was psychic.

Just when the evening was starting to roll, too. But that was my kind of luck. Wasn't it? "Thank you, Gerris."

The note said: *Must see you now. Critical. R.* The handwriting was primitive.

R? Who or what might R be? Who would know where to find me tonight? Relway? Who else? And didn't that stir up the mixed feelings?

"Now what?" Tinnie demanded, her psychic side simmering.

"I don't know. But I can't ignore it."

"Right now?"

"Maybe sooner." It would be significant. I didn't doubt that. Relway wouldn't contact me unless it really did matter.

"You're going to ditch your date?"

"What? Oh. Damn. No. I shouldn't be gone long. And she isn't a date, Tinnie."

"Maybe not. But I see how she looks at you when you're not paying attention. Like she wants to devour you."

"Kind of like I look at you even when you are paying attention?"

The ghost of a smile twitched the corners of Tinnie's mouth. "Right, Garrett. Try that line when I have time to notice. All right. I'll tell her why you ran out."

"Huh?" That didn't sound promising.

"I know you. You'll go out there and either get yourself knocked over the head and dragged off or you'll get interested in something and forget everything else or there'll be a pretty girl and your pig-dog nature will take over and—"

"You wound me, woman. Now that you acknowledge my existence again how can I possibly stay away more than minutes at a time?"

"I'm wearing new shoes, Garrett. Specially made. Don't pile it up too deep."

"And they're the most amazing shade of green I've ever seen. They set off your eyes perfectly." Maybe I didn't need to find out what Relway wanted. Not tonight, anyway.

I looked into Tinnie's eyes for a few long seconds. No. I definitely didn't *want* to find out what Relway had.

Her devil smile wakened. "Go on. Take care of it. Then get your big goofy self back in here. We'll see if maybe this threat to the Weiders doesn't require you to stay all night so everybody is protected."

Whoo-hoo! I moved out with a real bounce to my step.

"Mr. Garrett! Mr. Garrett!"

"Yes, Mr. Gresser?"

"Two more of my men have deserted. What am I supposed to do? How can I manage?"

Why me? Maybe Gilbey and Genord were fleeter of foot. "I'm here to handle gate-crashers and bad boys, Gresser, not to make sure Mr. Weider's guests are well served. You're the professional. Surely you know your business better than I. Why not grab a tray yourself?" I pushed past him.

I almost made it before Alyx caught up. She pushed up close, radiating availability. "Where're you going, Garrett?" She looked so damned kissable I had to bite my tongue. Why is it always feast when I can't do anything about it and famine when I can?

"I've had an emergency message, kid. I've got to go out for a few minutes. But I'll be right back." I glanced back to see if Tinnie was scowling. I didn't see her.

I did see Kittyjo watching from a shadow thirty feet away. She didn't look nostalgic for the good old days when we'd been very close friends till she changed her mind. She did look troubled. I winked at Alyx and headed for the door.

Maybe Kittyjo would warn her off me. That would be useful. I don't deal well with temptation.

Morley has a personal rule he recommends often: Yield to temptation whenever you can because every opportunity might be your last. I don't subscribe to that completely. Yielding could bring on the lastness. But I'm weak when blonds, brunettes, or redheads are part of the temptation.

On the other hand, a good rule of thumb would be: Never get involved with a woman crazier than you are. The trick there is to recognize the craziness before you get pulled in. Some hide it well. Kittyjo did.

As I departed a raw-throated Gerris Genord began to croak for attention. It was time Ty and Nicks made their announcement.

43

I stopped to see the security guys out front. They knew me. I told them I'd be right back. I stepped into the street, watching for the Goddamn Parrot as well as whoever wanted to see me. I didn't expect Relway himself. Relway prefers to stay out of sight. But the little guy emerged from the darkness like a whispering ghost. I squeaked, "You startled me."

"Sorry." Like hell. He smirked. "Sorry about interrupting your evening, too. But you have to see this."

"It's big enough to bring you out personally?"

"I'm here because every player in the rights game is here. That's significant. Something I have to look over with my very own eyes."

I wondered if he had people inside. I wondered again, aloud, as we walked. I got only silence in response. Which was answer enough for me. It was likely that several of Gresser's workers were secret police. Poor Mr. Gresser.

"It's quiet tonight," I observed. That wasn't a good sign, really. Not in TunFaire, where, by day or by night, completely quiet streets generally mean big trouble.

"Very."

The silence deepened as we walked.

The flicker of torchlight shone around a corner. We had walked only a few blocks, to the far side of the brewery. The torchlight had no noise attached. No excitement. We weren't headed toward a street party or toward a riot.

We turned a corner.

There was my missing wagon. There was my venomous new equine acquaintance. Four men surrounded them. Three carried torches. The fourth held a short spear to the spine of a man lying facedown in the street. Two of the torchbearers wore Gresser's corporate livery. How did they get away unnoticed? . . . Hell. They didn't. Gresser did complain. But the guys covering the front hadn't mentioned them. . . . Were they Relway's people, too? Of course they were. Which meant they were everywhere. Too bad I couldn't con them into doing my job for me.

The wagon was open on the side I'd been about to investigate when somebody decided to put me away for the night. Or a slab of sky had fallen on my noodle.

Relway told me, "These guys saw you get knocked down. They thought it might be interesting to trail the wagon and see what was going on."

I forbore complaint. I now had a notion about one guard who might be in with Relway.

The fellow with the spear forced the captive to keep his head turned away. Relway didn't want his face seen.

These four would be among his best and most trusted men, then. I tried to memorize their faces without being obvious.

"Shit!" I said softly when I looked inside the wagon. "This is what I was afraid of when—" Three corpses had been stuffed in there. Two were naked. Tom Weider still wore the dirty nightwear he'd had on when I was wrestling Carter and Trace. "Aw, shit," I said again. I couldn't express my despair any more articulately. This would crush the old man.

"You know them?"

"These two are Weider's kids, Tom and Kittyjo. The other one worked on the brewery's shipping dock. His name was Luke. He was helping tonight because he liked his boss. I don't think he was getting paid. He had four kids. We got a major problem here, friend. An enigma compounded by a mystery, as they say."

"Please be a little more specific."

"I saw all of these people in obvious good health inside the Weider place after this wagon left. I saw Kittyjo as I was coming out the door to meet you."

Relway grunted. "That doesn't sound good."

"Listen. We had gate-crashers who kept disappearing into the crowd whenever you weren't looking. But we never came up short on a head count."

Relway had to say the nasty word first. "Shapeshifters?"

"I'm willing to bet. Or, at least, somebody who always has some pretty tricky little spells handy."

"Changers have never been a problem here. But—"

"But?"

"The colonel got a letter. Off the Hill. Out of the blue. He didn't share all of it but it had to do with shapeshifters."

"We've got all these outsiders coming in. Some might be shapeshifters. Some up there would be interested." Traditionally, shapeshifters have preferred to play their deadly games where there are no sorceresses or wizards to winkle them out. They aren't a beloved breed. As they do with vampires, most races murder shifters as soon as they give themselves away.

"I didn't want to entertain the possibility until now," I continued. "You never want to see anything this ugly."

Shapeshifters have murdered people and replaced them for a lifetime, but not often. They prefer to hit and run, impersonating someone they've gotten to know well, briefly, without killing anyone. Even when they do commit murder they change guises frequently. Few have the ability to hold a shape and age it. And fewer can fool families and lovers for very long.

Their ultimate provenance is uncertain. They appear to be human most of the time. Maybe, like vampirism, their malleability is the result of some bizarre disease. What does seem to be true, or at least what everyone believes to be true, is that shapeshifters can't survive very long as themselves. They have to mimic. Maybe they even have to kill occasionally in order to appropriate a new soul.

They don't appear to be related to werewolves—though I expect they could become werewolves if they had one to pattern from.

"Anybody got any silver?" Relway asked. That made sense. As vampires and werewolves do, shapeshifters supposedly find silver poisonous. Relway wanted to run a test.

Nobody volunteered so I fished out one of Marengo North English's groats, the smallest silver coin I had. You've got to minimize your risks.

"Looks like your racket pays better than mine does," Relway chided. He knelt beside the captive. I repeated my morality tale about the nutritional value of idealism. Relway laughed. His life must be more fulfilled nowadays. He didn't use to have a sense of humor.

Relway slit the prisoner's shirt down it back. "I'll open his skin and flay it back so you can tuck the coin underneath." He tapped the captive's back in the spot you and I can't reach without a stick. "If they really don't like silver, we'll just let him hurt till he offers to help us find out what we want to know."

He never spoke to the captive directly. He carved with no more emotion than a battlefield surgeon.

The silver hurt the changer from the instant it touched him. He twitched, spasmed, shook, fought back a scream with every gasping breath.

Relway said, "Stay alert. That letter was right, this could attract more of them. They supposedly touch one another mind to mind."

I noted shadows moving in the surrounding shadows. "Did you bring a whole army?"

"Enough so I could handle any rightsist trouble if it happened."

Shapechanger minds were like a Loghyr's? Might that explain why the Dead Man hadn't seen what Trace and Carter were? "I've never heard that about them being mind readers. That could mean real trouble."

"Not like your roomie. They can only read other shifters. And only for general emotion, not specific thoughts."

"You sure?"

"No, Garrett. I'm not. Somebody told the colonel. He told me. Just in case. He didn't tell me why. He likes to pretend the Hill doesn't really influence him. Did anything interesting happen in the Weider place? Did you get a chance to spy on the big meeting?"

"I was mostly too busy. I got in once. By accident. Nobody gave anything away. But while I was there they asked me to investigate the Black Dragon bunch."

"You accepted that commission, I hope."

"That's what I said, did I? That groat you're abusing came out of North English's own purse."

"No. I thought he squeezed them till they squealed." The prisoner groaned. He would've screamed if he'd had any breath left. Relway covered his mouth and nose with a hand, just to make life more difficult. "Let me know when you're ready to talk."

A scuffle broke out in the darkness. It lasted for several seconds. I still marvelled at the absence of witnesses. TunFairens always scatter at the first hint of trouble but, once they feel safe personally, they usually come back looking to be entertained. Maybe the changers were radiating some stay-away emotion so potent even humans felt it.

But then why would I be hanging around?

"Damn!" I said. "If these things really do read each other from a distance, the ones at the house will realize that they've been found out."

"Not necessarily. Not if they just feel emotions."

"How did you know they were out here tonight? Block?"

"No. I didn't know anything till I stopped the wagon. Which I did because I thought it might have something to do with what the rights people are scheming. I wasn't looking for what I found."

"Seems like a lot of trouble just to keep an eye on the rights guys." I gestured at the surrounding night.

"They're dangerous people, Garrett. Until I caught this thing here I would've said that rightsists are the biggest danger Karenta faces. They get people hurt and killed and businesses destroyed and it's only going to get worse. I can't just let that happen. But the danger posed by these things might be even darker."

"I think he passed out." I indicated the changer.

"So he did." Relway let the thing breathe. "You know anything about shapeshifters, Garrett?"

"No. I ran into one once. A Venageti spy who'd replaced a Karentine counterintelligence officer. That's it."

Relway sat down on the changer, ready to use his hand. "I was afraid of that."

"Of what?"

"Not yet. Maybe this thing can confirm my suspicions."

Relway's men dragged someone over. This one shifted slowly between several sets of features. I recognized none of them. Relway searched it after making sure the other one would remain unconscious.

"This is interesting." He showed me a tattoo on the new captive's right forearm. It was black. It resembled a dragon, though the light could have been better. It incorporated a simple Karentine army crest.

"That *is* interesting."

"I do believe I'll have to do some digging. I suspect an untold story has begun to surface."

The changer recovered. His features became fixed. The tattoo faded. We pretended not to have noticed it.

I glanced at the wagon. "I need to go break the news. And grab the villains still inside. Bring the bodies back. The old man will want them."

"You need help?"

"Send your waiters back. Mr. Gresser will be infinitely grateful."

Relway grinned. He had an all-new and challenging bunch of bad boys to eradicate.

I told him, "Let me know what you get from those two."

"Goes without saying. Long as you let me know about the crowd in there."

"They're dividing turf, making peace with the Outfit and making rules about who they can and can't push around. They don't want to irritate anybody who can send troops out and they don't want to waste time fighting each other."

"Ah. Too bad about that."

"Belinda Contague is there. Speaking for her father."

"A genuinely hard woman. And so young. Out of a privileged household. Makes you wonder. You're a friend of the family. How come we see so much of her now and so little of her father?"

"Chodo had a stroke. He doesn't want people to see him until he recovers. They might think he's getting weak. But he's as hard as ever and getting mean-spirited besides. Anything new on Crask and Sadler?"

"No. But they're out there."

Those two were worth worrying about. They were nightmares.

44

"I'll take these three to the Al-Khar," Relway told me. "Drop by and find out what they had to say."

His people would wait outside the Weider shack while I rounded up the changers inside.

"I want these bodies," I reminded.

"Go ahead. Take them."

I folded the door shut before he changed his mind, pinned it, climbed to the driver's seat. I gathered the reins like they were covered with slime, told Relway's thugs, "You guys want to make sure this monster stays headed in the right direction?"

Monster and thugs eyeballed me. The horse smirked. One of the thugs—their names were Ritter and Abend but their attitudes left them undeserving of remembrance—said, "You can't drive a cart? Get down from there."

"I can drive a cart," I muttered. "If I really want to, I can drive a cart. But I'm going to let you do it this time." I *can* drive a cart. I learned in the Corps. But watching the south end of a northbound beast, knowing the critter is looking for a chance to visit disaster upon me, isn't my idea of fun.

The big bruno on the back gate was on the job now. He had let this very wagon scoot out—along with Relway's guys, whom he'd forgotten to mention, which you just naturally had to wonder about—but now nothing was going to get past him. "What's my name?" I demanded.

"You're Garrett."

"And what's my job?"

"You're in charge of—"

"Bingo! I'm in charge. And I'm telling you to let us in."

"But you never said nothing about—"

"I'm saying it now. I gave you some hard road about letting this wagon get away. Then I went and got it back. Open the gate."

"But—"

Relway's men ran out of patience. They vaulted the low wall and opened the gate. The guard raised a loud fuss. Gilbey arrived before I finished proving I could drive a wagon and got it parked. Of course, it might be sunrise before I got the best out of the damned four-legged snake pulling the vehicle.

Gilbey said, "I thought you went home with Dame Tinstall, Garrett. Your friend is fit to be tied."

"Which friend is that?"

"The one who came with you. What have you got here?"

I opened the side door. There was light enough from the house. Gilbey threw his right forearm up against the side of the wagon, closed his eyes, froze that way. He controlled himself before he asked, "What's going on?"

"Shapechangers." I told him what I'd been doing.

"It explains a few things. I just saw Kittyjo. Now I see why she was staying out of the way tonight when she was so excited about everything this afternoon."

"Any idea why a shapeshifter gang would want to take over the Weider family?"

"Because they like beer? Because they want a brewery?"

That wasn't some attempt at black humor. Gilbey meant it. "I'll bite. Why would they want a brewery? Why right now?"

"Better ask them, Garrett. Anyway, the brewery might not have anything to do with it. What now?"

"Much as I hate to, we have to tell the boss."

He seemed exasperated. "Of course we do. I mean, what do we do about these monsters? We need to catch them, don't we?"

"Sure. And we need to move fast. Before they get the word, change appearance, and get away. I *think* there are only three still here. The others took the corpses away."

Undetected and unchecked, I was sure the changers still in the house would have brought in more of their own. The Weider place would have become a changer fortress and haven.

But why the Weiders? There were other families as wealthy, others more iconoclastic, others better forted up.

But suppose the presence of the leaders of the rights movement had something to do with it. Suppose the changers had come in because of the guest list. Suppose Marengo North English and Bondurant Altoona got replaced? They were goofy already. Would anybody notice?

Whatever, it couldn't be meant long-term. Shapechanger schemes get found out. We liked to think, anyway. In TunFaire some real heavyweights would trample all over them once the news got around. By tomorrow there ought to be a hue and cry. The rightsists would be in deep clover.

Shapechangers scare everybody. Alienists make fortunes proving to losers that their loved ones haven't been possessed by demons or replaced by shifters. Or the other way around if that's where the profit is.

Alienists are like lawyers. Right, wrong, justice, the facts of the case, none of that matters. Results are what count. That's usually somebody else with empty pockets and a dazed expression.

The alienist's client doesn't want to believe his beloved no longer loves somebody as wonderful as him. The explanation has to be supernatural and sinister.

Changers have served as excuses for murder, too, though it seems the corpses never change after death. No murderer ever got off using that excuse.

I told Gilbey, "We won't make anything happen standing around trying not to cry."

45

Belinda was in the hallway outside Weider's study, standing delightfully hip-shot, listening to Marengo North English. The man had to have a side I'd overlooked. She seemed enthralled.

He seemed to have forgotten his niece.

Belinda spotted me. Her expression went colder than arctic stone. Then she recognized the damp around my eyes. "What happened, Garrett?"

"You two come with us. Max is there, isn't he?"

North English nodded. "He hasn't made it downstairs yet. Too many visitors." So Marengo and Belinda had been standing around chatting for a while. Interesting.

Gilbey remarked, "Ty will be getting cranky. He dislikes taking second priority."

I opened the study door slowly. Max was seated in front of his fireplace, deep in a comfortable chair. He'd built the fire high. The heat beat out in waves. He stared into the flames as though he saw through them into an age when the world knew no suffering.

"Back again, Garrett?"

"Yes, sir."

"Your friend was furious because you left."

"She gets that way." My friend winced. "I had to see about something outside."

"What's the news, then? How bad is it?"

"As bad as it gets. Tom and Kittyjo have been murdered. So has Luke."

Gilbey said, "That's the man we asked to look out for Tom."

I said, "The change happened before that."

"Change?" Weider muttered.

"They were replaced by shapeshifters," Gilbey said.

I added, "It looks like Black Dragon is a shapeshifter cover. It claims to be a rights group but it's really something else." Nonhumans wouldn't be interested in human rights. Not quite the way The Call is.

Weider sighed. "I'm tired, Garrett," he told me. He *sounded* tired to the marrow. "Sit down, Manvil. Garrett." He indicated chairs. "I just want to put my burdens down. I want to take a long, long rest. I don't have any fight left. If there was anybody to surrender to, I'd let destiny make me a prisoner of war."

"You did your share, Max," Gilbey said. "Take it easy. Garrett and I will handle it." Gilbey glanced at me. I nodded. He asked, "Should we enlist Lance?"

"Lance strikes me as more the executive sort."

Gilbey smiled. "Not far from wrong, Garrett. Though the man can surprise you sometimes." He twisted, looked beyond me. His eyes gleamed for an instant.

"I'll help," Belinda said. I'd almost forgotten she was back there, listening.

I didn't argue. Neither did Gilbey. I was beginning to develop a suspicion that Gilbey would be incapable of arguing with Belinda. He told us, "That junk in the corner there was mostly for decoration but there was a time when all of that was real weapons. Help yourselves."

Without hesitating Belinda selected a wicked fourteen-inch blade, examined it with a professional eye. Gilbey chose a bronze gladius sort of thing and added a small, coordinated buckler for the left wrist. "Stylish," I observed, sighing. Now that I was sitting down I didn't want to get back up.

Gilbey didn't smile. Except for Miss Contague he was all smiled out for the century. Nobody else smiled, either.

I miss the old days. Nobody grins into the face of the darkness anymore.

You need a sense of humor when the going gets grim.

Seldom do I lug lethal hardware but I couldn't find a simple headknocker anywhere. At least nothing sure to stand up to harsh commercial-grade use. A small crossbow, intended for use by cavalrymen or centaurs, caught my eye. I used to be pretty good with one of those things, though I hadn't had one in hand for a while.

Marengo North English considered the choices. Gilbey suggested, "Why don't you stay with Max? He's a little distracted."

North English relaxed visibly.

Obviously the great champion of humanity volunteered only because of Belinda. Oh, what to do when the delicate flower chose danger without thought?

Gilbey picked up a light, thin-bladed antique. "I've heard you were well regarded as a fencer." He extended the weapon to North English.

"When I was young."

"Good," I said. "Then we won't have to worry about Max while we're gone." I gave his shoulder a comradely pat. He puffed up like he'd been handed the key role in the mission. Maybe, in his mind, that's what happened. He seemed incapable of seeing himself anywhere very far off center.

46

We slipped into the back stairs. I told Belinda, "You don't have to do this."

"I know. And you didn't have to warn me. Don't waste your breath."

I wasted no breath. I'd argued with her before. And the stairs were steep.

I was shaky when we reached the fourth floor. I'd been pushing my luck a lot lately and Fate wouldn't give me time off for bad behavior. It was one damned thing after another, too often involving me getting hit over the head.

You can't roll the bones with the sickle-toting guy without crapping out sometime.

I controlled the shakes. I learned that trick in the Corps. The hard way. I took a deep breath, held it a moment, asked Gilbey, "Is there more than one way out of Tom's suite?"

"Possibly. There're servants' passages all through the house. But if we hurry, that shouldn't be a worry."

Indeed. And maybe I should have had Relway's guys stick with me, just in case.

Belinda said, "If I knew where we were going, I'd leave you behind just to make you stop thinking, Garrett."

All my life I've been told I think too much. Except at girl time, when I'm told I don't think enough.

So it goes. You can't win.

I stepped into the hallway.

The Luke replacement was standing guard right where Luke was supposed to be. His eyes narrowed suspiciously. I pasted on a big grin. Belinda and Gilbey marched along behind me. I said, "Hey, Luke. The Old Man says bring Tom down. He wants the whole family there for the announcement."

Whoever Luke was really, he couldn't argue without giving himself away. He couldn't let Tom out without courting disaster. And I didn't give him time to consider his options.

A crossbow isn't a customary accessory when you're just going to escort somebody somewhere inside his own home. *Faux*-Luke figured that out almost quickly.

He flung himself back just as I started to pop him with my free hand. He tried to run into Tom's suite. We didn't let him. But he did make a big racket not getting there.

He went down. Belinda had a knife pricking his throat before he stopped bouncing.

Gilbey and I burst into the suite.

And I said, "Well, there *is* more than one way out." It stood open.

There was no light behind the panel except what ambled in from Tom's apartment. That was just enough to show us that the shapeshifter could only head downstairs. This almost qualified as a secret passageway. It was barely wide enough for a grown-up my size. The stairwell was just slightly less steep than a ladder. I thundered down to the floor below. Another door stood open, exiting through a broom closet. The main hall lay beyond it. Gilbey stayed with me. We couldn't let the shifter get a big lead. It would change faces on us again.

A door stood open down the hall, still moving. My mother would have been all over this guy. He was a wonderful bad example. We blew into the room—and froze.

It was Hannah Weider's bedroom. It smelled of sickness and despair. The dying woman had been confined there for ages. Her face brightened when she saw us. She tried to say something.

Hannah Weider was so withered and liver-spotted she looked more like Max's grandmother than his wife.

Words wouldn't come. She wiggled a finger.

Gilbey got it. "It's under the bed."

Trace Wendover scooted out. He headed for the door, realized that I could get there first, flung himself back at the bed. He snagged Hannah, dragged her in front of him as a shield. A knife appeared. He didn't need to voice the threat.

Alyx appeared in the doorway. "Mama, I brought you some of Ty's—Shit! What the hell?"

Trace turned, startled.

Mama tried to admonish her baby about her language.

I shot Wendover in the forehead.

I used to be pretty good with one of those things. Evidently I still had the knack.

47

"She's gone!" Alyx wailed. "It was too much for her." There was no vinegar in her now. She was about to fall apart. She shook her mother like that might bring her back.

Belinda arrived. She had her changer under control. She looked at Alyx, shrugged, gave me a don't-look-at-me stare.

I didn't expect her to do any comforting. She wouldn't know how. I doubt that anyone ever comforted her.

"Get Tinnie," I suggested. She knew Tinnie. "Or Nicks."

Trace had a bolt in his head but he remained active. His shape shifted continuously until the bolt popped out. It clunked on the floor.

"There's a neat trick," I muttered. "Sure like to learn that one."

Alyx jumped on the thing.

It tossed her across the room.

I shot it as it got up. This time I followed up. I pushed a silver groat into its new wound.

The changer lost control of its muscles.

I asked, "Gilbey, you want I should tell the Old Man this one?"

"Still my place, Garrett. But this time might be the one too much. Hannah was the reason he kept going."

Belinda's changer kept sliding out of his restraints. He oozed like a slug. By trial and error I found that a whack on the side of the head would do to them what it did to me. "A few yards of silver wire would come in handy about now."

Nicks appeared on cue. "Here, Garrett." She shed silver chain necklaces. "Tinnie will be here in a minute. Alyx? You all right?" Then Nicks realized that Hannah really was dead. The look she gave the changer made me glad she was on my side.

I asked, "How come you're here?"

"Your vampire girlfriend told me to come." She had a sharp tongue on her, Nicks did.

I used her chains to bind the guy I'd bashed. He started shaking and flopping. I thought he'd break the chains easily but he didn't.

Gilbey knelt beside me. "Gag them. We don't want to upset anybody downstairs."

Tinnie marched in. Belinda was right behind her. The redhead said, "Ty will be here as soon as Lance gets somebody to help."

Gilbey shook his head. "He doesn't need to do that. Better he should meet us in his father's study. If you ladies will see to Hannah's dignity? Garrett. Let's drag this garbage downstairs."

"We have another one running loose still," I said as I gathered my share.

"I know. I know. We'll deal with it."

I wondered. If Relway was right, that one would know that something had gone wrong.

48

Max surprised us all. Horrible news piled atop horrible news prodded him back to life instead of finishing him. Maybe the pain was just too big to encompass. Or maybe he was too long in the habit of meeting Fate head-on. He glared at our captives but did not touch. He would take a practical, businesslike approach to revenge.

Both changers still twitched and flopped. They would've screamed if not for their gags.

Gilbey left to divert Ty and Lance.

Marengo North English, Belinda, and Nicks had been asked to step out. Max didn't want to share this with them.

Lance followed Ty into the study. Ty was on crutches. You didn't see that much. He was pale and angry. "Fuck up again, Garrett?"

"Be quiet," Max said. His voice was calm and flat and cold. Ty responded instantly. "Sit down."

Ty sat. Likely he hadn't heard that voice in a decade.

"This isn't Garrett's fault. He wanted me to be more careful. Somebody meant to murder us all tonight. Who knows why? We've stymied them. Because we let Garrett do a little. Blame the mess on me. We did capture five shapeshifters." He hadn't been surprised to hear that the secret police were watching the house. "Manvil. What about the other one?"

Gilbey nodded. He must have been up to something.

"Five?" Ty croaked. He stared at the two squirming in front of the fire. That had burned down some now but still put out a lot of heat. The changers didn't like that.

"Garrett dealt with three more outside the house." He didn't mention Tom or Kittyjo. Yet. He looked at me. "We'll get their story?"

"If it can be gotten."

"There's another one here in the house, Ty," Weider said. "I expect to deal with it momentarily."

So Gilbey *had* been up to something. I should've warned him that the creatures could feel one another's distress.

"That we know about," I reminded. "Changers are almost mythical around here. We don't know anything about them. We see the giant meat-eating thunder lizards more often." It was a bad time for thunder lizards, though. "Worst case I know of, and that's probably a fairy tale, involved a family of changers that operated in the forest north of town during the last century. I didn't figure out what was going on here just because changers are so rare. I wouldn't have thought of them at all if weird stuff didn't happen to me all the time."

I headed for the door. Weider frowned but understood when I leaned against the wall where I'd be out of sight when the door opened.

My timing was impeccable. The pseudo-Kittyjo walked in barely a minute later, insufficiently suspicious of a summons from the Old Man. That surprised me.

She didn't seem to sense the distress of the two we had collected already. Was the silver responsible?

Gilbey stepped over to hold the door. When it swung shut there were two of us behind her. She didn't understand till she got a look at me.

Ty broke the hard silence. "What's going on, Dad?"

"This isn't your sister. It's something that murdered her and took her shape."

"Dad?"

"Kittyjo is dead, Ty. Believe it. Tom is dead. Lucas Vloclaw is dead. They were murdered. They were replaced by these monsters." He indicated the roasting shapechangers.

I had my little crossbow ready. I let the changer have a look.

"What did you things want?" Weider demanded.

Ty didn't get it. "Jo, what is this crap?" He did see that there was something strange about her, though.

She seemed stranger by the second.

She was changing! She was maintaining the outward appearance of Kittyjo Weider but inside she was doing something that would, probably, improve her chance of escape. Or, if she was bloody-minded enough, she was becoming something fast and deadly.

I said, "It's changing, people."

The Kittyjo thing glared at me. Gilbey moved. The changer turned his way. I poked it. Felt like I'd slammed my fist into a leather bag full of rocks, too.

The shapechanger didn't go down. It just turned on me. Evidence was accumulating: Shapeshifters were not overly endowed with intelligence.

I ducked a blow like a lightning bolt. Gilbey applied a couple of kidney punches. Neither had much effect. He barked in pain. His knuckles leaked blood.

Ty hollered something about leaving Jo alone.

I plinked the thing with my crossbow, in the throat. My bolt penetrated barely an inch. The changer stopped to fiddle with it.

Gilbey was nearer the weapons collection. He seized a ferocious antique mace, topped the changer a few times. I readied another quarrel. The shifter decided it didn't want to play anymore. It left. Without bothering to open the door.

I loosed another bolt. It struck the small of the creature's back, right in its spine.

The changer sprawled forward, fingertips dangling over the brink of the grand stair. I told Gilbey, "I used to be pretty good with one of these things."

"So I see."

The shifter couldn't get up. It tried pulling itself forward. That worked. It tumbled ass over appetite all the way to the ballroom floor.

I galloped after it.

It looked nothing like Kittyjo now. In fact, it had a distinct thunder-lizard look. Developing armor plates clashed with Kittyjo's dress. A nub of a tail wiggled under the red cloth.

People shrieked. The orchestra stopped playing. A crowd collected. Lance joined me over the changer, shaking. I told him, "She was probably the first one replaced. She would have been the easiest."

Ty joined us, having come down by clinging to the stair rail. He wanted to hurt somebody. He stared at the thing that had replaced his sister and maybe grew up a little. He put his anger aside, found the hidden Weider steel. "I apologize, Garrett. I was out of line."

"That's all right. It's tough."

"This is too big for us to squabble amongst ourselves."

"I'll buy that."

Ty nodded. He scanned the crowd. "That spine shot was all that stopped it."

Worth remembering. "Still only looks temporary." This looked like one of those nightmares where the monster keeps getting up and coming.

Ty said, "Lance, Giorgi went up to Mother's room. Alyx is up there, too. They'll need some support."

I added, "Tinnie should be there, too." I wondered where Belinda was. And somebody needed to watch the changers in Weider's study.

49

Max joined us. "Am I presentable?" He was in control, but barely.

"You look fine, Dad," Ty replied.

"Then let's get our guests calmed down."

I hefted the little crossbow. I had a pocket filled with bolts. Guests backed away.

Presumably the shifter could become its nasty old self with a little effort.

I dug out another coin. These things were going to break me.

The shifter expelled my bolt but its legs still refused to work. Nothing human illuminated its face now. The creature was incapable of emotion in this form.

Max stayed with me. "Just a minor problem with a would-be assassin. It's over. No need to concern yourselves. Go ahead. Enjoy."

Marengo North English materialized among us, over the changer. Sword in hand, handsome, posing, he looked brave as hell. He registered no claim that could be challenged but his stance made it seem that *he* must have been the target of a bizarre murder plot.

My opinion wasn't improving as I learned more about the man. I hadn't seen any proof that he believed what he preached—except that he did put cash where his mouth was. I had a problem picturing a famous skinflint gushing coin without believing.

Maybe Tama Montezuma knew the truth. She appeared more stunning than ever when she rushed up to see if Uncle Marengo was all right, despite being rattled in the extreme. There seemed to be a certain ghastly hollowness to her.

Doink! I let the changer have it between the shoulder blades. "Cut its shirt open," I told North English. "I need to get to that wound." The changer flopped, again eager to go somewhere far from guys with crossbows, knives, and silver.

The guests backed away again but continued to watch. Even the musicians and servants wanted to gawk. There wasn't an ounce of compassion in the house.

What does that say about the human folk of TunFaire?

Valiant Marengo stepped forward heroically. With an elegant flick of his blade he slit the changer's stolen dress. The creature kept trying to wriggle away. Its limbs refused to cooperate.

I yanked the bolt out and pushed my coin in before the wound closed. "This's the last one. I hope." Six was more shapeshifters in one place than I'd ever heard tell of. A few more wouldn't be a real surprise now.

Weider stared at the changer. He shook his head. "I don't get it, Garrett." He was fighting the shakes.

He had a better chance of understanding than I did. It was his house, his family, his brewery. What I understood was, he was my friend. "We'll find out."

Ty agreed. "Whatever it takes, Garrett." He was shaking, too. "No prisoners. No quarter." He refused to sit down.

"I'll need help dragging these things out of here." On cue, Relway's thugs materialized. They must have been listening. They slipped through the crowd like they were greased. "Where were you guys when I needed some backup?" I grumbled. "This needs taking away. I have two more upstairs. I'll show you where."

Weider addressed his guests again. "Please, people. Celebrate. Be joyful." He couldn't fake any joy himself. His despair shone through.

My admiration grew. Max was like those old-time aristocrats who had built the empire. He soldiered on with what had to be done despite any personal pain. He would not yet yield before his duties were satisfied.

I led Relway's men to the study.

One prisoner had slipped his bonds. We got there just in time. It cost me another groat to get it under control again. I was grumbling like Marengo before we finished.

Ritter said, "We'll take them out the back way. You'll hear from the chief."

"Remind him. He promised."

Belinda was waiting when I went back downstairs. She asked, "Are we ready to go now?"

I watched North English entertain a gaggle of hangers-on, flourishing the borrowed sword. He seemed particularly animated. I must have missed the most exciting part of the adventure.

A frown darkened his face when he saw me watching—but he was too pleased with himself to worry.

Miss Montezuma offered me a speculative, enigmatic, almost frightened glance. She looked like a woman who had found a snake in the breadbox. Though I doubted she would know what a breadbox was.

Again Belinda asked, "Can we go now?"

"I can't. Not while there are guests still here." And then there was Tinnie.

Belinda scowled. "There was a time, not that long ago, when you would've dropped everything . . ." It wasn't true. We both knew it.

"Go if you need to, Belinda. I'll get in touch. If you'll let me."

She nodded unhappily.

Belinda Contague was powerful and deadly—and a sad little girl. Not to mention dangerously willful.

Sometimes I'd like to choke Chodo for whatever he did to her.

"I'll go, then." She glanced at Tinnie. "Don't forget me." Damn! She wouldn't get into a killer Contague mood, would she?

Chodo got rid of Belinda's mother because *he* couldn't stand competition.

"Belinda . . ."

She stalked away. She muttered something I didn't hear as she passed Tinnie and Alyx. She paused to say something to Marengo North English. He seemed startled, pleased, frightened all at the same time. He looked at me speculatively. Belinda swept up the stairs to the outside door and Gerris Genord. She and the *major-domo* were gone before I got my thoughts organized. Events had Genord looking bleaker than they did Max or Gilbey.

50

Nothing else happened. The do was not the ball of the season. Too much crude excitement for people of refinement. Our sort don't let these things happen. The bigger-name guests shortened their visits. They began leaving soon after Belinda. Those who stayed on were almost exclusively rightsists nabobs and men who wanted a private word with Max Weider. I'm sure Max wasn't much help.

Tinnie didn't stray far the rest of the evening. Alyx tagged along gamely, never grasping the truism that there is no outstubborning a redhead. I should have told her. I have some experience in the field.

Even diehard friends of the Weider and Nicholas clans packed it up before the orchestra finished playing. Ty was unhappy. Nicks was outright depressed. I caught the glimmer of a tear more than one time.

"This is sad," Tinnie mused. We were surveying the grand hall from the vantage of the front entrance. Gerris Genord nodded as though she had spoken to him. The man looked like he was fighting an ulcer. "I feel for Nicks, Garrett. If you make a huge sacrifice just to make your family happy, it shouldn't turn to shit around you the way this has."

"Woman! Such language for such a delicate—"

"Stick it in your ear, Garrett. I mean it. She didn't get any joy out of tonight. I don't think that would be too much to ask in exchange for the rest of her life."

"There's got to be a curse on Max Weider. On the whole damned family. It rubbed off as soon as Nicks decided to join up." I was beginning to wonder if such a curse could actually be managed. It seemed unreasonable that a man's only luck ever had to be bad.

Without really seeing him I watched Gresser bustle around frantically, as though his depleted crew had work to catch up.

Tinnie said good-bye to some straggler she knew, not bothering to introduce me. I asked, "You going to stash me in the flour pantry and only take me out when you want to play?"

"There's an idea." She gave me an arch look. "If I could keep the Alyxes of the world out of there. Are you going to stay?"

That was my secret plan. "Coy doesn't become you."

"Me? Coy? Since when?"

"You're trying to fake it. I don't think Dean would ground me if I didn't come home tonight. Especially if I make up a story that has your name in it somewhere." Tinnie remains one of Dean's favorite people.

One of mine, too.

"What I love about you is your wild enthusiasm when you decide to do—"

"Excuse me, sir." Genord was back from escorting the straggler to his coach. He looked grave. "There's someone to see you."

Again? "Not a gentleman?"

"Definitely not a gentleman."

Tinnie hissed angrily. "I knew something would happen."

I went out. It was Relway. Again.

Of course. Who else knew where to find me? Certainly not my least favorite pigeon. There'd been no sign of the little vulture since he got himself evicted.

Maybe the vampire bats got him. Or maybe he was just lying up somewhere, waiting for the light. He wasn't like the parrots in the islands who stayed up all night, mimicking the cries of the frightened or wounded.

Relway again. Definitely not a gentleman. Gerris Genord would have messed his smallclothes had he known who this runt was.

Relway looked beat. "It wearing you down?" I asked.

"Not yet."

"What's up?"

"I need you to look at something again."

"Not something happy, I assume."

"No, nothing. It's not a happy night."

51

It wasn't happy at all.

It wasn't far from where he'd overtaken the murder wagon.

This time it was Belinda's ugly black coach. Empty. One horse lay dead in the traces. A crossbow had caught it in the throat. The other beast was psychotic.

"Poisoned bolt," Relway explained.

One coach door dangled off a broken hinge. A man I didn't recognize sat in the doorway. He held his right arm and rocked slowly. He was in pain.

Two corpses lay in the street. I did know them. Again, spectators were noteworthy for their absence.

"This is Peckwood," Relway told me, indicating the guy with the broken arm. "He saw it happen."

Peckwood didn't look like he'd been content to watch.

Relway told him, "Tell it again for my friend."

Friend? Oh-oh. Keep an eye on that hand patting your back, Garrett. Watch for a glint of steel.

Peckwood spoke stiffly. "The coach came from back that way, not in no hurry. Then I see two guys come from up yonder, running hard." Up yonder meant northward, the direction Belinda should've headed if she was going home. "I figure they meant to do this someplace else, only whoever was in the coach crossed them up."

I'm sure Relway knew who was in the rig even if his man didn't.

Why would Belinda head west instead of north? Curious.

Peckwood continued, "They didn't look like they was up to no good. I tracked them. One guy tried to plink the driver. He missed. He was puffing too hard to shoot straight. The driver started whipping his team. The villain didn't have no choice but to shoot a horse or let the coach get away. I figure originally they planned to croak the driver and grab the whole rig."

A sensible strategy. And the whole rig would've included the beautiful Miss Contague, a lady with several deadly enemies.

One of the dead men was Two Toes Harker. He'd been cut hastily and deeply and repeatedly. His knife lay not far away. He'd had a chance to use it, too. It was bloody.

Peckwood got his wind back. "Soon as the coach stopped, the driver jumped down and that other guy jumped out and the blood started flying. Everybody was surprised to see each other. And the bad guys wasn't expecting a real fight."

"Know them?" Relway asked, meaning the corpses.

I indicated the smaller one. "Cleland Justin Carlyle. Usually called CeeJay. Chodo's current number one cutter of throats and stabber of backs." Carlyle had done some cutting tonight. A nasty blood trail led away from him. "Two men did this?" Carlyle was a pro, hard to take.

Peckwood nodded.

"And they took Miss Contague?"

"A woman. I don't know who she was."

"Tell him who they were," Relway said. "I know. You don't know. But I'll bet Garrett can guess."

"Crask and Sadler," I said.

"The very ones. And even all sliced up they worked Peckwood over when he tried to stop them from taking the girl."

"I got in my licks," Peckwood insisted, gritting his teeth. "They'll carry some extra scars."

"Belinda left the Weider place a while ago. Why was she hanging around?" And where did Carlyle come from? Was he shadowing us before? I hadn't noticed.

Belinda would know.

Crask and Sadler had Belinda.

I was tired. I didn't want to face those two even if CeeJay, Two Toes, and Peckwood had torn a leg off each one. They'd still bite. With poison fangs. "Got any idea where they went?"

"No," Relway said. "My people have orders not to leave a crime site if they're alone. Peckwood carried out his orders."

"Shit."

"I should encourage more innovation?"

"What good would it do if he'd followed them? We still wouldn't know anything happened. And he'd probably get killed for his trouble."

"Glad you see that, Garrett. Most people would argue."

"I want to argue. I just can't. I'm in over my head here. I don't know anybody inside the Outfit well enough to approach. Maybe none of them *would* help. Well, I could go to her father's place but by the time I went out there and got back it would be tomorrow night."

"I'll bet they were in too bad a shape to worry about covering their trail."

There was plenty of blood in the street. But nobody is filled with enough to leave a trail all the way to the sort of neighborhood where Crask and Sadler would hide.

"I don't like ratmen."

"Did I ask you to like them?" Relway smirked. "You need a good tracker, Garrett. When you need a good tracker you have to deal with ratmen."

Some races are just naturally better at some things. Ogres, trolls, humans, elves, dwarves, none of us are much good at tracking in the city. Ratmen with the talent can sniff out a trail through the worst alleys better than any hound.

Favorite trail-covering devices, among those who can afford them, include little sorcerous traps that crisp the nose and whiskers.

Still smiling, cognizant of my aversion, Relway said, "Never be a better time than now, Garrett. It's the middle of the night."

Absolutely. The ratpeople live on the underbelly of the night city. We were at the peak, or depth, of their day. "Any notion who or where?"

"I don't use ratpeople."

"And you sneer at my prejudice?"

"The problem is their prejudice. I don't use them because they start wailing when they find out who wants to hire them. They think we're the death squad branch of The Call, or something."

Ratpeople are timid. They've learned the hard way. I lug around a burden of prejudice but I'm nicer to them than most. I make an effort to control my bigotry.

I sighed. I'd wanted to stay away from Morley, as much for his sake as mine. Now that choice had been taken away.

Relway asked, "You'll let me know how it goes?"

Like he would not as soon as I did. "Why not?" I started walking.

Tinnie was going to promote me back to the top of her hate list. Who did I think I was, running off to save some woman in trouble? Some *other* woman. Especially *that* woman.

It was all right when I saved *her* sweet patootie.

52

The Goddamn Parrot plopped onto my shoulder seconds after I parted with Relway. He was shivering. It was cool out now. Or maybe he was scared. There were a lot of night predators around. They snacked on one another when nothing tastier presented itself. The small nocturnal flying lizards will attack anything smaller than themselves, including cats and dogs and the little people. And they are too stupid to figure out that doing the latter is suicidal.

The price of thunder-lizard leather and parchment might plummet.

"My luck ain't never gonna turn," I grouched. "I thought sure you were catfood by now."

Mr. Big had nothing to say.

"Cat got your tongue?" Snicker. What a joker.

Still nary a word. Apparently the Dead Man had no minds left over for me.

Nevertheless, I talked to the bird all the way to The Palms. Night people of all stripes watched nervously from the edges of their eyes. They gave me room. You had to be careful about humans who talked to themselves. Some conversed with ghosts or got messages inside their heads that resulted in attacks on imaginary foes with too-real weapons.

A ploy worth remembering, I told myself. Though with my luck nobody would be impressed the day I tried it. Or somebody would be rounding up recruits for the looney ward at the Bledsoe.

I ran into a new waiter three steps into The Palms. He demanded, "Can I help you, sir?" He eyed me as though I suffered from some grotesque skin condition—though his nose was so high in the air he must have checked me out with mirrors. Maybe I had bloodstains on me somewhere.

"No." I kept going.

I spied a familiar face. Dang me. Tama Montezuma looked better than she had at Weider's. She seemed recovered from her distress. She smiled like she wished we could be pals.

The fellow with her had a back that looked familiar, too. Aha! Marengo North English, brave and bold. Of course. Surprise!

I had my comradely smile on before he turned to see who his niece was ogling.

I nodded to both and kept moving. I noticed others who had been at the Weider mansion. Celebration becomes social disaster when people start dying. That stuff is entertaining only when it goes on between the families of the bride and groom.

"Well, at least ya tried ta dress decent oncet," Puddle grumbled. "Goes ta show. Anyting can happen, ya wait long enough."

"What?"

He ignored that. "What happent? Gang a pansies work ya over an' make ya play dress-up?" He whistled into the speaking tube. I didn't hear a response but one must have come. He said, "It's dat guy wit' da pet parrot. Yeah. Dat one. Agin, I don't know what he wants. I never axed. Garrett. What da hell ya want?"

"Plug your ears."

Puddle gaped.

"I mean it. Plug them up." Once he did shove beefy, grubby fingertips into his furry ear canals I leaned to the tube. "Crask and Sadler just snatched Belinda." That would get Morley's attention. "I need a tracker fast."

Dotes was still buttoning buttons and hooking hooks when he hit the bottom of the stairs. A plaintive call pursued him. He ignored his startled customers, eyed my apparel in mock astonishment. "What happened? They knock you out and dress you up before they made the snatch?"

"Snatch? What snatch?" Puddle demanded. "It was pansies done it, boss. I got dat on good autority."

"His own," I said. "He makes it up as he goes along. I wasn't there. CeeJay was. Got himself dead for his trouble. So did Two Toes Harker."

"Harker was a good man. Dog loyal."

"No virtue goes unpunished. They did hurt Crask and Sadler before they bought it. Maybe pretty bad. And so did one of Relway's guys who showed up during the excitement but couldn't keep them from getting away."

"They left a trail?"

"They were bleeding."

"Puddle. Run tell Reliance I want his best tracker right now. Tell him Garrett will pay top marks." He showed me sharp teeth, dared me to argue. I didn't. Ratpeople are venal.

Someday Morley will get his ass in a sling again and come to me. And I'll get even. And then I'll pile on the expense charges till I've got a lien on his soul. Then I'll shop around and see if I can't get a couple brass tokens for that.

I didn't warn him. If it comes as a surprise, it'll be more exciting for all of us.

Puddle took off.

"That shouldn't take long," Morley said. "Reliance is desperate for cash. Was it smart, you coming here? Being involved with rightsists?"

"My pal Marengo North English is right over there. With the gorgeous brown beast. Supposedly his niece. Incest is best. He's seen me already. I'll worry about that after Belinda is safe."

"That would be the infamous Tama Montezuma?"

"The very child. Which you should know, soaring at your new heights."

"I ignore gossip, Garrett. She's outstanding. And completely wasted on a sour old fart like that."

"Absolutely. So why don't one of us go over and offer to carry her away from her life of luxury and popular envy? Bet you she'll jump at a chance to elope with a guy who's poor but handsome." Then I stunned Dotes by going to squat beside North English's table.

I pretended to speak to the lady while telling North English, "Belinda Contague was abducted after she left the Weider place. Several men were killed. I know who did it. I'm collecting specialists to go after them. Would you care to join me?"

North English eyed me coolly. He glanced at his companion, who seemed very distressed by the news, then at the shadows to the rear of The Palms. It was hard to make out anything back there but he was, without doubt, cognizant of the management's background. He was the sort of man who would have found occasional uses for a Morley Dotes. He nodded graciously. "I appreciate the information, Mr. Garrett. And I wish I *could* join you. The young lady was quite charming. But, as you can see, I have preclusive obligations. Do let me know how this tragedy plays out, though, won't you?"

The preclusive obligation wasn't fooled. I winked. Miss Tama Montezuma awarded me a very friendly twitch of her lip. She seemed to be in a strange mood, feeling no affection at all for her uncle. North English seemed pretty cool toward her, too.

Montezuma was no bimbo, whatever her reputation.

When I rejoined him I told Morley, "I have a suspicion that that could be one very interesting woman."

"Darn! And here you are already up to your ugly, unpointed ears in interesting women. What a pity." He eyed the Goddamn Parrot. "What did you do to Mr. Big? He doesn't look right. Narciscio will be brokenhearted if you—"

"Nothing." Morley's vain nephew had a place on my list only a couple of slots below his uncle and the talking buzzard.

"He isn't talking. Not that I mind that right now, right here, understand." Like he feared that I would cozen that ugly jungle crow into being himself for a few minutes. Right here in front of the paying customers.

"This's where he learned to talk, isn't it? He really shouldn't hold back in familiar surroundings. Find him a cracker."

"Garrett!"

"Heh-heh. Come on, pretty boy. Say something for Uncle Morley."

The little vulture persisted in his silence. If there was a way to disappoint me, he was sure to find it.

Morley's anxiety faded. He put on a smug smile, offered me another fine look at all his pearly whites. He had more of those than two predators deserved. Made me wish I was a ventriloquist after all.

"Ultimate justice does exist, Morley. My hour will come."

"All things are possible. But it isn't going to happen tonight." Quietly, he had begun flirting with Tama Montezuma. Already.

"Don't you have something going upstairs?"

"When I have a friend in desperate need? I couldn't let myself be distracted by trivia."

"I could." And so could he when it suited him. Which was most anytime there was a Tama Montezuma type in the equation.

Puddle joined us. I indulged in silk purse and sow's ear anatomical reflections. However Morley dressed him Puddle couldn't look like anything but what he was. Morley takes care of his friends, which keeps them fiercely loyal. They go along with his every mad scheme. Even unto managing upscale vegetarian watering holes.

Personal loyalty tells you more about most individuals than any surface glitter or grime.

Puddle whispered to Morley. The name Reliance occurred several times. I knew it only by reputation. Reliance was a ratman getting just enough above himself to have become feared and respected within his own community. He was part civic leader, part gangster, but as yet not in any way big enough to arouse the ire of humans. Ratfolk respect Reliance because he has enough nerve to deal with other species. They respect any of their own who are strong, good or bad.

Morley beckoned, headed for the kitchen. Puddle oozed along behind us. I glanced back past him. Several people seemed interested in us, North English and his lovely niece in particular.

Could there be a connection between The Call and Belinda's predicament? Possibly, but it seemed unlikely. North English had thugs of his own by the battalion.

53

Three ratpeople awaited us behind The Palms. One was Reliance himself. He was bigger than most ratmen and had gray in his fur. He had survived longer than most ratmen did. He was dressed better than any ratman I'd run into before, colorfully, including a pair of tall black pirate boots and an ugly purple-and-white thing flopped on top of his head. He was unusually confident for a ratman.

He needed something to complement the red-and-yellow shirt and the green trousers. Mr. Big really belonged on one of those skinny, sloping shoulders.

Morley introduced me. Reliance produced a pair of specially designed TenHagen spectacles and examined me. Dotes suggested I state my case myself. I did so.

"Belinda Contague, Chodo Contague's daughter, has been kidnapped. The men who did it are notoriously vicious." I didn't name names because Crask and Sadler *were* so notorious. I didn't want to scare anybody off. "I need to track them so I can rescue Belinda."

Reliance glanced at his companions. Light escaping from The Palms made his eyes turn red at the right angle.

"Would be valuable to have the friendship of Chodo Contague,"

Reliance hissed. His Karentine lay just this side of intelligibility. Rat throats don't handle human speech well. They use a polyglot mess of their own.

Their speech, like most dialects, becomes intelligible if you're exposed continuously. Like my brother's speech impediment. I never noticed except when other people asked about it. Which doesn't happen much anymore. The Cantard wasn't as kind to him as it was to me.

"It would," I told Reliance. Chodo's friendships are unpredictable but legendary. He did well by me. I owe him, really. But how do you repay a debt to a human vegetable? Take care of his family? I was doing that now.

Reliance eyed us intently. Most ratfolk aren't bright. They fall between a brilliant dog and a slow human. This guy was a genius for a ratman. He indicated Morley, then me. "I have heard of you. You worked with Shote. Your reputations are sound." He spoke slowly, carefully, so that we could follow him. He knew neither of us ever did his people any willful harm. Shote was another tracker I'd employed. "I will help you. And Chodo Contague will owe me."

"Absolutely." He didn't want money? Ratmen always want money—despite being weak on the cause-and-effect relationship between wages and work. They can make dwarves look fiscally indifferent, though only at the pettiest level.

Reliance looked at me sharply. He suspected I'd committed Chodo too fast, too glibly. Tell the rat anything to get what you want. But he knew Chodo's reputation, too. Chodo always paid his debts. He nodded. "This is Pular Singe." All ratman sibilants tend to stretch out into syllables of their own while *r* and *l* sounds get confused. "She is young but very talented."

I checked his smaller companion. She? That wasn't obvious. Her apparel didn't differentiate her. Unlike most human girls she didn't have obvious female attributes. I guess if you're ratpeople you can tell. Or there wouldn't be any ratpeople.

A youngish ratman moved closer, bristling feebly. I said, "If you say she's the best, then she is and I owe you special thanks."

The ratgirl eyed me shyly, unaccustomed to the company of humans. I gave her a wink and a glimpse of one raised eyebrow. Gets them every time. "What do I call you? Pular or Singe?" Depending on the clan—and I have only the vaguest notion how you tell that, though it has to do with which sorcerer created their particular line—surnames can come front or back.

"She is hard of hearing," Reliance told me. "Her talent is a divine compensation. She does not speak human well. Her cousin Fenibro must translate for you."

Fenibro dipped his muzzle. "She prefers Singe."

"Thank you." Singe, I noted, followed every word, maybe reading lips. Easier done with humans, of course.

Time was getting away. I asked Reliance, "Will you join us yourself?" I meant the question only as a courtesy. It would be hard enough working with the other two. This one might think he had something to contribute.

"I do not think so. I am far too old and slow."

"I'll tag along, Garrett," Morley announced. "Come here, Puddle."

"You will? I thought you wanted out of this stuff."

"You can't go after those two alone." The ratpeople would scoot at the first sign of trouble. That was a given. "You think too much. You'd get your candle snuffed. I need you. You're such a wonderful negative example."

He could be right. Or maybe I owed him money I'd forgotten about. "We'd best go. They're getting farther ahead all the time." He couldn't possibly want to tag along just on account of being my friend.

Morley whispered to Puddle. Puddle nodded. He went back into The Palms. Morley pointed a finger at the sky, the moon, and said, "I'm ready."

I told Reliance, "Thank you again, sir. Singe? Fenibro? Ready?" I started jogging. Nobody had trouble keeping up despite ratmen not being built to run on their hind legs. When they get in a big hurry they bounce off their hands sort of like a gorilla. They move fast when they're scared.

The Goddamn Parrot remained dumb, which was a blessing. He roused only once, just long enough to emit a sort of puzzled interrogative squeak. If I'd had time, I would've been worried about the Dead Man.

54

"Took you long enough," Relway grumbled. He didn't look much like the Relway I'd left though the changes were cosmetic and subtle. He'd acquired a drooping shoulder and a slight dragging limp, a lisp and a marked preference for shadows. I doubted even Morley would recognize him later, changed and in a different light. The runt even smelled different. The ratpeople wouldn't recognize him later, either.

"Took a while to set it up."

"In the middle of the night?"

"I got the best."

Relway eyed the ratpeople. They were sniffing around and muttering. All the violence upset them. "The best is Pular Singe."

"That's her. You know her?"

"Only by reputation."

Good for Morley and Reliance. Maybe not so good for me. Now I might actually find Belinda fast, which could mean a big fight with TunFaire's two ugliest bad boys.

They would be like wounded animals, even nastier now they were hurt. Like cornered rats. Snicker.

Crask and Sadler were like a malevolent force of nature, beyond control, subject only to laws they created themselves.

I gave the ratgirl another reassuring wink. That seemed to calm her. She responded with the wedge-toothed grimace her kind thinks constitutes a smile.

There's a certain pathos to the ratpeople. Most of them desperately want to be just like the race that created them. Poor deluded beasts.

Trackers amaze me. Singe amazed me doubly. And she wasn't full-grown. She was going to be a legend. Once on the trail she was limited only by her ability to walk fast and mine to keep up. Fenibro kept giving me the ratman equivalent of a big shit-eating grin. You'd have thought *he* was running the trail. Pular Singe kept looking to me for approval. Boy, did I give her plenty. Evidently she didn't get much at home. Ratmen don't treat their young or females well.

Everybody needs somebody to look down on and treat bad. You wonder who's left for the young ratwomen, though.

Later I grumbled, "These guys must be headed for the arctic." We had covered several miles, leaving downtown's seething heart for a neighborhood called the Plain of Cavalry. Centuries ago, when the citizen militia was TunFaire's only army, the mounted troops assembled there to practice up for scrimmages with neighboring city-states. In those days the plain was outside the wall. Later the wall was extended to enclose the plain so it could be used as a bivouac in times of siege. They started burying dead soldiers there. Eventually it became a vast graveyard. It's not much used anymore. It's become the object of endless dispute. Those who want to build there insist that land inside the wall is too precious to waste on dead folks already forgotten by their own descendants. The descendants disagree. The traditional position has prevailed only because many of the dead are old-time heroes and imperials. But adequate bribes might silence the opposition.

The cemetery is a bivouac again, filled with shanties and crude tents slapped together by refugees. This isn't popular with the neighbors, who have to suffer more than their share of victimizations. The Call is popular around the plain.

Wary tension filled the cemetery air. There was very little light. There's no free fuel to be had anymore. I was uneasy because I hadn't thought to bring a lantern. The moon wasn't much help—though it gave Singe all the light she needed.

Squatter villages appear wherever there's open ground. They're unclean. They stink. It's only a matter of time till some plague gets started. It can't be long before the street conflicts engulf the camps.

"Hold up," I told Pular Singe. I gestured, too. She stopped, waited, watched me with a disquieting intelligence. I suspected her hearing problem was less severe than Reliance thought, more a convenience than a handicap. She got my deaf-and-dumb sign language right away, too, though I was rusty. It was a shame Singe had trouble with the common speech. I got the impression she had a real sense of humor.

She had to be some kind of mutant.

"Morley, wouldn't this pest-hole camp be perfect to disappear in?"

People were moving around us, despite the hour, looking for nothing they could have articulated if asked. Movement itself was the destination.

The squatter population was a volatile mix including every type of refugee. I saw people so exotic they had to be weird to themselves.

"Absolutely," Morley said. "You'd have to be a woolly mammoth to get noticed around here."

"Is the tracking getting harder?" I asked Singe.

She shook her head, a human thing, not natural for ratpeople. Pular Singe tried hard to emulate human ways.

Fenibro told me, "It is difficult but she can single it out."

"She's amazing."

"She is. There is blood in it still."

No blood had been visible for miles.

I observed, "She sure says a lot with a headshake."

Morley murmured, "The boyfriend likes to show off his talent, too."

"Which is?"

"Human speech."

"Oh. Think we're being led?"

"You asking me if I think Crask and Sadler grabbed Belinda hoping that you, personally, would try to rescue her?"

"It's possible, isn't it? They might even have counted on you coming with me."

"*I* might calculate a scheme like that, Garrett. Not those two. They aren't complicated thinkers. They saw a chance to grab Belinda. They grabbed her. They probably expected you to be with her. Things didn't go the way they anticipated."

Yeah? How did they know where to find Belinda? How did they know who she was supposed to be with? "You think they expect to be trailed here?" Morley wasn't giving Crask and Sadler enough credit. They weren't just mountains of muscle. They had brains. That's what made them scary.

"Once they have time to think. They left a heavy trail. But they shouldn't expect trouble this soon."

I glanced around. As a group we presented an unusual look but out there the unusual was the norm—and inquisitive noses tended to get broken. "Figure Relway had us followed?"

"Is the moon made of green cheese?"

"That's what I thought." The tail wasn't obvious, though. "Go ahead, Singe. You're doing wonderfully. But please be careful."

Fenibro looked at me like I wanted to teach granny to suck eggs. But Pular Singe practically purred. Whereupon Fenibro suffered a case of the sullens.

55

The change in our surroundings was miniscule but real. Surprisingly, I sensed it before Morley or Singe. I didn't need to prompt Dotes, though. Still, I gestured to point out the fact that the refugee hovels shrank back from one particular mausoleum.

It was an antique from imperial times, a family thing that had been used for centuries. It would be as big as a house inside with several levels below ground. The family must have fallen on hard times. All families do eventually. The mausoleum needed restoration though it remained sound enough for someone to have set up housekeeping inside.

Pular Singe sniffed, pointed, gestured uncertainly. She dashed off. She circled back before I figured out what she was doing.

She whispered to Fenibro but looked at me from beneath lowered lashes, eager for more approval. Fenibro told me, "The devils you seek are in there." He was scared. He wanted to get paid and go. His speech was barely intelligible. I understood Singe's rattalk almost as well. "They have bad odors, sir. They are evil. Even my blind nose tastes them now." He fidgeted, eager to go but afraid to ask for money.

Morley squatted on his haunches. I don't bend that way. I dropped to one knee. Dotes murmured, "Seems like we've done this thing before."

"The vampire thing?" I stared at the mausoleum door. It stood open just wide enough to admit a bulk the size of a Crask or a Sadler. It seemed to sneer.

Dotes asked me, "Do you have anything in case we prance into an ambush?"

"I was thinking about throwing you in there to see what happens."

Fenibro squeaked like one of his ancestors getting tromped. He suffered a sudden, sad suspicion that our natural inclination would be to elect him our tossee. Unlike Singe, he did not grasp the concept of humor.

Singe spoke rapidly in rat polyglot. I caught just enough to understand that she was telling Fenibro to control himself, then that their part of the adventure was over and it was time for them to take off. I started mining my pockets for coins.

Fenibro argued with Singe. He puffed his chest out, male demonstrating dominance. Singe hissed. Fenibro wilted. That left no doubt where real dominance resided. He whined, "Singe says to tell you Reliance requires no payment. Someday he will ask a favor in return."

I groaned. That arrangement always gets me into trouble eventually.

Morley ignored the ratpeople. He persisted, "I thought you might have something up your sleeve. You often do."

"Not this time. I wish, though."

"A light, then. Surely we can come up with a light."

A glance around suggested otherwise. The refugees and squatters had stripped the cemetery of everything burnable.

I nodded to Singe. "Go home now, darling. It might get hairy around here. And be careful."

She took off instantly, practically abandoning Fenibro. He whined as he tried to catch up. There was no doubt that Singe was his girlfriend only inside his own head.

Morley grouched, "You never put any forethought into anything you do, do you?"

"This was your idea. *You* should've thought about bringing a lantern."

"My idea? You're stalling, Garrett."

Yes, I was. In a good cause, too. I'm really fond of my skin. It's rough and it's scarred but it's the only one I've got. Crask and Sadler might decide to use it to make wallets or belts.

Morley heard the sound first but I caught it an instant later. Somebody was sneaking our way.

There was enough moonlight to show me Morley. He gestured. I waved. We sank down behind antique tombstones.

Fate handed me a wonderful opportunity to look goofy. Yet one more time.

I jumped out at the sneaker, expecting Crask, Sadler, one of Relway's goons, a squatter determined to share my wealth, anything but a terrified Pular Singe, who should've been miles away already. We bumped snoots. She squeaked and started to run. I caught her arm. "I'm sorry," I whispered. "I thought you'd gone home."

Her fright faded as quickly as it had come. She looked at my hand. If she'd been human, she would've blushed. She did shiver. I let go but stayed ready to grab again if she bolted.

"What is it?" I used my gentlest voice. And wondered where Morley was.

"I brought . . ." Those words were perfectly clear, if few. And she'd heard me just fine. She seemed too embarrassed to continue. She couldn't meet my gaze. She lifted a shuttered lantern and offered it.

"You're a dream come true, Pular Singe. I might just steal you away from Reliance."

She was painfully embarrassed. She had a sense of humor but didn't understand teasing. She was brilliant for her own people only.

I didn't want her expiring from a stroke of shyness. "Thank you, Singe. You know I didn't think about needing a light. I owe you. Not Reliance or Fenibro or anybody else. You. Personally. You understand?"

Still avoiding my gaze, she reached for the Goddamn Parrot. That critter remained deadweight. Maybe when I wasn't looking somebody did stuff him and nail him to my shoulder. Maybe some wicked sorcerer cast a spell on him. Thank you very much. "Pretty," Singe said.

"You want him?"

She looked at the ground, shook her head in quick little rolling jerks, then scooted away. Mr. Big has to be the most unwanted creature in this whole wide world. I can't get anybody to take him.

Singe made less sound departing than her unaltered cousins might have. The noise she'd made approaching must have been deliberate.

Morley materialized. "Another Garrett conquest."

"What?"

"Maybe it was just an illusion cast by that devil moonlight but these elven eyes saw Miss Pular Singe, brilliant young ratwoman, acting as smitten as any other teenager with a crush." He giggled. "You'd make a great team."

The curse again? I shook my head vigorously. No rat would find anything redeeming in me. Or vice versa.

Morley kept right on snickering. This was delicious. He lingered over wedding plans and what to name the children. "Or would you call them pups?"

"Let's get on with this," I grumped. "Before we're all too old to keep up."

"This is rich, Garrett. Now I remember why I liked being part of your adventures. They create so many memories for those lonely winter nights."

He exaggerated. I think. Elves—even breeds like him—just don't think the way us humans do.

56

"Whenever you stop snickering," I said.

"You armed?"

"Only with my wits. Never mind the cracks." I wished I hadn't left that little crossbow back at the Weider place.

"Take this." He offered me a small, flat-handled dagger I hadn't seen on him anywhere. No doubt he was lugging a whole arsenal not evident to the naked eye. He was such a prankster. He'd have a trebuchet on him somewhere. "Don't it seem awfully quiet in there?"

It sure did. Crask and Sadler really had it in for Belinda. A scream or two would have been reassuring. There'd still be somebody to rescue. "Think they killed her already?"

"Maybe. But let's be careful anyway."

"Good plan. After you."

He didn't argue. I had him at a disadvantage now. His night vision was better than mine. He had no sound tactical argument against leading the way—if we had to go at all.

Once we were close enough to make out details it was obvious that the mausoleum's builders had belonged to one of our more bizarre early religions. The doorway was surrounded by carvings of fabulous creatures who glorified ugly. I plucked the Goddamn Parrot off my shoulder, planted him on an outcrop. Maybe he could go for help.

"But for the color he fits right in." And the breathing part. I didn't clue him in, though. He might pick this exact moment to express one of his vulgar opinions.

Dotes grinned, revealing a lot of sharp white teeth.

Enough moonlight leaked into the mausoleum for Morley to see that no one lurked immediately beyond the doorway. He reached back, touched me, found the lantern, tapped it. I cracked the shutter. We'd stirred up a little dust already. The wedge of light swept around like a flaming sword.

It revealed nothing startling.

Morley pointed downward. There was evidence of recent traffic in the leaves and trash that had blown in over the years.

I fought back a sneeze.

Dotes kept moving. I kept a glimmer of light splashing out to

probe the way. Even Morley can't see in complete darkness. Again
I wondered if Crask and Sadler hadn't set me up. They knew I was
a white knight dumb enough to roll the dice with death over a
damsel in distress.

The trail in the rubbish ran straight to a wall. "Damn!" I muttered. "Not another secret door. How come people think they can
pull that off?"

But it wasn't one of those. The builder hadn't been trying to fool
anybody. This door was a massive wooden job. I stabbed its huge
hinges with my sword of light. Our friends hadn't oiled them. They
wouldn't operate quietly.

Morley shrugged, bounced into place beside the door, whispered, "Let's go."

What the hell. Might as well. It was only Crask and Sadler on the
other side of that damned thing. Only a couple of superhuman,
demi-demon, stone killers. A pair of walking nightmares. No big
deal at all. Did it all the time.

I grabbed the rusty ring and heaved.

A slab of human meat the size of a small barn tipped out and
crashed at my feet. One of the villains. I had no time to find out
which.

Morley slugged him in the temple with the pommel of a dagger
cousin to the one he'd loaned me. Air left the huge killer in a sigh,
like he'd never wanted anything more than he wanted to lie down
and sleep right now.

"Garrett?" The voice was weak but definitely Belinda's.

"I'm here."

A piglike grunt from the darkness preceded the wobbly rush of a
pallid behemoth bigger than the leviathan snoring at my feet. A
hand like a ham floated out of the darkness, grabbed me, flung me
at the voice just starting to tell me to look out. There were grunts
behind me, slaps and thumps and a growl of pain. Morley is good
but he didn't get the best of this exchange. Brute force sometimes
smothers style. Dotes cursed as he flew my way, apparently in the
feet superior mode. He crashed into the mess on the floor before I
could get my own feet under me again. The door slammed a moment later. I hit it with my shoulder an instant after that.

There can't be any nightmare worse than mine about being
buried alive.

The door gave a little. I let out a mad-sorcerer cackle and hit it
again. Something bashed it from the other side. The shock shot
from my shoulder down to my toes and back. Crask cussed me and

Sadler at the same time. "Get up! Get up!" he raged at his sidekick. His voice was feeble. Between them Two Toes, Carlyle, and Peckwood had dinged him badly and hurt Sadler even worse.

I shoved. Crask shoved back. "Give me a hand, Morley!" The lantern's shutter was all the way open, shining on the ceiling and showing me Morley making points with Belinda by asking if she was all right.

"Of course I'm not all right, you moron!" she snarled. "I'm lucky. They passed out before they could torture me much. Help Garrett. Unless you want to spend the rest of your life here, eating raw mice." Her voice was feeble but her will remained unflagging. She was a razor-edged chip off the old Contague flint.

Crask wedged something against the door. We banged into it until my shoulder ached. We moved it a fraction of an inch each time, till Morley was able to weasel through. He muttered continuously. This adventure was playing hell with his outfit.

He flung the blockage aside. I stalked out. Belinda clung to my left arm. She had no choice. She had no strength left. She grunted with every step. Crask and Sadler had given her a taste of joys to come.

We hit the moonlight. "What now, dauntless sidekick?" Morley asked. "We don't have a tracker anymore. You should have kissed her. She would've hung around forever."

"I did what I wanted to do. I got Belinda back." It was time to head home. Only, what were the chances I would run into Crask and Sadler in such reduced circumstances ever again? Less than zip. I grabbed the Goddman Parrot. "Which way did they go, bird?"

His Highness did not deign to speak.

A silent bird wasn't a problem I'd ever expected to face.

I was worried about the Dead Man. I'd heard nothing for too long. He should have been nagging me mercilessly.

He'd shown that he couldn't read shapechangers close up. Maybe they got to him while I was busy at Weider's. If one could pretend to be me long enough to get Dean to open the door . . .

Morley whispered, "Didn't we decide that Relway would have a man watching?"

"I counted on it when we went in there." Sort of.

"Then wouldn't you guess that Relway will know where those two went?"

Probably, come to think. But would he let me know if I asked? Relway just might discover that he had some use for Crask and

Sadler no one else could appreciate. I said, "They'll never be weaker. And you know they never forgive and forget."

Morley patted my arm. "Good to see my wisdom finally taking root. But Belinda is in no shape to chase anybody."

Belinda snapped, "Belinda will keep up! Belinda is in better shape than either of them. And Belinda's got another score to settle." Whereupon her legs melted and she had to grab a handy tombstone. "I don't want to hear a word, Garrett." Her voice didn't waver.

Something stirred out in the darkness. It trailed the faintest whisper of disturbed grass. It headed the direction Crask and Sadler must have gone. Dotes and I exchanged glances. I asked Belinda, "Where were you headed when they grabbed you? They meant to catch you on your way home, only you—"

"No. They were waiting on the way to your house. Originally. They were really pissed off because you didn't take me home. They wanted us both."

"Lucky for both of us I had to work, then. Eh?"

"Yeah? Isn't it?" Belinda didn't sound like she believed that in her heart, though.

"Where were you going?" I asked again.

She hesitated, then admitted, "To The Palms. People from the reception were going to meet there."

"Oh." Neutrally, recalling that she had spoken to Marengo North English in parting and he had seemed surprised. None of my business, though. Except that later the same gentleman had seemed quite unhappy about being at The Palms with his delectable niece. I asked Morley, "You want to take her back to your place?" She would be safe there, if she wanted to be.

"You're not going after them alone?" Morley's tone told me nothing I did would ever surprise him. Maybe because this wouldn't be stupider than anything I'd ever done before.

"I'm not going after them. They're Relway's now." For now.

I was very worried about the Dead Man.

57

There was no deadly silence in my neighborhood. The night people were out in force and they were busy. Commerce was king. No political dialogue was under way. I exchanged greetings with those I knew. There was no tension in the air. Nobody seemed interested in my movements. A stroll around the area didn't uncover anyone watching my house.

Even Mrs. Cardonlos was otherwise occupied.

I got a strange feeling as I climbed my steps. Not like something was wrong. No. It was more like something was missing. An emptiness I hadn't felt for years. "What's the story here?" I asked the Goddman Parrot. This close he had no excuse for being out of touch.

The bird was stubborn. He still refused to talk.

"Old Bones?" I tried my key. Miracle of miracles, Dean didn't have any bolts bolted or chains chained. I shoved the door, cocked an ear to the silent darkness.

The house didn't feel right.

It was darker than a priest's heart in there. Dean hadn't refilled the feeble lamp we leave burning in the hallway. I hoped he had a fire in the stove so I could light it again. I'm not big on flint and steel, though I manage if I have to. It was way too late to go mooching from the neighbors.

I felt the wall till I found the lamp. I took it and headed for the kitchen, carefully. There was no knowing what Dean would leave lying around.

I completed my pilgrimage without getting hurt.

The stove was warm. I dug in, found some live coals, got a kitchen lamp burning so I could find the oil to fill the hall lamp. Its wick needed trimming but I was bone-tired. I would mention it to Dean tomorrow.

Tinnie would be cussing me big-time now, I figured. I ought to start rehearsing my apologies.

Once I had a light I took the Goddamn Parrot to the small front room. He was just aware enough to move to his perch. Maybe he was worn-out, too.

I put the hall lamp in its bracket and shoved into the Dead Man's room. "All right, Chuckles. What's the story? If you've gone to sleep on me I'm gonna . . ."

He hadn't gone to sleep on me. Not this time. No way.

What he'd done was, he'd gone missing.

For a while I stood there with my mouth open. Then I retrieved the hall lamp and prowled the Dead Man's room like maybe a quarter ton of moth-eaten corpse might have gotten lost amongst the dust bunnies. I faced the unusual and weird as a matter of course but this was beyond comprehension.

The Dead Man was gone? How? He couldn't have gotten up and walked. Nor could Dean have carried him.

There were no signs of a struggle. There would've been had he been abducted.

He was just gone.

Dean was going to get rousted out after all.

No, Dean wasn't.

He didn't respond to my knock. "You awake, Dean? I need to talk." I pushed his door open hoping I didn't get him started cranking.

His room was empty.

It wasn't just untenanted or deserted, it was barren. Not one scrap of clothing or stick of furniture remained.

"My gods! They've eloped!" I didn't imagine Dean. When I imagine people I pick them put together like Tinnie or Nicks or Tama Montezuma.

I petitioned the air with the intensity of an actor in a passion play, "What the hell is going on?" A waste of time. I'd asked already and hadn't gotten an answer.

I went back down to the kitchen. A hasty inventory left me baffled. I made something to eat, drew a beer off the keg in the cold well, shuffled around the ground floor balancing food, drink, and lamp while I searched for messages or clues.

I found nothing. Not even a *Dear Garrett* note.

"Hell with it," I grumbled. "Hell with them. Hell with everybody." I dragged myself up to bed, enumerating the names of everyone who ought to join the infernal pilgrimage.

I don't recall lying down.

58

I don't recall getting up. My first clear thought surfaced when somebody groaned in pain. A moment later I realized that the groaner was right there in my bedroom and he was making those noises with my dried-out mouth. Then it dawned: The pain was caused by sunburn of the backs of the eyeballs. I was staring out at a morning where the gods, or devils, of daylight were putting on one of the great sunshine shows of all time.

It was almost noon. The sun seemed to span half the sky.

That information developed, I tried to reason out why I wanted to stare into that unholy furnace.

The proximate cause made itself apparent instantly. Which is to say that there were hundreds of idiots out there holding another political discussion. Sticks and stones and broken bones.

Hundreds of guys in brown, wearing a variety of rightsist armbands, showing colorful standards and banners, were proclaiming their message with enthusiasm, not only to the fey but to any handy humans who had a foreign look on them or maybe just parted their hair a little strange.

Maybe my mom didn't raise me right after all. I don't quite grasp politics. Despite claims to the contrary substance has no relevance. Apparently conflicts are decided by whoever shouts the loudest and whacks away with the biggest stick.

Why did they keep doing it in Macunado Street? Why couldn't they take it into the countryside? Nobody but farmers or mammoths or woods elves would be bothered out there. I wanted to grab a big megaphone and yell, "People, we got folks trying to sleep around here!"

I dropped the curtain. After a minute I felt fine. I didn't have a hangover. What did I drink? One beer? Good. Still, maybe I should ease up on the health food for a while.

As I descended to the kitchen I recalled my housemate shortage. I'd have to build my own breakfast. Boy. Life just ain't fair.

The Goddamn Parrot heard me moving around and squawked. He started the thing where he pretends to be a small child begging not to be abused.

He was back to his old self. I'd feed him if I started feeling generous and forgiving. Which could not possibly come anytime but later.

I got some bacon frying and some water heating for tea, then went over the ground floor one last time, hoping I'd find something I was too tired to notice last night. I came up with the same big batch of nothing. No getting around it. Dean and the Dead Man were gone. There was no suggestion of foul play. They'd gotten up and gone because they'd wanted to get up and go.

I sipped tea and nibbled bacon and snacked on halfway stale bread dipped in bacon drippings while I tried to get my mind wrapped around the notion that the Dead Man had moved voluntarily. That would make twice in my lifetime. Last time was when I moved him in here.

Give him another generation and he'd be dancing in the streets.

I glanced at the keg in the cold well. Tempting. But it was too early. And I had work to do.

I shivered. Events had left me a mighty hill to climb.

"Shut up in there!" I barked at Mr. Big, who was singing the marching song of ten thousand verses, each of which begins, "I don't know but I've been told . . ."

I poured tea, stirred in a spoon of honey, found a muffin young enough not to scar the hardwood if I dropped it, migrated to my office. "Good morning, Eleanor."

The lady in the painting smiled enigmatically, bemused by my morning dishabille. She didn't surprise me when she didn't have anything to say.

The Goddamn Parrot was stuck on a verse about ratgirls. It didn't flatter them. He must not have been completely comatose last night.

Me, I thought better of ratgirls since meeting Pular Singe. Hers was an acquaintance worth nurturing.

"So, darling. Did the Dead Man take off so he wouldn't complicate my life now that I'm involved with righsists? Or did he feel unfulfilled and had to find himself and realize his potential?" That was a chuckle. Without continuous nagging Old Bones has the potential of an iceberg. He'll slide downhill if he isn't at the bottom already. If you give him a push.

I finished my muffin and tea, went for another cup. I took the scenic route back to the office. The Goddman Parrot shut up as soon as I gave him some breakfast. Nestled in my chair again, I told Eleanor, "Listen to this and tell me what you think." I started where I thought it began, did Black Dragon, Crask and Sadler, Belinda, Relway, shapeshifters, the Weiders, Marengo North English, Tama Montezuma.

"So what do you think? Is it all connected? Or have I stumbled into several things all going on at the same time?" Occasionally it helps to bounce the facts off Eleanor or the Dead Man even though neither is inclined to respond. Sometimes the pieces fall into place.

I twisted and kicked and whacked away at the facts with a big faded steel hammer to conjure the mess into a couple of complete scenarios. I was sure neither had much to do with reality. Neither made sense of what was happening.

"I prefer the chaos theory," I told Eleanor. "Shit's flying everywhere and it's by chance a lot is raining down where I'm standing. I'm what ties the whole mess together. . . . Oh. Right. Isn't this exactly what I've been waiting for?"

Eleanor's smile turned more teasing than enigmatic. She knows how thrilled I am when somebody pounds on my door.

I don't always hear them, though. The door, replaced often lately, is heavy. I'm thinking about getting one of those mechanical bells so I can be sure there's somebody out there to ignore.

59

"Gods, Garrett," Colonel Block growled. "You been on a three-day bender?"

"You're looking good yourself. We saw one another just yesterday. Remember?"

"You really go to hell overnight, don't you?"

Maybe I did look a little ragged. "All right. So maybe I need a shave." I let Block come inside.

He doesn't come around unless he has something on his mind. "That would be a start."

"Want a cup of tea?"

The Goddamn Parrot broke off crunching sunflower seeds long enough to excoriate the head of the Guard, then the head of the household.

"Can I drown that thing in it?"

"I'll brew you a bucket if you'll do it and take the rap. What's up?" I shepherded him into my office. He helped himself to a chair.

"I wanted you to know what Relway got from the prisoners. And your thoughts about last night. Relway's devotion colors what he sees."

"It was pretty straightforward." I told him what I knew. Once I would've held out just because he was the law. I'm mellowing with age and accumulated head lumps. I concluded, "What I don't have is a clue what it adds up to."

"I find it productive to forget the big question while I root out little answers."

"Uhm?"

"Instead of worrying about what it all adds up to, work on why the shapeshifters chose the Weiders. There are a hundred questions you could ask. You can paint the big picture one brushstroke at a time."

He wasn't offering advice that was new. But there was a subtext, an unspoken message. He was reminding me that collecting brushstrokes would involve me in my least favorite pastime.

What I need to find is a way to cruise through life without having to work.

"So what's the word? Did Relway collect any brushstrokes?" He must have tormented up some random flecks of color.

"He's got a bunch of words for you, Garrett. But there ain't many of them ones you want to hear. The big thing is, we didn't get anything out of the shapechangers."

I must have looked doubtful. I don't know why. Maybe I'm getting cynical. If you can't believe the secret police, whom can you trust?

"Really, Garrett. Before Relway got back to the Al-Khar the prisoners tried to escape."

"The place is a sewer any sane person would want to get away from, but how—"

"They're shapeshifters, Garrett. They can't turn into mice or roaches or anything that's not as heavy as they are but they can turn skinny or plastic enough to slide between bars and—"

"I get the picture. Damn! We should've seen that coming." I selected a quiver of choice expletives, used them up. This could turn real bad if those things could turn into furniture or the carpet underfoot. "So they're all loose again—"

"Not all. Three got away. And they were hurt. The others died trying. Relway says you can study the bodies if you want to."

"Did they all have tattoos?"

"How did you know?"

"Wild and lucky guess. Let me guess some more. The tattoo was a dragon with a Karentine military seal worked in. It was hard to see even when they weren't trying to hide it."

"You've seen them before." He was squinting now, suddenly troubled.

"I have. Relway told me he'd try to find out what the tattoo means."

"He probably hasn't had time."

"My guess is that they're some special ops mercs left over from the war."

"That would be my guess, too. Which means that I made this walk mostly for the exercise. I'm not telling you anything new."

"Exercise never hurt anybody. I'm told. Come on in the kitchen. We'll get that tea." I was sure he had more to say. But maybe it was something he didn't want to tell me. I asked him to come along because in my house we try not to leave visitors unattended. Especially not Winger or officers of the law. Both are almost certain to get into stuff I'd really rather they didn't.

I poured. Block communed with his inner demons. I asked, "Do you prefer the uniform?" He wore a slightly fancy version of the vaguely military, undyed linen outfit recently adopted by the Guard. It did little for the dignity of his office. Most rightsists street thugs dressed better.

Block accepted tea. "We don't have much of a budget. So it's become a point of pride. Shows people we're dedicated."

Maybe. "*Anything* useful come from those changers?"

"No. Except that someone from the Hill, names I can't mention, want the dead ones." And there it was, his secret burden.

"And I thought you were saving them just for me."

Block sneered. "A bunch of shifters turning up stirred a *lot* of curiosity."

"Think someone knew about the tattoos?"

Block shrugged. "I haven't mentioned them. Yet."

"How come?"

"I wanted to see what happened when they figured it out. I'm just a dumb lawman. I wouldn't notice, anyway."

And what might he be holding out on me? "You'll let me know if anything comes of it?"

He nodded. My coconspirator. "Some big-toothed hounds are

going to be on this trail before long." Which was maybe as much as he dared tell me.

That didn't excite me. I don't like sorcerers. They're dangerous. And they're unpredictable. Like lawyers. You don't want to turn your back on one of them. Most of them aren't even kind to their mothers. Still, it would be stupid not to hear what Block was trying to say. "You guys have been awful nice to me lately."

Block shrugged again. "That's because you can help us. We need to make you want to cooperate."

He sounded like Chodo Contague about to offer an infernal deal. "It might be easier to leave town. My mother has cousins upcountry."

"Then you'd be stuck wearing scratchy homespun and couldn't indulge yourself in all this elegant luxury." He indicated my clothing. "I can't see you as a peasant, anyway."

"They raise sheep."

"That's different. You'd never have trouble finding a girlfriend."

"I liked you better when you were worried about hanging on to your job. You were crabby all the time, but . . ."

He smiled. "I'm a much better person now."

"All right, much better. Where're you headed on this? Let's not duplicate each other's work."

"Then concentrate on infiltrating The Call."

"My loyalty is to Max Weider. The Call isn't going anywhere. The Weiders might. I've lost three of them already, when I *was* paying attention."

"Can't fault your logic."

"Yeah? Relway mention that we caught up with Crask and Sadler?"

"You fishing?" Block isn't as dim as he pretends.

"I'd like to know."

"He did. You rescued the fair maiden."

Interesting. Relway apparently kept his boss informed.

Relway's boss continued, "You let them get away, Garrett. What kind of hero are you?"

"The living kind. I *thought* somebody was watching us."

"Lucky for you."

"We got out of the tomb without help."

"Not what I meant. You came home instead of running after the bad guys. Your unsavory friend also chose to abandon the hunt. We can only assume that he was concerned for Miss Contague." Looking out for Belinda was, of course, looking out for himself.

"You have a point?" I asked.

"Yes. Somebody did stick to the bad guys."

Came the dawn. "You know where they are."

"Sure do. And we wondered if you'd want that information."

"I took them on last night. With help and with them hurt. They still might've gotten the best of it."

"Did I say we'll stand around and watch? These are famous villains. And they don't have any friends now that Chodo don't love them anymore. That gives the Guard a chance to put on a big show for some very important observers. With the invaluable assistance of a certain public-spirited subject. You want to be the public-spirited subject?"

"That why you're here?"

"I want to be visible when the Guard is doing its job right. Let's walk up there and see what happens."

"Let me get myself organized. I wouldn't want your reputation bruised because of the company you keep."

"If that could hurt me, I'd have been exiled ages ago."

"You got a point. I won't be long. Go settle in my office. Try not to poke around."

I knew the Dead Man couldn't keep an eye on Block but Block didn't.

60

I was beginning to like Tad Weider's sense of style. I selected an outfit that he might have worn to the horse races. It included a lot of yellow and red and brown. There were ruffles at wrist and throat. I spiffied myself, considered the result in my little mirror. "Oh! The elf girls are gonna carry me off and make me their love slave." I stepped back. "But if I'm going to dress like this, I'd better get a new pair of shoes."

My ragged old cobblehoppers sported memorabilia of a thousand city adventures. They didn't complement the look.

"What happened to you?" Block demanded when I got back. He looked me up and down.

"The Weiders felt I should upgrade my wardrobe."

"People been telling you that for years. But . . . You really need new shoes. Those clogs look like you wore them in the service."

"That's on my list. I thought we had a riot to attend. I'm ready," I said.

"New door?" Block asked as I locked up.

"Yeah. Somebody busted the old one."

"There's still snow piled up here and there. You sure you didn't have anything to do with that? I hear rumors with your name in them."

"How could I make it snow in the summertime? Even if, according to Tinnie, everything is my fault."

"You put in a key lock? You must be doing pretty well."

I'd been doing very well lately but he didn't need to know that. He might let something slip around crooks or tax collectors. Or crooked tax collectors. Or is that redundant? Doesn't it take a unique breed of pyschopath to prey upon his fellows that way?

The street was quiet except for the moans of stragglers nursing injuries sustained during the earlier debate. "This is better," I said. "You should've seen it here a while ago."

"I did. I'd have been here an hour ago if it wasn't for that damned parade."

We walked. I didn't like the direction he chose. If he kept on, we would stroll right into the Bustee, the ultimate slum and the most dangerous neighborhood in a city famous for bad neighborhoods. The only law in the Bustee is the law you make yourself. Outsiders won't go in except in big gangs. "I hope we aren't headed where I think we're headed."

"North side of the Bustee."

"I was afraid of that. Another reason to make a show?"

"Yes. To show that the Guard won't back off."

Relway I could see playing to the Bustee audience. Relway doesn't have sense enough to be scared. I was surprised he got anybody to go in with him, though, let alone the sort of highlifes he and Block would want to impress. Maybe I was out of touch.

When we arrived it was evident immediately that the Guard had impressed both the locals and the observers already. They had a dozen prisoners in chains, none of them the great villains Crask or Sadler.

I'd expected troops or something. But Relway had brought only the dozen Guards he would have assembled for the same job anywhere else. Observers outnumbered working lawmen even after we arrived. Block introduced me around. I knew several of the witnesses, though none well. You run into people in my racket. Some are friendly. Some aren't. You rub some the wrong way if you're determined to do your job.

I was overdressed. The most foppish dude there wasn't showing any lace. They all wore grubbies.

I faded away from the Names, joining Relway. Sullen neighborhood brats watched from a safe distance, as friendly as feral cats, waiting to spring their friends in chains. Or maybe to murder somebody from a rival gang. They were filthy. None wore clothing fancier than a loincloth. Several weren't that dressy.

In the Bustee sanitation is the exception rather than the rule. The quarter doesn't have even the rudimentary street-center sewage channels found elsewhere. There are few streets as we know them, just stringers of space where there are no buildings. The Bustee has its own unique aroma, and plenty of it.

"Figure Crask and Sadler know something's up?"

Relway glanced at his prisoners, then at me like he'd suddenly discovered that I was retarded. "Probably. We've been standing around here way too long, waiting to get started."

"I'm sorry. But—"

"This's going to be a blow, I know. But, as important as you are, we weren't waiting on your account."

"I'm crushed. So what *is* the holdup?"

"A dashing young gentleman sorcerer who uses the business name Dreamstalker Doomscrye. Or maybe Doomstalker Dreamscrye. He wants in. We don't tell those people no. He was supposed to be here hours ago. Evidently as an apprentice he wasn't taught to tell time."

Relway's sarcasm was quite daring. I was beginning to think the man had no sense. In TunFaire we restrain our opinions concerning the lords and ladies of the Hill. They can do worse than turn you into a frog if you irritate them.

"Ulp!"

"What?" Relway asked.

"I forgot my bird."

"Then go fetch the prima donna chicken."

"Too late. Might as well enjoy myself." I didn't miss the fancy-pants crow at all.

Relway's man Ritter was headed our way. A kid maybe fourteen blistered out of a dark chink between tenements. He held a rusty knife extended ahead. I knew the tactic. He was a cutpurse. He just wanted to steal and run before his victim could react. It happened every day, everywhere in TunFaire, though elsewhere cutpurses usually selected more promising targets. This kid had to be counting coup.

His pals were all set to cheer when Ritter sidestepped, snagged the thief's long hair, slashed him several times with a knife that appeared as though by magic. The whimpering boy collapsed into the muck. Ritter came on as though he'd done nothing more significant than stomp a bug.

That kind of cold demonstration was why the Guard was becoming feared.

They were nasty, these new lawmen.

Believers so often are.

"Doomscrye is here," Ritter announced. "What a jerk. He's already complaining about us wasting his valuable time."

These secret policemen were *too* daring.

"He's young," Relway told me. "He'll learn."

Did he mean Doomscrye or Ritter?

61

As a place to squat the object of our interest was a long slide downhill from a tomb. It was an ugly little lean-to shanty hugging the hip of a three-story frame tenement that tilted ten degrees sideways while twisting around its own waist. "Good thing we don't have to go in there," I observed. "Our weight would bring it down."

"It's tougher than it looks," Ritter told me. "Ninety-two people live there."

That was probably a short estimate. The occupants might use the place in shifts. I asked Relway, "If the manpower shortage was so awful we let whole tribes of nonhumans immigrate, how come people down here didn't take advantage?"

"Some did. And some are unemployable in any circumstance." Relway's bitterness sounded personal.

He hailed from the underbelly of society. *He* had been able to get somewhere. He was outraged because so many people wouldn't even try.

Plenty willingly made the effort to be unpleasant, though. We were attracting more watchers the age of the kid Ritter had hurt. I saw sticks and chains and broken bricks, the weapons of the very poor.

My companions remained unconcerned.

Ritter pretended to be in charge so Relway wouldn't attract attention. A donkey cart appeared, headed our way.

The observers were getting nervous. Doomscrye complained incessantly. He was very young for a sorcerer. He hadn't seen military service. He might be the harbinger of a generation never to get its rough edges knocked off where *nobody* was special when the Reaper was on the prowl.

Doomscrye did not understand that real trouble could climb all over him any second. Likely he'd never faced even minor trouble.

Fate handed him the opportunity to discover that nobody thought as well of him as he thought of himself.

A hunk of brick got him in the chest. Block snagged him and dragged him behind the cart.

Ritter and several others struck back contemptuously, bashing heads. Other Guards shackled captives with chains from the donkey cart. The only kid to get in a solid blow died swiftly, his throat cut.

"Oh, shit!" I muttered. "We're in for it now." There was a lot of racket. I expected a riot.

I was wrong. The locals *were* intimidated by ruthlessness—particularly once Doomscrye set the brickthrower on fire. The kid was still screaming when we ripped Crask and Sadler's hovel apart and learned that all the buildup had come to an undramatic, anticlimactic conclusion.

There was no epic battle, no ferocious last stand by cornered baddies. Crask was delirious with fever. Sadler was unconscious. It took four Guardsmen to hoist the villains into the cart. Nobody insisted they be treated gently.

Me neither. Though I did recall times when we were less unfriendly.

Crask's delirium faded briefly. He recognized me. I said, "Good morning, Bright Eyes." But looking into them was like looking down a dark well at a remote mountain of ice.

Maybe The Call ought to work on the problem of humans who have no humanity in them.

Crask wasn't afraid. Fear to him was a tool used to manage others.

"You going to question them?" I asked.

"We're a little slower than we like to pretend, aren't we?" Relway sneered. "Would this exercise have a point otherwise?"

"I'd sure like to know why they jumped Belinda when they did."

Relway smiled. "I'll bet you would."

"What's that mean?"

"I expect *she* has some questions. Like how they knew where to find her."

"Is this all there is, then?"

"I expected more excitement myself, Garrett. But I'm pleased there wasn't. They don't seem so terrible now, do they?"

"Neither does a saber-tooth tiger when he's sick on his ass. You guys be careful. They won't be completely harmless even if you hang them."

"I'm always careful, Garrett."

That I believed. But was he careful enough?

I stuck with the gang only till we cleared the Bustee. Wouldn't do to be seen with them by my patriotic friends.

The chained kids would get five years in the Cantard. They would be aboard prison barges before the end of the day. The mines always needed a few good men. Or whoever else they could get. Already they were the catch-all sentence for any crime not a capital offense.

The mines would constitute a death sentence for many, anyway.

So what's changed since I was young? These guys would get shovels instead of swords—and worse odds of getting home alive.

62

My favorite venue for exotic research is the Karentine Royal Library, over where all the midtown government buildings cluster, clinging to the petticoats of the Hill. There are lots of books—and no wizards to make them a high-risk objective.

The most interesting books in town are, of course, squirreled away, under lock and key and deadly spell, up the Hill, behind imputed BEWARE OF THE WIZARD signs. Only brawn-for-brains barbarians try to reach them. Which supplies the wizards with leather for bookbinding.

The Royal Library is a Crown indulgence. It isn't supposed to be open to walk-in traffic. I get around that. I have a friend inside.

Linda Lee is a treasure. And cute, too. Especially when she's mad, which she always seems to be whenever I drop by.

"You're full of it up to your ears, Garrett," she snapped. "How did you get in this time? And how come you still have that trash-beak penguin parked on your shoulder?" I'd stopped by the house. Just in case my peripatetic sidekick had chosen not to cover up the fact that we were partners anymore. "You're one slow learner." She was no fan of the parrot. And was always very admiring of the way I put words into his beak without moving my lips. Even from another room.

The secret of getting into the library is you slide in through a small side door that has escaped the notice of most of the world. As a rule, though, most of the world would be more interested in getting out of a library than getting in. Books are *dangerous*.

The library guards are so poorly paid that none of them really gives a rat's butt who comes or goes. And the most indifferent guards get the side entrance. Young or old, the man on duty will be drunk or asleep. Or drunk and asleep. Or maybe not even there because he's gotten dry and had to go out looking for a drink.

I still have to go in on tippytoe. The guards have their pride. You don't make the effort, they are going to yell. You don't make the effort, they can't cover themselves with the gargoyle who rules the place.

Today's steadfast guardian of the priceless tomes was both drunk and snoring and had a huge, smouldering weed banger dangling from his left hand. Which would burn down to bare skin any moment. . . .

"Ye-ow!" echoed through the building.

A screech demanded, "What was that?" That was the head librarian, a wicked old witch with a temper so foul that on her best days she was like a troll with very bad teeth. She began to shift toward the guardroom in a streaking shuffle. She'd lost all sympathy for youth in recent centuries. Her sworn mission was to get in life's way.

I whispered, "She must've been sneaking up on us."

"You keep those hands to yourself, Garrett." Which is all that I had done. So far. Sooner or later she would have her way. "I always give in and give you whatever you want when you start that stuff so you just stop it."

I didn't argue. We both knew she never did a thing she hadn't made up her mind to do. But she's a last-word kind of gal.

"Wouldn't think of it, darling. According to Morley I'm practically engaged to a pretty ratgirl named Pular Singe, anyway."

"Is that thug going to be your best man?"

"Uh?"

"I came by your place last night. To see that Dead Man." They're pals, sort of, him and her. He's never explained how he overlooks the fact that she's a woman. "A neighbor told me Dean and the Dead Man moved out. That they just couldn't take it anymore. And that you were out whoring around with some trollop in black."

It took no genius to figure out which neighbor that would be. "You need to pick who you gossip with more carefully, darling."

"I try. But you just keep coming back."

"*You* went to *my* house." Me forgetting who the last-word kind of gal was.

"I enjoy those conversations with your partner." She gripped my arm, looked up. Her eyes were huge pools of mischief. "Sometimes I *do* just want to sit around and talk. He's so interesting. He's seen everything."

"Now whose hands are—"

"This is different."

Funny. I was breathing just as hard.

"What do you want, Garrett?"

"Huh?"

"The Dead Man doesn't get distracted."

"Uh . . . He's dead. Even then you'd probably . . . Shapeshifters. I need to know about shapeshifters."

"Why?" Always direct, Linda Lee.

"Shapeshifters murdered some people I know. We caught them and sent them to the Al-Khar but some got away before we could question them. The rest died. I need to find out whatever I can about them." Pant pant.

"I can't help much. The information we have here probably wouldn't be reliable." Linda Lee cocked her head. The head librarian was just warping into the guardroom, from the sound. Our whispers hadn't reached her. "What you want you'd probably only find in a specialized library."

"What's that?" I had a feeling I didn't want to know.

"A private library. On the Hill."

Sorcerers. "I'm psychic." I didn't like that answer.

"You don't know anybody up there?"

"I know people. Met another one today. They ain't our kind of people."

"You wouldn't know anybody in The Call?"

"Uh . . . Why?"

"You could try to get into the library at their Institute For Racial Purity. Where they research racial issues. They came here trying to hire a librarian. They have a lot of stuff from private sources. They wanted it cataloged and organized so they could use it to support their theories."

"Linda Lee, you're a treasure."

"I know. What made *you* realize it?"

"I do know somebody in The Call."

"Aha!" the chief librarian shrieked in the distance. "I've caught you, my pretty!" But she crowed too soon. She always declares before she has me in sight. I moved with trained silence and deliberate speed to the end of a stack. I could remain unseen there till the old woman committed to a particular path. Linda Lee would signal me, I'd take a different route and once again the old woman would be scratching her head and wondering what she'd really heard.

It's unnatural that anyone her age would hear so well.

Linda Lee whispered, "I'll see what I can find out." Then she glommed on and kissed me. Linda Lee knows kissing better than she knows books. I didn't start it but after about four seconds I was plenty read to continue. Weider who? Shapeshifter what? I don't know no Relway.

The chief librarian cackled.

"I've got you for sure this time, my proud beauty! I'll teach you to tryst with your leman in a holy place!" She stomped and clomped her way closer.

I slipped away from Linda Lee, who winked and made noise heading another direction while I sneaked between stacks on little mouse feet. We'd played this game before. Linda Lee probably more times than me.

"Awk! Shit!" said the Goddamn Parrot, with impeccable timing. "Help!" He started flapping.

I'd kill him for sure this time.

A vise closed on my right shoulder. It turned me. I gaped at the ugly grin of a foul-breathed ogre I hadn't seen before and whom I hadn't heard coming. He was twice my size and twice as stupid. I had a notion he wouldn't ask me to recommend a good book.

In fact, I suspected he was the kind who liked to hit people and watch them bounce. Exhibit number one: He had a gargantuan green fist pulled back three yards, all set to whistle my way.

The old lady had foxed me.

I kicked the ogre hard where a sharp knock will drop any reasonably constructed critter, puking. The ogre just showed me more green teeth and put some moxie into his punch. Only trolls and zombies are less vulnerable there.

I never got a shot at his ears.

Ogres drop like stones if you slap both ears at the same time. So I'm told. Nobody I know ever got close enough to try. The source is always a friend of a friend of a friend, but, "It's gospel, Garrett. It really happens that way."

Before the lights went out I had the satisfaction of knowing the old woman would need weeks to pick up all the books that scattered while I was flying through the stacks.

Might be wise not to visit Linda Lee at work for a while.

If anybody robbed me while I was splashed all over the alley behind the library, they sure overlooked the one thing I wouldn't mind losing. I came around to find the Goddamn Parrot muttering like one of those psycho guys who stomp around shaking their heads and arguing with ghosts. I hurt everywhere. I had book burns. That ogre had pounded me good after I couldn't see to make a getaway.

There'd been way too much of this stuff lately. I never recovered from one thumping before I stumbled into the next.

Was I nurturing some kind of death wish?

63

Time to tap an *old* resource.

Time to drop in on the Cranky Old Men.

I didn't look forward to it. It wouldn't be pleasant. But with my aches and pains and premature cynicism I'd fit right in.

They say there's more than one way to skin a cat. Undoubtedly true, but why would you want to? Whoever the first *they* was. Somebody with strange habits. Who needs to flay felines? I hear they keep right on shedding after they're tanned.

Maybe the saying was started by the guy who knocks out ogres with his bare hands.

The Cranky Old Men are an ongoing crew of antiques who pooled resources to purchase, maintain, and staff an abandoned abbey where they await the Reaper, many because they're so unpleasant their relatives don't want them around home. Somebody in a black humor named the place Heaven's Gate.

In its prime the abbey housed fifty monks in luxurious little apartments. More than two hundred Cranky Old Men live in the same space, three to the apartment and who's got any use for even one chapel let alone the three of the original setup?

The place is cramped and smelly and almost as depressing as the Bledsoe and makes me hope that in my declining years some twenty-year-old lovely with an obsession for chubby old bald guys who smell bad takes me in so I don't have to buy into anything like Heaven's Gate. Of course, with my luck and the way things have gone lately I shouldn't worry about getting old.

The abbey was constructed in a square around an inner court, two stories high, filling a larger than normal city block. Not an uncommon layout in TunFaire. Tinnie's clan resides in a similar though larger compound, which includes their tanning and manufacturing facilities. In a display of misplaced faith in their fellowman the monks had included ground-floor windows around the street faces. The Cranky Old Men had adapted to modern times by installing wrought-iron bars. Most people just brick them up.

There are two entrances, front and rear. Each is just wide enough to permit passage of a donkey cart. Both are blocked by double sets of iron gates. The place looks more like a prison than the Al-Khar does.

Somebody's grandson was on some scaffolding, installing bars on a second-floor window. The deeper poverty arriving with the immigrants might make the place attractive after all.

I eased around the scaffolding to the gate. It was comfortable in the shadows there.

"Eh! You! Move along!" a creaky voice insisted. "No loitering." A sharp stick jabbed between the bars too slowly to hurt anyone.

Everyone got this treatment, including favorite sons.

"I came to see Medford Shale." Not strictly true, but you do need to offer a name and I knew that one. The hard way.

"Ain't no Medford Shale here. Go away."

"That's him back there under the olive tree. On the cot." Which was true. And handy. So maybe my luck wasn't all bad.

The sharp stick jabbed again. I didn't go away. The old man on the other end came out of the shadows. I said, "Hello, Herrick."

The old man squinted. He scowled. He tried to stand up straight. "I ain't Herrick. Herrick passed. I'm his kid brother, Victor."

"Sorry to hear about Herrick, Victor. He was good people. I need to see Shale."

Victor's eyes narrowed again. "You ain't been around lately, have you?"

"It's been a while." Medford doesn't make you want to hurry back.

"Herrick passed two years ago."

All right. It had been a big while. "I'm really sorry, Victor. I need to see Shale."

"You got a name, boy?"

"Garrett. We go way back."

Victor sneered. "Shale goes way back. You're just a pup." He started to shuffle off, thought better of it. Maybe he decided he'd given in too easily. "What you got there?"

I didn't think he'd miss the bundle. "Little something for Shale." There was more on the way. These sour old flies would need a lot of sweetening.

"Bigger than a breadbox," Victor muttered. He considered the Goddamn Parrot. "You better not be carrying no birdcage there, boy. We got no truck with useless mouths."

I patted the bundle. "It's edible." The best bribes are the wonderful things the Cranky Old Men know they shouldn't eat. Or stuff they shouldn't drink.

"Got a creme horn?"

"I do believe. If Shale will share."

Victor fumbled with the inner gate. He muttered to himself. He didn't sound optimistic about Shale sharing. He had reason to be pessimistic. Great-granduncle Medford is a cranky old man's cranky old man. Maybe he had a little ogre or Loghyr in him somewhere, way back. He hasn't aged obviously since I was a kid and my Great-grandaunt Alisa was still alive. He's one really nasty old man.

But he's got a soft spot for me.

As long as I come armed with molasses cookies.

Victor opened the outer gate.

The instant it opened wide enough so Victor couldn't stop me the Goddamn Parrot revealed his secret relationship with a lady pig.

The old boy just stood there, poleaxed, as I started toward Shale. I said, "Bird, these codgers don't get a lot of meat in their diet. Costs too much. A buzzard in the pot might put smiles on all their faces."

I could see the little monster only from the corner of my eye but,

I swear, he sneered. Somewhere, somehow, he'd gotten the idea that he was invulnerable.

Probably my fault.

"Hey, you!"

I sighed, stopped, turned. "Yes, Victor?"

"Whyn't you say you was one of them ventriloquisitors? A guy with a good and raunchy routine would be a big sell around this dump."

"I'll think about that." Might be a good career change. I never saw a ventriloquist with his head bandaged or his arm in a sling. "Let's see what Shale thinks." I just can't seem to get by without people thinking I'm flooding the dodo's beak with nonsense.

How come his big silence couldn't last?

Was some petty little god still carrying a grudge?

64

Shale appeared to be asleep. Or maybe dead. His chest wasn't moving. Maybe he was hibernating. Maybe that explained why he never got any older. I hear you don't age when you're sleeping.

He'd been in the same place so long the olive tree no longer protected him from the sun. He was all wrinkles and liver spots and if all his fine white hairs were tied end to end, they might reach his knobbly ankles. His clothing was threadbare but clean. Medford Shale had a thing about cleanliness.

"Shale thinks you're a no-talent little peckerwood and it's probably that mallard doing the actual talking and putting words into mouths." Shale's withered lips scarcely moved. Maybe somebody from the great beyond was ventriloquising him. "You found yourself a wife yet?"

"Good to see you well, Uncle Medford. Nope. Still playing the field."

Any other old boy in the place would've done a wink and nudge and boy-do-I-envy-you number. Medford Shale snapped, "You some kind of nancy boy? Ain't gonna be none of that in this family. What the hell you doing, coming around here dressed like that?"

No relative of Shale's ever did anything that didn't embarrass him. The more sensitive sort never visit him. Generally, that includes even those of us with hides like trolls.

"Your life is so full you don't have a minute to come ease an old man's last years?"

"That's right, Uncle. Given a choice between watching grass grow and listening to you bitch there ain't no contest." I'd always wanted to say that. When I was a kid my mother stopped me. Later, respect held me back—though I think respect should run both ways. Shale is too self-engrossed to respect anything. Right now, with a fresh crop of ogre-inflicted bruises atop the other aches I'd collected recently, I was crabby myself.

"That's no way to talk to—"

"You want to be treated right, you treat people right. If I want to be pissed on and cut down, I don't need to trudge all the way over here."

Shale's eyes widened. He sat up more spryly than you'd expect from a guy three times my age. "That parrot has become confused about what words to put into your mouth. No kin of mine would talk to me that way."

"All right. I'm no kin. And the buzzard is quacking. He says, you want things easier here, help me. I know where to find a baker's dozen of those molasses cookies you like." I gave him a glimpse of the bundle.

Medford Shale wasn't stupid. He wasn't the kind of character who didn't look out for number one, either. I learned to deal with him when I was a toddler, before Aunt Alisa died and he bought into Heaven's Gate thinking the staff would cater to him the way his wife had. And they did. Almost. But he could begrudge the most reasonable request. Human nature made paybacks inevitable.

One of the staff heard me mention cookies. She was wide and ugly and tough, neither tall nor entirely human, probably a war veteran despite her sex. She had the air. Female combat nurses did visit the Cantard.

"Nothing sweet for him, you. Nothing spicy. They make him cranky."

"Really. All my life I've thought he was just a nasty old man."

"No shit. You fambly?" She was so solid she recalled things I'd seen in foreign temples, the sort of wide, steadfast, imperturbable creatures that guard doors and windows and roofs.

I nodded.

"I see the resemblance."

Shale observed, "A cookie never hurt nobody, you ugly witch. Don't listen to a word she barks, boy. She tortures us. She comes around in the middle of the night . . ." He thought better of continuing his rant. Possibly she did visit the troublesome ones in the night.

"What do you want?" she asked me.

"Why?"

She was surprised. "I'm in charge. I need—"

"The residents are in charge. You work for them."

"Very definitely a fambly resemblance."

"I didn't come to see you. Unless you know something about shapeshifters. Then your company would be very welcome."

I was cranky not because the endemic crabbiness there was catching, nor entirely because of all my pains. I was going to have to pan a ton of fool's gold to get any useful information here. But gather a few nuggets I would if I persevered. It never failed. Between them Shale and his cronies knew something about everything. And they'd lived most of it.

"Boy," Shale growled at me, "you can't talk to Miss Trim like . . ."

65

You bark at some people, you make nice over others, you spring for a barrel of beer, suddenly you're an honored guest at Heaven's Gate. Even Medford Shale mellowed for six minutes before he passed out.

"Lay him out on his bunk like it's for his wake," I told Miss Trim. She did say she was in charge, didn't she?

Her given name was Quipo, she said. I could keep a straight face when I used it.

It turned into that kind of evening.

"That old fart is so mean he'll outlive me and any children I might father so I might as well enjoy a fake wake."

Miss Trim was all right once she got some beer inside her. But she'd never be a cheap date. She put it away by the pitcher. She chuckled a manly chuckle, slapped me on the back hard enough to crack a few vertebrae. "I like a man wit' a sense of humor, Garrett."

"Me, too. There's a guy I know, name of Puddle, you really got to meet."

One of Quipo's henchwomen appeared. She hadn't acquired her job through sex appeal. Few of the staff had. "The new barrel is here."

I groaned. I hadn't ordered up this latest soldier but I knew who would pay for it. And I hadn't gotten much out of anyone yet, though I'd been offered the impression that I'd learn plenty if I just hung on.

"Have them bring it right over here where I can keep an eye on it. Some of them are indulging a little too much."

The old men were doing their damnedest to get ripped. The staff were one scant stride behind. Boys and girls alike tried to light lanterns and swat bugs in the courtyard. They did more harm than good but laughter filled the air.

"This is a good thing you're doing, Garrett." Quipo waved vaguely. "These men need a party."

"It's an expensive thing that I'm doing." Not that my employer—employers—couldn't afford it. I would bill them. If ever I rooted out anything useful. "They're lubricated now. I really do need to find out something about shapeshifters."

For a moment Miss Trim looked like she might contribute something. Then she asked, "Isn't that kind of an exotic concern?" Her hand brushed my leg. The Goddamn Parrot noticed, stirred restlessly, muttered under his breath. How steep was the bill here likely to be?

Word was out that I wanted information. Shale had said plenty, most of it untrue, wrong, or just plain libelous, and nowhere near the subject.

Old or young, rich or poor, saint or sinner, the human males of TunFaire have one thing in common. We're all veterans. The tie binds us. Once invoked it can, however briefly, shove aside most other concerns.

One peculiar geezer named Wright Settling, who never recovered from having been a career Marine, drew himself a sputter off the dead barrel. He grumbled because the new one wasn't ready. I told him, "Jarhead, I really need to talk about—"

"Yeah. Yeah. You kids. Always in a hurry. After all these years it can wait a minute."

"What can wait?"

"Hold your horses. Trail and Storey, they'll tell you all about it. Endlessly." Evidently hearing all about it was one of the more painful costs of sharing Heaven's Gate. He glanced at Miss Trim and snickered. "Maybe somebody else's got something for you, too. In more ways than one."

Ever notice how some older people stop caring if they're rude? Jarhead was a case in point, often less politic than Medford Shale, without complaining as much.

"People's lives do depend on me solving this." Solving what? I had only a shadowy notion what was going on.

"That's Storey right there. I'll get him soon as I get my beer."

I fooled Jarhead. I didn't play his game. I broke Quipo's heart by abandoning her, too. Me and my delinquent feather duster went to Storey.

"Mr. Storey? Mr. Settling says you're the one man here who can really help me." Never hurts to mention their importance.

"He did, did he? Jarhead? Why the hell is that old fool putting it on me? Who the hell are you?"

"I'm Shale's great-grandnephew."

"I'm sorry."

"More significantly, I'm the guy who bought the beer. And I may not tap the new barrel. I seem to be wasting my time. Why waste my money, too?" I turned toward the newcomer.

"Me and Trail was in the army together," Storey said, not missing a beat. I had a feeling I was about to hear one of those stories that define a lifetime. "During the Myzhod campaigns we saw more shapeshifters than you'd think could exist."

Myzhod campaigns? Could've been the bloodiest phase of the war but that didn't mean anything to me today. "A little before my time, Mr. Storey."

"I didn't expect you to know." He smiled resignedly. We all learn to do that. "There must have been a hundred huge campaigns that nobody remembers now but them that survived them."

"Yeah." Don't I know it? Most times I mention what it was like in the islands, guys who weren't there just yawn and come back with a story about the really deep shit they got into. "So you ran into shapeshifters down there? Were they Venageti?"

"They was supposed to be ours. Folks forget that they worked for us first."

"Special ops?"

"They wouldn't waste them as infantry, would they?"

"I wouldn't. But I'm not the brass. You never know with them."

Storey chuckled. "You got that right. I recollect one time—"

"So what about these changers back then?" I didn't expect much. "Anything might help."

"They took the point on the Myzhod offensive." Storey seemed a little dry. I made sure he got first crack at the new barrel. He sipped, saluted me by hoisting his mug, continued, "The Myzhod is a dried-up river. The Venageti had a string of bases on the south side. They used them as jump offs in a bunch of different operations. Those bases were tough. They'd stood up to some heavy attacks. Some big names were getting embarrassed. High Command was pushing hard. They come up with a plan where shapeshifters would infiltrate a base and open the way for us commandos. We'd bust everything open for the regulars following on behind.

"First night us guys carried off the bodies of the guys the changers replaced. Second night, after those things wormed deeper inside, where they would cause confusion and grab the inner gates, we were supposed to attack where they'd prepared the way. We'd rip the belly of the base open before the Venageti knew what was happening."

Storey paused for a long drink. A tear dribbled down his cheek.

Another old man joined us. "This the Myzhod massacre, Will?"

"Yeah. Garrett, this's Trail."

"Glad to meet you, Trail."

Trail said, "Will an' me was almost the onliest ones what got away. That's on account of we smelled a rat because things was going too slick. We'd already switched livery with some dead Venageti so we just ran around like a lot of other scared crazy idiots till we figure it out. Then we cut out soon as we got a chance."

"It was a setup," Storey explained. "The whole thing was from the beginning. The Venageti line troops wasn't told up front they was part of a trap so they didn't give it away. The fact is, them shapeshifters sold us out. They led the whole damned army in there and got most of Karenta's best soldiers killed. Which probably made the war last forty years longer."

I guess the powers that be wouldn't brag about a defeat so severe it took two generations to recover.

I knew I'd learned something interesting but didn't see a connection with my situation now. This was the first I'd heard about shapeshifters serving on our side. Except for what was implied by the dragon tattoos with their Karentine motif, of course.

"When was this, Storey?"

"Forty-one or forty-two."

"Forty-two," Trail said. "It was the year my mother died and my brother was killed. That was forty-two. You remember, Will. The news was waiting when we finally got back to friendly territory."

"Yeah. Would you believe they wanted to charge us with desertion?" Storey grumbled.

Trail grumped, "We demanded a truthsayer. Even then they didn't want to believe us because a disaster that big would ruin lots of careers. But eventually enough others got back that they had to believe a story everybody told."

"We won a kind of battle, just getting back with the truth," Storey said. "The gods smiled on us. We had to cross two hundred miles of desert without getting caught by the Venageti or the natives. If we didn't get back, them shapeshifters could've pretended to stay with Karenta and led even more troops into the cauldron."

"It was bad," Trail told me. "I still get nightmares about that desert. I wake up and try to convince myself it was worth it 'cause if'n Will an' me didn't make it back, maybe there wouldn't have been any war for you kids to win."

"Most of us try to think that way, Mr. Trail." I shuddered, recalling the islands. Mostly we'd just wanted to stay alive but there'd been a flavor of hanging on so somebody else could bring the slaughter to a favorable conclusion someday.

In forty-two, eh? Over fifty years ago. And these old friends were still scrapping with the darkness. Maybe there was one more trick they could play on the nightmares.

"You ever see those shifters up close?"

"Up close?" Storey growled. "Shit. We practically slept together the three months before the attack. I reckon we saw them up close. One I'll never forget. We called him Pinhead. Pinhead sounded something like his name in his own language. And it fit. None of them was really bright. It made him really mad when we called him that."

Trail said, "They were so dumb we figured the gods made them that way to balance off how they could turn into something else when you wasn't looking. Like they had to be too stupid to take complete advantage."

Storey said, "I don't think they had the ability to appreciate the blessing. Some of it they couldn't control. Some of it they had to do whether they wanted or not."

"Yeah," Trail said. "There was this one called Stockwell. He made a chicken look smart. He was only a kid by their standards. The rest of them rode him—"

"Whoa! Stockwell? For sure?"

"He was another one that got called what his name sounded like. Most of them did. We turned this one into Carter Stockwell. It was kind of a joke, too, on account of—"

Couldn't be the same clown. Could it? After all these years? "I've been butting heads with a bunch of shifters. Believe it or not, one of them calls himself Carter Stockwell."

"Really?" Trail asked. For the first time he seemed completely interested. "Ain't that interesting, Will?"

"Sure is. I'd like to run into Carter Stockwell again some time. When I have a sack full of hot irons and silver knives. You know it's almost impossible to hurt them unless you use something silver?"

I nodded. "I noticed."

Trail said, "Always been my pet theory that silver is the reason they got involved in the war in the first place. That they never was on nobody's side but their own. If they could glom onto the silver mines, they'd control the best weapon that could be used against them."

"You could be right," I said, though that sounded like a stretch to me. "Interesting. Have some beer, gents. Keep talking. Name some more names." Not that I believed their Carter Stockwell was mine. He might be a grandson, though. "Talk to me about tattoos."

That drew blank looks and puzzled grunts.

"The changers I'm running into all have a dragon tattoo right here. It's about six inches long but hard to see when they're alive."

Storey shook his head. "I don't remember nothing like that."

"Me neither," Trail said.

"I do," Miss Trim told me. She was well sloshed now, sliding out of focus. She wore a lopsided, trollish leer. Was she making it up to get my attention? "It's a dragon squeezing the commando insignia in its claws."

I grunted. "We're onto something, Quipo."

"They were commandos. Mercenaries. I didn't know they were shapechangers, though. They called themselves the Black Dragon Gang. Said they came from Framanagt."

"Which is an island so far east of nowhere that nobody would ever check. Was anybody named Norton involved?"

"Colonel Norton was their commander. But he was Karentine."

Stockwell and his pal had expected me to know something about their crew. "What did Black Dragon do to get famous?"

"Nothing. It was the other way around. They did everything they could to hang around Full Harbor. They only went out when they couldn't avoid it. You don't make a name doing that."

"That's where you were? Full Harbor?"

"For nine wonderfully miserable years."

Full Harbor was where I'd had my only previous encounter with a shapeshifter, a Venageti agent masquerading as a Karentine spymaster. Was there a connection? Should I have made one? "When did you separate?"

"Six years ago." Quipo didn't want to talk anymore. She wanted to act but the only guy around young enough wasn't interested.

Six years was long before my own encounter.

I reminisced silently, trying to discover if I knew something I didn't know I knew. Apparently I did. Or Black Dragon didn't realize that I didn't know. "Was there ever any suspicion that the Black Dragon Gang might not be trustworthy?"

"Uh?"

The beer was hard at work now. I was about to lose Quipo. "Is there any chance those guys were really working for Venageta?"

Miss Trim's eyes focused momentarily. She gave it a good try. "Uhm? 'Dwould 'splain a lot. Never fought a dat."

Plop! She melted on the spot.

The Cranky Old Men became excited. Only the fact that Quipo had a few sober sisters chaperoning saved her from a catalog of minor indignities and vengeances.

I became the crowd favorite. I was an ear that would listen. Every old man wanted to tell his life story. None of those had anything to do with shapeshifters.

Part of the cost of doing business. I might have to come back someday.

I hung in there bravely, almost as long as the moon did, but eventually the beer ran out and I fell asleep.

66

I had a hangover. Again. Surprise.

It was not yet a classic. It was just an infant. But it had potential. This was practically the middle of the night still. Dawn was only a hint of color in the east.

Victor nudged me with a toe in a spot that the ogre had thumped yesterday. I woke up sprawled under an olive tree, supported by cold, damp stone. The Goddamn Parrot was on a branch overhead, muttering. He made no sense but occasionally my name entered the mix. "Get up, Garrett," Victor insisted. Pain blazed through my side. Oh, no! Not another cracked rib. "Some guy is looking for you."

Some guy? That didn't sound good. I hadn't mentioned Heaven's Gate to anybody, ever. Nor had I noticed anybody following me. Not that I'd made much effort to keep track. Crask and Sadler were in the tank. The shifters ought to be licking their wounds. Nobody else should be interested.

"Get up, damn you!" Victor let me have it again, in the identical spot, harder. He knew what he was doing.

Victor was a teetotaller, a member of TunFaire's smallest and most viciously bizarre cult. He was the only born-again alcohol hater at Heaven's Gate. He'd let me know again and again what he thought of me dispensing the devil's sweat.

"Victor, you do that again, you'll need to get fitted for a wooden leg."

Victor chose discretion. "Your party is outside the front gate."

My party was Ritter from Relway's deck of jokers. Brother Relway was looking like a mojo man who sees all and knows all. I asked, "Don't you guys ever sleep?"

"Sleep? What's that? Wait! Yeah! I remember. They used to let me do that when I was in the army. Once a week whether I needed it or not. Don't have time to waste on it anymore, though. This is Card." Somebody unclear, clinging to a shadow, lifted a hand but didn't speak.

I told Ritter, "I always knew you groundpounders had it sweet but you're the first one who ever admitted it. What's happening?"

"Boss wants you back at the Weider place."

"That doesn't sound promising. How come?"

"There's been another killing."

"Shit. Who was it this time?" I should've gotten Saucerhead in there.

"I couldn't say. Nobody told me. I'm just supposed to get you."

"How'd you know where to find me?"

He looked at the thing on my shoulder. "Followed the parrot droppings."

"No, really."

"The boss told me you were here. I don't know how he knew. I didn't ask." That cut me off quick. "I'm just a messenger, Garrett. He picked me because you'd recognize me."

"You guys bring any transport?" Besides being hungover and achy from the ogre's handiwork I was stiff from sleeping on cold, damp stone.

"You kidding, Garrett? You know what kind of budget we've got?"

"Can't blame a guy for hoping. Though I expected the worst. You do that and you're never disappointed. Sometimes you're even pleasantly surprised."

"It isn't that far, you know. Just a couple miles."

"More like four. And I have a hangover and fresh bruises."

"That ogre thumped you pretty good, eh?"

Relway's crew seemed to know every breath I took. Relway had to want me to know that, too. Ritter was hardly so dumb he'd give it away if it was supposed to be a secret.

"Just don't get in any hurry. I'll hike as fast as I can. I gotta do one thing before we go, though."

I limped over to Shale's apartment. He lived alone. His personality guaranteed his privacy. I slipped the packet of cookies into the crook of his arm. He was a nasty old thing but he was family. The closest I had anymore.

67

Colonel Block met us on the Weider front steps. "Good morning, Garrett." He was in uniform. He dismissed Ritter and Card, eyed me as though he had developed major reservations. A large, muscular, nameless bruno lurked close by in case Block needed a ton of muscle in a hurry.

The mansion looked deserted from the outside. I saw no light and heard no morning bustle. People should have been stirring.

"You came yourself?" I asked.

"This is getting big. A definite high-level interest has developed. Things are going on that we can't see from down here in the bushes." I got the impression that he was understating—and was not about to go into detail why.

"I didn't want to hear that. Where's Relway?"

"Good question. I haven't seen him since yesterday."

"He sent for me."

"I sent for you, Garrett. Because you know these people. They need to deal with somebody familiar. They're like trapped animals right now."

"Ritter told me there's been another murder."

"Yeah. Guy name of Lancelyn Mac. He had a head-on with somebody who tried to force his way into the house. The cripple was there but didn't see that part happen."

"Ty."

"Ty, then. Talk to him. I can't tell you anything he can't."

"Where is he?"

"Everyone in the house is in the family dining hall. Anybody who leaves has to go with someone else. That rule applies to everybody. My people included. Nobody should be alone, ever." Which explained the muscular behemoth attached to him like a shadow, jabbering like a stone.

"You think changers killed Lance?"

"Maybe. Nobody else is interested in the Weiders. Are they?"

I shrugged, sketched what I'd learned at Heaven's Gate. Block listened without interrupting.

"Interesting," he said. "The same name cropping up, then and now. You could cobble together some weird hypotheses if you made a few assumptions about shapeshifter thinking."

You sure could. I had one notion I wanted to bounce off the Dead Man. It regarded his hero Glory Mooncalled and plans the man might have regarding TunFaire. "They have a strategy. They have a goal. If we knew what that was, we could figure out what they'll probably do next."

"Next time we catch one I'll be sure to be more careful about keeping it caught. They're in here."

"Here" was the family dining room that had served as Mr. Gresser's staging area during the ill-starred engagement gala.

Tinnie ambushed me at the door. "Where the hell have you been?"

"Out white-knighting around. I rescued a maiden, then I rushed to the bedside of an old man who doesn't have long to live. I took him some cookies to ease the pain."

"We heard about Belinda Contague. I want to talk to you about . . ."

Alyx materialized. Her bounce and deviltry had gone missing. She was a kid who needed somebody to tell her everything was going to be all right.

The whole crowd seemed possessed by a universal despair.

"Hi, Alyx. Hang in there, kid. We're going to turn it around. Gilbey. Max. Nicks. Ty. Can we get right to it?" Ty was in his wheelchair. Nicks sat nearby at a long rosewood table. Earlier that table had been shoved against the wall and piled with the goodies Gresser's people had been serving to the rest of us. Nicks was nowhere nearby mentally although she did grunt in response to my greeting.

I needed to hone my charm skills.

"Ty," I said. "Come walk me through what happened." All business is my middle name—even when I have a beautiful woman hanging on both arms. In my dreams.

Block wanted to see a re-creation. Ty had refused to do it for him.

Ty pushed his wheelchair away from the table. "I guess." His voice was flat. He was ready to give up but was going on because he was expected to go on. I'd seen it before. It might armor his soul till he passed through the dark fire.

Nicks positioned herself behind Ty's chair. She moved like a sleepwalker.

The remnants of this family would need a lot of help. Though if I didn't get somewhere soon, there might not be a family much longer.

I followed Nicks into the great hall. Block followed me. I heard feet shuffle. Well. Max had invited himself along. Gilbey paced him, ready to help. Max looked like he'd aged thirty years.

"This way," Ty murmured weakly.

Alyx trotted along. She might be up for a fight before long.

Ty directed Nicks to the foot of the steps to the front door. He beckoned me. "I couldn't sleep, Garrett. My back was aching and my leg was burning. I decided I'd get some work done if I was going to be awake anyway. I dragged poor Lance out and made him come down here with me to talk about how we were going to bring the furnishings back. I was in the chair, right here, looking back along the hall, when Gerris said something from up there. I was surprised to see him. He said someone was at the door. He wanted instructions. He seemed rattled. Lance said he'd take care of it."

"Nicks," I asked, "would you walk through Lance's role? Alyx, scoot up there and be Genord."

A snooty voice suggested, "Why not let Genord be Genord?" Genord stepped out of the gallery, which continued to grow behind Max and Gilbey.

"Perfect. You be Genord, then. And we'll walk through it."

Nicks positioned Ty according to his instructions. He told me, "I was saying something to the effect that I hoped Dad wouldn't insist on putting that ugly rust-bucket suit of armor back by the green colonnade when Gerris spoke."

Genord, now at his post, stepped into sight and announced, "Sir, there's a very abusive young man here who insists on being allowed inside."

"That's not quite right. I think he used the word obnoxious," Ty told me. "What's he want, Gerris?"

Genord replied, "He just wants in, sir."

Ty said, "That's when Lance said he'd take care of it. He was exhausted. He didn't want to be awake. He was in a mood to be very rude to somebody. I told him, 'Kick his butt down the stairs if you have to.' He went straight to the door."

I looked up at Genord. He told me, "I stayed with him. Just in case. I wasn't alert enough. Something did happen. And it was over before I could react."

I nodded. "Go ahead. Nicks?"

Genord moved Nicks into position at the door, returned to his own place.

"Freeze," I told them. "Genord. Is this where everybody was? Exactly. Ty? Were you still looking up the hall?"

Genord nodded. Ty told me, "No. I was looking over my shoulder like this. But I couldn't see anything. Lance or Gerris."

I didn't have to bend or squat to see that he was right. You had to be two giant steps to his right even to spot the tail of Nicks' skirts.

"But you saw it all?" I asked Genord. I was down to the unexpected eyewitness.

He nodded. "The man was in shadow, though. And I was turned toward Master Ty when Lancelyn squawked."

"But you got a look at the visitor when you answered the door, didn't you?"

"I'd recognize him if I ever saw him again."

"Did you recognize him then?"

"Excuse me?"

"I'm wondering if he might not have been here for the betrothal party. Possibly as one of Gresser's serving crew."

"I see where you're going. I don't think that's possible. Though if you assume that the assassin was a shapechanger, he could have been here before in a different guise. But didn't you lock all of them up?" Genord seemed to be enjoying himself now. Was he fond of being the center of attention?

Block observed, "Evidently the guy wasn't out to kill just anybody. Otherwise, he would've sliced you up when you opened the door. And he must not have wanted in all that badly or he would've just made his entrance over you and Ty. He's already made one kill. He'd have nothing to lose by another."

I snapped, "He say anything to you?"

Genord appeared rattled again. "Uh. Yeah. Let's see." Genord's snooty accent evaporated. He closed his eyes. After a deep breath he uncorked a string of rude demands for the return of a missing girlfriend. I frowned. So did everyone else. Genord stumbled. "Uh. That's what it sounded like to me. I was puzzled. That was one reason I deferred to Lancelyn. I couldn't imagine that the man had come to the wrong house." There is no other residence near the Weider mansion.

I exchanged glances with Block. The puzzle was growing bigger. I said, "I mean did he say anything after he hit Lance. But before you answer that, tell me, are you saying that this killer was accusing Lance of stealing his woman?"

"No." Genord appeared to be surprised by the question. "Not exactly. Well, he didn't use any names. But he must've meant Lacelyn because he kept accusing Lancelyn directly. Then he did what he did and I think he was completely stricken by it afterward. I think he panicked and ran away."

Ty said, "There couldn't have been any girl, Genord. And you know it. I didn't hear what was said but I know a girl couldn't possibly have been the real problem. Lance told you why himself, Garrett."

"Yeah. His thing for Kittyjo." Not to mention that only a psychic killer could have counted on Lance answering the door if he had a quarrel with Lance. "What was this guy wearing, Genord?"   •

"What?"

"He wasn't naked, was he? Give me an overall impression. Upscale? Down? Neat? Rumpled? Threadbare? How was his grooming?"

Genord paused. He didn't seem to have thought about his much. "Uh. . . . Almost military? Yeah. That's what I'd call it. His manner was crisp. Like the training sergeants we all recall so fondly."

He could have been describing himself.

He was recovering fast, turning almost cocky again. A changeable guy, Gerris Genord.

Block asked, "Did you notice an armband? Or medals. Or anything else that might connect him to a freecorps or a rightsist group?"

"I didn't see anything to connect him to anybody or anything but death. But he stayed in the shadows."

I took a couple of steps to the side, looked up toward the door. I told Block, "Colonel, let's you and me walk through this ourselves."

Block looked puzzled but his instincts had been right when he had asked for a re-creation.

Genord frowned, troubled again.

I said, "I'll play the killer. You go be Genord. Genord, get out of the way. Nicks, you be Lance again. Ty, don't move at all. All right?"

"Not a muscle."

"Ahem," Tinnie said. "What're you trying to prove?"

"I'm trying to understand what happened. Something isn't right. This doesn't make sense."

Genord glowered.

I checked the layout. The players were in place. I stepped outside—without closing the door, so the bogeyman couldn't get me without somebody noticing—then walked through the murder with Gerris Genord directing. Reluctantly. Then we did it again so I could see things from Lance's viewpoint. Then I told everybody, "Go back to the dining room."

Tinnie tarried. I winked. She went but not without a frown.

Block asked, "You got something?"

"Maybe. It all may hinge on what could turn out to be a stupid question."

"Seemed to me . . . I had a gut feeling . . . But a lot of times murder just doesn't make sense."

This one might not make sense even if it was right. "I think it happened pretty much the way we walked through. Nobody contradicted anybody."

"But?"

"The question. What was Gerris Genord doing awake and answering the door in the middle of the night?"

"Shit. You're right. I never thought of that."

"You felt it. Or you wouldn't have had a hunch. You didn't see it because Genord is supposed to answer the door."

68

"Sorry. Just family right now," I told Tinnie. "Nicks, you qualify." I considered before telling Gilbey, "And you."

He was irked because I'd thought about it.

"Let's go to yonder corner. Drag over some chairs." I dragged one for myself. I gathered them in a circle, knee to knee.

"What is it, Garrett?" Max Weider was experiencing a resurrection of will. Maybe he thought something was getting accomplished. I hoped I could maintain the illusion.

"Some of you may think this is a stupid question. But the answer could be critical. Can anybody tell me why Genord would be answering the door in the middle of the night? Even I'm not superhuman enough to stay on the job all day and all night, too."

Ty chuckled weakly. He said nothing. In normal times he would've spoken just to remind us he was there.

His eyes went cold when the substance of my question connected. "I didn't think of that. Gerris is always just there."

"You don't have a night porter? Somebody like that?"

"No."

"Let's take it a step further, then. How do we know there was anybody at the door? We just have Genord's word."

"Shit," Ty growled. "I never thought of that even when I was there. But Genord wouldn't—"

Max snapped, "Why *was* Genord up in the middle of the night?"

Nobody told me maybe I was good at what I do. Nobody said,

hey, Garrett, maybe you're onto something. I suggested, "Why don't we ask Genord?"

Gilbey muttered, "I'd hate to pick which one I didn't like the most, Lance or Genord, but under the circumstances—"

"Take it easy. We don't know Genord is telling stories." I didn't want to lynch the majordomo. Yet. But I sure didn't buy the tale he'd told.

Max raised a hand, glaring. Hard Max was back. "Get him, Garrett."

"I'll do it," Gilbey said. He was right. In normal times he'd summon Genord.

Manvil stayed a step behind Genord as they approached. Genord looked worried. He felt the string running out.

I said, "I've got a problem with this thing, Genord. It goes right back to that guy at the door. Nobody saw him but you. Ty says he never heard the guy. But you said he was shouting."

"Maybe I was so scared it just seemed like he was shouting." Genord shrugged. "I can't tell you anything else."

"Sure you can. You can tell us what you were doing up in the middle of the night. You can tell us why you were at the front door when Ty and Lance came into the great hall."

Genord shuffled his feet. He looked for a way out. He didn't answer me.

"They took you by surprise, didn't they? They couldn't help but notice you. Sooner or later somebody would ask you what you were doing. You panicked. You didn't think. You just did the first damned thing that popped into your head. And that was something really stupid. Which you compounded by making up an incredibly stupid story."

"I just answered the damned door!"

"Sure. You heard the knock all the way up to your room on the fourth floor. Come on, Genord. You're not that clever. It's obvious you were sneaking in after being someplace you shouldn't have been. Unless you were waiting for somebody. Or maybe you really were squabbling with somebody. Somebody who didn't get out of the way fast enough when Lance came up and maybe recognized him . . ." That couldn't be quite right. But it might be close. "Colonel Block."

"Uhm?"

"You did have somebody watching the house, didn't you?"

"The shithead supposed to be out there wasn't. He sneaked off, he claims to get something to eat."

"But don't your men operate in pairs?"

"The other now former Guardsman wandered away even earlier. He hasn't turned up yet."

"You kept a few too many Watchmen on the payroll."

"Evidently. Though the first shithead did yell as soon as he found out something happened. Give him that. He did the right thing even though he knew his butt was in a sling."

Genord relaxed visibly while Block delivered his bad news. Not a soul missed that. I asked, "Anybody got a silver coin? And a knife?"

69

Gerris Genord was no shapeshifter. But he was a villain. I had no doubt about that. He refused to talk, though. Block predicted, "He will. Eventually." A regular sibyl, he was.

I suggested, "Check his room, Gilbey. See if there's anything there to tell why he'd blow such a cush job."

Block's men took Genord away. He went silently but with defiant pride. I asked, "Anybody know that man well?"

Young, old, male, female, human, or otherwise, none of the staff knew a thing. That this betrayal came hard on the heels of the other tragedies suggested treacheries of incalculable depths.

"Did he have any particular friends?"

Nobody even heard of Gerris Genord, suddenly. He'd never had a friend. Gerris Genord? Is that some tropical disease?

Gilbey returned. "I've got something I want you to see, Garrett."

"What?"

"We didn't know Gerris well at all."

"The man was a pig—" I started, but then intuited, "He was fanatically neat, wasn't he?"

"He was." Gilbey offered me a scrap of burnt wool. I saw nothing remarkable.

"What about it?"

"Would you burn your clothing?"

According to some I should. "Oh." Genord's room contained no fireplace. There was a small charcoal brazier, though, that had seen use lately, despite the season. It contained curled fragments of burned paper mixed with shredded wool remnants and crumbled charcoal. The air still stank of burnt wool.

I said, "Genord had some time to himself before the Guard arrived."

"Obviously. And there were comments about the smoke when we gathered everyone downstairs. I didn't think anything of it at the time. The chimneys do need work."

I stirred clothing with a toe. "He didn't have a lot of time."

"Only a few minutes, really."

"Then we might still find something."

"And look here." Gilbey indicated a large sack in a corner.

"Looks like an army duffel bag."

"And it is." Gilbey upended the sack. Clothing, small personal items, and trinkets cascaded to the floor. "Well. It looks like Brother Genord meant to leave his position without giving proper notice. And in a hurry. This explains why we've had so many valuables turn up missing lately."

It did look like Genord had tried to provide himself with a handsome separation bonus. "He didn't wear jewelry, did he?" He never seemed the type.

"No, Garrett. It's obvious he expected to have to run someday. Soon." Gilbey extracted a heavy gold pendant from the pile. "This was Kittyjo's. It was a gift from Lancelyn."

I glimpsed something blue beneath a tattered shirt, pointed. "Bingo."

"A rightsist armband. I never suspected that. Genord came across as a political eunuch. What group?"

I plucked it out. "This's freecorps. Brotherhood Of The Wolf."

Gilbey frowned. "Isn't that? . . ."

"An armed branch of The Call. With a really serious, hard-core reputation. This gets interestinger and interestinger." Not to mention scarier and scarier.

We turned up nothing else. Genord had found time to do everything but get away. Which made me wonder if the armband wasn't a plant. Or if it hadn't been so special to Genord that he kept it nearby even though discovery would deepen his troubles.

As we went back downstairs I told Gilbey, "Let's don't tell anybody but Max. If everybody knows one of The Call's people got himself arrested here, some of the goofier members of the movement might decide they have to give the Weiders lessons in how to treat their betters."

We didn't know that could happen. Genord might have kept his work and his politics compartmented. But I didn't believe that. Not with the family and its brewery attracting so much attention lately. Not with the hard-core reputation of the Wolves.

"Good idea. But it won't stay quiet forever."

"Probably not." Which suggested that my next move, inevitable but one I didn't want to make, had to be undertaken soon or the opportunity would evaporate.

I pulled Block aside as soon as we got back to the dining room. "More trouble." I slipped him the armband. "That came out of a duffel bag Genord packed after the murder. Looks like he meant to take off but didn't move fast enough."

"The Wolves were tough, Garrett. Commando types. Genord don't fit the part."

"Maybe he's honorary. Or he's a good actor. You never know about a guy who managed to survive the Cantard. He sure didn't stop to agonize over the morality of killing Lance even though ultimately it was a stupid thing to do."

"There is that. But people do do stupid things when they panic. What do you think?"

"I don't know what to think. I don't want to but I'm going to try to get inside the movement. Maybe I can find some answers there. I want you to take care of these people. Whoever's been trying to hurt them isn't finished. He hasn't gotten whatever it is he wants."

"I'll keep this armband. I'll discuss it with Genord. You shouldn't know anything about the connection if you're going to get close to his friends."

Good point.

"And you might clean up a little. You'll do better if you're presentable. Consider stashing the wonder buzzard, too. Some of those people have fairly refined sensibilities."

"They even hate parrots?"

"They especially hate parrots with an attitude problem. You see what's happening on the streets. Call people don't believe in self-restraint. And the more they get away with the harder they push."

Worth remembering.

"You be careful what stories you tell about yourself, too," Block told me. "They'll know when you're stretching the truth."

"Uhm?"

"Relway isn't the only one watching you."

"Really? Shit!" I have my pride. And one thing I'm proud of is that I'm good at working a tail or detecting one set on me. I hadn't noticed anyone.

There aren't many guys that good.

I had a bad feeling. I asked Block. He told me, "I don't know how they're doing it. Relway hasn't figure it out yet, either. You know it's a trick he'd like to have in his bag."

I'll bet. "How bad is it?"

"Sometimes you have an entourage."

More agony for my bruised pride. Time for a subject change. "What do you know about the Institute for Racial Purity?"

"I've never heard of it. What's it supposed to be?"

I told him.

"Something else to check in my spare time. You be careful, Garrett."

"I'm not leaving yet." I was ready, though. But not for the place I had to go. I preferred a destination where the beds weren't stone, where I could sleep off my residual hangover without fear of interruption.

70

I plopped into a chair, told Max what I knew, what I was doing and thinking and suspecting. He was attentive. His anger burned hot enough to heat-treat steel. He didn't blame me for his pain, as a lesser man might have done.

I started awake as an arm snaked around my neck. A taut bottom began making itself comfortable in my lap. "Ulp!" I said.

The Goddamn Parrot chortled. He was watching from the chandelier.

The behind belonged to Tinnie Tate. She was in a snuggly mood. "You fell asleep. Mr. Weider said to leave you alone because you've been working so hard." She leaned back to let me see an expression saying she thought I had him fooled.

"And now?"

"Go home and get some rest?" She wiggled.

My head was so cluttered with sleep I missed her point. "I'll just find a spare room and grab a nap before I hit the road." Then, belatedly, the message soaked in. "On the other hand, there're some mysteries at home that need solving. If I have the help of an amenable assistant."

The Goddamn Parrot snickered.

I did need to be seen around there once in a while or some bad boy from the neighborhood would try his luck against the fear the Dead Man had woven so powerfully around our place.

Tinnie growled. She was tired. So was I. I said so. But, like everyone who didn't have to be somewhere else, I didn't want to abandon the dining room's relative security. Block had left several men on guard there. For what good their presence might do.

Alyx heard me talking. She decided to come over. "Want me to show you a safe place to nap, Garrett?" The devilment was back, if weakly. The stay-together-in-pairs rule remained in effect.

"No thanks." I winked.

Tinnie shifted to a less uncomfortable position. My reward for saying the right thing. She murmured, "How about I show you *my* guest room?"

"A man's gotta do what a man's gotta do."

71

Tinnie followed me to the Weider front door. She was dressed for travel in a peasant frock and sensible shoes. Stupid me, I asked, "Where do you think you're going?" Stupid me should have started discouraging her about an hour ago. Not that I could have gotten anything through all that red hair successfully.

"With you. You need somebody with you. That's the rule."

"I've got my talking feather duster."

"What good is he in a fight?"

"He squawks a lot and—"

"Be careful how you answer this one, Garrett."

Oh-oh. Time to make that extra effort. I had to remember my lines just right. Only I hadn't seen a copy of the playscript yet.

Redheads will do that to you.

So will blonds and brunettes and all the lovely ladies of every other hue.

"All right, then. You're in. That'll cure you of wanting in. Real quick." What could happen? I was just going to visit one of Karenta's most beloved subjects at his big, safe country estate.

I learned quickly that the countryside is still infested with country. It isn't my favorite part of the world. I prefer domesticated bugs, cockroaches and fleas and bedbugs. They don't get greedy if they bite at all. They don't rip off an arm and hang it in a tree to come back to later.

It was well-groomed out there, close to town, but still way too green. "You getting tired?" I asked Tinnie. She didn't look tired. She looked fresh, sexy, full of vitality and likely to be all of those still when I collapsed.

"You trying to get rid of me again?"

"Again? I never . . ." One foot starting to swing out over the abyss, I shut up.

Maybe I was learning.

"Oh, look!" Tinnie took off running, frisky as a fifteen-year-old. She leaped into a patch of cornflowers.

I told her, "The blue detracts from your eyes."

"I like them anyway. Yikes!" She jumped higher and farther than you would have believed possible for such a trim slip of a gel.

A tiny face peered up out of the flower patch. It belonged to a grinning miniature man. Or boy, actually. He was a pint-sized teen. His grin was humorless. It was a conditioned response to the presence of big people. He was terrified. The grin was supposed to buy time while he figured out what to do.

Flower stalks swayed behind him. I glimpsed brown-and-green homespun in motion, a flicker of golden hair tossing, tiny heels flying. Well. I chuckled. The Goddamn Parrot chuckled. I took Tinnie's hand, pulled. "Let the kids have their privacy."

"What? You mean? . . ."

"Yeah."

"Oh. Actually, that's not such a bad idea, Garrett. When you think about it."

I do that a lot. "Well, if you really . . ."

"All this fresh air is getting me giddy. There's a wonderful big patch of cornflowers over there in that pasture."

"Not to mention cows and horses."

"I didn't know any little people still lived outside the wall. Because of the thunder lizards. You're worried about a few cows?"

No. There were horses over there. Eventually they would recognize me.

But the company went to my head. "I didn't want you worrying about the livestock."

"If they bought bullshit by the pound, you'd be the richest man in TunFaire."

"I'll never be anything but a poor second," I replied. "While Morley Dotes is alive."

Tinnie hiked her skirts with one hand. She ducked between the rails of the split log fence. "I'm only giving in because you keep pressuring me." She showed me a couple of hundred taunting pearly whites.

This was my Tinnie. The argumentative evil twin her family doesn't see. Very often.

I leaned on a fence post, the tip of my nose an inch from hers. "I just had a thought." I glanced back toward TunFaire.

We'd passed through a small wood a while ago. The top of the Hill, a few towers, and the general miasma of evil air hanging above everything were all that could be seen of the city.

"A naughty one, I hope."

"Actually, it's more a troublesome one."

"There you go getting serious again."

"Sometimes I don't have any choice."

"All right. What is it?"

"Colonel Block warned me that I'm being followed around, all the time, by some very clever tails. Which would mean that somebody might be following me now."

"Doesn't that just mean somebody takes you serious? Aren't you always complaining because people don't take you serious?"

"Right. It's great for the ego. But it occurs to me that if I yield to temptation and vanish into a flower patch with the most stunning redhead north of the Cantard—and I can't think of anything I'd rather do—I might get trampled by watchers running to find out where I went."

That tree line back there offered the last good cover for someone tracking me.

Tinnie leaned a little closer. Her eyes were only halfway open. Her lips were parted. She breathed, "Most stunning?"

"You witch."

She laughed. "See? You forgot all about—" She stopped, stared to her right.

Somebody had left the wood. Somebody who was in no hurry. Somebody who whistled while he scuffed along the dusty road.

Staying close, Tinnie whispered, "It's still a good idea, Garrett. Maybe on the way home."

"Sooner or later."

A rumble like the stir of remote thunder came from up ahead. We would reach another tree line in half a mile. The rumble came from beyond that. "Now what?" Tinnie asked.

"Horsemen. A whole bunch."

The stroller behind us caught the sound. He vaulted the fence and disappeared into tall pasture grass on the other side of the road. Hmm.

I got myself over on Tinnie's side fast. "Head for those tall weeds."

"Why?"

"Because we don't know who's making that racket. It could be somebody we don't really want to know."

"Oh."

The war taught me to suffer inconveniences and discomfort stoically, so I only grumbled a little about the thistles in the weed patch. Tinnie was more vocal. Poor spoiled city girl. But she did clam up, bug-eyed, when a squadron of centaurs hove into sight. They were all males with the hard look of campaign veterans. They maintained a warlike traveling formation. They were armed and alert. The army wouldn't like this. I didn't count them but there had to be at least sixteen.

They might have been looking for something. They didn't see it in the pastures, though. They moved on quickly.

"What was that about?" Tinnie asked when the coast was clear. "What are they doing all the way up here?"

We had watched centaurs from hiding together before, a while back, in the Cantard, which is where centaurs properly belong.

"I don't know. But those guys weren't your everyday refugees."

"I don't like it."

"It isn't far now. North English's dump is just past the next bunch of trees." I hoped. I'd never been invited out.

72

Marengo North English's digs were typical of Karenta's ultra-wealthy gentry. The centerpiece was a huge red-brick manor house that crowned a knoll half a mile behind a tall hedge of some plant consisting mostly of thorns. There was a lot of green grass, numerous well-groomed trees, sheep, cattle and neat military squares of tents. An illustration of the place would have overlooked the livestock and bivouac. Workaday aspects of the rural idyll always get overlooked.

"You ever been here?" I should've asked earlier.

"No. I always heard he's kind of reclusive." She indicated the tents. "Lot of relatives visiting. You been here?"

"My folks never moved in these circles." Tinnie started putting on her shoes. She'd been going barefoot, claiming she wanted to feel the dust squish between her toes. They were very nice toes, even dusty-dirty. But I decided to study the hoofprints outside the gate instead. Numerous oddly shod hooves had milled around there recently. Or maybe it was just a trick of the light. The day was getting on.

"Why isn't anybody on guard?" Tinnie asked, between shoes. She danced on one foot while she tried getting a shoe onto the other, tucked up behind her. Her effort had its moments.

I'd been wondering myself. Was North English that confident? I didn't believe it. Not in this world. Not this near TunFaire. The gods themselves aren't that confident. I kicked at hoofprints. "It worries me, too." Those centaurs hadn't looked like they'd been in a fight.

"Should we head back?"

"It's late. It'd be dark before we got to the gate." In darkness, outside the wall, is nowhere I want to be. Call it prejudice. The owners and workers of manors, farms, orchards, and vinyards get by just fine. Those without stout walls just dive into deep cellars via twisty, tight tunnels if the big thunder lizards come calling. Anything else they kill before it kills them.

I don't take risks if I don't have to.

The night can hold things worse than death in the jaws of a hungry beast.

"You scared, Garrett?"

"Sure. You understand what I'm doing? If you don't, you'd better start—"

"We're a team, big boy. You and me and our ugly baby."

The Goddamn Parrot lifted his head long enough to give her a baleful look. I looked balefully at our surroundings. The spread seemed almost lifeless.

"Something I can do for you folks?"

Here came the missing guard, out of a cluster of evergreens not far inside the gate, next to the road. He was buttoning his trousers. He had trouble concentrating on his fingerwork. He was stunned by Tinnie.

I know the feeling. I get it all the time.

"Name's Garrett. I'm doing some work for Marengo. He was supposed to leave word—"

"I guess he did. I recognize the name." His nose wrinkled. "But he's not here. There's a big rally tonight." He checked Tinnie again, probably wondering if she'd like to change her luck in men.

Things are bad when groat-a-dozen brunos take on airs. Maybe belonging to The Call boosts your self-confidence.

He said, "Go on up to the house. Front door only. Someone will be waiting."

I lifted an eyebrow, started walking. Tinnie grabbed my arm. The gateman looked sad, soulful, constipated. Life just isn't fair.

"You little heartbreaker," I told my little heartbreaker.

"What?"

"You completely destroyed that man just by walking away with me."

"What are you talking about?" She never noticed.

Then she bumped me with her hip.

Devil woman.

73

Somebody was waiting. She was long and lean and looked surprisingly regal observing our approach from above. She also looked like she had a sudden toothache come on. I don't think she was glad to see me.

Tinnie offered me another solid hip bump. "That's for what you're thinking."

The woman must be half Loghyr.

Miss Montezuma seemed less than thrilled to see Miss Tate, too, but put her disappointment aside. She was cool, elegant, imperial. This lady was always in control. "Welcome to The Pipes, Mr. Garrett. Miss Tate. You've chosen an inopportune time to visit. Everyone's gone to town. Tonight is supposed to be important for the movement."

We joined Miss Montezuma on the porch. I considered the manor, which dated from the middle of the last century and was supposed to be a minor fortress. Some tightwad had been skimping on the maintenance. It needed a lot of exterior work. The surrounding protective ditch hadn't been cleared out in a generation. If I had friends like Marengo's, I'd keep it filled with acid and alligators.

I surveyed the vast lawns. Or pastures. They were pretty enough. One frazzled kid was trying to convince some sheep that they wanted to head back to their paddocks. "Everybody went? Even Marengo?" North English never included himself in The Call's public exercises. "What happened out there?" One area of lawn was torn up, as though cavalry had fought there. Maybe the livestock had been folkdancing.

Tama Montezuma frowned. "The cattle or sheep must have done it. Tollie has no help at all."

"Why did everybody go?"

"Marengo doesn't tell me everything. But he did say tonight will be a turning point for The Call and Karenta."

"It's a shame I missed him."

Miss Montezuma's gaze brushed Miss Tate. "Isn't it?"

My luck turns fantastic when there's no possibility of benefiting.

Tinnie kicked my ankle. I glanced at her. She had a flower petal in her hair.

The Goddamn Parrot snickered.

"So what do I do now?"

"'Come in. Have supper. I was about to start my own. Then I'll find you rooms. It's too late to go back to town. And you might not want to be there anyway. We could talk about why you came out. Maybe I can help."

I said, "Ouch!"

"Sorry." Miss Busyfeet took her heel off my big toe. "I'm so clumsy today." The Goddamn Parrot snickered again.

Who am I to argue with a beautiful woman?

She could've left her shoes off, though.

The Goddamn Parrot began to dance on my shoulder. He had not yet eaten today. He said something. It was just a mumble, garbled, along the usual lines but intelligible only to me.

I hoped.

The impact of the presence of two beautiful women must have weakened the spell binding his beak. Or we were too far away from the Dead Man for him to control that beak completely. Or His Nibs had become too distracted to stay on that job—or maybe he had turned routine buzzard management over to one of his less attentive subsidiary minds. None of those were very bright.

Certainly he would not have taken his attempt to mislead rightsist observers so far as to abandon completely his ability to spy on me. That would deprive him of so many opportunities to gather ammunition for future nag sessions.

Yes, Old Bones was still out there somewhere, playing his own hand, involved in some way, whatever appearance he tried to project. This case touched upon too many of his fascinations for his defection to be complete and real.

"You're so sweet," Tinnie said. She scratched the quacking feather duster's head. "How come you never say things like that, Garrett?"

Tama Montezuma offered me a dose of my own medicine. She raised one eyebrow and smiled a thin little smile that *dared* me to open my yap.

I took that dare. "Shut your beak, you perverted vulture." To the multitalented Miss Montezuma, I said, "Besides reporting in I hoped to do some research on shapeshifters."

She jumped. "Research? On shapeshifters? Here?" Ha! I'd blindsided her with that.

"The Royal Library referred me to The Call's Institute For Racial Purity. Which is supposed to have a library chock-full of books about nonhumans."

"Oh. That. I'm amazed any outsiders take it seriously. The books are piled all over the old dining hall. They keep collecting books without knowing what to do with them. They can't get anybody who knows anything to come out here. I suspect because they think a librarian should work out of conviction instead of for a salary."

"They" probably meant Marengo North English, well-known skinflint.

Tinnie said, "Sounds like a job for Garrett. He can read and everything."

"I'm no good at organizing." Which was why I hired Dean, way back when. The old boy started out part-time. Next thing I knew he'd moved in.

"You hungry?" Miss Montezuma asked.

"Famished," Tinnie chirped. I didn't doubt it. The woman could eat a whole roast pig and never gain an ounce.

I smiled over her shoulder, nodded. I didn't want Miss Montezuma thinking my friend did all my talking for me.

Tama was amused. "I'll take you past the library on our way to the kitchen. You can poke around there after we eat."

"Marengo won't mind?"

"Marengo isn't here."

"Doesn't seem to be anybody here." There was no sign of staff although Marengo's shanty dwarfed the Weider hovel. "Though how you can tell in all this gloom . . ." Hardly a candle was evident.

"There aren't any servants anymore," Miss Montezuma replied. "And we're frugal with all consumables. If we need light to work, we'd better get the job done in the daytime. Though I suppose I could find a lamp for *you*."

They just fall at my feet, willing to do anything.

"There aren't any windows in the old dinner hall."

The Goddamn Parrot snickered.

"You better do something about that sneeze, bird." I asked Miss Montezuma, "What's going on? They say Marengo is tight, but . . ."

"The Cause is a vampire. Its hunger never goes away. He has to cut back somewhere."

Did North English start out less rich than everybody thought? The impedimenta of great wealth seemed plentiful enough, if old and mostly threadbare. "At least he hasn't had to sell the candlesticks to make ends meet."

"Don't be cynical. Marengo believes he has a divine mission."

I doubted that, being a cynic. "What about Miss Tama Montezuma?"

"It doesn't matter what Miss Montezuma thinks. She's just Marengo's fancy woman."

"If I buy that, will you try to sell me maps to hoards of fairy gold? Bargain-priced?"

"I'm sure Miss Tate is far too alert and levelheaded to let me take advantage of you."

I didn't look at Miss Tate. I had a feeling Miss Tate would be hard at work restraining her redhead's temper. My smirk might overtilt the load.

"I'm curious," Tinnie said, reasonably enough. "If you have no servants, how do you eat?"

"I cook better than I do what I'm famous for."

Whew!

Miss Montezuma cooked very well indeed. With Tinnie and I following her instructions we collaborated in constructing a meal featuring a wild rabbit Tama claimed to have caught herself. "A woman of many talents," Tinnie observed.

"Yeah." I made a mental note to check Miss Montezuma's background. Street legend didn't dwell on her antecedents, which was unusual. Everybody loves a scandal.

74

During supper I was ordered to call Miss Montezuma Tama and learned that North English's place really was deserted.

The man from the gate was named Stucker. He avoided conversation with a passion. Tollie was a Montezuma-stricken fourteen-year-old who managed the livestock. There was a silent old man who had one eye and a hook for a right hand. Venable constituted security at The Pipes. Venable thought thunder lizards were the most wonderful things the gods ever created. He couldn't understand why they were unpopular. He could go on about them forever. He kept a pack of his own as pets and security associates. They would have the run of the estate tonight. Venable claimed his babies only ate strangers.

I suspected that, if you got yourself eaten, Venable's position would be that you couldn't possibly have been friendly.

An advantage of thunder lizards as guards is their stupidity. You can't bullshit them. But stupid is exploitable, too. They'll forget everything and go for the snack if you toss them something like, say, a squawking parrot with his wings clipped.

Tama discouraged table talk, though Venable wanted to bring me up-to-date on things to do with thunder lizard fandom. Tollie couldn't stand to look at Tinnie or do much more than croak if he tried to talk to Tama.

After supper we headed for the library. I insisted. Marengo might say no if we waited. His racist treasures might be damaged by eyetracks.

Long ago I learned that nobody wants to share information that looks like a resource.

The room set aside for the library was huge and cluttered. Most of the stuff there had to predate any notion of a specialized library. Some, I'd bet, predated any notion of Marengo North English.

Tama said, "Marengo wants to set up his research center here. But he's never found time to get started."

I got the impression she'd heard talk till she didn't listen anymore. "It's not like he's short on manpower. He could drag in a bunch of true believers and set up in a day."

"He's too paranoid."

"Yeah?" I set my lamp on a dusty side table, assayed the job ahead. Books were jumbled into small wooden crates in no obvious pattern. Scrolls were tied in bundles of four or five. I selected a bundle. "How do you feel about what he's trying to do?"

"My thoughts aren't consulted." She wasn't going to offer an opinion.

Did she know anyone well enough to take that risk?

Tinnie prowled the room slowly. She used her lamp to illuminate books where they lay, maybe hoping to luck onto something. Luck did seem as sensible a strategy as any. She harrumphed.

I said, "Miss Montezuma, you're being disingenuous. I asked your personal opinion, not if you're a consultant to the Inner Council of The Call."

"Tama, Garrett. Tama. Listen to me. I'm Marengo's companion. His mistress. Strictly utilitarian. What I think doesn't matter any more than what the chamber pot thinks. Unless one of us actually says something. I like my life here." *Most of the time,* her eyes said.

"And when the bloom begins to fade?"

She understood. She'd thought about that. That was obvious immediately.

I recalled how North English had slobbered over Belinda.

Uncle Marengo was in a mood to expand his horizons.

I dropped the subject.

Tinnie exercised uncharacteristic self-restraint. "Here's something." Her timing was flawless. The volume she handed me looked like it might actually be useful. It was *Werebeasts: The Monsters That Walk Like Men.*

The title turned out to be the most interesting part of the book. It dealt only with people who turn into wolves or bears or big cats or critters of a more mythological conviction. Those gods or devils who turn into eagles or snakes or whatnot, with no problems in the weight differential department, were the only self-directed changers mentioned. The creatures I wanted to demystify were anything but divine.

Tama neither dug in nor read over my shoulder. Was she illiterate? Probably. A pity but common enough, especially among women. I learned to read and write because that was a good way to kill time in the long, dull intervals between war's storms of high terror. A lot of guys did. It was encouraged. Written communications get less garbled over time and distance. Karenta's more literate forces proved marginally more efficient and effective than Venageta's over the war's final generation.

Now Karenta's masters are troubled. They have begun to suspect that allowing commoners access to books may have been a grave mistake. Literacy puts crazy ideas into heads more useful when empty. Books let guys who have been dead for a hundred years pass on the one original notion they ever had, which meant immortality for countless social insanities.

There was scare talk about the mob possibly teaching their young to read, too, thereby perpetuating the abomination. Today's free-thinking insanity might continue for generations. It might destabilize the natural order.

Few girls get much education. Tinnie is an exception because amongst the Tates everybody produces. The Tates are more like dwarves than people, some ways. Tinnie manages their bookkeeping.

In time, Tama said, "I'm no night person, Garrett. And I've been up late a lot recently. I need to get to bed."

I missed her point. She reiterated, more directly.

"I need to hit the sack, Garrett. Marengo will strangle me if I leave you unsupervised."

"Oh."

"I'll show you your rooms. I'll trust you not to sneak off with the North English family treasure during the night."

Without light, tippytoeing between the thunder-lizard pups? Wouldn't Venable be pleased?

I didn't run with Tama's straight line. Tinnie waited for it, watching me with smouldering eyes.

Tinnie noted Tama's mention of rooms, plural, as in closed doors for everybody, maybe with nobody knowing where anybody was.

I got assigned first, presumably on the assumption that Tinnie was less likely to go rambling.

It was very dark in my room, beyond the circle cast by Tama's lamp. "There's your bed," she told me. "The chamber pot is underneath. I'll see you and the bird tomorrow." She took off with Tinnie.

I had returned to the door without killing myself on stealthy furniture, leaned into a hallway filled with darkness. The women were out of sight already. Tinnie hadn't left a trail of bread crumbs covered with foxfire. Bad girl. Or maybe not bad enough.

The Goddamn Parrot chuckled softly.

I was beginning to wonder if having the old gutter-beak version of the bird back might not be preferable.

"There are things in the dark," I told him. "Beware!" I shuffled to the bed, undressed.

75

The bed was a fine great mass of down that gulped me whole. I was asleep in seconds, too exhausted to be long disappointed by my solitude.

Nor was I disappointed when, later, I wakened to discover solitude's end. "Did you use a ball of string to mark the way?"

Tinnie hissed, "How did you know it was me?"

"Who else?"

"How about that gaunt witch Montezuma? Or has she been here already?"

I know it's you because I know the scent of your hair and the shape and feel of the rest of you, I didn't say out loud. Also, you are less bony than, not to mention shorter than, the aforementioned gaunt witch. "Not yet, she hasn't. I find it hard to believe myself but not everybody finds me as irresistible as you do."

"Oh? *I'm* the weak one? You want me to show you just how resistible you really are?"

"Hold it down, will you? You'll wake the parrot up."

"Now you're trying to shush me up?"

I knew just the thing to shush her up. But it didn't take for very long. It never does, partly because Tinnie really likes being shushed up.

Two unpleasant things happened at the same time. The Goddamn Parrot broke out in some kind of sea chanty about swords and silver and dead men while someone else gave me a quick, savage finger poke with a nail probably specially sharpened for the task. A soreness upon my ribs suggested that the offending digit had struck several times previously. A whisper accompanied the pain. "Garrett! Somebody's in here with us!" It was not a quiet whisper. The woman was not ashamed.

I groaned, "You're evil. Let me rest."

The bird shrieked like his just deserts were trying to get hold of him. Tinnie snarled, "Garrett! There's somebody in here, dammit!" Which pronouncement was followed immediately by a racket as somebody tripped over some sly and belligerent bit of furniture.

The Goddamn Parrot screamed rape. Tinnie screamed fire, presumably on the assumption that that was more likely to get attention. I yelled, "Be quiet!"

As I climbed out of bed, feeling around for something suitable for bashing undesirable visitors, furniture crashed nearer and nearer the door. Said door opened. For an instant a hunched shape shown in silhouette against a ghostly light from the corridor. Before the door closed I had taken advantage of that light to navigate past two pieces of furniture that would have ambushed me otherwise because they did not seem to be where I remembered them. A third piece, more patient than the others, waited till the door closed to move into position.

The impact of plunging headfirst into a wall—even with my arms thrown forward to absorb it—was enough to leave me groggy and seeing double. Which I was doing when I opened the door and leaned out cautiously.

My night visitor was moving away fast, vaguely illuminated by a weak lantern trailing from her left hand. Her? The figure looked something like Tama, and also a little like the herd boy Tollie, yet distorted. Perhaps by the crack taken by my noggin. So maybe the sweet thing had considered offering some special hospitality and been panicked by hearing Tinnie speak as she was sneaking up on me. Maybe. It could happen.

I could not think of a reason why the kid would want to sneak in on me. Unless he thought he was entering Tinnie's room.

Whichever, how come the wannabe visitor's other hand was

hanging on to a hatchet or cleaver or some such large, heavy, sharp piece of metal?

"Who was it?" Tinnie whispered from behind me.

"I don't know."

"I'll bet I can guess."

"No doubt you can. To the bleakest possibility. And make it all my fault."

"Hey, that's your place, lover. In the wrong. You think we should barricade the door? Just in case?"

"I think we should barricade the door." If what I thought I saw was real, that was one nasty piece of iron. "Just in case. But you'd better hope they don't hold bed check over to your room."

"I sleepwalk."

Right. We moved some furniture. Then we went back to bed. Then, somehow, I got distracted and ended up falling asleep before I had a chance to spend any time figuring out what had just happened.

76

If Tama Montezuma knew anything about or had had anything to do with or had any feelings about the previous night's events, she gave no sign at breakfast. "Good morning, Garrett. I would've wakened you earlier but Tinnie told me you haven't been getting much sleep lately."

Damn! I never warned Tinnie. But she was all right so it didn't matter.

"He seldom gets up before the crack of noon, anyway," Tinnie said. "This's way early for him."

"Hey!" I protested. Then, "Never mind. Tama, Tinnie tells me you've had word that Marengo is headed home."

"A messenger came a few hours ago. Said Marengo is on his way. And that he won't be in a good mood." For just an instant her eyes seemed shifty, evasive, troubled. "Last night didn't work out for him."

"How come he left you here?" I had been thinking about that and, not being a major aficionado of Marengo North English, had developed some suspicions concerning Marengo and his interest in

female persons who were not his wife or niece. I refused to believe
that North English was so devoted to his convictions that he had
gone off to help bully TunFaire's nonhuman population.

"A dangerous level of confrontation was anticipated." That
sounded like a quote from Marengo. "But before you jump to any
conclusions, I chose to remain here." And that sounded like the
truest thing she had said for a while.

I glanced at Tinnie. Her thoughts had taken her elsewhere.

I hadn't seen anything yesterday to suggest that something dramatic was going happen. On the other hand, I had spent the whole
day distracted. Tinnie's presence seldom left me with attention to
spare.

Still, you tend not to overlook big gangs of guys all dressed in
brown marching back and forth singing and busting heads wherever they find somebody not dressed in brown and marching and
singing their favorite songs.

I didn't pursue my question. Tama volunteered, "He said it would
be too dangerous." Her mask of control had begun to show cracks.

The missing mob began returning.

First to appear were a dozen freecorps types who roared through
the house demanding food. They were ragged. I observed, "The
other guys must really look bad." Slings and head bandages were
plentiful. Smiles and laughter were not.

Maybe the other guys never got their hands dirty.

Rightsists kept turning up, alone, in pairs, in small bands. Many
were injured. The mood was grim. I suspected some wouldn't return at all.

They paid me no attention. They even ignored Tinnie.

"What's with those guys?" I asked Tama, back in the library
at last. She'd spent some time helping feed them. "They don't act
human."

"They got their butts kicked. Their big show turned on them."

Damn! TunFaire had long dreaded some huge demonstration by
The Call. And I missed it. Out of town. Gone fishing.

Was I lucky, or what?

"How come they don't notice you or Tinnie? None of those guys
is over a hundred."

"Marengo is inflexible when it comes to what he considers correct behavior. He has made it clear he considers correct behavior a
hallmark of the superior being. These men are all superior beings.
Therefore, they must conform to the highest standards. Your friend
and I are spoken for. It would be incorrect behavior for them to sur-

render to their natural inclinations. They must show themselves to be the superior creatures they claim to be. Marengo insists. And Marengo pays the bills." Tama said every word with a face so straight you knew she wanted to explode in giggles. She whispered, "I'll tell you a secret, though. When they're in the city, surrounded by persons of other stations and Other Races, they act their ages and classes."

"You can take the boy out of life but you can't take the life out of the boy."

"I'll bet you know what you're talking about, too. Tut-tut."

I had tried to talk to several men, in passing. I'd gotten nothing but grunts and scowls for my trouble. It didn't seem politic to press. "Did they get into it with centaurs?"

"Centaurs?" Tama seemed startled. She recovered quickly. "I don't think so. It just seems all the Other Races were ready to fight. The rioting grew bad enough that troops were sent in, some places."

Bet that didn't do much good. Short-timers who thought just like The Call weren't going to be fanatics about defending nonhumans. Their real mission would be to ensure the sanctity of the property of wealthy friends of The Call, anyway, probably.

Call me cynical.

The Call's strategy was no secret. They'd been pursuing it on a small scale for weeks. They wanted to terrorize nonhumans and destroy their property so they would flee TunFaire. Last night's riots would've been intended to become so intense and widespread that the Crown could do nothing but let them run their course.

The Inner Council of The Call had expected the night to be a watershed. They'd counted on the fire of human resentment to flare out of control everywhere.

It hadn't happened. They'd gotten limited support and unlimited resistance.

The fire had blown back into their faces. The most militant nonhumans had been ready for them. Somebody had snitched on The Call.

It wasn't an ignominious defeat, though. It was just an acute embarrassment.

77

Tinnie and I—ever chaperoned by Tama—worked out a system for identifying and reviewing books of potential interest. She sorted and identified. I read. Nothing turned up quickly. I fell behind Tinnie, normally an intriguing place to be.

She asked, "All right if I start a separate pile for stuff that's not in Karentine?"

"I guess." We'd need translators, too? I sneezed. "Wish we could do something about this dust."

The door opened. "Miss Montezuma? Are you? . . . Ah. There you are." The speaker was an old man with a bad artificial leg. His trip to town must have been hell. "The chief is expected soon. He's probably wounded."

"Probably?" Tama was moving already.

"Reports vary. Sometimes he's in critical condition. Sometimes he's only scuffed up a little.

"But he *is* hurt? Garrett. Tinnie. I have to go."

"Have fun." I was sure that the direst reports about North English's condition would originate closest to him. I'd seen him in action.

"Come on, Garrett. You know I can't leave you alone."

I let another great line slide.

As we strolled the hallway in Tama's wake Tinnie remarked, "You're learning."

"Huh?" Wasn't I?

"You've stopped sticking your foot in every time somebody opens a door a crack."

"Did I miss something?"

"I doubt it. But if you did, so much the better."

Pain is a great teacher, darling.

Tama went out onto the same high porch where she'd awaited us. We joined her in time to see Marengo North English's coach arrive. Armed horsemen accompanied it. They were ragged. Bandages were common.

Somebody loved Marengo. A military-style honor guard turned out. So did a haphazard medical team.

How bad had it gotten? There was no smoke over the city so

folks hadn't started burning each other out yet, but if there were many casualties, it could turn nastier fast.

Clearly, the fun had gone out of dressing up and bullying the neighbors.

An ugly little devil-worm of a word wriggled through the muck in the pit of my mind. I hoped it didn't get out and infect these guys. They were in a mood to embrace the demon.

Its name was War.

On Marengo's estate, where there were no pesky nonhumans to make them look bad, the members of several Call freecorps sparkled, though guys with different armbands seemed to have scant patience with one another. Did they fight each other when nobody else was handy?

The medical crew whisked North English out of his coach, onto a stretcher, headed for the house fast. From where I stood Marengo looked like a genuine casualty.

Up close he was grimly pale, like he'd lost a lot of blood. He was still leaking. His clothing had been destroyed by people eager to patch him up.

He was awake and aware. He frowned blackly when he saw me. His gaze jerked to Tama suspiciously. Tinnie joined me. North English's suspicion faded. He knew about us.

What was his problem?

Tama fussed over North English. Sounded like she meant it, too. It wasn't necessary to fake everything in the deal she had.

She moved with the litter, spewing orders. She knew what she was doing. She'd had practical medical experience sometime.

The Pipes crowd seemed accustomed to the presence of mysterious strangers. Nobody questioned us. We were with the boss's woman. He'd seen us himself and hadn't had a stroke. We must be all right.

I did have to field questions about my shoulder ornament. Fortunately, the Goddamn Parrot kept his beak shut. I didn't have to explain how I'd become a ventriloquist. Unfortunately, none of those bold young warriors were in the market for a pet. "Think what a wonderful mascot he'd make," I said. "Put him on your standard and have him squawk insults at dwarves . . ."

The bird squawked an insult at me. It was incoherent but it was there.

Few of the returnees were alert. Mostly they just flopped down somewhere and closed their eyes, safe for the moment.

I remembered that from the islands. After a long, hard, emotionally draining fight, the moment we felt safe we surrendered to exhaustion by collapsing on the spot.

I picked a guy who didn't look as beat as some. "What happened?"

He focused on me momentarily, remembered seeing me with Tama. He shrugged. "Somebody tipped them off. I thought it was gonna be the great big ole hairy-assed mother first night of the Cleansing. I thought we was going to hit the skells and skuggs everywhere, all at the same time. Not just The Call and Theverly but all the groups and freecorps."

That's what they were doing at Weider's the other night. Slapping the last coat of paint on their plan. Using a joyous occasion to mask the stir of darkness. "So somebody leaked it, eh?"

"They was waiting." Like that said everything that needed saying. Misfortune hadn't robbed him of his sense of humor, though. He observed, "Ogres is bad in a street fight."

"They are hard to dent. I speak from joyless experience."

A blond character, shorter and younger than me, born with a board strapped to his back and a chip on his shoulder, stalked into the morning light. He spotted Tinnie, used her as a landmark by which to locate me, came over. "You Garrett?"

I confessed.

"The commander wants to see you."

"North English?"

"Is there another?"

"I'm new at this. I thought maybe Colonel Theverly—"

"Follow me, please."

I did. I caught Tinnie's hand as I passed her.

78

Tama was working on North English when we joined them in a room reminiscent of Max Weider's study—though this was much larger. If the weather turned bad, the freecorps goofs could hold their maneuvers indoors. A world of plotting could be managed from there. The gloomy nether reaches contained maps hung above sand tables boasting miniature structures that looked familiar.

Two guys with spears for spines and no imaginations were camped between us and the tables, I guess in case I suffered one of my outbreaks of curiosity.

Good to see they trusted me as much as I would've had I been the old boy getting mummified. "Sir," I said as the officer and I approached, "you wanted me?" He looked less determinedly antagonistic now.

"Tama says you came to see me." His voice was weak and high but stronger than I'd expected. He winced as Tama swabbed an abrasion. Naked to the waist, he was a pasty, doughy sort of man.

Also a lucky sort. He hadn't been treated kindly. He had suffered cuts and stab wounds and bad abrasions most men couldn't have survived.

I said, "I wanted to bring you up-to-date." He lacked enthusiasm. In his position it would be hard to be enthusiastic about anything less than life itself.

I edited my story only slightly. If I was being followed, my movements were no secret. Anything I'd learned, if I'd learned anything, could be learned by others. There was little point holding out. And none to revealing that I was reporting to Block and Relway, too.

I was up to the centaurs. "They were a military unit. Disguised but definitely veterans."

North English waved a hand. "Wait a minute." He pushed Tama away.

I waited while he ordered his thoughts. That took a while.

"Let me get something straight. You had no idea The Call would begin the Cleansing last night?"

"Not a glimmer. But you're the only one I know who'd know about it. You didn't warn me."

"But you're generally well informed and a keen observer. You would have noticed anything obvious." He seemed to be having trouble thinking.

"I thought so myself."

"If you didn't notice, then it wasn't something we did that gave us away." My guess was, he'd just realized that he had a rat in his walls. "Tama. Miss Tate. I want to chat with Mr. Garrett privately. Ed. You and your men step out with the ladies."

Ed was the officer who had delivered me. Apparently bodyguarding was among his duties. He was scandalized. "Sir, I wouldn't recommend—"

"Do it, Ed."

Ed stopped arguing.

Tinnie didn't want to leave, either. Tama didn't want to leave. They did not argue. Marengo North English was in charge.

I chuckled. "You got Ed worried, boss."

North English frowned at my familiarity. "Possibly. And that's my fault. He took the same attitude yesterday, I told him to go away—and I ended up lucky to be alive."

"How bad is it?"

"I told you, I was lucky. Damned lucky. They meant to kill me but a gang of dwarves looking for rightsists to fight popped up and attacked them."

"I'm confused," I confessed. "Maybe you started in the middle. Dwarves saved you? From human attackers? Why would they do that?" It was interesting that terror and pain would put him into such a talkative mood. But why with me?

"They didn't recognize me. And the men who attacked me were disguised as members of the movement."

"Maybe they were."

"Possibly. That's not a thought I cherish. But I do have rivals. Although I don't think any of these men were that because I didn't recognize any of them. Even so, I did want Ed and the others out of here so we could speak freely."

"About what?"

"You must look into what happened while you're doing whatever else it is that you're doing. I'm particularly interested in knowing who those men were. I am confident that they were specifically committed to the extinction of Marengo North English and my survival is due only to an ironic twist of fate."

"I still feel like we're going sideways."

"I'll start from the beginning. Last night was a big night for The Call. We'd planned for months. We put it off several times because we thought we could make a bigger splash later. But now we were coming up on the dwarfish New Year. We had to move before all their rustic cousins came to town for the holidays."

North English composed his thoughts carefully before he continued. He was much more businesslike than he had been at Weider's.

"As you may suspect, like you, I have a taste for toothsome ladies. Not long ago I met someone new and intriguing. She seemed equally interested. Last night presented a perfect opportunity to pursue the possibilities. The Cleansing provided a reason to be away from The Pipes. And there was nothing I could contribute to actual operations short of getting out in the street throwing brick-bats with the others."

I listened for hints of hypocrisy. I still had trouble picturing Marengo North English as a true believer.

Maybe the insincerity existed only in my imagination.

"So you had a date. Rough trade, too, looks like."

"I walked into an ambush. I couldn't have been much stupider. Ed warned me but I wouldn't listen. It's the way men get."

"Sometimes," I admitted, having been there.

"It's only sheer fool luck that I'm here now." He snuck a glance to see if I was conscious of the irony.

I eschewed any observation about fools and drunks. "Are you heading somewhere?"

"I am. Yes." Pause. Deep breath. "Eight of the most influential men in the movement were murdered last night. Somebody tried to kill Bondurant Altoona. Burned his house down. But he wasn't inside." Did I near disappointment? "Ladora Ankeny was hurt worse than I was, poor woman. I was attacked, of course. Set up and attacked."

"Thought you and old Bondurant didn't get along."

"We don't. He's not well liked. We left him out of our plans. But he did hear somehow and left home—to get in the way, if I know the man at all—just before the fires started."

Maybe. "Were the attacks coordinated?"

"I believe they were."

"Why?" I meant why did he think that but that wasn't what he heard.

"The assassins were all human. I can't believe that there's that kind of opposition among our own people. There're only two kinds of humans." Eyes calculating, he paused to read my expression. "Those who're with us and those who're with us but haven't yet awakened."

You might be surprised, boss. "You know who got killed, right? Who they were could tell you why. What did they have in common?"

Evidently North English didn't want to face that question. He had an answer already that didn't please him.

"So?" I asked, noting that he was still trying to read me.

"Everyone attacked was involved in fund-raising. Or made decisions concerning raising funds. I think I might be the only one who could see that connection. So maybe *that* was why *I* was targeted."

Which offered us both an answer he didn't want to face—along with a reason why.

He'd slipped off to meet Belinda, jumping right into a honey trap. And now his ego hurt worse than his body because he feared he'd been set up from the beginning.

Belinda was her father's daughter, with extra weapons. She could blind men with their natural weakness. And she had no concept of mercy.

I said, "If you play on their ground, you obey their law. Only the strong survive. You mess with their money, they kill you. Unless you kill them. They don't think like kings and generals. Or like you. They don't send soldiers to attack your soldiers. They'll kill your men only if they get in the way. They want you. Once you're dead your soldiers are no longer a problem."

That seemed the obvious way to operate, too. I've never understood why, when we caught a big-time Venageti wizard or general or noble, we'd always ransom him. Or even just let him go if he promised not to fight anymore.

I wondered what Belinda would say about last night. Not that I'd ask. I try to separate business and friendship. If a friendship is what we have.

I told North English, "I've known these people a long time. I'm surprised they've been as tolerant as they have."

That startled Marengo. "Tolerant?"

"By their standards."

"It wasn't my intent to engage in criminal activities, Mr. Garrett. I'm the most visible Call leader but not the only one. Not even the supreme one. Other groups started raising money that way a long time ago. I opposed the plan when the Council proposed it. I reminded them that The Call wasn't founded as a criminal conspiracy. I reminded them that one of our missions is to set an example. We can't cut corners because our cause is just. If we do, we're no better than the Other Races. And it sets a precedent we'll pay for later."

The man was heated up for a speech. Maybe he *was* a true believer. I cut him off. "Looks to me like you've got a good counter-argument now."

"Possibly. But I doubt it." He paused. I had nothing to say so that's what I said. He continued, "It's all out of control, Garrett. It's like riding a lion. The beast answers the reins if the mood takes it. And the gods help me if I try to get off." And again with the calculating look.

"What do you want from me? Looks like the Outfit sent a message. Emphatically. You were lucky. You survived it. They'll let you alone if it looks like it took. I say don't aggravate them. Chodo is way less friendly than Belinda."

"Did she set me up?"

"Probably." My guess was, Belinda just thought on her feet and improvised. "Maybe that was why she wanted to meet you."

His pride was bruised more deeply than his flesh. Marengo North English thought well of himself. What kind of world was it where a woman could use him as knife fodder? "You know Belinda. Talk to her."

Was he going to whine? "If you've checked me out, you know I know Chodo better than I know Belinda." Unless she'd developed a true-confession habit.

North English smiled enigmatically. Maybe he knew more than I thought he could. He winced, closed his eyes. His wounds still hurt badly.

79

"What actually happened last night?" I asked North English, after we took time for him to rest and take a painkiller.

"I'd arranged to meet Belinda at a rooming house on the far north side. She said the place belonged to her family."

"Remember the name of the street?"

"I don't. That was the driver's responsibility." When I frowned, he said, "I don't think it had one." He colored slightly.

"You went into an elven neighborhood?" Elves don't get excited about frills like street names or house numbers.

"Just the edge. Nobody would expect to find me there."

"No. But somebody did."

"Yes." North English proceeded to describe the attack on his coach, which occurred soon after it entered that street. It mimicked the attack on Belinda's coach.

Was that coincidence?

Quite possibly he'd had an earlier close call and didn't yet realize it. Belinda had asked him to meet her at The Palms. And CeeJay Carlyle had been with Belinda when she headed for her postparty rendezvous. Did Crask and Sadler mess everything up?

I asked, "Should I talk to your coachman?"

"If you know a good necromancer, you might. I'm the only survivor. They didn't get me dragged out of the coach fast enough."

There'd be no way of double-checking details short of consulting the men who had tried to kill him. I had a suspicion that was a long-shot daydream.

The details didn't matter. Had to be Belinda's doing. And Marengo knew that. But I wondered if she might not have had more than one motive.

Her attack had been extremely vigorous, even for her. If, indeed, she had ordered the attack. It risked warfare now and persecution later if The Call enjoyed any enduring political success.

She must've decided that the Outfit had to make a clear, definitive statement incapable of being misunderstood by anybody. Which might mean she hadn't just been responding to business encroachments.

Just suppose Marengo had had some remote connection with the attack on Belinda . . .

I decided that he must have had. Based upon no evidence whatsoever.

Poor Marengo! That made him a zombie, dead but still walking toward the knife.

Somebody had brought Crask and Sadler back. Those two were fearless but they weren't stupid and were only marginally crazy. They knew lots of people wanted to carve them up.

They must have been sure they could do their work quick and dirty and profitably and be gone before death could pick up their trail.

So somehow North English got word to them when Belinda showed up with me, cleverly grasping the moment. He might not have known that those two thought they owed me. But would he have cared?

I didn't think so, either.

Then Belinda made a date, probably hoping to let North English meet Carlyle for an exercise in comparative knife techniques. And North English agreed, probably thinking he'd have fun with Belinda if his hitters missed.

No proof. None whatsoever. All speculation. But I thought the Dead Man would agree. And he'd looked inside Belinda's head, where the snakes and spiders lurk.

I can conclusion-hop with the best. I've run with villains for years, people who play those kinds of games. You can smell them out if you know the stakes and luck onto a few hints up front.

These scenarios fit the facts neatly.

They didn't toss light into the shadows surrounding the shapeshifters and the Weiders, though. They gave me no mention whether or not The Call was trying to strong-arm the Weiders, or was connected to the shapeshifters somehow.

Damn it. The one thing I'd figured out didn't help much. Belinda and The Call could work out their differences, with bloody steel or rattling jaws. That wouldn't touch me.

Belinda might have let the nonhumans know about the advent of the Cleansing. The Outfit had tentacles reaching inside shadows Relway only dreamed of penetrating. Everybody owes them something, somewhere, somehow. Though in this case Marengo was, probably, the leak himself.

I asked, "Any way you can bully your council into backing off?"

"Backing off?" He got that air of struggling to concentrate again.

"To quit trying to horn in on the rackets."

"I can try. If I had a good reason. If they're really doing that."

"How about staying alive? Is that a good reason?"

"They wouldn't do anything just on my say-so, Garrett. Again, if they're really involved."

Why did he keep pretending? "Here's a reason they can understand. If you get in a war with the Outfit, it won't just be Marengo North English who gets dead. They can get to anybody. Eventually. They'll find somebody close willing to be corrupted. They won't be impressed by who you are, who your parents were, how much you're worth, or who you know. You should've gotten that message last night."

"Last night is why I hope you'll find us a basis for negotiation."

I was puzzled. It showed.

"What?" North English demanded.

"What's to negotiate? They'll tell you to go away or get dead. Then they'll kill as many of you as it takes to make you understand."

I exaggerated a little. The Outfit is no monolith and the people inside are as venal as any other. It could be tamed by somebody who wanted to focus a lot of energy and resources. Somebody like Relway, someday, when he doesn't have to deal with all the other distractions.

Assuming Belinda didn't get to him first.

"Why go for the rackets, anyway?" I asked. "The Call is festering with rich people."

"Not many of whom want to open their purses for the Cause. They're investing their leadership skills." Yes, he was sarcastic. And bitter. "I've financed almost everything. I've fed and armed and clothed a thousand men for Colonel Theverly. Before Theverly it was the Brotherhood Of The Wolf."

"What became of those guys?" I still wanted to figure out where Gerris Genord fit.

"They wouldn't be controlled. They were disbanded when Colonel Theverly came aboard. Some joined the new corps. The hardheads dropped out, went somewhere else." North English waved a hand weakly, dismissing the Brotherhood. It was old news. He had a hobbyhorse to ride. "Do you have any idea how much weapons cost when you have to buy them from dwarves?"

Wouldn't it be something if the dwarves used this crisis to strip humans of their wealth?

Wouldn't it be something if the dwarfish weapons were used to exterminate the dwarfish race?

Life gets funny that way.

I grunted. He could take that as thoughtful commiseration if he wanted.

He changed the subject. "Have you found anything in the library?"

"No. And I really hoped I could root out something about shapeshifters. That bunch at Weider's were part of something big. If I can learn more about the race I might be able to guess what."

North English didn't get excited. "Tama says you're sorting as you go. I appreciate that. I know gathering information and studying it is important but somehow we just never get around to the library. How did you know about it?"

"I went to the Royal Library. They said I'd do better here or in some wizard's private library. I don't know any friendly wizards."

"Does anybody?"

"You kidding?" But he was talking to himself, bitterly. Maybe he had had an unhappy experience.

I must have risen in his consideration. He was treating me like an old retainer now. Almost with respect. But with cautious lack of trust.

"Did you have a problem with one of our sorcerers?" Wouldn't exactly be unique if he had.

North English realized he had given something away. He didn't like that. "Didn't everyone who visited the Cantard?" Quick shift of subject. "Tama overstepped herself by allowing you into the li-

brary without consulting me but it was a good idea. Let me know if
you find anything interesting. Max Weider is my friend, too."

I was dismissed. He accentuated the point by closing his eyes.
He wanted to rest. He wanted to think, to conjure some way he could
take his special breed of liberty to TunFaire with better effect.

I left the room.

I found a crowd outside, frowns prevalent, everybody afraid
they'd missed something important. Lost in thought, I ignored them.

Marengo had a connection with a wizard? Should that surprise
me? He was a powerful man. Wizards prefer the company of powerful men to that of slobs like me. Why? I can be charming.

Did it even matter?

Tinnie and Tama eyed me expectantly. I told Tama, "He'll live.
And he's in a more charitable mood than I'd have thought. It must
have been love at first sight, Tinnie. He wants to adopt you. Offered me three shiny new groats if he could have you for a niece."

"That's not funny, Garrett."

"That's what I told him. I said you don't have any sense of humor. He said, 'Just wait till I tickle her fancy.' "

Tinnie snapped, "Why're you laughing, Tama?"

"I'm trying to visualize those words coming out of Marengo's
mouth. It isn't a pretty picture."

I said, "He told me to go ahead with the library. And let him
know if we found anything."

Tama said, "Since you have his blessing, you and the niece-
apparent go to it. I have work to do." Tama pushed through the
crowd. Even mistresses have responsibilities. Freecorps officers
continued to gather. Maybe they were worried they might have to
look for work.

Tama did what none of them dared. She entered Marengo's
sanctuary.

Tinnie murmured, "I don't know what to make of that relationship. Most of the time she acts like she doesn't care."

"She can't afford to, too much," I said. "And she probably wonders about you and me, too."

"What's that supposed to mean?"

"That I don't understand, either, but my New Year's resolution was to stop trying to figure out relationships. I'll deal with what people show me."

Tinnie paused to think. She's bright but she sometimes forgets to wake her brain up before she lets her mouth take off. Two of us doing that at once causes problems.

Dean says we were made for each other.

Dean has said the same thing about me and several bright, picturesque young ladies. He's even said it about me and take my pick of his platoon of homely nieces. Real nieces. Dean believes I need more stability. He doesn't like the way I live.

"Now you're drifting off on me?"

"Didn't get enough sleep last night."

"Bragging or complaining?"

"I was thinking about Dean."

"Why?"

"He's gone. They both are."

"Really?" The news startled Tinnie. "I never thought—"

"It's the times."

"Uhm?" She became very quiet. She didn't say anything until we were back among the books. "Is it permanent, Garrett?"

"What?"

"The split with your partner."

I glanced around. I tapped my ear. You couldn't be sure who was listening. The Call were paranoid by nature. After last night they would be doubly so. "It had to happen. My sympathies aren't what they used to be. Dean wouldn't see things my way. He wouldn't listen to reason."

"And?"

"So they sneaked out."

The facts awed me whenever I recalled that the Dead Man actually let himself be moved. Maybe even *asked* to be moved.

Ah. I could find him. If I could unearth Saucerhead. Tharpe must have been in on it. He was one of very few people the Dead Man would trust to help.

I'd be expected to figure that out for myself. Far be it from my pet fruit bat to speak up.

"If the split is permanent . . ." There was an edge to Tinnie's voice. She had something in mind. Maybe something risky.

The Goddamn Parrot shuddered and twitched, fell of his perch. He flopped around amongst the books. Dust flew. Inarticulate noises spewed from his beak.

"I don't know." I stared. Had something happened to the Dead Man? The bird seemed to be trying to talk. Maybe His Nibs was making a desperate effort to get through.

Or maybe darkness was overtaking him at last.

Maybe, before he checked out, he would be kind enough to share his thoughts about what he'd overheard.

If he'd been paying attention. Chances were he'd fallen asleep and this was one of his nightmares leaking.

Tinnie said, "He's been acting strange for a long time."

I opened a book. "How would you know what's strange for that runt condor? You weren't in on getting me stuck with him, were you?" Her sense of humor could include a prank like the Goddamn Parrot. Especially if she thought I deserved it.

"No. But I think Morley showed a lot of flair, finding him."

"That Morley is a piece of work, isn't he?" I grumped.

"Are we going to move in out here?" Tinnie asked. "I haven't been home for days. I imagine Uncle Willard is starting to steam."

"He'll boil over when he finds out you were with me."

"He likes you, Garrett."

"Sure. From a distance."

"He's not blind or stupid."

In a minute we'd be back to me moving into the Tate compound. "You want me to take you home?"

"I don't think my cute new uncle can do it for a while. Besides, he tickles."

I looked around. We'd been through scores of books. That didn't amount to ten percent of the heap. Less if some of the drifts had formed atop dunes of documents not immediately evident.

I didn't want to leave. The library was a great excuse to hang around the heart of The Call. Just being at the North English place would put me next to a lot of interesting stuff. Nobody would notice me after a while. I would become part of the furniture.

"This is a great opportunity . . ." No sense letting Tinnie in on everything. What she didn't know she couldn't share with friends whose politics were suspect.

"I understand that. I don't want you to waste it. But Uncle Willard will be foaming at the mouth."

"Especially when he hears what you've been doing."

She grinned. Those devils wakened in her eyes. "We could give him one more reason for—"

"Wicked, wicked woman. Right here?"

"Look around. Nobody ever comes in here—"

Click! The door opened. "Excuse me. I hate to interrupt, but—"

"That's all right, Ed," I told the stiff-backed officer.

He winced. "The old man asked me to include you in our response to a problem that's just come up. He told me I'd find you here."

"He was right again. What kind of problem?"

"Murder."

"Ah, shit. Not again." I shed some dust and the book I was pretending to skim. "What can I do?"

"The old man says you're the expert." Ed looked Tinnie over. He had no trouble with his sexual identity and was one hundred percent in favor of redheads.

The guy might be all right after all.

"Let's go."

81

As we descended the front steps, I said, "Ed, I need to take Miss Tate home sometime today. She's overdue. Her folks will be worried."

"Why tell me?"

"I didn't think Venable and his lovable lizards would care and you've got the next closest interest in security here, right? I thought you'd want to know who's coming and going and why."

"If you want to do me a courtesy, I'd prefer you called me Lieutenant, not Ed." His voice was brittle.

I was supposed to be cowed. "All right, Ed. I won't call you Ed no more. But don't look for any military crap. I'm out of that. I don't need it, don't appreciate it, don't like it. If it helps, think of me as a civilian contractor."

He didn't warm to that idea. Civilians are not to be trusted. You don't have enough control. But he said, "All right, Mr. Garrett. On that basis. Call me Mr. Nagit."

"Or Lieutenant?"

"Or Lieutenant. Yes."

Tinnie was tagging along. The Goddamn Parrot had adopted her shoulder for the time being. One of them snickered. I have my suspicions which though both my trials showed straight faces. I asked, "You interested in a parrot, Mr. Nagit?"

"I don't think so."

"He can talk."

"Then definitely not, Mr. Garrett. But when you decide to get rid of the other one . . ." He chuckled.

"Make me an offer." I chuckled, too.

"Garrett!"

"Sorry, darling."

Mr. Nagit smiled. We'd made peace. For the moment.

Mr. Nagit led us toward the front gate. A crowd had gathered out there. More men were headed that way. I said, "These guys need something to do."

"The old man said give them a day to recuperate. But you're right. Uhn! What's this mess?"

We had come to the torn-up part of the lawn. I said, "I noticed this yesterday. I asked Miss Montezuma about it. She didn't know what happened."

Mr. Nagit eyeballed the hoofprints. He moved a few steps this way, a few steps that. I tagged along. He observed, "There were at least a dozen animals involved. Pretty light. And poorly shod. Came this way from the gate, swung around there, then went back. They were galloping when they came up to the turn but they walked back down."

I agreed. "They were chasing somebody."

"This may connect with our murder." Nagit started toward the gate, reconsidered the battered ground. "Sure made a mess."

A mess. Bane of the military mind. "Maybe they were playing with their prey."

"What kind of people would? . . ."

"Tinnie and I saw a band of centaurs when we were coming out here." I described the circumstances. No point being secretive. I'd told North English already and suspected he might have said a word to Mr. Nagit.

"Centaurs? Hmm."

Meanwhile Tinnie tried to shush the Goddamn Parrot. That clown rooster was having a mild fit. I asked, "Do birds behave strangely around here, Mr. Nagit?"

"Not that I've noticed."

"That buzzard's had two seizures this morning. I thought he might've picked up something."

"Not here."

We soldiered on. Toward, it developed, the cluster of evergreens just inside the gate.

I observed, "These people shouldn't be tracking all over the murder scene."

"I understand that. I told everyone to stay out of the trees."

"The body in there?"

"See for yourself."

82

I saw for myself.

Mr. Nagit bullied the freecorps thugs into moving back. I did admire their discipline.

There wasn't much smell yet but the flies were plentiful. They're always the first to know. I heard them before I saw anything.

The first dead thing wasn't human. It used to be a wild dog. Before something left nothing but a head and some feet and fur and odd bits of bone scattered amongst the well-tossed pine needles.

I heard a little "Tee-hee." I looked over my shoulder and wasn't surprised to see my one-eyed, lizard-loving buddy Venable checking another savaged remnant of wild Rover.

"Did your babies do this?"

He tittered. "Killed the wild dogs and ate them, they did, yes. And never laid a claw on Stucker. He was dead already. They won't touch carrion unless they're absolutely starving. Even then, sometimes, the strong males will eat the weak ones before they touch cold meat. Hee."

The dining preferences of his pets didn't interest me. Mr. Nagit was less intrigued than I. I asked, "What's this about Stucker? He looked pretty healthy when I saw him a few minutes ago."

Venable looked baffled.

Soon I saw why.

Stucker's corpse was naked. It was dirty and far from fresh. The wild dogs had been at him during the night, long before my glimpse of him in the house a while ago.

There was no doubt he'd been dead half a day before the dogs found him. I muttered, "But he was at supper with us last night."

The pine needles were well stirred. Here and there, in the soft soil beneath, were clear hoofprints.

"Why didn't they bury him?" I wondered aloud.

"They did. Over there," Venable told me. "Just not deep enough. The dogs dug him up. We pulled him over here and brushed him off before we sent for the lieutenant."

I wanted to scream and give Venable a good throttling. But that would do no good now.

I reminded Mr. Nagit that, "We saw centaurs on the road just north of here yesterday. And nobody was on the gate when we got here. We were talking about that when Stucker came out of here still pulling up his pants. I figured he'd gone off to take a dump. But . . ."

Mr. Nagit looked puzzled.

"The boss will understand. It's a matter of shapeshifters. Killer shapeshifters."

The light dawned. "He told us how he handled a couple of those at the Weider masque. I thought they'd all been captured."

"Some were. And used their abilities to get away. There seem to be an awful lot of them around. They keep turning up."

"We'd better grab the Stucker back at the house."

"Good idea. Only I'll bet we don't find him."

"Why not?"

"If you were him up there and saw this mob down here, what would you think?"

"That we found the body." Mr. Nagit showed me his comradely smile.

It wasn't that endearing. Venable's pets smiled that way while they waited for your friendly status to evaporate.

"Exactly. What else strange has happened the past few weeks? Any assaults? Unexplained deaths? Mysterious thefts? People supposedly seen two places at the same time?" The shifters seemed to have the solution to that difficulty worked out, though.

"No." Mr. Nagit barked at the freecorps fighters gradually pushing into the grove, wanting to sneak a peek at disaster. He finger-pointed half a dozen. "You men go up to the house. Grab Stucker."

"But—"

"If you see Stucker it won't *be* Stucker. Stucker's right there. Already starting to ferment. Get moving."

I observed, "That'll teach those guys to get so close an officer notices them."

Nagit smiled again. This had to be a record day. "I suppose it will." He glared around like he was thinking of something else that had to be done. Men backed away.

There was a lot of soldier in those guys still.

"Settle down!" I snapped at the Goddamn Parrot. Having decided he didn't love Tinnie anymore, he had jumped to my shoulder where he was practicing some weird tribal fertility dance.

Lieutenant Nagit said, "Looks like he's trying to see the body but you keep moving."

He was taking up for the bird? "Maybe he's hungry. He's a vulture in disguise. Venable. Think he could play with your pets?"

No?

That wonder buzzard is so damned useless I can't even turn him into lizard bait.

83

There was no sign of pseudo-Stucker. Surprise, surprise. The shifter was somebody else now.

So I was not surprised when I spied one Carter Stockwell, known shapechanger, drifting behind the crowd, moving toward the front gate. Evidently it never occurred to anyone else to wonder why an unfamiliar fellow would be wearing the same clothes Stucker had had on for the past two days.

"There's our man," I told Nagit. "Right there. That face is the one he wears whenever he's not replacing someone."

Nagit looked at me narrowly, briefly—then gestured several men closer. "How do you know that, Mr. Garrett?"

"I've run into this shifter before. He always collapses into this shape." Did that make sense?

It did to me.

The creatures really did have to be psychic when it came to

threats. Carter looked at me suddenly, as though responding to my interest. He lengthened his stride immediately.

"He knows I've made him, Mr. Nagit."

The lieutenant gave orders quickly, softly. Everyone hurried to execute them. These freecorps boys took their military stuff seriously.

The mob took off after Stockwell, determined little turtles vainly coursing a hare. Stockwell changed as we watched, his legs lengthening until a foot of calf showed below each cuff. He bounded away, gaining ground fast. He circled the tent city and disappeared into the woods beyond.

"Wow," Mr. Nagit said. "That's what I call putting on a burst of speed." He kept a straight face.

Stockwell dwindled into the distance. What was his connection with the centaurs?

There had to be one. Tinnie and I had run into centaurs just up the road. Minutes later the Stucker look-alike, still buttoning his trousers, comes out of the very copse where later we find what's left of the real Stucker. Just downhill from a lot of ruined pasture. "The torn-up turf. The way it was torn up. Those centaurs helped catch the real Stucker for the changer." Which meant that there must be a common mission between the centaurs and shapeshifters. Which I thought the Dead Man, with his special interest in things and personalities out of the Cantard, would find very intriguing indeed. I might even tell him about it. Someday.

The Goddamn Parrot took flight. That little traitor would give the news away first chance he got. For free. Apparently out of practice flying, he had trouble staying straight and level getting across to Tinnie.

"How do I spot one of those things if they come back? Or if there're more of them around?"

"I'm trying to find out. That's why I was in the library. But I hadn't found anything yet. I do know they don't like silver. Not even a little. You could whap everybody with a solid silver ugly stick every once in a while. Why would they replace a low-level guy like Stucker?"

Nagit looked at me like he had sudden doubts about my smarts. "He was on the gate eighteen hours a day. He saw everyone who came and went. Valuable information to a lot of people, I'd think. Plus he had the run of the house in his free time. He could've dug around in there whenever he wanted."

"The perfect spy. He was good, too. I didn't know him so he had no trouble with me but he did fool Miss Montezuma at dinner last night."

"Stucker was the perfect target. He was a loner. Nobody knew him very well. Everybody knew he was totally committed to the movement, though. He did everything possible, in spite of his social handicaps. So the boss always said. You'd never suspect him."

Unless the replacement Stucker never got a chance to bury the man he replaced deeply enough. On account of that meddlesome Garrett turning up. I shivered, thinking a dark wing had brushed my soul. In Stockwell's place I might have paid me a deadly visit during the night.

I assumed the boss was right about the original Stucker. "You had doubts?"

"About Stucker? Never. The man had a minor job. He did it well. I notice people only when they don't do their jobs well."

"I see." I also saw that Tinnie was headed our way, oblivious to the moon-eyes around her. The woman put a definite strain upon these superior beings' commitment to correct behavior.

Every man in sight hated my bones the instant she slipped her arm inside mine.

She purred, "How much longer are you going to be?"

"I don't know, darling. This's another shapeshifter incident. The gatekeeper was a changeling."

"Too bad. He seemed nice."

"We only met the shifter. The real gatekeeper was dead before we got here."

Tinnie glanced that way. She flushed.

I said, "It isn't pretty. Wild dogs got after him. Then Venable's little pals got after the wild dogs."

"I know that, Garrett. What about you being much longer?"

I wasn't looking forward to facing Uncle Willard. "Mr. Nagit, I'm going to take the lady home. I'll be back."

Mr. Nagit wasn't completely thrilled. "Do what you need to do. I'll leave word to let you in."

In parting I suggested, "Venable might try to set his pets on that shifter's trail. If you do catch him, I definitely want to talk to him."

Nagit scowled. "I suppose—Now what?"

The soldiers had begun to stir.

"Looks like somebody's coming."

Yes, indeed. And it was somebody who liked his ceremony. He had outriders out, fore and aft, in numbers sufficient to stave off

small armies. A guy who didn't look old enough to be a veteran
hobbled up. "It's Colonel Theverly, Lieutenant. He's coming."

And he'd be in a bad mood after last night, too, I expected.

Tinnie scrunched up close. "This looks like a real good time to
start hiking, boyfriend."

"Probably."

"Uncle Willard won't be the only one mad at you if these people
suddenly get all paranoid about us." Which, on reflection, seemed
entirely possible. The returning freecorps people we were about to
encounter had no way of knowing that we were accepted guests.
And good old Colonel Theverly always had been one to leave a lot
of unfamiliar bodies around for the gods to sort out.

Renewing acquaintances with Theverly could wait. I expected
to be back before nightfall. We could get together then.

Tinnie and I got out of the gateway to The Pipes only moments
before the leading horsemen turned in. We stood across the road
and gawked at the cavalcade. Quite a few cavaliers gawked right
back at the redhead. Me, I just stood there wrapped in my cloak of
invisibility.

Once we did start toward town the Goddamn Parrot began to get
excited. He sounded like he was trying to talk again. What language wasn't clear, however.

"He can't stand country life," I explained to Tinnie. "Heh-heh.
Maybe I can lose him in the woods."

84

"Speaking of woods," Tinnie said. She gestured to indicate the last
copse we'd traversed before we'd gotten to The Pipes coming out.
"What became of all those people you said were following us?"
She'd seen the feather of smoke leaning above the treetops.

"A question definitely worth consideration, my dear," I said.
"Perhaps I should've offered to borrow something sharp before we
left your new uncle's establishment."

"You sure should've. It's obvious we can't rely on your rapier
wit."

"How sharper than a frog's tooth. I shouldn't have run so fast when that goddess wanted to be my girlfriend."

"You? Run from anything female?"

"She was green and had four arms. And teeth like one of Mr. Venable's pets. But she was affectionate."

"I'll bet. There's somebody in those trees."

Her eyes were better than mine. I didn't see anything. But I took her word. She wouldn't joke about danger. Much. I picked up a stick. "This would be handy if it wasn't rotten." It would shatter the first time I knighted somebody. But if I carried it maybe folks would be discouraged from getting close enough to find out that it was mostly decorative. I mused, "I need to stop by the house and arm up."

"I'd help but I really need to go home. Uncle Willard's probably going crazy."

I told the Goddamn Parrot, "The lady's a gold seam of straight lines but I'm a gentleman." I spotted movement at the wood's edge. Someone wasn't good at sitting still. Then I spotted more movement elsewhere. "I hope those people aren't all working together."

They weren't, apparently, but they were aware of one another and wanted to stay out of each other's way. Which made for a lot of rustle and scurry as Tinnie and I strolled through the wood.

"These are the people you never noticed before?"

"They're city boys. They don't do quite as well when they're surrounded by a whole lot of country."

"A not uncommon problem, evidently."

"Hey!"

"I'm starting to think that you've been telling tall tales about you and the Marines. Tell the truth. You were really the guy who mopped the floors at expeditionary headquarters, weren't you?"

"You found me out. Don't tell anybody. They'll kick me out of The Call. Then what would I do for entertainment?"

"You could always harass yourself."

"Wouldn't want to horn in on your only hobby."

Tinnie took my hand. We ambled. We strolled. She didn't appear to be in a real hurry to ease Uncle Willard's anxiety.

Those following me didn't intrude. Guess they just wanted to play follow the leader.

85

"It's a different city."

Tinnie felt it, too, though nothing was immediately obvious to the eye. There were ample crowds of all ethnic persuasions working hard doing the things that need doing to keep a city going. "Nobody's talking to anybody."

She was right. And it wasn't just that. People were being careful to give one another room and especially careful not to expose their backs to anyone not of a like ethnic conviction.

It was a wary city. Everybody expected something big to happen. Probably sometime soon.

The Call's adventure hadn't been quite the disaster the boys at The Pipes imagined. The world was waiting for the other shoe to fall. When Marengo figured that out . . .

I was alert, yet not paying close attention. If you can figure that. I ran everything through my head again, trying to find a thread of sense to pick at. But it wouldn't hang together in one big, stinky lump no matter how much I twisted and shoehorned and ignored the usual rules. I could only get it going if I assumed two or more things were going on at the same time. But something down inside me wanted it to be just one big thing that I wasn't seeing right.

"You're the common factor," Tinnie said.

"Huh?" I looked around. We were approaching the Tate compound.

"You were muttering. Doing pretty good, too. You might have a future as a street character. You've already got the wardrobe."

The Goddamn Parrot released a startled blat more like crow slang than the king's parrotese. He flung himself into the air and flapped away. I barked, "What the hell?" Couldn't be my luck turning good.

Tinnie asked, "How did you wake him up?"

"I don't know." But I had a suspicion what was behind his excitement. What's big and sits in the dark and doesn't breathe a lot? "I'm a common thread but I came in after the fact." The Goddamn Parrot disappeared between buildings. "The way my luck runs nothing will get him."

"You going to come inside?" Tinnie asked. She grinned. She knew I didn't want to deal with Uncle Willard.

"I have to get back into that library." We crossed the street. I noted that most people moved around in large groups and that more weapons than usual were in evidence, some of them quite illegal.

"Can't stay away from Tama Montezuma's bony butt, eh?"

"Has she got a bony behind? I never noticed. I see no one else but you." I damaged my case by noticing a devastating set of twins exiting the Tate retail outlet.

"When you stop shaking and get your heels off your tongue you might try for something a little more convincing."

"Damn." Right behind the twins, chattering at them, came Tinnie's cousin Rose. Rose is a brunette as gorgeous as her cousin but she's got snakes and spiders for brains. Her face lit up like a bonfire when she saw me. "Here comes trouble," I said.

"She's not bad if you understand her," Tinnie said. "She'll try to make something out of me being with you but Uncle Willard will say, 'So what?' and she'll go off and have a good pout." She planted a long, unsisterly kiss on me. "Be careful. Come see me. And stay away from strange women."

"Make up your mind." I kissed her back. Rose was scandalized and excited. "I won't be gone long." I hoped circumstance wouldn't make a liar of me. It did have a habit of doing so.

86

I moved carefully homeward. I hadn't spotted a tail since we left that woods, but I was getting used to the idea that I could be followed without being able to catch somebody doing it. I didn't like it, though.

I was more concerned about the new malice in the streets. Trouble has a way of finding people who look like they're vulnerable.

I spent a little concern on the Goddamn Parrot, too, but because I had no control over that situation I did not let it interfere with business.

Approaching the house cautiously is ancient habit. It felt justified today, though I saw nothing indicating trouble—unless the absence of Mrs. Cardonlos constituted a harbinger. Nor did I note any damage to the house itself. Clearly, the bad boys had not yet worked up the nerve to give it a try.

I let myself inside—and froze before I shut the door all the way. Something was wrong. I smelled an odor that didn't belong.

Somebody had been inside. Somebody who wore lilac water to disguise the fact that he found bathing an unhapppy chore. Maybe Saucerhead? Tharpe wasn't a stickler when it came to personal hygiene. Or maybe Winger?

Not Winger. Nothing was disturbed. Winger couldn't keep her hands off stuff.

I moved along the hall slowly, avoiding the creaky boards. I don't know what cues there were, other than odor, but I knew I wasn't alone. Which meant somebody had gotten past the wonderfully expensive lock that Dean had had installed.

I told him that damned thing was a waste of money.

I slipped sideways, not into my office but into the Dead Man's room. Amongst the memorabilia were tools useful for removing uninvited guests. I returned to the hallway prepared to repel boarders. I had everything but my eye patch and my parrot.

A mountain of blubber wobbled out of the kitchen, a platter in each hand. "Puddle!" I barked.

"Hey! Garrett! I was just havin' a snack while I was waitin'. How the hell did ya get in wit' out me hearin'?"

"How the hell did you get into my house? And why? To swipe my food?"

"I come in tru' da door. Ya got to get ya a better lock, Garrett. Dem Hameways ain't shit, ya know what ye're doin'. Ya get out an get yaself a Piggleton combernation with da t'ree tumblers . . ." As he nattered Puddle eased into my office. It was obvious that he'd made himself at home there and that he'd been around for a while. And that he was used to having busboys there to pick up after him. He plopped the platters onto my desk, atop the abandoned battlefields of previous snacks. My personal chair groaned as his ample behind settled.

"Make yourself at home, Puddle."

"T'anks."

"To what do I owe the honor?" I wondered where the food had come from. Puddle definitely wasn't thoughtful enough to have brought his own supplies. Dean must have taken pity. Obviously, I couldn't take care of myself. Well, the whole move-out thing was just for show. For the benefit of my new political pals. I hoped.

"Boss wants ya, Garrett. Sent people out wherever ya might turn up."

"What's the story?" I snagged a chicken drumstick I knew hadn't been in the house last time I was home. I supposed I could hunt up

Mrs. Cardonlos and sweet-talk her into telling me what I'd been missing.

Was that a gang of pigs oinking as they fluttered around my chimney?

"Boss'll tell ya all about it." Puddle had his mouth full. Maybe it was him making the porker noises.

"Give me a few minutes, then we'll do it." I headed upstairs. There's a linen closet in the second-floor hall that has no linens in it. I spent a few minutes filling my sleeves and pockets and shoe-tops with assorted instruments of mayhem. I should think about buying a couple of eggs from Venable when I got back to The Pipes. I could hatch them and keep pets around the place if the Dead Man decided not to come back. If I kept them a little hungry, even wizards off the Hill would have trouble sneaking in.

When I got back downstairs Puddle was digging around in the kitchen again. He had no shame. "I don't get much a dis tasty stuff 'round Da Palms."

"You could've picked a boss with fewer quirks."

Puddle grunted. "Ya ready ta go?" He shoved a couple of pieces of chicken into his pockets.

"Not quite." I needed to get outside some food myself. It had been a long time since breakfast.

87

Sometimes I've got an edge like a brick. We must've traveled half a mile before I realized, "Hey! We're not headed for The Palms."

"An' I tole da boss ya'd never notice. Dey's people followin' ya, ya know? An' dey's maybe not all da kind what ya want to know ya got da boss for a fren'."

"There's times I wonder about that myself," I grumbled, having noticed a green and red and yellow and blue ringer amongst the nearest gang of eaves-perching pigeons. A puff of cooler wind raced down the street, which seemed unnaturally calm for late afternoon in a city mad for bickering. Autumn would be along soon. Maybe, if I got lucky, the Goddamn Parrot would have a little goose in him and would head north for the winter.

I suspected we were headed for Playmate's stables, though, as a gods-fearing, righteous man Playmate doesn't have much use for Morley. Any tail who knew much about me probably developed the suspicion before I did. I wasn't concentrating. I had found a thread to worry.

We rounded a corner, turning left. Puddle was street side of me. Two steps later he leaned into me. Hard. I staggered through an open doorway. Before I could growl Puddle started pushing. I just glimpsed an old woman squinting at something she was sewing and a homely youngster probably of the female calling who shut the door behind the fat man. Then we reached the end of the narrow, almost barren tailor shop. I looked down steep steps. A light burned a long way below. "Go," Puddle urged.

I went.

A door closed behind us. It hung crookedly. The stairs had no business surviving our combined weight. Puddle picked up the light off the earthen cellar floor once we got down. It consisted of a cracked teacup half-filled with oil. The wick was a floating glob of lint. Puddle could carry the damned thing. It looked hot. And he knew where we were headed.

"Morley really this concerned?"

"Bad tings goin' on out dere, Garrett. It don't hurt none ta be careful."

Everybody in town was more paranoid than me. Maybe I should get a little crazy myself. "It'll all work out. History's drama has got a way of doing that." But it sure can get rough on the cast and crew.

"Ya ever go ta da plays? Dey's a great new one at da Strand, I been ta see it t'ree times already. Called *Atterbohns da Toid* on account of it's about King Atterbohns, one a da ones from way back."

I was surprised. The Strand doesn't put on the kind of show I'd associate with a mind like Puddle's. Hardly anybody would take their clothes off.

The more excited he grew the denser his speech became. "Dat's da Atterbohns what murdered his brodder and married his sister an' had a baby by her dat grew up ta help his gran'ma raise dis army aginst his fodder . . ." He whooped off and gave me every detail, half of which were historically inaccurate. Not having seen the drama myself I couldn't tell if the fault was his or the playwright's. The historical Atterbohns married his brother's widow, his sister-in-law, a perfectly respectable thing for the time, though murder was a bit of a gaffe. Less respectable was the fact that the sister-in-law orchestrated everything, including numerous other murders and the revolt of the son—who perished, along with his grand-mother, in questionable circumstances later, to be followed to the throne by a six-year-old brother whose paternity was somewhat dubious.

A play about Atterbohns III would have to be one of the new tragedies. Its moral would be too dark and heavy for a passion play or traditional comedy. "I might go see it just to see how much license the playwright took with history. Who wrote it?"

"I dunno. We get ta da end a dis tunnel, ya gotta be quiet. It runs inta anudder one dat ain't ours. We don't wanna attrack no attention."

TunFaire has a million secrets. They probably extend two miles down into the earth and two up into the air. Were there enough overlapping tunnels for me to sneak all the way downtown to the brewery caverns? That sent me into a tumult of speculation. If all the tunnels and caverns under TunFaire *were* connected, control of them would be a major asset.

There were rumors and legends about people and things suppos-edly living underground. One beaut involved a king of the rat-people who was a sort of cross between a high priest and Chodo Contague, a ratman wish-fantasy, something a Reliance would be if he had a whole lot of brains and guts and luck.

Surprisingly, none of the legends featured dwarves.

Puddle made a right turn when the tunnel ended. I stayed quiet, as instructed. Eventually we found a stairway from the same litter as the one leading down from the seamstress's shop. A door stood ajar at the top. A gray light outlined it. I let Puddle get all the way up before I risked the steps myself. Having survived him I knew they would support me.

I stepped into the entry foyer of a tenement that decades ago had entertained middle-class pretensions. Not a soul was around. The place even lacked the usual squallings of infants, yellings of hus-bands and fathers, shriekings of wives and mothers, whimpers of despair that characterize such places. But you could almost feel the tenants holding their breaths behind their curtained doorways. The cellar door standing ajar must be an omen of dreadful portent.

Puddle was puffing so hard I thought he'd collapse. He wasted no energy. He used his gasps to extinguish the light, which he left on the step behind the cellar door. He closed that.

We hit the street. Five blocks later we joined Morley in a dwarfish hole-in-the-wall. None of the hairy folk seemed to mind his elven blood.

"What was that all about?" I asked. "Other than the obvious."

"The people following you have a supernatural knack for keeping track. It wanted to test its limits."

"That's all?"

"There's more. In back." He nodded. I preceded him past a dwarfish staff who saw nothing. We were ghosts.

The quest for profit makes for strange bedfellows.

88

Spooky people were waiting in a back room. Belinda Contague and Pular Singe sat beside a crippled table with rags piled on top. "What's this?"

Morley let me have it behind the ear with a sap.

I said, "Wha de grungle frunz ya? . . ." It made perfect sense to me but apparently not to anyone else. At least nobody tried to answer me.

The darkness never really came. Not entirely. I remained vaguely aware of being manhandled and womanhandled and rathandled and half-elf handled around till I was the vain wearer of a tonsorial array fit to embarrass most guys who haunt alleys for a living. Puddle stuffed everything in a bag—including my proud tools of mayhem—and vanished. Morley and Belinda tied me to the rickety chair formerly occupied by Pular Singe. Singe said something apologetic and drifted off after Puddle.

The scow of consciousness pitched and rolled across heavy seas. The thump had reawakened every headache I'd enjoyed lately. I talked some more but only a drunk would have understood. Or maybe Singe. I'd understood her.

Morley said something about if I was the real thing, he'd treat me to the gourmet best of The Palms. I could not express my joy.

Belinda's apologies sounded more promising.

The two of them rubbed me all over with silver.

A dwarfish voice gobbled something. Morley responded in the same tongue. Belinda began letting me loose. I tried to turn her over my knee but had barely strength enough to raise a hand. I said something in a tongue that sounded sufficiently dwarfish to me but drew no response from anyone else.

I understood Belinda when she said, "You hit him too hard."

"I hit him just right. Too hard and he wouldn't be breathing."

"I think you scrambled his brains."

"Be a little hard to mix them up more than they already are. He'll come out of it."

Bless him for his optimism. I would take it into account when I got even for all his abuses.

"Sorry," he told me, not sounding the least bit contrite. "We had to make sure Puddle got the real you. Been several Garrett sightings lately and I'm sure that, talented as you are, you're not yet able to be two places at once."

"I'm gonna work on it, though," I promised. "I'm gonna be having dinner with Relway and Colonel Block while I'm stuffing that talking vulture down your throat. Sideways."

Some of that dribbled out in comprehensible Karentine. Morley seemed surprised by my attitude. But he didn't let it get in his way. "Something that looked like you turned up at The Palms last night asking for Belinda."

I glanced at Belinda. She was still hanging out there? "Not what you think, Garrett," she said. "Crask and Sadler did such a good job I can still barely move."

Morley continued, "We knew it wasn't you right away."

"Uhn?" So a shapeshifter went there pretending to be me. If there was an easy way to recognize one, I wanted to know. Later. After my head stopped hurting.

"Sarge offered you a mixed pepper platter. One of his little jokes. But you took it and dug right in."

"Now I know they're completely stupid." Even a hog has more sense than to eat peppers. Morley's pepper platter is a gorgeous mix of colors and shapes. Kind of like parrot on a plate. Just the stench, though, would've had me gagging—if I'd been into self-abuse far enough to let Sarge shove something that nasty under my nose in the first place. "What did you do with it?" In a few hours one of those critters could destroy a reputation I've worked on for years.

"We caught him but he got away as soon as we turned our backs. Those things don't have bones, apparently. It got out through a crack barely big enough for a cat."

My brain was up to about half speed. And I had a cup in hand, brought by the dwarf, which smelled strongly of boiled willow bark.

I'd only have to suffer the headache another hour, then make sure I never ranged too far from a chamber pot. "Let me see. It was after Belinda. With harm in mind?"

"We took more hardware off it than we did off you just now."

"Stranger and stranger. We have shapeshifters attacking the Weiders. We have them attacking The Call. We have them going after Belinda. . . ." I stopped. My mouth hung open. A small but significant fact had caught up. "Belinda. You've been at Morley's place since we dug you out of that tomb?"

"Mostly sleeping."

"But you've been in touch with your people."

"As much as necessary."

"How about with Marengo North English?"

"North English? Why would I? . . ."

I raised a paw. "Wait." I let the brain limp along for a minute. "The Call tried to bring on their season of Cleansing last night."

"It fizzled," Morley said. He showed lots of pointy teeth in a wicked grin. He wasn't disappointed.

"While the rest of his gang were having a good time bopping heads and busting shop doors Marengo North English was up north on the edge of Elf Town expecting to meet Belinda for a night's indulgence in the labors of love."

"What?" she barked. "How could?. . ."

"He got a message. It told him to meet you up there. He believed it was real." I'd believed it was real when he told me. "Men sometimes surrender to wishful thinking." If I'd thought about her condition, I'd have been suspicious as soon as North English mentioned getting the message. Her family owned tenements in the area. It seemed a handy trysting place if you thought in sneak-around terms. Obviously, Marengo did. "When he got there a gang dressed up as righsists tried to murder him. They got interrupted by a gang of dwarves looking for rightsists to pound."

"A marvelous irony," Morley observed, absolutely straight of face.

"I thought so myself." I managed a feeble smile. The first weak efforts of the tea had begun to make my fingertips tingle and my headache less assertive. "There is a common thread in everything," I said. "However confusing. Shapeshifters. All evidently members of a group of commando mercenaries once known as Black Dragon Valsung."

"What about Crask and Sadler?" Belinda asked. "They aren't shapechangers."

"Maybe I'm not thinking as clearly as I imagined." My headache gave a particularly unpleasant throb. Probably Crask and Sadler wishing me evil from their cell, if they were still healthy enough to entertain wishes. "They were hired by shapeshifters." Just to keep my theory alive.

"Or by a somebody who hired the shifters, too," Morley said, knowing that would put a twist on the evidence that I wouldn't like.

I grunted. "Keep in mind that Glory Mooncalled has got to be shoehorned in here somehow, too. I'm pretty sure." Seeing those centaurs had convinced me. Organized, disciplined, military centaurs always have something to do with Glory Mooncalled. No other commander had ever been able to to hold their attention long enough to sell them on the military virtues. No other captain ever got them to fight for ideas instead of money or plunder.

Pular Singe eased into the room diffidently. I wondered what had become of Fenibro. Maybe she'd decided she could get along without the boyfriend. I had yet to see her affliction handicap her very much. "The watchers have followed the parcel of clothing." She spoke slowly and carefully. Her diction was the equal of Fenibro's. She was proud of herself. "I will have no trouble tracking any but one. One leaves no trail at all."

I frowned at Morley. He shrugged. Belinda said, "It shouldn't take them long to figure out that Puddle doesn't have Garrett's bones in that sack."

"Point taken. Can you walk, Garrett?"

"In circles."

Pular Singe said, "The one who leaves no trail is like the one who pretended to be . . ." She pointed at me. "That one had no scent, either."

Interesting. Could that be a way to detect changers? Add a ratman to your bodyguard?

89

"Who had a chance to plant something on you?" Morley asked. We were headed toward Playmate's for real. Dotes was the only one of us walking normally. At a glance we must have looked like beggars. I was dressed the part.

The clothes I'd been wearing lately all came from the Weider place. All Tad's stuff. Could have been anyone there though the list of suspects that occurred to me was very short. And it had to be somebody at the Weider mansion. Nowhere else had anyone had a chance to get to all the clothes. And only a few people there had known I was getting them.

The actual mechanics did not interest me much. Somewhere in each pair of trousers, perhaps, would be a scrap of paper or a loose button with a spell attached. I could round up a dozen half-baked hedge wizards in an hour who would sell me something similar for enough to buy a bottle of wine. There would be some gimmick like an enchanted tuning fork or a feather floating in a bowl of mineral oil that would point at me all the time.

"It's starting to come together," I said. "I don't know who or why but I'm beginning to sniff out a how."

"Well?" Morley asked after I failed to go on.

I turned to Pular Singe. "Singe. The parade following me . . . following Puddle and my stuff. Was the shapeshifter the one who was actually on my trail, with everyone else following him?"

Singe had to think about it. Although she was intensely interested, she hadn't been included in on everything so wasn't sure what mattered. Also, some of what she had was human stuff that made little sense to ratfolk, anyway.

"The one who had no scent. Yes."

Morley asked, "What's that look mean, Garrett?"

"It means the haze is clearing. The clothes were marked so I could be tracked and watched. By shapeshifters. The clothes were delivered straight from the Weider place. Before the engagement party. But there were no shapeshifters inside the house before the party preparations began. Belinda. You promise me you didn't have anything to do with the attack on Marengo North English?"

"I promise, darling. Cross my heart and hope to die. Though I would've done it if it needed doing."

"Does that extend to all his crackpot pals? The human rights movement lost several big names."

"I'd reached an understanding with those people. They would stay off our turf. They hadn't had time to violate it. I'm sure they would've gotten around to it, though."

"Not even using Crask and Sadler?"

"I'm not as hotheaded as you think, Garrett. I considered that. I decided that the Marengo I met thought too much of himself and his prejudices to have hired those two. He'd use his own people. I suspect that argument holds for other rightsists chieftains as well. First try, at least."

I recalled Tama telling me they were having trouble finding a librarian because Marengo and the other big fish were reluctant to pay actual wages. I muttered, "That fits."

"What does?"

"Singe. How would you go about tracking the one who leaves no scent?" I added deaf sign so we were sure to meet on a common border between our languages.

Pular Singe was a serious young woman, determined to get the most out of the abilities she had. She would go far if she remained motivated. Desire and determination do seem as important as raw talent in this world. She thought hard. "I would track those who follow it. The sight-hunters. If they do not give up that when they discover that you have outwitted it."

I hadn't outwitted anybody but myself lately. Didn't seem to be much point in reminding Singe, though.

Morley and Belinda both sneered at me when Singe was looking the other way. Friends always have to get those little digs in, just to let you know they love you. The evidence suggests that the whole world loves me.

"No point me hiding out at Playmate's," I said. "If they've done any digging into my background, they'll know we're friends. I'll go to the Weider place." I'd abandoned hope of getting back to The Pipes. It was getting dark. "Singe . . . Where'd she go?"

"Off to tail your tail, probably," Morley said.

"She's infatuated, Garrett," Belinda chided. "It happens to a lot of women when they first meet you. This one's still at that stage where she'll do any damn fool thing to make you like her back. Give her a week. Reality will catch up."

They both had a good snicker. So did something on a windowsill two stories overhead. Morley failed to catch the flash of green and yellow and blue and red as the little buzzard took off, but I did. Possibly I was supposed to, now that it knew where I could be found later.

90

"Pardon the expression but you look like shit on a stick," Max told me. "I've seen better-dressed bums. What happened to the clothes we gave you?"

Gilbey said, "That's what he's come about." Manvil was a little cool.

"I didn't turn up here sometime in the last twenty hours and do something unpleasant, did I?"

"No. Why?" Gilbey was just tired.

"There was a copy of me running around trying to do naughty things. And you seem a little standoffish."

"Excuse me. Unintentional. Possibly it's because you haven't gotten anywhere. Or because bad things happen when you're around."

I took it like a man. It was true. "I think that's about to change. It's coming together. What I want to know right now is who handled the clothing you sent me. Because somebody tagged them all with a tracking spell that let the shapeshifters stick to me wherever I went." Too bad I couldn't be two places at once. That would be a really useful skill in my racket.

"Genord," Max said. "Gerris Genord handled the clothing." And as soon as he said that I recalled Genord being mentioned at the time. The evidence was there. Maybe I'd gotten bopped on the noggin a time too many. Maybe I ought to stick to working for the brewery.

The news relieved me some. I hadn't wanted to suspect Gilbey. I liked the guy. "Maybe a connection with the shifters is why Genord overreacted when Lance and Ty caught him sneaking in. Maybe there really was somebody at the door, somebody he didn't want to be seen with . . . *How* would he be connected with them? We know *he* wasn't a shifter."

I'd already recognized one commonality between Genord and Black Dragon. The commando connection. Whether or not he seemed the type Genord had had an armband that was worn by a small freecorps made up of former commandos. Once the fair-haired thugs of The Call, the Brotherhood Of The Wolf had fallen out of favor since Colonel Theverly's arrival. But I was willing to bet they were still in business, still associated with Marengo North English. And a shapeshifter had been flushed at The Pipes. "Uhm?"

Gilbey repeated, "I said, 'Why not ask Genord?' The Guard do have him in custody, don't they?"

I couldn't imagine why they wouldn't. But I didn't feel like walking back up to the Al-Khar. I'd put too many miles on me already today. "Can my friends and I get space to rest for a while?" The willow-bark tea was wearing off. I hurt. And I needed a nap.

"Find them a place, Manvil," Weider said. His tone suggested he'd begun to grow disappointed in me, too. I didn't blame him. I was disappointed in me myself.

Carefully failing to alert the staff to our presence Gilbey installed all three of us in a guest room probably reserved for visiting tradesmen. Belinda he failed to recognize. Morley he knew only by distasteful type. He remained rigorously polite throughout.

Gentlemen that we are, Morley and I let Belinda have the one narrow bed. I took the bedclothes to make a pallet for me. Dotes wasn't in a napping mood. He kept muttering about how trying to do a small favor had become a career. I asked, "You want to make yourself useful while I'm snoring, work this out. What could you do with a brewery? Besides make beer?"

"Why?"

"That's where this mess started. The shapeshifters wanted to replace the Weiders. Which makes sense only if they wanted control of the brewery." I snuggled down and went to sleep. The floor was softer than the most yielding cobblestone.

A toe ground into my ribs. I didn't have to open my eyes to know it belonged to Belinda. Only a woman would use a toe like a forefinger. A man would just kick you.

I grunted.

"That's four hours, Garrett. Dotes and I don't have a life to devote to your snoring, entertaining as it is. If I'm out of touch much longer I'm going to find myself out of touch permanently."

I sat up, groggy and disoriented. But I remembered, "I wanted up sooner than this."

"You needed the sleep," Morley said. "You really ought to go home and stay till you're completely recovered. You look a little ragged."

Maybe I did. People kept mentioning it.

I pulled myself together. Belinda looked ragged, too. I felt a twinge of guilt. She needed rest worse than I did. But here she was chasing wild geese with me. "There something going on that you guys forgot to mention?"

Morley looked at me askance. Belinda ignored me. Mostly.

"I appreciate you ambushing me and getting me loose from whoever was following me." I rubbed the back of my head. "I think. But I don't see why you bothered."

Morley shrugged. Belinda, without looking me in the eye, said, "The ratgirl insisted. She was scared those people might do something bad to you."

I smelled a scheme. Some kind of three-cornered deal between the Outfit, Reliance, and Morley Dotes, that would put me right in the middle. I hoped their little hearts weren't broken when I wouldn't go along.

Morley sneered. "I don't know how you do it, Garrett. That Singe would gleefully follow you into Hell. And be your love slave besides."

Sourly, putting herself together for travel, Belinda said, "And that blond bimbo walked right in here a while ago. She was really put out because you weren't alone."

"Alyx? Alyx is just a spoiled kid."

Morley grinned at me and flashed me his own version of the raised eyebrow trick.

"Maybe," Belinda begrudged. "She did come back with some food."

"And we didn't even eat it all," Morley said. "Your share is in that sack over there."

We saw no one as we left the house. The place was a mausoleum infected by despair. Maybe that spread from Tom's room. I felt a sudden fear that more evil might be headed the family's way. "This would be a good time for the shifters to come back." Unless Block's troops were on the job and alert.

91

The city was darker than usual, the night people fewer than normal. We drew unfriendly looks but never a challenge. I did see evidence that some fainthearts, especially among the refugees, were getting ready to move on. The Call's botched Cleansing had had an impact.

I didn't need to talk to anybody to sense the tension. TunFaire's population is half nonhuman, most of whom operate nocturnally. But numbers won't mean much if we humans gang up. Most of the other races don't get along with each other any better than they do with humans. For some, like dwarves and elves, the enmity goes back millennia.

I said, "The Call didn't splatter a lot of blood around but they won anyway. You can smell the fear."

"That's true. But what you don't see is the people who aren't running."

Morley probably knew something he couldn't share with me. Though he wouldn't be involved directly in anything, of course. Neutrality was a commodity he'd marketed most of his life.

Belinda said, "If Marengo has half the brains I think he's hiding, he won't do anything for a while. Allegruan and Dryzkaksghul Gnarrisson and the others really sucked up their pride to hold it together long enough to face the Cleansing." Allegruan and Gnarrisson were what you might call the urban elven and dwarfish war chieftains. "That'll all fall apart now if The Call gives them time to remember old feuds."

"You're right," Morley said. "There's talk about that already. One of Allegruan's brothers got into a shouting match with Dryzkaksghul's uncle *during* the rioting because Gnarrisson's great-grandmother was a sister of the Burli Burlisson who ambushed the elves in Zhenda Canyon when they were headed home after attacking the dwarf caves in Wrightwight Mountain."

"Nerve of them, hitting back like that." I didn't know the incident. The history of the Karentine kingdom and its imperial predecessor is more than I can encompass and there's not nearly so many centuries of that. Nor does it carry such a burden of treachery and betrayal. Among fundamentalist, rustic-type elves, treachery and betrayal are high art forms.

"The brother's point exactly. If nothing else Burli and all his get forever are guilty of boorish manners."

I guess history sometimes is one of those you-had-to-be-there things. "I've always treasured your ability to see the absurd, Morley."

"It's only absurd by modern Karentine standards, Garrett. By those of the time, dwarfish and elvish alike, Burli showed very bad form. He didn't even take prisoners. He killed all the raiders and cut off their heads and set those up on stakes outside the entrance to the forest Thromdredril, supposedly all because he spent a few years in old-time TunFaire and contracted human insanity. And this is where we part ways. Enjoy the Al-Khar."

He and Belinda scooted, deaf to my questions.

92

"Don't do it!" I barked as somebody wound up to bop me from behind, right after I asked to see Colonel Block. "It's the real me. Rub me all over with silver. Make me walk around with a crown under my tongue. Just don't hit me on the head anymore."

In seconds I was surrounded. Relway's was the only face I recognized till Block wandered in. He took me at my word. His troops held me down while a guy with a silver dagger tested me for a tendency toward morphism.

Nobody apologized. Block said, "You've turned up here once already today. But the first time you weren't you."

"No shit. But how'd you know?"

"We knew you were out at North English's manor. I can picture you being guilty of a lot but not of screwing up in two places at the same time."

Relway demanded, "You learn anything?"

"I had a long, private talk with North English this morning. I could tell you word for word but I don't think you'd learn anything you don't already know. That bunch aren't as secret as they pretend." I told Relway everything anyway, almost, figuring that would save time. Then I asked Block, "What was this other me up to?"

"Tried to get the duty jailer to release Crask and Sadler in his custody. He sold his cockamamie story, too. We'd have lost them if they'd been able to travel. But the jailer came to me to try to arrange transportation. I understood you were out of town. I went down to check it out personally. The shifter knew trouble when he saw it coming. He took off before we could close in on him."

"So the bad boys are still here?"

"We have a full house. But there's pressure from the Hill to release everybody being held for being public pains in the ass yesterday night."

"What about Gerris Genord? Gotten anything out of him yet? I just turned up evidence that he might be tied in with the shapeshifters." Or to somebody in between, which is more the way I thought it would be. I didn't think Genord deliberately hurt the Weiders. I suspected he hadn't been knowingly involved in the infiltration of the shapeshifters. I thought he was a pawn moved so that bad things happened around him. His belated recognition of that fact might have caused the irrational state he was in the night Ty and Lance caught him sneaking around.

Relway said, "We haven't talked to him yet. There hasn't been time. Too much excitement to cover outside."

Though, I noted, he did have the resources to keep track of me. "Can I talk to him?"

"I'll collect a team and we'll visit him together."

"I don't want to pull his toes off. I just want to ask a few questions."

"He'll be more eager to answer if I'm behind you with a bunch of rusty tools. I'll keep quiet."

Relway, being Relway. He would be as interested in watching me ask as he would be interested in hearing Genord answer.

That wouldn't cost me. "Let's do it."

Genord was asleep when we got there but he woke up fast. He looked around wildly. He was confined in a cell every bit as evil as imagination could make one. The only positive was that he didn't have to share. Elsewhere captured rioters were piled in on top of one another.

"Comfy down here?" I asked. "I stopped in to see if they're taking good care of you." There'd been a change in Genord and it wasn't what you'd expect of a guy who found himself buried in the Al-Khar. He'd hardened. His eyes had gone cold. He looked like a commando after all. He *was* a shapeshifter but only inside his head.

He didn't respond.

"I've had a thought," I told Relway. "About the changers and our friend here. You think they know we've got him?"

"They do now. If they didn't before. The one who pretended to be you saw him when he came down to visit Crask and Sadler."

"Meaning if Genord does know anything, they'll want to get him out or shut him up."

Relway and Genord both thought they saw the direction I was headed. I took a quick turn on them. "Suppose we cut him loose? What will they figure happened?"

"That he ratted them out," Block replied. "I like it. Turning him out would solve a problem for me, too. It'd free up a cell that wouldn't have to be a single anymore. And if we do hang on to him and his own buddies get in to cut his throat, we're spared having to feed him till a judge lets us hang him."

Relway stage-whispered, "We got a budget. We don't got to account for what we don't use."

That was bullshit. I'd heard a little about the Guard's finances from Block.

I told Genord, "Brotherhood Of The Wolf is made up of elite-forces types. These shapeshifters operated as Black Dragon Valsung in the Cantard. A mercenary commando group. Is there a connection from the war?" Then I floated the suspicion I'd had for some time. "Is there a connection to Glory Mooncalled?"

Not that Genord knew of. That notion startled him momentarily. Then he nodded. "Yeah. Mooncalled's behind everything."

"He's lying," Relway said.

"He thinks he's lying. Thought he was when he said that. He's already wondering, though." You could almost hear Genord pondering the question of whether or not he'd been duped.

He chose silence as the safest route. He hadn't been in charge. He had to have faith that his superiors knew what they were doing. That they would come to his rescue.

Commandos are like Marines that way. They don't leave their own behind.

I mentioned that to Block. He growled, "We're prepared!" like how stupid did I think he was.

I might not have gotten names or a bloody knife but I was now satisfied that there was a connection between Genord's bunch and the shifters. I needed to go back to The Pipes to find out more.

I said, "Hang on to him for a while yet, just so I can get a head start and drop his name a few places. Then go ahead and kick him out." Ty was a vindictive sort. He would find this kind of vengeance particularly satisfying. Provided, of course, Genord couldn't talk his way out of the deep shit.

He hadn't shown much talent for that yet.

Block left a man with Genord in the unlikely event Gerris opened his heart. We were headed for the relative sanity of Block's quarters.

Relway had disappeared. Block asked, "You need to check on Crask and Sadler?"

"I don't think so. Long as they're locked up tight I'm happy. They shown any signs of recovering?"

"Unfortunately."

"You be careful with them. And don't forget there's people outside who're worried about them."

"I have some ideas about those two. Assuming somebody really does want them out. Or dead." He gave out a mock-evil laugh.

I suggested, "You're gonna use them as bait in some stunt, don't forget brother Genord." Like he needed reminding again, already.

"He's already moved, I expect." Block played with the evil laughter again. "We're going to get them, Garrett."

"I don't doubt it. I just hope I have some friends alive when it happens."

"They get to Hell before you, they can have the place all fixed up. A keg in every room. Platoons of panting females."

"That's your idea of Hell?"

"Oh. You won't get to touch."

"I don't get to do that now."

Block made like a man playing a funeral flute. "I've heard about your bad fortune."

"My reputation is entirely the product of Mrs. Cardonlos' imagination."

The name seemed to startle Block. He asked, "What's your next step?"

"Back to North English's manor. I'm almost convinced that he isn't behind any of this. Though clever actors have fooled me before. Do you think he's a born-again believer in The Call's mission?"

"I try not to judge the sincerity of his type. Nor that of people off the Hill. I keep an eye on what they actually do."

"You said there was pressure from up there. . . ."

"It'll slack off."

"Thought a lot of Hill types support The Call."

"Only if it's successful. They don't want to be caught out dangling in the wind if North English's gang goes batshit and fucks up completely."

It was getting on toward the hour of the wolf, the coldest, cruelest time of night, when despair rises up and gnaws the bones of even the strong. And also the hour when the worst trolls and ogres are out. When it's plain common sense for a lone human investigator with too many enemies not to be wandering around alone. "You got a cell I can borrow for a couple hours? Just till the sun comes up?" I would nap my way into whichever future successfully conquered the city.

"There's probably one around here with your name on it, reserved. But for now you can use the cot in mine. I won't bother you. I'm up, I might as well work. Maybe interview a few of our clients." Block understood the hour of the wolf, too. There was no better time to question somebody who was chained up in a mass of filthy straw, shivering in the cold, desperately outnumbered by the rats and lice.

"Thanks. Get somebody to waken me at the crack of dawn." Before he could cut me down with a wisecrack, I said, "I ought to see the damned sun come up once before I die."

I found the cot and stretched out. Wow! Two naps in the same night. This was pure luxury. And there wasn't one damned talking bird within miles.

93

The somebody who wakened me wasn't one of Block's regularly sanctioned gangsters. The somebody was Pular Singe. I almost whooped as I popped up, startled. "How the hell did you get in here?"

I scared her. I had to calm her down before I could get any sense out of her. She lisped much worse when she was frightened and her hearing went north. In time I learned that she'd just walked into the Al-Khar, following my scent. There'd been nobody on guard. She hadn't thought anything of that.

"Did you see any bodies?"

"No."

"Damn! I hope that means they were ready for an invasion and just ran away." Because that was what a lack of guards meant. Somebody unfriendly had gotten inside but hadn't found anybody to kill. Not right away. I suffered no overwhelming impulse to find out if Block and Relway were all right, though, "Why are you here?" I had myself together now. I started easing her toward the nearest street door. Seemed a stroke of strategic genius to get ourselves far away from whatever big trouble was afoot.

"Reliance sent trackers after everyone following you, Garrett. He believed they would run to their masters as soon as they knew you had shaken the one with no scent. I teamed with two others to follow that thing. It can be done. I learned."

We were at the door. I thought I heard Block's fake evil laughter from deep inside the jail. "How'd you manage that?"

"By sight. This creature is not smart. It does not look back. It does not see those who are not people. That is why others were able to follow it. Even Fenibro is smart enough to look back sometimes. We took turns being closest. It is easy to track one another."

"Hmm." The ratpeople were working real hard to put me in their debt. I had a bad feeling about that. People who do that sort of thing always want something back. Usually something that involves me having to work.

There was enough light out to see. A modest fog had come in off the river. I understand that happens frequently but I'm seldom up early enough to see it.

For some early is late. Singe was uncomfortable being out after daybreak but she stuck with me, valiantly trying to communicate everything Reliance's people had found out about my personal road show. I must say, I appreciated the unflagging interest of all the friends I'd made recently. Even though they were watching one another as much as making sure that they knew every little thing I found interesting.

Only Max Weider wasn't watching me. But Relway was doing Max's share as well as his own. *He* had a whole crew on my backtrail.

Where did he find them all?

That fact that he could round up that many people fanatically devoted to law and order was as scary as the fact that our Marengo North Englishes and Bondurant Altoonas could find all the friends they wanted.

Human folks were flooding the streets now, starting their day. Many were the sort who worshipped Marengo. They did not like what they saw when Singe and I strolled by.

It constituted a little lesson on what it means to be a ratman.

Singe's courage was not up to a prolonged test.

Mine wasn't much less feeble.

Singe told me, "I cannot remain with you."

"I understand. Before you go, though, tell me, did your people track the scentless one to others like it?"

"It went to a place where others of its kind waited."

"Ah! And where might that have been? How many of them were there?"

"Three and the one we followed. We did not understand the language they spoke. Nor could I get very close. They were alert. They were very troubled."

"You did get close enough to listen?"

Singe made a dramatic effort to respond with a nod. "We are often closer than you think."

I hugged her with one arm. She barely came up to my brisket. Somehow, she seemed bigger when we were just walking, talking. "You are the bravest child I've ever met."

Did you know rats purr? I'd heard cats and raccoons do it, but never. . . . Singe did.

I tried to be stern. "You can't take risks like that. These creatures are extremely dangerous. They think nothing of murder. I'd hate myself if you got hurt."

Singe's purr grew louder. I could hear Morley and Belinda mocking me now. I cautioned myself not to let Singe make too much of my praise.

"Where're they hiding?"

She had trouble explaining. Ratpeople don't think in terms of street names and addresses. Not that we have the latter anywhere but on the Hill. Mostly you locate yourself as being so many doors some direction from an outstanding landmark. Like, say, a tavern. Most of those draw their names from signs easily recognized by the illiterate. The Merry Mole. The Gold Seam, for dwarves. The Palms for people overburdened with wealth and self-opinion.

She made me understand. "A lamp, is that it?" She got that across with finger speech when I proved too dense to get it verbally. "Down by the river? There aren't any taverns. . . . The Lamp brewery? That's been closed up and abandoned for twenty . . ."

What a wonderful place to squat. The Lamp brewery was no sprawling monster like the Weider place but in its day it was a leading producer of working-class lager. It went before my time but the old men remember it fondly. I suspect time improves the beer, as it will do. Had the Lamp product been superior, the brewery would still be in business.

"That's interesting, Singe. Very interesting." I'd have to let Relway know. We could give the place a look when I got back from The Pipes.

The shifters had themselves a brewery. But not a functional

brewery. Nor one that could be made functional, probably. Anything of any use whatsoever would've been sold or stolen long ago.

I told Singe, "I owe you." She purred some more. "But I really don't want to be indebted to Reliance. I feel like he's up to no good."

The child wasn't completely smitten. Nor wholely thick-witted. I didn't lead her into any verbal ambush. She didn't volunteer anything.

I chuckled. "You're the best. Look, I have to go out to the country. You go home and rest. You should stop taking risks for that old schemer."

She stopped walking. For a moment she found the courage to look me directly in the eye, which ratpeople are almost constitutionally incapable of doing. Then she extended a paw. I extended my own. She gave me a light, nervous handshake. "Thank you for not being cruel."

"Cruel? What? . . ." Pular Singe vanished into an alley more quietly than one of the creatures from which her race had been wrought.

94

Headed toward the city gate I discovered that I was being tailed again. There were three of them, working as a team. They were good. But they didn't have the advantage of having tagged me with a spell. Somebody had to stay close to see me. Which meant I could see him if I paid attention.

One was a Relway thug I'd seen in the background around the Weider place. So my pals at the Al-Khar did have time and manpower to watch me even when there was excitement going on right inside their own house.

Who were the raiders? If the shifters were all holed up at the Lamp brewery, crying in their beer? Could I assume they were Genord's pals?

Relway or Block would let me know. If the mood took them.

Mine was not a comfortable journey, even with the Guard watching over me. I was without defensive resources again. And I was alone. My passage drew concerned or calculating looks everywhere. Already there was a general assumption that a man alone either had reason to be supremely confident or was a complete fool.

I tried to maintain a confident swagger.

I felt a puff of cool air. I hadn't paid much attention to the weather. Clouds were piled up to the south. We might be in for some thunderstorms. This time of year they usually hold off till late afternoon. If I really hustled, I could get back to town ahead of the showers.

By the time I reached The Pipes the temperature had risen and the clouds had become less impressive. They would grow again when the temperature began to fall.

Hey! I don't recall anybody ever paying much attention to that kind of thing. Well, maybe farmers. But you'd have a hell of a racket going if you could predict the weather. Stormwardens make a hell of a racket out of just creating small spots of weather. . . . But that's a tough way to make a living. The magic is harder on the magician than it is on the world around him.

There was steady traffic on the road but I never worried. I didn't draw attention to myself. I was just one more vagabond drifting. Call uniforms and freecorps armbands were plentiful, suggesting a lot of messages moving between The Pipes and Marengo's satraps inside the city. I expected trouble getting past the gate but Marengo and Mr. Nagit had left word. The gate was well-defended now. Still not strongly enough to whip a troop of centaurs but, probably, enough to discourage that crew from attacking in the first place.

What had become of them? Did Block and Relway mention them to their military contacts? Or Mr. Nagit or Colonel Theverly might have done so. It needed doing. We couldn't have random armed bands roving the countryside.

A youngster who reminded me of me six or seven years ago went to the house with me. "You walked all the way out here?" Like he found that hard to believe.

"You must've been cavalry."

"Yeah."

"Figures."

"What's that mean?"

"Nothing personal. I just don't like horses. Anything interesting happened since yesterday?" Probably better change the subject. Cavalry types are goofy about horses. You can't find an ounce of rational paranoia among ten thousand of them.

"Been a campout. Bigwigs been busy, though. The Old Man got mad once he got over having his feelings hurt."

North English let word of his pecadillo get out? I asked.

"Nah, he ain't bragging. But other people know. Word gets around."

Interesting. Marengo told me he was the only survivor of the ambush. I should've been the only one he told the real story. "Just out of curiosity, what story did you hear?"

His story matched Marengo's.

Interestinger and interestinger.

Why would he want everyone to know? Most of us prefer to conceal our humiliations and screwups. Marengo North English struck me as very much that sort of man. What was the tactical advantage?

Or had he confided in someone who hadn't kept his secret? Or . . . Might one of his attackers have retailed the story?

95

My return must have been portentous for North English. Fifteen minutes after I entered his house I was alone with him in his dimly lighted sanctum. His expression suggested he was unnaturally interested in what I would have to say. Before he could ask me anything I inquired, "Are you aware that every man on the grounds knows what happened the other night? Not the official version but the version you told me?" If the men knew, then Tama must know. Might be a good time to find out if she had formed any opinions.

A darkness stirred behind Marengo's eyes. Perhaps it was veiled anger. He growled, "I didn't tell anyone but you." He watched me intently. I don't know what he expected.

"And I never told a soul," I lied. Then I mused, "You did say that the men who attacked you looked like they belonged to the movement."

North English grunted. He must've thought about that more than he wanted to admit. He must've taken it to heart. The kid who had walked me to the house had told me Marengo was hiding out today, letting no one in to see him but Tama. There were no bodyguards around so maybe he was getting paranoid about everybody.

I told him, "I saw Belinda. She swears she had nothing to do with the attack, nor was she responsible for that invitation. I believe her."

North English's style was becoming plebian. He grunted again, evidently preoccupied with rearranging furniture inside his head. He didn't seem surprised by what I'd just said. Eventually he pulled himself together, and urged, "Tell me what you think."

I offered some ideas that had occurred to me during the walk from town. Marengo continued more attentive than ever before. Somehow he must've come to the conclusion that I was a real person.

"You're convinced there's a connection between Brotherhood Of The Wolf and this Black Dragon gang?"

"There's no absolute proof but the circumstantial evidence looks strong to me."

"And this's something you just came up with on the way out here?"

"Oh, no. The Guard are looking at the possibilities from another angle. There may have been a previous connection during the war. And the shapeshifters may be associated with Glory Mooncalled somehow."

It was obvious that was something Marengo didn't want to hear. "You have a plan?" The North English I wanted to believe in, the one who could contemplate mass extinctions without qualm, seemed about to emerge from behind the mask. Marengo sounded harder and more angry by the minute.

I said, "I have some ideas. There'll be risks. Do you have any men you trust completely? Bearing in mind that the Brotherhood Of The Wolf was practically your bodyguard."

Hard Marengo glared. He didn't like my plan already.

"I can find men on my own. If you prefer." Like he was in whether or not he liked it.

"Talk to me."

I explained. He frowned a lot. He seemed confused by several points, like his memory was a little rocky. He muttered to himself, interrupted himself to ask, "Does this mean you've lost interest in the library?"

"Pretty much." What the hell brought that on? I reviewed briefly, then continued.

Marengo asked, "Will Weider cooperate?"

"I think so." Putting words into the Old Man's mouth.

"I'd guess so, too. He'll want to balance the books. How many men will you want?"

"Say twenty? Enough to put up a fight even if a few aren't trust-worthy."

"Good. Good. When do you want to do it?" He seemed eager to cooperate now.

Marengo North English seemed a different man when he wasn't "on" in front of his followers. No sense of conviction came off him at all.

"As soon as we can. Which would be tomorrow night at the earliest, probably. There's a lot to pull together."

"At this end, too. But I think we need to do it. Find Nagit. Don't tell him anything, just send him to me. I'll talk to him, then send him along with you to run messages. So you don't have to ride out here and back every few hours."

"All right. But I wouldn't be riding, I'd be walking."

As I started toward the door he demanded, "Why the hell don't you get a horse?"

I thought he knew. "I need the exercise." They must've done some research on me. That was common sense.

He smiled wickedly. "That's right." And now I got the feeling he did know all about me. I had the feeling that he was taunting me somehow. Or maybe he was just letting me know that I wasn't inside anything here yet and there was no way I was going to get inside. This was a marriage of convenience only.

North English suggested, "Tell Nagit to dredge you up some decent clothing. It'd be a shame if everything went in the shitter because you got dumped into a vagrants' home."

The shitter? Why would he, suddenly, start using language like that? It didn't fit the superior-race image.

96

I ran into Tama in the hallway outside. She was carrying tea and rolls for two. The tea smelled good. She seemed delighted to see me, yet infinitely suspicious. "Will you stay a little longer this time?" Her voice husked. My spine quivered. My knees jellied. Boy, could she suggest a lot without saying anything.

Her smile broadened. It told me Tinnie wasn't here to save me this time. I gobbled, "I wish I could." She slithered closer. Long, dark fingers spidered up my chest to my hair, my cheek, then drifted down again. The woman was pure devil.

"Some chances come once in a lifetime. Are you done in there?"

"Uhm." I was done. I was crispy around the edges. "I need to find Mr. Nagit." I gulped. Seemed like I needed an awful lot of air suddenly.

"He went out to the stables. Probably trying to stay out of Colonel Theverley's way. They don't get along. Do take advantage of the *tea* while it's hot."

She stepped very close again. That demon hand . . . Marengo North English was one lucky man. She never stopped smiling and never turned off the raw animal attraction. I took a cup and stared and tried to find my lost breath as she went on to serve Marengo.

I don't know what Tinnie meant. Tama's behind didn't look bony at all. In fact . . .

I found Mr. Nagit out back. He couldn't have been more thrilled to see me if I'd been the old boy with the sickle. But he was a gentleman. He was polite. I told him what I thought he needed to know. "He's going to plug the leak? Wonderful. Then the attack did wake him up."

"Do I detect a tremor of distrust of the high command's wisdom?"

Weak smile. "You *are* a detective. Yes. I've had to stand around in the background, keeping my mouth shut, during an ongoing debate about how much it matters if somebody warns the Other Races that we're coming. I thought the boss had yielded to the majority opinion, that it doesn't."

"The boss might be smarter and tougher than people think. He might be sandbagging."

Nagit grunted. "The one thing they're all forgetting, or just don't want to remember, is that Glory Mooncalled is out there somewhere. Nobody wants to listen when I say he's dealt himself into the game."

"I'll listen. Because you're right. I think he's in the game big. I just don't know how. Yet. But you're right. Marengo didn't like that idea at all when I brought it up."

"He's been a little odd since the attack. More so today. Today he's staying locked up in there, not letting anyone in but the Montezuma woman. You'll want a change of clothes before we go. Right?"

"So many people disapprove of my wardrobe, I just have to assume that that might be appropriate. And I wouldn't mind borrowing a few knives and whatnot, so I'll feel more comfortable while I'm roaming around."

"I expect we can find you a nice outfit and a suite of cutlery." There was something sly about the way he said that. "Pick yourself a horse while you're out here."

"Uh . . ."

"I'm giving up my time to help you, Garrett. You'll make a few accommodations for me, too."

What was this? Did everybody in Karenta know I don't get along with horses?

Probably everybody who's already fallen under the sway of those monsters did. They gossiped behind my back. Those strange people who actually like the beasts probably understand what they're saying, somehow.

I grumbled, "Point me toward the old plodders."

"If that's what you want. Personally, I'd rather have something that could get up some speed if we ran into those centaurs."

"What?"

"There's a large band of centaurs in the area. On the move. Just as you told us. The colonel has patrols out looking for them." Mr. Nagit sounded like he begrudged having to say anything positive about Theverly. "The patrols haven't been able to pin them down. They're doing better watching us than we're doing finding them."

I made masculine noises. "As long as we know where they're not."

"Luck won't love you forever, Garrett. Pick a good horse."

Seemed to me luck wanted a trial separation already. "All right. I'll go to the library and wait when I'm done. Don't forget to see the boss."

"I'd like to. I've got troubles enough without having to hold his hand and run his errands."

Dang me. Sounded like there was disillusionment in paradise. "What's going on?"

"Besides the centaurs? I've got another dead man. I've got a missing man. And I've got a man missing a limb. I've got livestock scattered everywhere. I've got berserk thunder lizards staggering around biting everything that moves—including each other. And I've got a self-proclaimed hero-of-the-soldiers colonel who's completely indifferent to all those problems."

I lifted an eyebrow high. That works differently when you show it to a man. "What happened?" In a tone hopefully dripping empathy.

"The shitstorm started last night when Venable's pets went crazy. They spooked the cattle and sheep, went after each other, tore up Venable's other arm when he tried to get them under control, and killed somebody, apparently an outsider, who's torn up too badly to identify. Tollie was missing this morning but the corpse isn't him because the dead man was shorter, fatter, and older than the kid. I say the dead man must be a stranger because none of the other men are missing."

"And Venable's pets only attack strangers."

"Says Venable."

"Even this morning?"

"Even this morning. He claims they had to be poisoned or ensorcelled. Which is a troubling notion, too. And Theverly could care less about that, either. I'm not a man who swears much, Mr. Garrett, but I do wish this shit would come to an end and we could concentrate on our mission."

I asked several professionally oriented questions, all of which had occurred to Mr. Nagit and none of which had yet generated conclusive answers. He grumbled, "None of that matters anymore because right now I've got no greater mission than to go get orders to join you in your adventures, probably mainly so I can bang you over the head if you manage to irritate the boss or his honey."

"I detect a note of disaffection, perhaps complicated by a dollop of cynicism."

"Not a note, Mr. Garrett. A whole damned opera. I'd leave if there was anywhere better to go. But where? Bondurant Altoona? Arnes Mingle? The sad part is, this, here, is as good as it gets. Parker! I need you."

Mr. Nagit drafted Parker to help me with a mount, then stalked off. I started my search. I looked each beast directly in the eye, hunting for fast and strong but stupid enough to have no intellect left over for malice. Reluctantly, I made a choice and had her prepared.

On my way I encountered Mr. Nagit's favorite colonel, Moches Theverly. Evidently Theverly didn't remember that we'd served together in the islands. At least he didn't seem inclined to drop everything and rehash old times. He didn't seem inclined to acknowledge my existence. And that was fine with me. There might come a moment when I didn't want him to recall who I was.

I noticed that he still surrounded himself with the same cronies he'd had years ago. And still projected the same air of immense competence. And still bore the scars of the wounds that had gotten him pulled out just before the big Venageti hammer came down on those of us who stayed behind.

I studied him while I had the chance and soon decided that he probably didn't signify in anything that was going on with me. He was just somebody who happened to be around, an actor who walked across the stage.

I amused myself sorting books and snatching peeks at anything that sounded intriguing until, after a much longer delay than I expected, Mr. Nagit showed up with a selection of personal weaponry and a change of clothing I didn't find quite suitable. "A uniform?" I complained.

"It's all that's available." That amused Nagit. No doubt he'd conspired to contrive a shortage of more normal apparel.

"Don't get the idea that because I'm wearing the suit I'm one of the troops. Next time I enlist I plan to start my career as a general."

"And work your way to the bottom, I suppose. Listen, Garrett. The Call wouldn't take you in if you did want to join. You're one big old tangle of unanswered questions and nobody wants to bother digging."

And just a few days ago everybody in the rights racket wanted to sign me on, for the full nightmare. When I still had a nonhuman partner and friends of questionable ethnic purity. I must've stopped being the ideal recruit while I was looking the other way.

Maybe Black Dragon Valsung still wanted me. Or Brotherhood Of The Wolf. We could let bygones be bygones. Couldn't we?

As I dressed I chewed on the sour certainty that my position had been marginalized all along, by everyone. They'd all wanted me to poke hornets' nests somewhere else but hadn't wanted me getting intimate with their own schemes. I was a ball bouncing randomly off any number of walls. No more than what Morley would call a finagle or a confusion factor. A bee annoying everybody.

"Not a bad fit," I said, checking over each shoulder. "The styling is a little too army but I do look almost dashing."

"The ladies will swoon." Mr. Nagit fought a smile.

I asked, "You ever see Glory Mooncalled?"

"What?" I'd startled him with the sudden shift. "No, I don't know anybody who has. Why?"

"I just wondered. I used to have a partner. He practically worshipped Glory Mooncalled. Because of his irreverent attitude." Though I couldn't imagine how someone could be more establishmentarian than a Loghyr gone sedentary. For folks like that revolution or change were not Good Things.

"Used to be a lot of that going around. You don't hear much of it anymore. Suppose we get this circus rolling? The sooner we handle it the sooner I come back home."

"I'm ready." I looked myself over again. I wasn't pleased. I looked like one of the boys. I hoped that didn't confuse me or anyone else.

Tama Montezuma was in the hallway talking to somebody when we left the library. The guy scowled at us. Mr. Nagit glared back. I paid the man no mind because Tama turned on the heat and made herself the focus of my existence. "Garrett? Look at you. Why'd they ever let you out of uniform?" The guy she was with sidled off past Mr. Nagit, plainly unhappy that anyone else was getting Miss Montezuma's attention. Men are that way. We can't help it.

Tama's eyes seemed twice as big as normal. What a case! Every woman I ran into seemed determined to fry my brain.

Mr. Nagit said, "Garrett."

"Uh. Yeah." He was Marengo's right hand. "Sorry, Miss Montezuma. Got to run. Work to do."

She smiled a smile both promising and predatory, moved on down the hall.

I just couldn't imagine where Tinnie got the idea that Tama was bony. "Whew!" I said.

Mr. Nagit agreed. "Yeah. What was that all about?"

When Tinnie was with me he'd seemed a normal, red-blooded Karentine sort of guy. "What?"

"That woman doesn't take a deep breath unless it has something to do with her meal ticket. And she just took you over the jumps."

"My ego can't handle it."

"Huh?"

"She wants to throw the boss over for me."

"Exactly. I thought she seemed extremely nervous."

Were we speaking the same language?

When we stepped out of the house I checked to see what the clouds were doing. My earlier expectations wouldn't be disappointed. Rain was coming. A real disappointment stood closer to hand. The horse I'd chosen now looked terribly ferocious for a swaybacked mare almost my own age. And then there were the dozen guys in freecorps outfits all looking like they were headed for the parade ground. I did a quick, paranoid scan of armbands, making sure noboby was dumb enough to wear his Brotherhood Of The Wolf allegiance on his sleeve.

"Is this necessary?"

"Somebody has to run messages. And those unfriendly centaurs are still out there."

Unfriendly to you, fellow.

I felt vulnerable despite having acquired a cutlery sampler.

Something slammed down on my shoulder. For an instant I thought an ogre had jumped me from behind, but when I turned my head I found myself beak to beak with the Goddamn Parrot. "Damn! I thought I lost you for good." I told Mr. Nagit, "You know, these things live a really long time. Someday you're going to want to have a family. Think how much fun your kids could have with their own talking bird."

"I wouldn't deprive your own future scions of the opportunity to enjoy such a wonderful experience." He laughed.

Him and his pals found my plight entertaining. Not one of them wanted his own talking shoulder ornament, no matter how dashing the look. I gathered my dignity and mounted up, getting it right way forward first try. I mouthed the notes of the trumpet call for charge and off we rode. A three-legged centaur would've had no trouble running me down.

97

Gilbey didn't like my idea even a little. "We don't want any more trouble here, Max."

The Old Man turned the letter Mr. Nagit had given him, as though Marengo might have scribbled a secret postscript on its blank side. He saw only what I saw, which was the North English seal. "We'll do it, Manvil." He turned the letter again. Whatever North English's message, it made a difference; but it left his old friend Max puzzled. North English's word obviously was gold to Weider. "Clear the great hall again." Wan smile. "Let this young gentleman's friends help." That was a subtle dismissal of Nagit and Gilbey both.

"Will this work, Garrett?"

"I don't know. My record hasn't been outstanding lately."

"No. It hasn't. On the other hand, most of our troubles could've been avoided if we'd listened to you in the first place. I understand that you're handicapped by the head start I allowed evil. But who could believe that such things might happen?" The latter he directed toward himself.

"North English will send in freecorps people he trusts. I assume you trust him. But, even so, I intend to bring in friends of my own."

"Whatever *you* think of the man, Garrett, he's my friend."

I confessed, "I do see him through different eyes. I'll also bring in some Guards people that Colonel Block trusts. Everybody can watch everybody. It'll be like party night at the pickpockets' hall."

Wan smile. "You missed the funerals."

"You had them already?" Of course he had. It was summertime.

"This morning. Early."

"I'm sorry. Nobody told me. I would've been there."

"No matter. You were doing the work of the Lord. I hope."

Max wasn't demonstratively religious but he did belong to one of the old-time hellfire and brimstone, rip off an arm for a finger and a head for an eye type of cults. Because of Hannah's incapacity he'd gradually lost interest in the workaday details of brewing the world's best beers. He remained the grand lord of the brewery with the final say about everything but he had abandoned the detail management to Ty and the brewmasters. I feared Hannah's passing might cause him to turn away from the business altogether and possibly even from life.

"Vengeance is mine."

"Can you pull it together by tomorrow?"

"I can." But I'd be one tired boy when I was done.

"Good. You'd better get started."

Now I was being dismissed.

As I opened the study door, Max said, "Lose the uniform, Garrett. If you're going to be roaming around alone, you don't want to ask for more trouble."

Max was right.

The comings and goings of freecorps messengers got noticed. The news spread at the speed of rumor. Tension soon filled the streets. Tempers grew shorter fast.

I had arrangements of my own to make. I couldn't use Nagit's men or brewery hands to complete them.

My proud destrier and I put on the miles.

I visited The Palms. Morley told me he could make it and he suspected that Puddle and Sarge and a few of the boys wouldn't mind
a party, either. I left a message for Belinda, which Dotes promised
to have delivered. Then I dropped in on Playmate, who not only
was available and willing but saved me several hours by knowing
where Saucerhead Tharpe was holed up. I then swooped down on
Heaven's Gate where I talked to Trail and Storey and Miss Trim and,
unfortunately, Medford Shale. Since I didn't have a keg under either
arm or any treats for Shale any welcome was less than enthusiastic.

Shale could just keep on wondering why nobody came to visit him.

My weather-prediction skills proved acute. It was late afternoon
when I went to see Saucerhead. It was raining. At times the down-
pour turned unseasonably ferocious.

Through everything the Goddamn Parrot never made a sound.
That critter had to be trying to spook me out. Not that I missed the
old, foul-beaked Mr. Big. Not even a little.

"Playmate's in. Morley's in," I told Tharpe, who wanted convincing. "The Dead Man might be in. If I can find him. And I particularly need you in. I don't think I can make it all happen without
you." Of course I could. But everyone wants to be wanted, Saucerhead more so than most. And I had some special requests, each of
which I explained carefully.

The big guy grumbled, "Gonna be a major pain, Garrett. That's a
lot of work."

"You got something else going?" In the past he'd always had a
good work ethic.

"Not really. Winger had an idea about—"

"You've got to get away from her, man. You ever notice how *she*
never gets hurt in any of her schemes?"

"Yeah. I know. It's not real nice but . . . All right, Garrett! Don't
start that shit. I really hate it when somebody reminds me that I
owe him."

I offered an evil chuckle reminiscent of the one I'd last heard
from Colonel Block.

The head Guardsman was next on my list. I hit the street once I
finished twisting Saucerhead's . . . uh . . . giving Mr. Tharpe his instructions. With cold water drizzling down the back of my neck. I
have to get myself one of those big-ass riding cloaks now that I'm a
cavalier.

"That a horse?" Saucerhead called after me, from the tenement
doorway. "Are you riding a horse?" He didn't mention the condition of the monster. "I've seen everything now. It really must be

important. I better get on this right away." He had a hat on his head already.

How many times have I said he and Winger didn't have sense enough to get in out of the rain? Made me wonder. He did have sense enough to wear a hat while he was out in it.

Pular Singe caught me leaving the Al-Khar, after I made arrangements with Block, who guaranteed Relway's cooperation. The good colonel was in a festive mood. An attempt to rescue Gerris Genord had been crushed without Guard casualties. One invader was dead. Two now shared Genord's cell. A couple of others, whose interest had been Crask and Sadler instead of their old pal Gerris, had gotten out again.

Very interesting.

I hated myself for thinking Singe looked like a drowned rat. But I couldn't help it. She did. A drowned rat in a wet shirt. "I hoped your people would notice me running around. . . . Where'd you get the shirt?" It used to be mine. It was Tad Weider's before that.

"From the stuff you threw away. It would be a sin to let that go to waste."

The shirt didn't flatter her. Ratpeople just aren't put together like human people. "You could get trouble from the shapechangers."

She tried to smile. It was an obvious, conscious effort to ape the human expression. "They have been disappointed already. Many times."

The clothes had gotten scattered amongst Reliance's dependents. And they didn't care if the shirts had been tagged.

"I'm glad to hear it. What about my tools?"

"Tools?" She didn't understand. I reminded me to keep it simple and slow. She might be a genius of her kind but she was still ratpeople.

"The weapons I was carrying." That stuff wasn't cheap. Even when you took most of it away from the bad boys you ran into. Still, with a little creative billing amongst my various employers . . . Heh-heh-heh.

"I do not know."

I tried to recall if any could be traced to me or the Weiders if they turned up at the scene of some major villainy. I didn't think so. "Would Reliance let you go out to a party tomorrow night?"

I knew I'd picked the wrong words even before the Goddamn Parrot loosed the first noise to pass his beak in hours. Slow and simple, stupid. Before she leapt too far in her conclusions.

I said, "I'll be working there. I want to hire you to unmask the creatures with no scent. Nobody is as good as you are." I couldn't restrain a grin, which seemed to help. But it was sure misplaced.

What must people think of this rain-bedraggled crew, hatless me, a soggy parrot scrunched on my shoulder, leading a moth-eaten antique horse, practically hand in hand with a ratgirl who looked like she'd been drowned once then thrown back for good measure?

The thought made me look around for witnesses. By chance I glimpsed another drowned rat. "Did you know Fenibro is following you?"

Singe's immediate anger made it clear the wannabe boyfriend hadn't been invited. "I told him not to . . ." I couldn't follow what she said.

"It isn't important. Maybe Reliance sent him to watch out for you."

"One day Reliance will learn that I am not a belonging." I caught that easily enough. She added, "It may take a very painful lesson. I will help you look for the shapechangers." In seconds her enunciation had become nearly flawless.

"Speaking of whom. Are they still holed up in that old brewery?"

"Yes." Singe looked over her shoulder. She showed her teeth in an unfeminine threat display. If I'd been Fenibro I'd have gotten the hell out of there fast.

98

Max waved me to a seat. "Lay it out."

"This's only tentative. Subject to change as—"

"Don't bullshit me, Garrett."

The man had exhausted his store of patience. With everything.

"All right. In temporal sequence. Gerris Genord was a plant. Part of a part of this that goes back a few years. And just one of a bunch of plants that put Wolf people inside rich families and businesses. They were after money, plain and simple. It was the Wolves who approached Ty. He or the brewmasters may recognize some of the prisoners.

"Gerris would've known when Alyx decided to bring me in. He would've reported.

"At some point some of the Wolves would've run into some of the Dragons. They'd remember each other from the Cantard. The Wolves asked for help. Or maybe hired the Dragons. But the Dragons had their own agenda. They started using the Wolves when the Wolves thought they were using the Dragons. For their own reasons the Dragons decided to make your family their main target.

"When Genord reported that Alyx was trying to contact me the baddies did some research and decided I could cause trouble. They tried to distract me by involving me in the rights movement. The Dragon crew tried to recruit me. They were recruiting guys at the brewery already. When I showed up there one of those guys reported me and the shifters sent over a team from the Lamp brewery ruins. They failed to discourage me. Genord marked the clothing you gave me so I could be tracked. My part in events since then you know." More or less.

Manvil Gilbey stirred the fire. Max needed a lot of heat to keep going. Weider mused, "Dragons and Wolves using each other. The Wolves after money. What did the changers want?"

"A functional brewery. Don't ask me why. I still have to figure that out. Maybe changers came with a big thirst. But I've got a feeling, supported by not much more than intuition so far, that Glory Mooncalled is in all this right up to his mysterious neck." An implication in part dependent upon my interpretation of my partner's arcane nonbehavior. "I also think that whoever is managing the Wolves has been blackmailed into helping the Dragons. I keep picking up little whiffs of disharmony.

"I have a hunch that that manager brought Crask and Sadler back to deal with the blackmailers. Belinda turning up complicated life. Belinda is dedicated to turning those two good old boys into fish food. So this mystery Wolf decided to uncomplicate life by getting rid of Belinda and me. He gave Crask and Sadler the go-ahead without consulting the allies he planned to ambush later."

Oh what an elegant theorist am I. I was probably off the mark on half of this. But I didn't let a little thing like maybe being wrong slow me down. "After the excitement at the engagement bash Genord began to understand how badly he and his pals were being used. He sneaked away to raise hell about it. He got no satisfaction and, possibly pursued, was in a highly disturbed state when Lance and Ty surprised him at the front door. Since then things have been falling apart fast for the Wolves and Dragons both.

"Meantime, not one person involved in this has dealt with me straight. Everybody, including you, has had an agenda they didn't want to abandon. Although everybody told me a little something here and there so I could have a tool or two to go make things uncomfortable for some other guy. I don't know what your problem was, boss. Maybe you just didn't want a guy with dirt under his nails making the guests nervous by tracking real life all over the place. I'm offended but I'll stipulate that it's your house, your party, your call."

Max's gaze flicked to Gilbey for an instant. Ah. His idea, huh?

Gilbey asked, "You have any idea who this mysterious manipulator is?"

"Just a feeling. No evidence. But if this turns into the pressure situation I want it to become, somebody will point a finger, and say '*He* made me do it.' "

Gilbey stirred the fire again. Max looked thoughtful. I said, "There's more but those are the assumptions I'm working with tonight. We'll see how things come together."

99

I stood at the head of the grand staircase, overlooking the Weider great hall. Tinnie wriggled in under my left arm. Morley had reminded me to add her to the guest list, possibly saving me several centuries in Purgatory. Or what she'd make seem like several centuries. Morley's thoughtful effort balanced off about one talon's worth of the Goddamn Parrot.

Tinnie said, "If it wasn't in bad taste, I'd ask who died." There were a lot of people of various persuasions and allegiances below us, mostly gathered in sullen clumps. The main folks circulating, other than Mr. Gresser's serving crew, were hard-eyed men from Theverly's freecorps, the brewery, my friends, and even a few of Belinda's.

"Some parties just never come to life. Damn!"

"What?"

"Saucerhead brought Winger." Winger might decide that being up to her eyeballs in toughs and lawmen represented a challenge. I glanced up. A gaudy glob remained perched on the main chandelier, gawking at the mob. The bird was vitally alert and his beak hadn't gushed an abomination in the past hour. He was way out of character. I was concerned. But even Morley hadn't noticed. If we could just keep it that way . . .

Manvil Gilbey came out of Max's study. "Going to be much longer?"

"Still missing some key faces . . . Speak of the devil. Here come Colonel Block and the secret police." More hard-eyed men, probably *not* Relway's undercover goons because he wouldn't want their faces this exposed, came in through the front door. Some pulled chains. A few of my guests wouldn't be willing participants. Examples hove into sight: Crask, Sadler, Gerris Genord and his captive friends. Genord seemed particularly unhappy about returning to the scene of his crime.

Him and his buddies got dragged to a bench that was chained to a pillar. They wouldn't be lonely there. The bench already supported eight desolate Brothers Of The Wolf who hadn't scooted fast enough to avoid Lieutenant Nagit's roundup at The Pipes. Apparently Nagit even caught North English by surprise with that. He'd told me that Marengo had been put out in the extreme . . . according to Tama Montezuma, who continued doing most of his talking for him.

Alyx joined us. "That's an awful lot of men who don't like each other crammed in nose-to-nose in one place." She'd dressed. Gorgeously. She looked like she wanted to go down and set the mob at one another's throats. "I'm surprised you got them all to come."

"Hey. We serve the best beer in town. And it's on the house." My gaze drifted to Trail and Storey and Miss Trim. And Medford Shale. Shale had refused to be left at Heaven's Gate. All four were demonstrating an heroic dedication toward making sure they got a fair share of Weider's best.

The real reason most of these people had come was that they were afraid not to. They might miss something critical. It was a tense time in the history of TunFaire. It was a time not to let yourself fall a step behind. It was a time when the future was rewriting itself from minute to minute and you wanted your hands and nose right in the middle of anything that might nudge the pen of destiny.

"Manvil, tell . . ." He was gone. "Oh, good. Better late than never." Saucerhead had completed his mission. Below, Ty had entered the hall from the family dining room. He was on crutches.

Nicks was beside him, trying not to look like she was there to catch
him if he fell. Ty was directing a crew from the brewery who were
dragging one of those huge, thousand-gallon wooden settling tanks
where beer sits briefly while the grossest sediments settle out.
Later the holy nectar would migrate onward to occupy the kegs and
barrels the customer sees. Questions about the tank stirred every
little cluster but people were too wary of their neighbors to ask outside their own cliques. Ty gave me a thumbs-up. I blew him a kiss.
We were getting along today. I told Alyx, "Go tell your pop. I just
dealt myself another ace. Everything's set and we're just waiting
for Relway."

"Waiting for Relway. Right."

"He'll understand."

She went. Tinnie asked, "Think she'll remember all the way
over there?"

"You're vicious. And she's *your* friend."

"You keep that in mind. All right. You've got everybody that
you've ever met gathered in one place. What the devil do you plan
to do with them?"

"Oh, I'm going to make them all unhappy. Real unhappy. Unless
I manage to make me real unhappy by making a complete fool of
myself."

"You think the bookies are giving odds? Is there a point
spread?"

"Lift your skirt."

"Right here? I can be conned into a little adventure sometimes,
Garrett, but. . . ."

"Three inches will be far enough." Her hemline dragged the carpet. "Ha! I thought so."

"What?"

"You're wearing the green shoes. I don't know if they turn you
wicked or you just wear them when you're feeling wicked, but—"

"Somebody's here."

Yes. Somebody was. The boys from the Lamp brewery had arrived. They looked sexy in their shiny new silver-plated chains. I'd
expected the logistics to be a problem but Relway had been on the
job already, having anticipated having to control shapeshifters
again, and better.

"Five . . . six of them. I thought there'd be more. There *should*
be more. Hell, there're only five of them." The sixth was a ringer,
Relway himself, in disguise and not really part of the coffle. He

was pretending to be a little hunchbacked torturer's apprentice, jingling the ends of the chains. Probably no one but Singe and I recognized him.

Singe showed more courage than I'd thought possible. Not only was she on the scene, she was out where people could see her. She stayed close to the walls, though.

The rightsist types were surprised by her presence but it didn't distress them. Not nearly so much as did the presence of Morley Dotes and Belinda's swaggering toughs. Ratpeople knew their place.

Everyone I wanted there had arrived. Singe had not yet found any shapeshifters other than those Relway was delivering but she kept on looking. I was counting on surprise visitors of several kinds.

Marengo North English wove his way through the crowd hurriedly, headed my way. He seemed to cringe from the touch of the crowd. He wanted out of the press, fast. His lovely niece trailed a step behind him. Tama seemed uncomfortable and deeply troubled. Maybe that was because there were so many really bad people around, though I couldn't picture her having much difficulty managing in even the direst circumstances. She'd already impressed me as a first-class survivor capable of cool thinking and quick decisions.

While Marengo had been eyeing the Belindas and Tinnies and Wingers and developing an itch, she had been formulating plans of her own, I was sure. Whatever silverware Marengo still had lying around The Pipes might not be there much longer.

Now Colonel Block was whispering with a fawning Relway. Both kept glancing my way. He nodded several times, started toward the stair himself.

Marengo arrived first. He asked, "Are you ready to start?" Oddly, Tama seemed more interested in my answer than he did.

I was, though I hadn't achieved the perfect and optimal mix I'd hoped for. But the crowd was better than the one I'd expected. The front door had been locked. Sarge and Puddle stood between it and the room, looking like some pudgy guardian temple trolls. Them dressed up formal was a vision to behold. Out of a bad dream. Unfortunately, I'd never get joy out of having seen them looking pretty. I was outfitted in Ty Weider's second best get-up. I looked like some limp-wristed, lilac-scented lordlet bent on embarrassing his family publicly. "Yes."

Singe moved around the edge of the room. Marengo glanced

down at her frequently, unhappily. Playmate, Saucerhead, and Winger were never far from the ratgirl. Winger cleaned up astonishly well. Marengo's gaze brushed her a time or three. I wouldn't interfere if they decided they were made for each other. They deserved one another. And I had a parrot that would make a wonderful engagement present.

A glance showed me that the future nuptial knickknack was still paying attention.

Singe drifted off to check Mr. Gresser's crew and Neersa Bintor's kitchen gang.

Block puffed his way to the head of the stair. He clung to the rail, sucked in a bunch of air, gasped out, "You've got to stall, Garrett."

"But—"

"Got a good reason?" Max demanded from behind me, as I made a small gesture that brought a colorful lightning bolt down to strike my shoulder. I guess Alyx had gotten all the way there with the message. Her old man sounded darkly suspicious. Which is probably the healthiest attitude if you're dealing with minions of the Crown.

"I think so," Block said. "Though you're free to disagree, of course."

"What?" I asked. I knew it would be ugly. The Goddamn Parrot cocked his head, the better to hear.

"An acquaintance took the liberty of inviting himself down." Slight weight on the last word. I understood perfectly but Max didn't catch it. Block's way-so-mysterious chum from the Hill had decided to stick his nose in. That was wonderful. That was more than I'd hoped for. That made my evening nearly faultless. That was one snake I hadn't really expected to lure in out of the weeds. Now if just one more old shit-disturber, lately of the Cantard republic, couldn't control his curiosity and chose to become a surprise guest, I would've contrived a flawless machination.

Block continued, "He can't make it for a while yet. And I'll tell you, you'll feel more comfortable once he is here." He winked, a very unBlocklike action. "I think." Meaning Block was going to feel more comfortable. His mystery guest must have been riding him hard.

Max clucked his tongue, irked. Max's opinions of folk from the Hill were blacker than mine.

Marengo didn't seem to be disappointed. In fact, he seemed more relaxed. Then I realized he wasn't listening to us, just to the crowd on the floor below.

I asked, "Is your buddy's identity a secret?"

"He's the Stormwarden Perilous Spite."

Never heard of him, I didn't say because Max got in the first word. "Why?" He seemed distinctly unfriendly now. Could this be somebody he knew and disliked? Did everybody know Spite but me? I'm supposed to know things. It's what I do. Know where to make connections. But I couldn't connect this glorified witch doctor to anything.

"Because the stormwarden is extremely knowledgeable in matters having to do with ranger, commando, special forces, and covert operations inside the Cantard. He was involved. He has unfinished business. He's been following this since he heard about the dragon tattoos."

How did he hear? I wondered. Would Colonel Westman Block be saddled with standing orders to report certain discoveries to certain interested parties? Might such reports be a condition of his appointment? Why, Garrett, how could you be so cynical? You developing a case of creeping realism?

Block surged onward, ingenuously "I don't know why, Garrett, but that got his attention in a big way. He's been nagging me like the proverbial fishwife. And seems to know more about what's going on than Deal does . . ." Block decided he was talking too much, which is a liability in his trade. He finished, "Him joining us was his idea."

"But he keeps Hill time, of course," I grumbled. Meaning I figured the stormwarden couldn't be bothered catering to the schedules of us lesser creatures. But that was all right. I wanted this devil out in the open where I could see him. "Tell me, old buddy, how did this guy hear about my party in the first place?"

Block shrugged. "I don't know. Not from me. I told you. He's well informed."

"Hmm." I glanced at Marengo, there with his old pal Max Weider, being mousy quiet. The very man who was grumbling and muttering about the caprice of sorcerers the other day. "I see."

North English lacked the grace to be embarrassed.

"I see," Max said, too. "So we'll wait, Garrett. Use the delay to build the pressure till these fools blow smoke out their ears. Then let the stormwarden land in their midst like a cat in a mouse nest."

I said, "You're the boss." A little time sweating might indeed make somebody a tad more amenable. "Excuse me." Block had retreated halfway down the stair, then had stopped, looking my way. He had something on his mind.

I went to find out. The colonel whispered, "Relway says to tell you you have to come visit the Lamp brewery."

"He find something interesting?"

"Apparently so. He wouldn't explain. He did say that he didn't understand it but that you might and you probably ought to see it before you go ahead with what you're doing here."

Now? "Maybe he didn't notice but here is just a wee bit busy. And every time he wants me to see something that turns out to be dead bodies. I've seen enough dead people . . . Oh, shit!" Medford Shale and his Heaven's Gate cronies had been admiring the settling tank like it might be the doorway to paradise. I'd been keeping an eye on them in case they decided to try tapping it, the results of which were sure to amaze and distress almost everyone. "Bird, go down there and get those drunks headed in another direction. Go on. Shoo."

The arrival of the talking bird had the desired effect. The old folks retreated toward the kegs already tapped. But their bickering orbit around the settling tank brought them face-to-face with the arriving prisoners.

Storey went berserk. He flailed away at one of the shapeshifters with his walking stick. I murmured, "Apparently it *can* be the same Carter Stockwell who was involved in the Myzhod campaigns."

"What?"

"Long story. Those old men were soldiers a long time ago. Some shapeshifter mercenaries sold them out to the Venageti. It was a big disaster for our side. Looks like these could be the same shapeshifters. Storey—that's the guy being so stylish with the walking stick—mentioned the one he's whipping by name."

"I do believe I'm beginning to get an idea of why the storm-warden is interested."

Me, too, if Perilous Spite was what I suspected. "Let's go calm them down."

"Let's have a whisper with Deal."

100

Storey settled down only after, for a moment, it looked like Trail had suffered a stroke. Several shifters bled liberally. The silver fetters took the strength right out of them. Trace whimpered like a whipped puppy. The voice of the guy who'd been in the stable and on the stair to Tom's room said, "We should've killed the sonofabitch when we had the chance." I couldn't tell if he meant me or Storey.

The boys from Brotherhood Of The Wolf were chained to the next pillar over. Several seemed stricken. They saw faces they recognized. Faces that belonged to people who weren't even human. People who had been manipulating them . . . A glance at Gerris Genord told me he'd figured that out already. Maybe while he was in the Al-Khar, maybe even the night he killed Lancelyn Mac. Maybe he knew the key answer, too.

Who.

I had an idea, name of Mooncalled. Only I couldn't make him fit. Going strictly by the available evidence, Marengo North English seemed more likely.

There was no coolness toward Genord on the part of the other Wolves. Block and Relway hadn't sold them a thing. They trusted their buddy. Kind of touching, that. These days trust is moribund and fading fast.

It did mean I had guessed wrong about Genord not being the commando type. It takes going through hell with a man to develop that kind of trust. I asked Genord, "You want to put somebody on the spot?"

He looked through me. He wasn't going to tell me jack. If there was any settlement due, his pals would handle it. We couldn't hold them forever.

That attitude came out of the going through hell together, too. I remember that attitude. I miss it. But all the guys I shared it with are gone. I'm left with just the pale ghost of it in my friendships with Morley and a few others.

An uproar loud enough for all the guests to hear erupted out in the kitchen. Neersa Bintor bellowed like an angry she-elephant. Before I finished making sure everybody didn't rush that way and thereby leave the rest of the mansion unwatched the big woman

stormed into the great hall. She had a body over her shoulder, a
shifter caught in mid-change, flopping like a crippled snake. In her
off hand she carried a kitchen maul that looked like it could be used
to drive the stakes that hold up circus tents. She searched the gawking crowd, spotted me, flung the shifter from thirty feet away. It left
some skin on the uncarpeted floor.

"I an' I, I be tryin' to manage de kitchen, you Garrett, you. You
be gettin' me better help dan dat t'ief, you. You be keepin' you rat
out a dere, too, you." Behind her Pular Singe managed to look sheep-
ish and proud at the same time. She'd winkled out the interloper.

It occurred to me that we'd neglected our obligation to inform
Neersa Bintor of our full plans. Not an oversight the goddess of the
cast iron would easily forgive. In the heirarchy of the Weider mansion Neersa Bintor ranked right behind Max and, just possibly,
Manvil Gilbey.

I apologized profusely in front of the mob. A certain gaudily
constumed woodpecker had a grand laugh at my expense. "Lend
me your cane there, Storey." I whacked the side of the settling tank
three or four times. The bird said "Gleep!" and flew back to his
perch on the chandelier.

"You listen, you bird-boy, you. I an' I got no room in my kitchen
for vermin, be dey talk or no. You unnerstan', you? I will catch my
own t'iefs, I an' I." The shifter at my feet stirred. Neersa Bintor
raised a prodigious sensible shoe, brought it down hard, then exor-
cised her venom through a hearty application of her maul. She kept
her foot in place while a couple of Guards got the changer fitted
with chains.

I whispered to Singe, as though she hadn't understood what had
been said, "Maybe you'd better stay out of the kitchen."

She whispered back, "You tink so, you?"

Singe the wonder child. She was being sarcastic. "Yeah. Scoot."
When I turned back to the crowd I saw the Bintor phenomenon
withdrawing.

I told the Guards, "You guys better get this thing shackled to its
friends before it remembers what kingdom it's in." I suspected the
passivity shown by the changers was partly due to their psychic connection, which must be charged with a communal sense of despair.

Block, near Relway, beckoned impatiently.

101

Relway is predictable some ways. For example, you can count on him to bring out the melodrama in any situation. He did that at the Lamp brewery, where he had guys with torches creeping around the interior ruins generating wonderfully creepy, dancing, slithering shadows. "It's in worse shape than I thought it would be," I told the little guy. The brick exterior remained sound but the inside walls and floors were falling down and caving in.

"Smells odd, too," Morley said. He drifted over and through rubble and ruin without attracting a speck of dust.

Relway grumbled, "The smell comes from what we're here to see." He wasn't pleased with his pal Garrett. Garrett had let Morley Dotes and Pular Singe tag along. Deal Relway wasn't dim. He knew Morley would try to memorize some identifying detail about him and that Singe, without even realizing it, would accumulate a battery of olfactory clues. I hoped he didn't feel threatened enough to consider some unpleasant form of rectification later.

"Through here." Relway ducked under a sagging floor joist. I had to duckwalk in order to follow him. The dust showed that there had been a lot of traffic before us. "What a glamorous life they lead."

Relway grunted. Block made a small speech about evil always seeming glamorous from a distance but being squalid and ugly when you saw it up close. It was hard to argue with that. I saw proof every day.

On the other hand, the wicked do prosper while the upright perform hopelessly in the theater of their own despair.

"Kind of like my shoulder ornament, you mean?"

The Goddamn Parrot, who hadn't wanted to miss this adventure, made a sneering noise—really! And Morley announced, "I resent that. That avian gem was a gift from me."

"For which you'll never be forgiven. Yech!" The smell was getting stronger fast. Though repellent it had a familiar edge, a malty—

"Here," Relway said, indicating a couple of old copper fermenting kettles that should've been stolen for their scrap value ages ago. "Take a torch and climb up there." He indicated a crude platform fashioned from old crates. "You too, Wes."

I borrowed a torch from a Guard. Colonel Block snagged another. We accomplished the climb with a minimum of injuries, though the wonder buzzard also lost some tailfeathers to a waving torch.

The kettles were full of *stuff.* A big bubble broached the surface of the one nearest me. "Oh! That's foul. Some people shouldn't be allowed to brew their own." That's what they were doing. Badly. That's why the stench seemed familiar.

Relway said, "That's right. Take that paddle and push the scum out of the way."

A six-foot pole with a wide, square end lay across the top of the pot. I followed instructions.

"Shit!" Block exclaimed. "What the hell is *that*?"

I had to keep pushing the surface gunk aside to see it.

It was a slug olive drab thing four feet long and human-shaped. No. Monkey-shaped caught it better. Its limbs were long and skinny and it had a tail. It had a round head with large round lidless lemurlike eyes. And no ears.

There was another in the other kettle, not as completely developed.

"What do you think?" Relway asked. "Think what's in them pots maybe's got something to do with why they'd want to grab control of TunFaire's biggest brewery?"

"They're cooking up baby changers. Damn! Makes you understand their behavior. Some. Makes you kind of sympathize—if that's how they have to reproduce." I smelled ancient sorcery of the same sort that had created Singe's people. "But they're still dangerous monsters from where we stand. I wonder if it'd make any difference to Max that his family didn't die just because of somebody's greed."

"Grief ain't big on caring about why," Block observed.

Singe suddenly squeaked, "Garrett! Danger!" and scooted into the darkness like. . . Well, like a scared rat. Something stirred back the way we'd come. Somebody barked something. Relway started to drag out a black knife. That started everybody else grabbing for weapons.

"Deal!" Block snapped. "Relax."

Relway froze instead.

A wicked vision seemed to materialize slowly from the uncanny shadows, like that mythical breed of vampire that spends part of its unlife as a mist capable of passing through the finest fissure. As it moved into the torchlight I saw that it was someone in black robes with golden lightning bolts embroidered on, his face concealed behind a silver mask. Clearly the aforementioned Stormwarden Perilous Spite, clinging to the traditions of his kind, which have spooky behavior and bad clothes as their foundations.

But people off the Hill dress like they're expected to dress. I sometimes wonder where they find their tailors. I also wondered if I really wanted this guy to turn up after all. Already he felt like clabbered bad humor.

The Goddamn Parrot decided he wanted to go for a fly with Pular Singe. Probably a good idea. I didn't want him attracting attention.

Block caught my eye. He jerked his head. I stepped down. He followed. His pal the wizard took our place. He stirred the kettles and examined their contents.

I call him *he* for convenience. There was a one in three chance that a woman lurked behind that mask. Not that sex made much difference. Those people are all misery on the hoof.

Block tugged my sleeve, gestured with his head. It was time us grunts made ourselves scarce.

I departed still reflecting upon whether or not it was a good thing to have the stormwarden join us. His presence might be enough to guarantee the continued sinister shyness of the specter general from the Cantard, whose appearance would be much preferable to me.

As we strode toward the Weider mansion Relway asked, "You gotten anywhere finding out anything for me, Garrett?"

"Nope. And I'm not going to, either. They've flat out told me I'm not getting inside anything, nor am I getting anywhere near any information they don't already want the whole world to share."

"But you're the perfect recruit."

"I think I was the perfect recruit until I started talking to you."

"Hmm?"

"Just a hunch. But if I was you and Block, I'd keep an eye out for one of your guys who maybe feels as strong about human rights as he does about law and order."

The ugly little man's face turned to cold iron.

Thou shalt have no other gods before me.

102

Max stared the length of the hall at the stormwarden. The sorcerer had come inside just far enough to be seen and cause a stir. He'd made himself shadowy and nine feet tall. Teensy lightning bolts slithered through the nimbus surrounding him. He was accompanied by two apparently ordinary men-at-arms who, on closer inspection, showed a slight golden shimmer. Sarge and Puddle were pleased to abandon their posts to the newcomers.

The hall had become a tomb with Spite's advent. Everyone anticipated the moment when he no longer just stood there. The shapeshifters seemed particularly unhappy, which suggested they recognized the sorcerer and knew him well enough to believe they had reason to be unhappy. And Marengo North English seemed to have faded into the very woodwork.

Weider listened closely while I explained what we'd found in the ruined brewery. He nodded occasionally, then observed, "They might've created themselves a small army if they'd gotten hold of my place, then."

"Which was probably their plan."

"But why would they get help from a faction of The Call?"

"We still need to dig that out. But I'm pretty sure the Wolves thought the help was going the other way. We know these shifters are old, now. We saw that when Storey had his fit." Trail and Storey and the Heaven's Gate contingent remained dutifully attentive to the keg they had staked out. "They've had lifetimes to practice telling Karentines what they want to hear and showing them what they want to see."

"Hadn't you better get on with the digging? That spook-wrangler gives me the creeps. He's got a bad feel to him. Try to get him out of here before he starts something I'll regret."

"You heard of him before, boss?"

"Perilous Spite? No. But I don't cross paths with those people much. I'm in trade. A brewer. A brewer doesn't have much contact with anybody but people who buy beer. Even during the worst days of the war the brewery had no intercourse with the war's managers and manipulators. I want to keep it that way. Go to work, Garrett."

"Quit swearing." I surveyed the mob and grimaced. I'm not big

on getting up in front of crowds. Not when I have to share the spot-
light with a lord from the Hill—especially when that lord is a complete unknown. Block seemed impressed by him, though, and
now-invisible Marengo hadn't too far from being petrified.

"Quiet down!" I bellowed. Immediately every thug from The
Call and the brewery and the Guard redoubled the racket by trying
to shush everybody else. I would've done better just standing there
letting them come to the notion that things were about to ripen.
Though tardily, silence did find its way among us.

A sea of ugly faces turned my way. Not a one looked happy. I
wasn't overflowing with joy, myself.

I hadn't thought this part through. Get them all together, let it
turn into a pressure cooker. Slip a couple cards up my sleeve that
nobody but Ty knew about. See what the situation produced. That
was the plan.

Should I explain? Some of these people had no idea why they'd
been summoned. The rest probably had the wrong idea.

I decided to let the thing unfold.

"Mr Trail. Mr. Storey. You gentlemen became exercised a while
ago. Please explain why to everyone else." I could imagine the rumors that had begun to go around already.

Trail couldn't get a word out while surrounded by so many people who outranked him socially. Storey didn't have that problem,
though. He had bolstered his courage mightily at Weider Brewing's expense. He repeated the tale of the Myzhod campaign. I let
him ramble and editorialize but he didn't embellish much. The
stormwarden demonstrated an intimidating willingness to bestow
cruel attention on any member of the audience inclined to become
restless. I suspected that a lot of my guests knew more about Spite
than I did. I suppose if I'd had one of those posh army sinecures instead of a real job as a Marine, I might have heard something about
him, too.

Storey made it clear that he and Trail believed these shifters right
here, right now, in this very room, were the same damned treacherous shifters who'd led an entire Karentine army to its destruction
fifty years ago.

Once Storey depleted his store of vitriol I announced, "Miss
Quipo Trim, lately of His Majesty's Royal Army Medical Corps, is
going to tell us whatever she recalls that might be germane."

Quipo told the crowd what she'd told me, adding details she'd
remembered since then. Then, in succession, I got statements from

everyone else who'd had contact with the shifters. I revealed my own history. I exempted only Relway, who wasn't present anyway, according to official information. Almost everyone had to see that this assembly wasn't about me and the Weiders, as many might have expected. Ultimately, it was about the security of the Karentine Crown.

The stormwarden weighed on my mind when I said, "That establishes the picture. These creatures have pretended to serve the Crown for ages but everywhere they go disaster follows. Rather like Glory Mooncalled. I haven't dug out much more about them. They're a big secret. Their commander in modern times was a Colonel Norton Valsung. Miss Trim tells me Valsung was Karentine but she's the only person I've found who ever met the man. I consider his existence problematical. He may have been a particularly clever shapeshifter."

I was fishing. But somebody might remember something and volunteer it. Heck, somebody might even volunteer to tell me who was behind the Brotherhood Of The Wolf and all The Call's embarrassments. Somebody might, but I wasn't going to bet the family silver that someone would.

The stormwarden moved ever so slightly, over by the front door. A sourceless whisper sounded beside my left ear. Years of practice with the Dead Man kept me from jumping. "Valsung existed. His continued survival is, however, indeed improbable. He was of use to them no longer."

I nodded slightly, letting him know I'd heard. I guessed I was supposed to use the information somehow. I didn't see what use it might be, though. I glanced up at the Goddamn Parrot. The old hen was observing alertly from the chandelier while taking care not to draw attention. Excellent. Remarkable. Bizarre. But excellent. Because if the stormwarden figured out how the wonder dodo was being used, I was going to have one very irritated sorcerer on my hands.

It wasn't possible that anyone would get the blame for me. That's Garrett's law.

I murmured, "I hope you stay very, very quiet and let the wizard carry the load."

The pressure hadn't yet had the effect I'd hoped. Nobody had lost control and started spouting secrets.

I turned to Brotherhood Of The Wolf. With them my footing was speculative and personally dangerous: They remained an enigma despite being subject to human motives. They were in bad odor with The Call but I couldn't question the purity of their politics. Those remained rigorously correct by the strictest standards espoused by the most fanatic of rightsists.

The silence in the hall continued but the overall restlessness quotient kept rising. To hold the crowd's attention I began moving down the stair. As I did so, I said, "There's a circumstantial but evident connection between the Black Dragon creatures and Brotherhood Of The Wolf." The fact that your dialectic might be impeccable and your treason accidental would not impress some true believers, lack of imagination and compassion being leading marks of the beast.

I made no direct accusations. I wanted Genord's friends to come to the light on their own, to decide that they owed amends. Genord himself was hopeless. He had decided to protect somebody.

I hollered back up to the balcony, "Boss, you want to weasel your goofball pal back out of your den?"

Max grunted, nodded to Gilbey. Manvil went. He returned leading a Marengo North English still trying to avoid being noticed by the stormwarden.

I had no mercy. "Tell us about the Wolves. Where did they come from? Why did they go away?"

Marengo didn't want to talk. That sorcerer really had him spooked. North English must have pulled some truly stupid stunt. He spoke only with the greatest reluctance, hastily, stumbling, obviously not always certain of his facts.

Morley materialized beside me. He whispered, "Why do you keep talking? Cut their throats and be done with it." City elves are direct folk. They'll chuck out the baby with the bathwater counting on the gods to look out for the tad if he deserves it.

"Because if I go slicing shifters up, I'll probably piss off about half the people in this zoo. Look around. Every one of these clowns is looking for an angle and trying to figure out how to use this. If they can sneak around the stormwarden—beforehand. Anyway, we need to find out how widespread this changers cancer really is. Which we can't do using dead men. That being a stormwarden over there, not a necromancer." And I, for my part, being obsessively curious, wanted to ferret out a few whys as well as the whos and whats. And that took getting people's minds into the right frame by asking the right questions so the right answers would float to the surface.

Marengo didn't say much interesting about Brotherhood Of The Wolf. They'd been his first effort to give The Call real muscle, a band of unimpeachable war heroes, accomplished, skilled, and dedicated. But having grown accustomed to deal with the King's enemies unsupervised, for weeks or months at a time, they tended to act without consulting their superiors. When they tried to drive the Inner Council to adopt policies they favored, by means of an unspecified intervention that left the council no other option, said council ordered them disbanded. They would be replaced by less elite, more pliable believers. The new groups grew haphazardly till Colonel Theverly came along. Most of the Wolves joined the new freecorps. A few, like Gerris Genord, dropped out and went elsewhere.

Marengo insisted that the Wolves, disaffected or not, would never knowingly ally themselves with Karenta's enemies.

Only the thickest-witted witness would have failed to understand that just from observing the captive Wolves.

Devotion to the Crown is a foundation stone of the freecorps ethic. We had plenty of evidence that shapeshifters did not share that dedication.

North English said his piece and retreated as fast as he could. His courage was extremely inconstant tonight. Perilous Spite really worried him.

I got the impression that the reverse wasn't true. The sorcerer was indifferent to everyone but the shapeshifters.

103

I studied face after face while others spoke. Those not anticipating punishment were growing impatient. Only the stormwarden's presence held them in check.

I went down to Genord, tried one more time. "You meant well but you were conned. And not just by these things." I indicated the shifters. "That's not really your fault. You didn't know they weren't human even though you'd worked with them in the Cantard."

Genord showed me the same blank face he'd worn since he'd come through the door.

I got down on one knee. "Look, guy, I'm trying to give you something to work with. They don't hang you for stupid. But they sure will for stubborn. Who got the Wolves back together? Who got you into this? Who are you covering for? You think maybe he knew about the Dragons? Eh?"

Genord and I both knew that Brotherhood Of The Wolf never disbanded. But we could pretend.

"Who decided to target the Weider family? And why them?"

Genord wouldn't talk but his buddies weren't as single-minded. They'd gotten a grip on the notion that they didn't have to throw themselves on their swords. There might be a way out of their fix. If they'd been tricked into serving evil . . .

"You guys haven't killed anybody, have you? Except Lance?" There wouldn't be any getting out of that for Genord.

Gerris remained donkey stubborn. He believed he was a good man fighting the good fight. Too bad his determination was wasted.

One of the Wolves volunteered, "We haven't killed anyone." The restlessness around us lessened immediately. People jockeyed for vantage points. They might hear something interesting.

Genord gave the talker a black look. His attitude was shared by none of the other Wolves. The man speaking looked like he was used to being in charge. "We're guilty of nothing but striving to serve the movement and the Crown." He glared at the balcony, at the unseen North English, angry, clearly feeling betrayed.

"Suppose you explain that." I surveyed the audience. I leaned back to check the chandelier. The ugliest bird of the century stared back. Still alert. Good. I glanced at the settling tank. I had hold of a thread, now. Finally. Things might start to unravel. Which could mean some real excitement. "Get away from that tank!" I yelled. Trail, Storey, and Shale were back trying to figure out how to get beer out of the vat. Quipo Trim, though, had established herself permanently beside an active keg of Reserve Dark. She muttered with Winger as she sucked it down. Winger was putting her share away, too, instead of looking out for Singe.

No beer disappears faster than free beer.

With my luck the women were swapping Garrett stories.

I growled. I did not want Winger getting drunk. She loses all sense of caution once she's had a few.

The Goddamn Parrot launched himself off the chandelier, swooped around the room. People ducked. People cursed. The bird landed on Winger's wrist just as she started to take a drink. Beer flew. She glared up at me. I indicated Morley. "Remember, the jungle chicken was his fault." The bird roosted on the chandelier again. I glared at Winger's mug. She began to get the idea. But how long could it stick?

Upstairs, Belinda and Nicks joined Alyx and Tinnie. They must've gotten a cue from Max or Manvil. They had North English surrounded and were keeping him out where he could be seen. If they added Tama Montezuma, they'd create a coven of heart-wreckers of diabolic magnitude.

Where *was* Marengo's favorite niece? I couldn't see her for the surrounding crowd. Hadn't seen her for a while now, come to think.

The Wolf continued his story. "Privately we were told that we weren't disbanding. That the announcement that we were would get that asshole Theverly down off his high horse." The Wolf spokesman seemed determined to stare a hole right through North English. Weider and Gilbey had joined the ladies, now, compelling Marengo to face his critic. Max was extremely unhappy with his friend. "We were told we were going underground to do the stuff we'd trained for. Some of us should take positions in the private world. Openings would be arranged. Some should join Theverly's command and monitor it from inside, taking as much control as we could. Some of us should move over to other rights groups so we could keep track of what they were doing. These were all things we were convinced we should've been doing already."

I gave North English the fish-eye myself. That was exactly the sort of stuff a guy like him would pull. But he called down, "That's not true. I told the Brotherhood to disband because I wanted it disbanded. I agreed with Theverly. They wouldn't be managed. Obviously, time has sustained the wisdom of our decision." Nevertheless, he remained shifty-eyed and kept his face averted from the stormwarden.

The man in chains didn't buy North English's protests. "We got orders from you every day. The last couple of months you've sent word three or four times a day. It got to where you were practically controlling every breath we took."

The man believed what he said. I didn't doubt that a bit.

The Wolf had said, ". . . sent word. . . ." And it hadn't been that long since I'd mentioned the changers' talent for telling Karentines exactly what they wanted to hear. This Wolf had been fed a story exactly suited to his emotional need.

North English looked baffled. Maybe he believed what he said, too.

The Wolf plowed on, "The Call was going broke. They wanted to get ahold of a lot of wealth fast. Two, two and a half weeks ago, not long after we started working with Black Dragon, we got word that the Weider brewing empire would be taken over. We'd worked on that project for a long time. Just in case. The Dragons tried to recruit brewery workers in our name. That was hard for us; you kept us tied up in meetings all the time." The man's conviction began to waver in the face of North English's steadfast headshaking. North English was getting angry enough to ignore the presence of the sorcerer.

Marengo said, "I haven't spoken to you three times in the last year, fellow."

"You couldn't, could you? Colonel Theverly would throw one of his tantrums. You—"

Pular Singe squealed. Saucerhead Tharpe bellowed. Playmate boomed something. Sarge roared. The Goddamn Parrot shrieked. A sorcerous voice whispered "Beware!" in my ear just as *Look Out!* rumbled inside my head. A woody crash came from the direction of the dining room. Shrieks followed that. Something was headed my way.

That something was a whirlwind of horror that looked like a troll with a bad case of the uglies. It had claws like scimitars. It had fangs like a saber-tithed tooger, top and bottom. It was preceded by breath foul enough to gag a maggot. It bulled straight toward me. Bodies flew and people screamed.

There wasn't a hero in the place. Whatever direction the thing looked it saw flying heels. My first impulse was to show it one more pair. So was my second. I listened to that one.

"Down!" said the little voice in my ear. *Down!* insisted the big voice inside my head. I'm a bright boy. I can take a hint. I flung myself down and clung to cold stone like the gods had announced that they were going to do away with gravity.

Came a sound like somebody slapping a brick wall with the flat side of a big wet board. The sound of big bacon frying followed instantly. The ugly apparition shrieked louder than all the shrieking around it put together. It collapsed upon itself, passing through repeated twisting changes before it assumed the shape like those in the Lamp ruin tanks.

A huge, sourceless voice filled the hall. "Stand back. It's stunned, not dead." The thing began to assume human shape. Evidently young shifters adopt some base form to which they'll revert automatically if they can't maintain a shape they've chosen.

The shifters bound in chains made unhappy noises. Their despair was so strong I felt it—maybe because I'd been exposed to the Dead Man for so long.

Stunned didn't last. An arm grew to an impossible length. One incredibly nasty, sicklelike claw tipped it. That claw slashed at me. I was just fast enough to dodge or the shifter was just slow enough to miss.

A waterlogged blanket slapped a stone floor. Big bacon crackled. The shifter leapt into the air, shrieked, then flopped around like its back was broken. I told Morley, "I think I'll back off a ways."

"Clever fellow. Sign me on as your assistant."

I noted that he wasn't watching the shifter. "Whatcha looking for?"

"Just keeping an eye out." He used his "I've got an idea but I'm not ready to talk about it" tone. I looked around, too.

Block and Relway were busy making sure men kept guarding every entrance. I looked up at Tinnie and the girls. They hadn't fled. But they had let Marengo get away again. Two large gentlemen from the shipping dock had joined the ladies. Max, Manvil, and Ty now formed a glowering knot at the foot of the grand staircase, evidently concerned that my new playmate might develop a taste for toothsome wench. A taste I can't say I begrudge almost anyone.

I limped over to Genord. I'd banged my hip good getting down onto the floor. "Here we go again. Want to tell me anything now?"

Gerris *still* wasn't talking.

"Live a fool, die a fool—Now what?"

Another racket from the kitchen, that's what. Neersa Bintor was *very* upset about something. Had Singe? . . . No, Singe was there by the dining-room door, just steps away from Relway, shaking like a last autumn leaf, looking at me, in a stance that begged forgiveness for failing to expose the changer in time.

Still looking around, Morley asked, "You want some bad news?"

"No. I'd cherish some *good* news, though. Just for the novelty. What?"

"Crask and Sadler went missing during that excitement."

Gah! "You're shitting me."

Sure enough, their fetters were empty. How the hell? . . . They'd

been out of the way and everybody had been distracted, but . . .
I stormed toward Relway. "You want to tell me how Crask
and Sadler could do a disappearing act in the middle of a hundred
people?"

"What? They couldn't. I've got the only key . . ." A twisted hand
came out of a pocket empty. "Hunh?" He was flabbergasted. It's a
memory I'll cherish. Relway is seldom at a loss. "Somebody
picked my pocket." He started growling at his own people, forgetting, for the moment, that he didn't want to reveal himself.

I went to Pular Singe, told her, "You did just fine. You couldn't
be everywhere at once. Once the shifters understood that you could
identify them they just stayed out of your way. Are you all right?
You think you can work? I might need you to track those bad men
again."

"Never mind the bad men," Morley said from behind me. "She
turned them loose strictly for their diversion value."

Slap and bacon crackle happened again. People who should've
been concentrating on that last shifter had let themselves be distracted by trying to keep track of me. That changer was off the floor
again. It lurched toward its brethren, sprouting scissorlike claws
capable of snipping silver. It seemed to be developing an immunity
to the stormwarden's sorcery. A double application was needed to
put it down this time.

"Someone would have to know me pretty good to think I'd drop
everything if they . . ." Of course. Somebody who controlled the
resources of Brotherhood Of The Wolf and Black Dragon Valsung
could find out all about me. Somebody who'd had me dogged since
before I knew I was getting into this mess. Somebody who . . .
Who? I could look around me and see everybody involved in the
case except Crask and Sadler. But they were pawns. Of the rest
only Marengo remotely fit. Like the lead Wolf said.

North English might be one hell of an actor. But he had been be-
having strangely ever since he'd gotten hurt. A fact which left me
squinty-eyed with suspicion.

104

Wait! What about the redoubtable Lieutenant Nagit? Mr. Nagit was an excellent candidate. He probably felt underappreciated. . . . Then I recalled something he'd said. Something I hadn't taken the trouble to hear at the time.

An evil globule of bright feathers hit my shoulder hard. "Goddammit! . . ."

"Do not be willfully stupid, Garrett. Do not be willfully blind."

People stared. Only Morley Dotes grasped the full significance right away. He turned, stared at the settling tank briefly, said, "You're one sneaky bastard, Garrett." He showed about a hundred pointy teeth in a grin. "I've taught you well, my disciple."

I ignored him. I told the bird, "No. I'm not being blind on purpose. I really just got it. Block! Colonel Block." He was close enough that I didn't really need to yell. "Find the woman. The mistress. Montezuma. It's her that ties everything together." Stupid, Garrett. Stupid. It was right there in front of you all the time. But she was gorgeous so you just didn't think she could be anything else. If she'd gotten lucky with you, you might have ended up as thick as Gerris Genord. Or well nicked by a meat cleaver.

How did she know Crask and Sadler? From her old days, before she got her hooks into Marengo?

We didn't know much about her. Nobody bothered to find out, no matter what we'd discussed. Why back-check a whore, however remarkable she might be?

She might have grown up with the nightmare twins.

Above, Marengo had found nerve enough to show himself. His mouth was open but nothing came out.

Mr. Nagit had told me the woman never did anything that didn't relate to her meal ticket. That explained why she had hooked up with Marengo in the first place. It explained why she'd work all the angles against the day Marengo lost interest. She'd started that as soon as she'd arrived at The Pipes, already old enough and wise enough to know that the ride couldn't possibly last.

Tama Montezuma would be one more reason Marengo North English couldn't finance his bigoted revolution. Tama would have found a hundred ways to suck herself a comfortable retirement out of Marengo's and The Call's cash flows.

It was amazing what vistas opened once I embraced the possibility that the luscious Miss Montezuma might be a villain. The probability of a connection with Glory Mooncalled laid itself out as though announced by trumpeters. I already believed that Mooncalled was behind the shapeshifters somewhere. I had hoped tonight's festivities would somehow lure him to the Weider mansion, too, probably in deep disguise. But no disguise would help as long as he came within a hundred feet of that settling tank.

Mooncalled would've gotten his claws into Tama the instant the Brotherhood Of The Wolf included Black Dragon Valsung in their plans. How she'd manipulated the Wolves was clear enough, based on the testimony of our witnesses. She'd pretended to be Marengo's go-between. Which the Wolf acknowledged when asked directly.

Tama wanted to be rich. She had only one thing to sell. The shifters wanted a brewery. They had nothing to market but their talent for infiltration. Glory Mooncalled wanted . . . what? Where Mooncalled came from and where he was going never had been clear. Even my partner, who made a hobby of studying the man, no longer understood what he was about. And the rest of the world knew only that Mooncalled traveled his own road and was a real pain in the ass about letting himself get pushed off of it.

The vistas stretched but I still had questions. Lots of questions. How did Tama get them to attack Marengo that night? Why try to eliminate all the main leaders of the rights movement? Or was that all staging? Where was Glory Mooncalled now? Why hadn't I pulled him in? Because of Perilous Spite? Or had he sensed the trap? And where was Tama Montezuma? Had she worked her magic on Mooncalled? That would be a real marvel, those two getting all tangled up in each other.

And: Where were Crask and Sadler?

The noise volume rose as everybody decided to do something. They teach that in leadership school. *Do* something, even if it's wrong. Karenta might have been a lot better off for a little more inertia in recent decades.

I have to confess some admiration and sympathy for Tama. She might not have lost me if people hadn't died. I understood what moved her. But she was too selfish and too sloppy.

All the despair now haunting the Weider mansion could be laid directly at her feet.

Mooncalled is in the area, Garrett, said the voice inside my head. *He is upset. I sense that he had plans for tonight, too, but nothing has gone his way. There may be trouble.*

We didn't have trouble already?

"Let's don't just stand around, Garrett," Block said. "We've got people on the run."

Morley chuckled. "I don't think anybody will get very far. Right, Garrett?"

"I'm not that optimistic, old buddy. Something will go wrong. It always does. Singe!" I couldn't mention Mooncalled. That would spark too many questions. I waved but Pular Singe didn't have courage enough to risk the center of the floor. Which wasn't a good idea, anyway. Almost everybody not in chains was now headed somewhere else in a hurry, many with their eyes closed in fear or in sheer determination not to become a witness to anything.

The gang from Heaven's Gate, however, remained preoccupied with their personal hobbies so didn't contribute to the general uproar. Trail and Storey remained determined to tap the settling tank. They wouldn't enjoy that particular vintage if they succeeded, though. It was particularly bitter, well beyond skunky. I headed that way. "Will you two leave that damned tank alone?" Shale, at least, had had the grace to pass out. Or just fall asleep. "There's all the goddamn beer you can possibly suck down over there by Quipo. Miss Trim! You're supposed to keep these antique idiots under control." But Quipo had reached a point where she was having trouble managing herself.

"Garrett. Heard 'bout you from your fren'. Winger." Quipo was speaking fluent drunkenese. "Where'd she go? Winger. Where'd-jou go?"

"Garrett." Max wanted me.

"What?"

"*Must* these people destroy my home?"

"Block!" I bellowed. "North English! Get your people under control!" Speaking of control, bigger trouble was on its way. Nobody was managing the shifters, especially that last one. It *still* wasn't yet properly shackled in silver.

The stormwarden descended into the chaos. He went among the handful of shapeshifters like a Venageti triage sorcerer, specialists who had used their talents to decide which wounded should go to the surgeons and which should be put out of their misery. Those guys hadn't saved many Karentines.

This guy ended two lives just like that, suddenly, vilely, noisily. Shifters never went easily, it seemed.

The survivors evidently tendered an offer of submission. The stormwarden's golden buttboys got them up and moving. They went docilely, chains tinkling. I wondered what would happen if the sorcerer turned his back. I asked Max, "You want I should do something about that?"

"What?" Weider demanded.

"It's your house." I kept my outrage well hidden. Karentines learn to do that when our lords from the Hill are out. People who won't control their emotions will suffer severe humiliations—at the least.

"Let him have them. They deserve him. Tell Marengo to shut up and get his ass down here. He's been acting like a fool."

North English was harassing his own people from the balcony, apparently convinced that by yelling insults he could make them catch Tama sooner. I didn't yield to my urge to give him a swift kick. Nor would I give in to my inclination to let Tama get away.

While I got North English rounded up so Max could calm him down Morley assembled his friends and mine. He beckoned me. "You've got to get Singe on Montezuma's trail, Garrett. If she gets a big lead, we'll never catch her. She was ready for this."

"Why do you care?"

"Ooh, he's thick," Winger observed. "Dumb as a stump, we'd say back home." She had a strong beer flavor even from six feet away.

"I've got a notion I don't want an explanation if you're interested in it." I noted the not-yet-departed stormwarden watching us from near the front door. I shivered.

Morley said, "Garrett, even Saucerhead figured out that Montezuma has to have a cash stash. Possibly a very large one. She's been milking North English for several years."

"Oh." Exactly what I'd expect of the whole gang, barring Playmate and—maybe—Pular Singe. Hustle out there and disappear the stolen riches before the rightful owner could reclaim them. Then look innocent. I'd seen Morley do it before. The problem was, Winger was the sort of accomplice who wouldn't have enough sense not to start spending like a sailor before the sun came up. Dumb luck and brute strength keep that girl alive.

I don't think Saucerhead understood that. Someday he'll be genuinely unhappy about letting her talk him into things.

I glanced up at Marengo. He still didn't want to mix with us peasants on the main floor. All right. Go, Tama. I didn't mind him losing his money. And him being broke wouldn't hurt Max. Or any of those gorgeous ladies up there. In fact, it'd be a better world if Marengo North English couldn't afford to be a shithead. "What do you think, latrine-beak?" I asked my shoulder ornament.

The Goddamn Parrot was out of words again. Which was just as well. He'd given too many people too much to think about already.

I had a few of my own left, though. "Crask and Sadler are out there somewhere."

Morley replied, "Your pal the secret policeman can handle them. If he hasn't caught them already."

Relway had vanished while I was blinking. Many of his people were missing as well. I asked Singe, "You want to be part of this?"

"Double share," Dotes offered generously, which made Winger sputter. "You wouldn't have to kowtow to Reliance anymore." He knew his ratfolk. Or this ratgirl, anyway. But this ratgirl was smart enough to know when somebody was blowing fairy dust, too. She did a credible job of lifting an eyebrow when she looked to me for my opinion. A double share of what, Garrett?

I said, "I can't go. I've got work to do here. You guys catch her, you bring her back to me." I tried warning them with sudden shifts of my eyes toward the sorcerer. But the fire of the hunt was upon them.

"Winger, stuff it. Bring her back here. I know it sounds improbable but there're issues in this world as important as your greed."

"Ohh!" Saucerhead purred. "Listen to the man growl. Shut up, Winger. He's probably right."

"Be careful," I told Singe and she understood that I meant she shouldn't ever trust her present companions completely.

Their expedition never hit the street.

Garrett. Beware. We are about to enjoy a badly misjudged and mistimed rescue effort.

"A what?"

A racket broke out up front. A centaur galloped in through the front door, a javelin in each hand. It bowled over the stormwarden's glitzy henchmen while seeming utterly amazed to find them there. Another minute and the collision would have taken place outside. The stormwarden had just given up staring at me suspiciously.

"What's this?" Morley asked.

"Glory Mooncalled's been watching," I said. But evidently not closely enough to have seen the truth because that centaur had come inside with no idea whatsoever what he was charging into. He was astounded by the mob looking his way. After toppling the guards he tried to stop suddenly but shod hooves just won't do that on polished stone. He skidded. He howled. He tumbled. He whooped. He reached floor level traveling chin first. His language was enough to make the Goddamn Parrot cover his ears. It wasn't

Karentine but every man in the place had been to the land where that language was spoken.

More centaurs arrived. Each was as surprised as the first. Their faces revealed their determination to free Mooncalled's allies and an equal intent to stifle the man's enemies. But they faced big problems achieving their ends, not the least of which was that they hadn't come prepared to deal with so many enemies. I got the feeling that they'd expected to just prance in and prance back out. I guessed the first wave of people rushing out had lulled them.

None of the later arrivals suffered the full ignominy endured by the first. That fellow started getting thumped before he stopped sliding. Funny, though. At first only my friends and Colonel Block's showed much enthusiasm for the sport. You'd have thought the guys from The Call would be particularly unfond of centaurs. Centaurs are the most treacherous natives of the Cantard.

In a moment the stormwarden had a nebula of slithering lights clutched to his stomach. The ball persisted less than an eyeblink. There was another splat of waterlogged board against stone. The latecomer centaurs got a mighty assist in their efforts to get back out of the house. Sadly, none collided with the doorframe along the way. What must have been sold as an easy massacre had turned into a rout of the killers before they ever got started letting blood.

I looked around. I didn't need outside help to realize that the centaurs had expected to get support from allies already on the ballroom floor. But nobody raised a hand to help. Which suggested that Mooncalled had staged his rescue in near-ignorance, trusting too much in unreliable allies. Which didn't fit his reputation at all.

Did I smell desperation?

Love is blind stupid.

"Oh, no!"

Oh, yes, I fear. Your craziest speculation was correct.

There were more centaurs outside. The uproar out there made that clear. It sounded like a pitched battle. I grinned. My more noteworthy guests must have brought extra help. Just in case.

It's getting to be a sad old world. People just don't trust each other the way they used to.

105

The excitement had ended. The centaurs had fled. The rescue attempt had failed without ever having become clearly identifiable as such to some people. Colonel Block and a badly shaken, poorly focused Marengo North English soon worked out a tentative, fragile alliance. They would work together to catch Tama Montezuma. I suspected that alliance would collapse about as soon as somebody actually caught sight of Tama. Both men had plans.

Both were counting on me, too. If I couldn't get Pular Singe to track Tama, she might never be caught. She might not be anyway. She was a survivor. She'd had a long time to get ready for the inevitable. I figured there was a very good chance we'd find no trace of her.

I told Max, "It didn't go the way I planned. . . ."

"Does anything?"

"Yes. Sometimes. Sort of. We did get to the bottom of it, didn't we? Sort of." And some good might come of it. Suspicion would attach to The Call for a long time. Plenty of people would believe Marengo was behind everything and had sacrificed his mistress to cover his ass. I planned to keep a foot in that camp myself until Tama offered a public confession, no matter what my sidekick claimed. I had a need to demonize North English, to see him as slicker and slimier than he could possibly be.

Perilous Spite departed, leaving echoes of sorcery fading in the street. With him went the surviving Dragons *and* the Wolves. Brief, feeble protests from the rightsists had had no effect. Being a cynic, I suspected the stormwarden's captives might not enjoy the full rigors of justice. A tame shapeshifter would be a handy tool if you were in the sorcery and dark master rackets. Guys like Spite have no interest in justice, anyway. Most are incapable of grasping the concept.

"Why didn't you do something?" I asked the Goddamn Parrot.

Perhaps because I had no inclination to become a part of the stormwarden's booty, Garrett.

I knew that but it still seemed he should have done something.

I am doing something. Rather more interesting than what you would have me waste myself doing. Spite will reap no benefit from those he has taken into his possession. His conscription was far too public.

That sounded a lot like one of those circuitous mollifications he always claims I'd misunderstood when things went to hell later. I couldn't recall why I'd been worried about him the past few days.

My friends stuck around, still hoping I'd give them the chance to beat everybody else to the bad girl. Miss Trim and the crew from Heaven's Gate wouldn't leave. There was still some beer left. I told Saucerhead, "You and Winger and Playmate take the old guys home. Make sure Winger's pockets are clean before she leaves. After you deliver them come back here and help get rid of that settling tank."

Garrett!

"Remove the tank, then."

Kindly get on with your chores. I am expecting company. It will go much easier if the crowd is smaller.

I threw up my hands in exasperation. That told me that he had managed his end not so he could be a card up my sleeve but in order to hook a fish of his own.

"Am I going with you?" Morley asked.

"I'm not going anywhere."

"Bullshit, Garrett. I know you. You want to duck out with your furry girlfriend so you can get to Montezuma first. Not so you can grab some money but because you don't want the pretty lady to get hurt."

I'm not as squishy as Morley thinks. I'd done some thinking about that night at The Pipes, about the would-be visitor and the knife or cleaver I might have seen. I wanted to think I'd seen a changer in Montezuma shape. But I was keeping an open mind. My failing to survive that night might have solved several problems for Tama. Particularly if she knew what was supposed to happen to her uncle Marengo up on the edge of Elf Town.

I was sure she'd known, now.

She almost certainly did. Will you quit dawdling?

"What do you mean, *almost* certainly? You had plenty of time to dig around inside her head."

Easier said than done, Garrett. Her thoughts were terribly murky. She had some sort of protection.

"Well, of course." Was he lying? His motives aren't often clear. Hell with it.

I turned to Morley. I don't mind him thinking I'm soft. It's an edge. "You figured me out." I turned away again. "I talk to the wind." That left him looking puzzled. "After all this excitement tonight I thought you'd want to run back to your place and snuggle up with your favorite squash. Unless you're romancing an eggplant these days."

Winger was leaving with Saucerhead, shooing the old-timers and Quipo, but she wasn't happy or moving fast. She snarled at Block as she passed him where he was hanging around hoping I'd help him. Marengo North English lurked on the balcony above, nursing the same foolish hope. I'd have to ditch them both without being obvious.

Morley and I had been whispering so Singe hissed, "What do you want me to do?"

Morley offered a show of teeth, amused. I told Singe, "This's your choice. You want to be independent. To do that you have to make your own decisions." That would be tough. Ratwomen are more oppressed than most human women. They never learn to think in terms of self-determination.

A smirking Morley Dotes drifted off to send his henchmen home.

"Do you want me to do it?" Singe asked.

"Of course I want you to do it. That's why I asked you. What I don't want is for you to decide to do it just because I want it. I want you to make a choice that's your own, made in your own interest." Gah! That sounded like one of Tinnie's serpentine evolutions.

It's certainly easier being the kind of guy who just uses people.

A stir at the door saved me any more skiprope. A man who appeared to be in his seventies paused to survey the hall before descending to its floor. The guard who should've kept him out seemed not to notice him. Maybe the old fellow was a ghost. He stood stiffly erect, partially supporting himself with a walking stick carved to resemble a fat black cobra. His skin was dusky but not dark like Playmate's or Tama's. His eyes were gray. He seemed to be going blind. He came downstairs slowly, with a marionette's jerkiness, feeling his way with his stick. He looked nothing like the image I'd carried in my head across the years since he'd started acting up in the Cantard. Dammit, this guy was just too old!

Manvil Gilbey, directing a crew already starting to clean up, asked, "Friend of yours?"

"Not hardly. Friend of a friend. Maybe. He should be harmless and he shouldn't be here long." I said that directly to the Goddamn Parrot. "Try to work around him. Don't bother him unless he misbehaves." Which didn't seem likely. I could recall no instance when that old man hadn't had somebody else do his dirty work for him.

Glory Mooncalled walked stiffly to the beer keg. Jerkily, he drew a drink in a mug formerly used by Trail or Storey. A glimmer of fear burned in the backs of his eyes.

I was sure that a lot of calculation and clever manipulation had gone into making this moment possible. No doubt I'd been played like a cheap fiddle for days just so my pal in the tank could manage a sitdown with his hero. With none of that having any real impact on everything else that I was doing.

He was good, Old Bones was. Or I was getting *too* cynical and suspicious.

It's an occupational disease.

"That who I think it is?" Morley whispered.

"I expect so. But nobody's ever seen him. What do you think, bird? Was the mystery man plooking Tama Montezuma?"

The Goddamn Parrot said, "Pretty boy." With a sneer in his voice.

"That does it. Into the pot. Singe?"

"I will help. Not because you want my help but because by doing so I can help myself."

"Excellent. Makes you just like the rest of the team. Morley!" Damned if he wasn't flirting with Alyx. Or maybe Nicks. Oblivious to the fact that the Weiders, father and son, were looking at him in a way more often seen in rightsists observing nonhuman behavior. "Don't do this to me, Morley."

He grasped the situation instantly. "You're right. Not smart. But it'll be torture holding back."

"Tell me something I haven't had to live with for half of forever." I collected Block and joined North English, who still refused to come down from the second floor. "Singe says she might help track Tama. But she refuses to help either one of you." I doubted that she knew who either man was, really, but neither was beloved of ratpeople and a refusal would be no surprise to them.

"Why is that old man here?" North English asked. I noted he kept his back to the visitor. Did he know the man? Was he afraid he might be recognized?

The old-timer took his mug and settled into a chair he dragged over beside the settling tank. There was a quiver in his drinking hand. I had a distinct feeling that it would be a long time before Glory Mooncalled was again a major factor in Karentine affairs. After this interview it would take him an age to reclaim his confidence and build a new underground, the secrets of which were

known only to his friends. He would have no secrets after this interview. And he looked too old to start from scratch.

I hoped the bag of bones inside that damned tank had the gods-
given good sense to do like I'd asked and rifle the minds of
Marengo North English, Bondurant Altoona, and their like tonight.
If we robbed them of all their secrets, we could disarm them, too.
In fact, if he hadn't been just too damned lazy, he might've spared
a mind to sneak a peek at what was going on inside the heads of
Block and Relway and maybe even that scab of clabbered misery
off the Hill, Perilous Spite. But I doubted he had the nerve to try the
latter. Too much personal risk involved.

"Nobody. Friend of a friend." I went back down to Singe. "Do
you have a scent?"

"Yes."

She was a marvel, picking it out of the mess that had to be in
that hall.

I was surprised immediately. Instead of heading for any door
Tama had marched right into the kitchen, past a flabbergasted
Neersa Bintor, into the pantry, and from there had descended to the
cellars below the house. Which, I shouldn't have been surprised,
connected to the caverns beneath the brewery.

"This woman definitely had everything worked out ahead of
time," Morley said.

Absolutely. I hadn't known about this way out. Or in, maybe, if
you had connections at the brewery end. Had Tama been through
there occasionally, say to visit Gerris Genord? Having someone
special to protect certainly would explain his stubborn silence.
And Tama knew how to get her hooks into a man.

I wondered what she would've done if Mooncalled's rescue
gang had shown up on time. Would she have pretended there was
no connection and have tried to stick with Marengo?

As we dithered trying to get lights for my feeble human eyes the
Goddamn Parrot squawked, then abandoned me.

*Garrett. Do not overlook the chance that a great many watchers
will be prepared to follow you.*

"A possibility very much on my mind." I ignored the odd looks
that remark earned me.

106

Morley cursed softly. Somehow, cobwebs had gotten onto the lace of one of his cuffs. Soil was supposed to avoid him. "This isn't the fun it used to be, Garrett."

"Fun? Fun doesn't have anything to do with it. We're the last righteous men, standing with jaws firm in the face of the chaos."

Pular Singe giggled.

Morley cursed again, but conceded, "It is a great way to meet interesting women."

"Can't disagree with that." Strange ones, too. "What is it?" Singe had stopped. She sniffed. I couldn't see a thing. The one lantern I'd come up with hadn't lasted all the way through the underground passage.

We were in the wagon lot behind the brewery loading docks, having exited the brewery through the storage caves. I hadn't been able to stop and share a tankard with Mr. Burkel, who'd been disappointed. But he'd told us we were only minutes behind Tama, who hadn't been able to negotiate the tunnels with our ease.

"She got aboard a wagon," Singe told me.

There were at least twenty of those crowded into the lot, waiting for sunrise. Morley grumped something about have to search them all. Singe said, "No, the wagon left."

I glanced back at the dock. There were two dock wallopers on duty, snoozing on stools under a single feeble lantern. Nights, of course, they only loaded independent haulers.

I woke them up. With sullen cheer they admitted having loaded a small wagon a short time earlier. "One driver," one told me. "Out of Dwarf Fort. They're fixin' to celebrate one of their holidays."

"She's on a cart out of Dwarf Fort," I told Morley.

"Then we'd better move fast." Dwarf Fort wasn't far away.

"She won't be headed there herself. She knows about Singe and she's improvising. She'll get off before the wagon goes inside."

Embarrassed, Singe informed me, "I cannot trail her well if she is riding."

"So how about you follow the wagon? Or the horses, if you can stand the stink? You knew she got into a wagon and there's only been one go out of here lately, seems like you could."

Singe brightened instantly. That hadn't occurred to her. Yet. It would have. She sniff-sniff-sniffed, then headed out.

"Not only brilliant and talented and beautiful but fast as well," Morley whispered. "You don't want to let this one get away."

"Did Marengo North English and Bondurant Altoona rub off on you?" He was ragging me at Singe's expense.

"Whoa!" He started to argue but decided against. "All right. Let's abuse the parrot." Who, conveniently, wasn't around to defend himself. He'd chosen to stay behind. Apparently. I was always the last to know what that overdressed crow was up to. Or even what that critter who figured everything out for him was up to, for that matter. We were in for some headbutting after this mess settled out.

"Wish you'd decided that a year ago. Then maybe held him underwater to see how long he could go without breathing." Singe flinched. She still wasn't used to our banter. It always took her a moment to realize we weren't really about to skin each other. "I'm thinking about spiking your goulash with catnip. Then you'd wake up married to Winger."

"Couldn't. She's already got a husband somewhere. And I'm engaged."

"Really? When did that happen?"

"Oh, back before I was born. I just don't talk about it much. My grandparents arranged it. They were immigrants. They stuck to the old ways. They still try to."

"I'll bet you're a major disappointment."

"They weep human tears at every family gathering."

"When are you supposed to start making this poor woman miserable?"

"Oh, a long time ago. But she never showed up for the ceremony."

"Smart woman."

"She just hadn't met me. If she had . . . I don't know if I could've talked my way out of that. The old folks are stubborn as rocks. They still carry on like it was my fault. They can't blame it on Indalir's family. They have royal blood. As if every elf who ever walked doesn't, the way those people tumble anybody who can't outrun them."

"I'm glad you aren't the kind of lowlife who finds women interesting."

"Definitely one weakness you can't pin on me."

Pular Singe stopped. She turned slowly, nostrils flaring. Morley shut up and began searching the night, too. He loosened his sword-cane. I said, "I hoped they'd lose us because of those tunnels."

Singe said, "No. Not watchers. It is the two evil men who escaped. They met the wagon here." She dropped to all fours, circled, sniffed.

I muttered, "Coincidence? Or prearrangement?"

Morley asked the important question. "How could they know where she'd be? She didn't know. She was just running."

"If she thought tonight might be the end of her run, she might've had somebody waiting outside. Who's going to pay any attention to a dwarf making a beer run?"

"There is the smell of fear," Singe said. "Mostly from the driver but also from the woman. I think she did not expect to encounter the evil men."

"She wouldn't want to run into them," Morley said. "After what they've been through they'd have a few bones to crack with her."

"If they got this far, I'll bet it was because they were allowed to," I said. "There'll be somebody else on this trail real soon, Singe. Probably the little man who tries so hard to hide who he is."

Morley tested his cane again. "You carrying anything?"

"I'm not military but I'm fixed." I did wish that I had my head-knocker. I needed to have some more of those made up.

"Notice the streets are empty."

"They're never busy down here. And there were centaurs around. Maybe there still are." It *was* unusually quiet, though.

Singe squeaked. "Blood. The direction changes. That way."

"I'm blind here," I reminded them. "I'm cursed with human eyes."

"Over there," Singe said.

I went. Morley followed. He confessed, "Her eyes are better than mine, too."

The treasure at the end of this dark rainbow was a broken dwarf. He wasn't dead but that was only because Crask and Sadler hadn't felt any urgent need to kill him. They'd only wanted his wagon. We left him for Master Relway. Singe picked up the trail again. She wasted no time getting on with the hunt.

The cynic in me, or maybe the practical businessman, told me I had to get in good with her now because she was going to be a phenomenon later. All she needed was a little more confidence, a little more experience, and a little more force of personality.

I kept up, puffing. I gasped, "I'm worn-out. These last few days just never made much sense. Everybody I know was mixed up in it, all of them banging off each other and getting in each other's way. . . ."

"Sometimes the world works that way, Garrett," Morley replied. "When everybody heads a different direction nobody gets anywhere."

I understood that but it didn't satisfy my sense of propriety. Everybody jumped into the mud. They all clawed and slashed in squalid pettiness, all the while espousing grand ideals.

I grunted. Morley chuckled, then said, "Here you go launching another clipper of despair because all the humans you know act like human beings."

We really are a tribe of sleazeballs but I don't like being reminded of it. It would be nice to believe that at least some of us are climbing toward the light without pursuing a hidden agenda.

Singe slowed. I took the opportunity to recapture my breath before it got away completely. The ratgirl whispered, "The wagon is just ahead." I knew that. I heard its iron-rimmed wheels banging the cobblestones. "It is a small one drawn by two ponies." Which was no surprise, dwarves not being inclined toward big wagons and plowhorses. "I smell fresh blood."

The coldness that always comes when I think about Crask and Sadler began to engulf me. I was almost superstitious about those guys. I wasn't, strictly speaking, scared of them but I dreaded a confrontation because facing them was like challenging forces of nature.

Morley observed, "They'll still be in bad shape. Their jail time couldn't have been any holiday." In tone more than word he sounded like he wanted to convince himself. So maybe he had his own reservations.

The villains had set a course headed north. Soon they'd leave this quiet neighborhood for one where the night people thronged. Nobody likes to work with strangers looking over their shoulders. We had to do something soon.

"You go along the right side and grab the driver," Morley said. "I'll take the left."

"Me?"

"You're taller and heavier. You'll have more leverage."

No point arguing with the obvious. "Now?"

"Without all that stomping. You don't want them to know you're coming."

Stomping? I wasn't making a sound. All I could hear was the whisper of Singe's nails on the paving stones.

Now there was enough diffuse light that I could make out vague shapes and keep from crashing into walls and watering troughs. Soon I made out the dwarf wagon. Morley loped beside me, in step. I murmured, "I see it."

"Do it."

My heartbeat increased rapidly. This confrontation had haunted me for years.

From somewhere came a loud, "Awk!" in distinct parrotese. It didn't sound like a warning so it must have been only to let me know there was a friendly witness. Which wasn't much comfort since it was hardly possible for reinforcements to arrive in time if I screwed up.

Singe must've been more scared than she let on. She began to fall behind.

Any noise I made got covered by the curses of the man driving. He couldn't get those stubborn ponies to move faster than a walk. Dwarf ponies have one speed. Slow. The only alternative gait is dead stop, inevitably exercised in the event of excessive brutality. Funny. Dwarf ponies are a whole lot like dwarves.

I grabbed the driver's right arm, used my momentum to pull him down. I couldn't tell which man I'd grabbed but that didn't really matter. Crask and Sadler might as well have been twins. I didn't see the other one. He had to be inside the wagon, probably in worse shape.

I glimpsed a surprised face as my victim hit the cobblestones. Foul air blew out of him. He groaned, then lay still. I moved in warily.

There was no need. The anticlimax was real. Sadler had bashed the stuffing out of the street with the back of his head. Shaking with the letdown I tried to decide how to tie him up so he'd still be there when Relway's crew arrived. "I got mine!" I said.

The Goddamn Parrot offered a pleased squawk from somewhere overhead.

The wagon stopped. Morley said, "Crask's inside. He's unconscious."

"Another anticlimax."

"What're you talking about?"

"For years I've expected this. It was going to be an epic battle. Bodies flying around, knocking down houses, busting holes in the street. Going on for hours. Everybody'd have to bring a lunch. Instead we butt heads with them three times in the last few days and hardly got a scratch for our trouble."

"So we caught them when they were weak. That's the smart way to do it. Hang on. This one's bleeding. Hell. He's got a knife stuck in him! I'm not so sure I want to snuggle up with Tama Montezuma after all."

I used strips torn from Sadler's jail smock to bind his wrists behind him. He made vague gurgling sounds. I asked, "Where is she? She in there?"

"Bad news, Garrett. More bad news. There's nobody in here but me and Crask and ten kegs of Weider's cheapest beer. And the dwarves will come looking for that before long."

"Awk!" Eight pounds of outrage in a three-pound package slammed down onto my shoulder. I lurched toward the wagon.

Morley was right. There was no beautiful woman in there at all, let alone the marvelous Miss Montezuma. "Where did she go? How could we lose her? Singe? Singe, where are you?"

Singe didn't answer me. I scurried around calling her name. Morley started laughing. He gasped, "We've been had, Garrett. You realize that? We've been snookered by a ratgirl."

"Yuck it up, you glorified greengrocer."

He kept laughing. "We can't go anywhere without Pular Singe. Not if we want to get there ahead of Relway or North English or Belinda. Only question left is, did the kid do it on her own or did Reliance put her up to it?"

"You really think it's that hilarious?"

"Well, no, actually. I don't enjoy getting slicked, either. I'd rather it was me doing the slicking. But you and I don't really need the money. We just think it'd be nice to keep North English from getting it back. And you want Montezuma for what she did to the Weiders."

I grunted, grumped. "I think I'll just go home and go to bed now."

"Why?"

"I should've expected this. Nothing in this whole damned mess had gone the way you'd expect it to or made any sense while it was going to hell. So I think I'll just wish Singe good luck, drop out now, and let the loose ends tie themselves up on their own."

"Garrett, there's sure to be a fortune involved."

"You just told me you don't need the money."

"I didn't say it wouldn't be nice to have it."

"Tinnie is still back at the Weider place." So was my sometime partner. But he could look out for himself. I was little peeved with him.

"You want Winger to score on this one?"

"You think she'd ditch the old guys?"

"I think Saucerhead will actually have a thought somewhere along the way, will say it out loud, will get no answer, and will discover that he no longer has one of his companions."

"Playmate . . ."

"Is so honest he's easier to flummox than Saucerhead is. He won't suspect a thing if she tells him she had to step into an alley to get rid of some of that beer. Tharpe would be suspicious, though. He's dim but his light isn't all the way out. And he's had experience with Winger."

Relway's troops began filtering out of the darkness. That put an end to all speculation.

The Goddamn Parrot began swearing his black heart out. Maybe my partner took Singe's coup personally even though it didn't really have much to do with him.

107

That really should've been the end of it, I thought. Most of the guilty had been exposed as villains. The whys and some of the wherefores of their crimes had been dragged sniveling into the sunlight. Clever exposure of truths dredged from evil minds and a judicious stimulation of wicked rumor by my sedentary sidekick, mainly behind my back, resulted in an indefinite postponement of the Cleansing. It particularly disarmed Glory Mooncalled by laying waste to his beloved rebel image. The more exciting rumors even stirred a Royal Inquest into the behaviors of Perilous Spite when some of his peers began to wonder if those rumors had substance and Spite might plan to use captured shapeshifters in some wicked scheme of his own.

The Dean Man hadn't dared touch the stormwarden's mind at Weider's but four centuries of observing human misbehavior closely had allowed him to manufacture rumors that got the Hill churning like an overturned anthill. Spite's enemies soon resurrected old questions about his management of the secret and special services during the war. Even his friends began to wonder aloud about several mysteries surrounding his tenure.

Working with Ty Weider, whom he liked for some reason, His Nibs even helped fashion a face-saving formula whereby Ty Weider and gorgeous Giorgi Nicholas could honorably evade an alliance not even their parents found particularly desirable anymore. That mostly took exposure of the truth that only inertia was keeping any of the principals committed and quiet revelation of the "fact" that Ty would be unable to father an heir.

Life was good for Garrett. I had plenty of time to do what I do best, which is nothing.

But Tama Montezuma was still on the run. And Pular Singe hadn't been seen since she'd deserted me, though Reliance and Fenibro both accused me of having squirreled her away in my harem. Neither Belinda nor Relway eased up on their machinations and malfeasances. Neither gave a rat's whisker if the Dead Man did know what they were doing. The Dead Man, of course, didn't make their mischief public, as he did with The Call, Perilous Spite, and his won personal fallen angel, Glory Mooncalled.

The stormwarden was particularly not happy but didn't get a chance to look for the source of his embarrassment. Odds were he never would. He had to devote all his genius to the manufacture of plausible explanations of how a man with his talents could blunder so often and so egregiously while Karenta's chief spymaster and still have grown filthy rich. Rumor began to speculate about possible past connections with the Dragons.

The day had been saved. I think.

At times I wonder, though, if TunFaire really deserves saving—whether the threat is from our own homegrown monsters or those from outside our experience.

If we didn't have a thousand religions already, I'd get me a black outfit and a big black book, grow a scraggly beard and start squawking about salvation and redemption. I know where I can get a black goat.

Grudgingly, of course, I admit that the Dead Man's efforts had made it possible for life to return to normal at the Garrett homestead. Or as nearly normal as a place can be while infested by a menagerie. It was a good week. Not one wannabe client came pounding on my door.

Dean had the place looking respectable again. Saucerhead and Winger had gotten the Dead Man back onto his wooden throne, not obviously the worse for his adventure. He looked like he'd never left home but certainly didn't think like it. He remained way too excited to fall asleep. Strategically, it would've been a great time to take on another tough case. Old Bones was up for anything that would let him show off. The only downside was that he just would not leave off complaining about having been stuffed into that settling tank. And never mind the fact that the ruse had been his own brainchild entirely. I'd nothing to do with the planning or execution of his scheme. I'd had only the shortest and most ambiguous warning that he intended to come to the party.

Dean complained more than the Dead Man did. He hadn't enjoyed having to move out, even for just a few days, never mind that it had been for appearance's sake. He refused to accept that explanation. He was going to make sure I shared his unhappiness.

Fortunately, Tinnie came around several times to help him clean and to cheer him up and to make him feel guilty about being alive. Her visits offered me blessed respites from both cranksters.

I caught up on my gossip with Eleanor. I scandalized Mrs. Cardonlos by telling her that I knew she was a police spy but I didn't mind that. I'm now convinced that she is Relway's creature. But I don't care. Me telling her I know she is a police spy has her backing off. It's clear she doesn't want such ideas to afflict her less tolerant neighbors.

To my complete and eternal astonishment everyone who had hired me paid all the fees and expenses I claimed. I was boggled because there were so few quibbles. Marengo North English astonished me by not holding a wake for each copper he had to let go. I got the distinct impression that he was in a huge hurry to get me the hell out of his life.

Despite all the good news my life was not very satisfying. A lot of people had gotten hurt and not many of the ones who did had deserved it. I couldn't help feeling there must've been more I could've done to keep evil at bay. Something I should probably be doing still.

Sometimes life may make no sense but you can't give up on it. You've got to soldier on. You probably can't win but if you abandon the struggle the darkness rushes in and swallows everything. But, on the other hand, you do get tired fighting the good fight. Me, Block, even Relway sometimes, we all feel faded, like the steel has gone, leaving no heat.

108

I was relaxed. I was comfortable. It was time to go review with old Chuckles. He had to be over his worst grump about how unfair it was that everybody had done things exactly the way he'd told them to.

I strolled across the hallway. Up for'ard Cap'n Beaky rehearsed his lines for his next effort to incite mutiny or mayhem. Once I entered his room I found that His Nibs still hadn't started snoring. "Can we talk now? You've had a week. That's time enough to get over it."

He didn't say no.

"That old man at Weider's the other night. That really was Glory Mooncalled, wasn't it?"

Yes.

"He was a big disappointment, eh?"

Indeed. Time, as ever, is a villain.

I waited. He added nothing, though, so I had to ask, "What wicked trick did time play you?"

Time caused change. The fiery idealist of yesteryear has become a cold blooded, cynical, power-seeking opportunist indistinguishable from those he wanted to displace when he was younger. My illusions are dead. My innocence is gone.

"Pardon me," I gasped once I regained control. My stomach muscles ached, I'd laughed so hard. "That's the best story I've heard since the one about the blind nun and the snake with no teeth. And I was just about convinced that you didn't have a sense of humor."

Your sophmoric jocularity provides striking evidence in condemnation of that entire concept. Which is an entirely human conceit, I might note, and highly overrated.

"Humor, you mean? Hell, even ratpeople have a sense of humor, Old Bones." In fact, fewer humans have a good sense of humor than do members of almost any other race.

Speak of the humorless. Dean interrupted before we got going good. He was carrying two chairs. He dropped them and left. He was back a minute later with a sawhorse, then left again. Next time he lugged in a couple of planks.

I asked, "What the devil are you doing?"

"Making a table."

"Why?"

"For a dinner party. This's the only room that's big enough."

"Dinner party? What dinner party?"

I invited several friends in for the evening.

"*You* invited several friends? Without bothering to consult your landlord?" Or even bothering to invite him? "I want to talk about my friends. You had a couple of hours to burgle brains. What did you learn? Give!"

Nothing of significance which you do not already know.

He seemed unusually reticent. That suggested his ego was involved. Which meant his productivity had disappointed him. "You didn't get anything? What were you doing? Helping Trail and Storey suck down the beer?"

Dean brought two more chairs. I hadn't seen them before. He must've borrowed them somewhere. He reported, "Both Mr. Weiders send their regrets but Mr. Gilbey will attend. Miss Alyx and Miss Giorgi will accompany him."

The proximity of the stormwarden made extreme caution necessary. And a great deal of attention had to be invested in tracking and, in time, controlling Glory Mooncalled. Likewise, the parrot. I had little attention left for mental espionage. He wasn't usually so defensive. His testiness was a clue to his mental state. He couldn't brag about his efforts that night. Which suggested he had done very little that I might find useful. Normally, he can discover something self-aggrandizing in almost anything.

"But you already gave me enough to wreck the stormwarden and cripple The Call. So what was going on inside North English's head? Did he put Tama up to running the Wolves?"

I do not know. I was not able to penetrate the man's mind.

What? "Uh. . . . Not able or didn't try?"

Some of each. Mainly the latter as it appeared it would be a difficult task. He appeared to possess the same protection that the Montezuma woman did.

But he had had time to shop through the heads of Nicks and Ty and Max and discover that nobody really wanted the wedding to go on.

Many is the time I have had to remind myself that he isn't human, that his priorities aren't human, and, especially, that what might seem important to me will be trivial to him. "You did dig into Bondurant Altoona's head, didn't you? And Belinda's? And those of other principals?"

*I attended that confabulation, humiliating myself by allowing
this once proud flesh to be embalmed within a demeaning, noxious
cask, only because by doing so I could at last come face-to-face
with Glory Mooncalled. I invested a great deal of effort in making
that meeting possible. Anything I did on your behalf was inciden-
tal. The appearance of the stormwarden, which I did not anticipate
because I had been out of touch with your researches, complicated
matters immensely. In any event, you brought the matter to a successful conclusion.*

"But not a satisfying one. And now I have to deal with yet another dark suspicion."

Old Bones simply wasn't interested in my problems. He shifted
his attention to Dean, who was back with more lumber and another
report. "Mr. Relway won't come. However, Colonel Block has indicated that he will be present. Lieutenant Nagit will attend." The
old man never glanced at me. This was between him and the Dead
Man and my opinion was irrelevant.

And it was my fault alone that both these vipers resided in my
house. Not to mention that bundle of colorful snake snack camped
out up front. Though that I could blame on Morley. . . .

He did say Lieutenant Nagit? The Dead Man shouldn't know
Nagit from a hitching post. Nor did he know Manvil Gilbey, for
that matter. What the hell was he up to?

Lieutenant Nagit, though? We might could have become friends
if he wasn't so bigoted. His taste in redheads was impeccable.

I might want to keep an eye on him in that area. Unless a redhead
with malicious intent to make me sweat was behind his having received an invitation.

Dean continued, "Marengo North English won't be here."

Now there was a surprise. Would Marengo dine with the hired
help? Who, coincidentally, had become far too familiar with his affairs *and* who had a tame Loghyr on staff? Not likely. Particularly
in light of my sudden new suspicion, which shouldn't have been
that new, come to think of it.

I had to take a few minutes to settle and reflect upon our interactions.

"Miss Tate will be here." Well, of course she would. Would she
ever be far off if Alyx or Nicks were close enough to cause palpita-
tions? Again, not likely.

"What's the point?" I asked. "We can't learn anything new from
any of those people."

The Goddamn Parrot's laughter echoed down the hall. The little
monster launched a rant almost certainly stimulated from outside.

Occasionally I have an agenda of my own, Garrett.

Only occasionally?

"Miss Contague will come as well."

What? Why get Belinda in here amongst the gentler lovelies? She was in one of her manic, deadly phases these days. People who had challenged her rule or who had just irritated her lately were finding themselves dead in alleys or turning up missing all over town—though, to Belinda's credit, she did restrict the mayhem to the realm of business. But when she got into one of these moods where she heard murderous commands in her father's voice inside her head I preferred to avoid tickling her interest in me. I had hopes that interest would fade into complete indifference eventually.

"You left out Shale and his pals?"

Mr. Tharpe and Miss Winger, too. This is neither a reunion nor a rogue's ball.

What was it, then? "Is Morley coming?"

I believe Mr. Dotes is arriving now.

Somebody banged on the door. Dean responded. Evidently he was so excited by the challenge of managing a real dinner that he was willing to assume his other duties without quarrel.

"Why?" I asked. I wanted the Dead Man's plan. He was up to something.

"Not much to do around The Palms," Morley said from the doorway. "Things are slow. Nobody wants to come out while that's going on." He inclined his head toward the street. The racket raised by a really bad marching band was winkling rotten mortar out of old masonry for half a mile around.

The less disciplined and crazier rightsist gangs were attempting to cash in on recent embarrassments suffered by Marengo North English and The Call. They were everywhere, day and night, often armed, usually in the biggest crowds they could muster, trying to appeal to the disenchantment swamping North English's troops.

In the short run the rightsist movement was on a roll. As the faintest of heart of the Other Races hit the road their stronger cousins became more cautious. Fringe rightsists were making themselves ever more menacing by riding the crest of a wave of fear not ameliorated by the relative restraint characteristic of The Call. But they were just more public, not more numerous. I thought the absence of The Call from the streets would hasten the collapse of the more marginal, radical, crazy factions. Without the image of The Call they couldn't maintain a credible camouflage of respectability, rationality, and patriotism. I was sure their popular support would evaporate.

I expected the whole rightsist mess to collapse within a few months. And I hoped recent emotional shocks were enough to keep Marengo North English from pulling himself together before it was too late to keep his curdle-brained brother idealists from stumbling over the precipice of chaos.

It amazed me that nobody agreed with me. Even the Dead Man seemed convinced that the madness could only feed upon itself and grow worse—instead of eating itself up.

The Other Races—those who hadn't yet run for the boondocks—contributed to the misapprehension with their bickering and finger-pointing. I'd bet Bondurant Altoona and his cronies were feeling pretty cocky about their chances of replacing The Call as the flagship goof troop. But all that would change. If I was right.

Strange thing is, the streets are actually safer today then ever before during my lifetime. Bizarre but true. Only the stupidest, craziest, most desperate crooks try anything with dedicated rightsists everywhere, making sure the rest of us humans live up to their righteous standards.

109

"Anybody remember to invite Pular Singe?" Morley asked. He couldn't resist a smirk. Like it was all my fault that the ratgirl had outsmarted us.

"I didn't invite anybody to anything," I grumped. "I don't have anything to do with this. Whatever this might be. It's the chubby guy's shindig. I just live here. I just own the place. I'm going to go up and take a nap while you all party."

Miss Pular has been invited.

"That must've been some trick." He was chairbound and could get word to her when I couldn't dig up anybody even willing to admit knowing her name during my infrequent outings? "She wouldn't come here."

"She'll be here," Morley crowed. "Count on it."

Which meant he was in on the Dead Man's scheme. Whatever that was. "She isn't your average rat, Morley. You couldn't trick her that easily. Anyway, we don't know that she had any luck robbing Tama Montezuma." And outstanding luck that would've had to be. Tama Montezuma was older, smarter, stronger, more experienced, harder and deadlier than the baddest ratperson around.

The hunt for the missing mistress was one undertaking The Call had not deferred. Marengo's snoops were everywhere. He had told them Tama had been the spy responsible for the failure of the Cleansing. And I would be amazed in the extreme to learn that he was wrong. Although sabotaging the Cleansing might not have been her primary purpose, she would've had to keep her changer allies posted and they would've jumped at the chance to embarrass The Call.

Morley showed me more pointy teeth than might one of Venable's babies after deciding that I'd make a nice snack. I knew Dotes meant to mention how disappointed Tinnie and Dean would be once I revealed my new infatuation with Singe. But he restrained himself. So I would owe a moment of charity when I got even for the Goddamn Parrot.

Dotes said, "She is smart, Garrett. You're right. And she's as cunning as a rat. But we've both had ample opportunity to discover that brilliance alone won't protect you from what you don't know. And what Pular Singe doesn't know is that the rumors she's been hearing are pure fairy dust."

"What rumors? How's she going to hear any rumors if she's hiding from Reliance?"

"Oh, we're counting on her being underground. If she is, she can't check out the stories."

"What makes me think something has been going on behind my back?"

Intuition tempered by experience?

"You're behind this? What're you trying to do to me, Old Bones?"

Make you rich? Right after we save you from your dread, terminal disease, of course.

"Ask a foolish question. What disease? I'm healthy as a horse—No, healthy as something decent and sane. A randy thunder lizard, maybe."

No one outside this house knows that. You have not been seen since the day you bearded Mistress Cardonlos.

"She'll come because she worships you, Garrett," Morley said, still wrestling with inner mirth. "She'll come because she won't be able to miss the opportunity to say good-bye. She'll come because, despite what she's heard, she doesn't really believe in this glob of carrion you call a partner."

"I don't call him a partner. He does. Far as I'm concerned, he's just—"

In the meantime Morley said, "Gleep!" and leapt into the air, goosed by the glob of carrion. He didn't come down. The glob was not amused.

I grinned some, enjoying his predicament. I wondered if I could get him to take the Goddamn Parrot back in return for my good offices in getting his feet turned back around below his head and maybe even on the ground. "Chuckles, I don't have a clue what you expect to accomplish tonight. Sounds like you've been spreading rumors that I'm dying. If I'm that sick, why do I want a bunch of people cluttering up the place?"

"You want to say good-bye," Morley said. Hanging bottom up from the ceiling like some kind of pretty-boy bat evidently didn't bother him much. "So you've asked some of the important people in your life to come visit one last time."

"The pain and despair must be overwhelming me. I can't remember why I'd invite Marengo North English and Lieutenant Nagit but not Saucerhead and Winger and Playmate."

All my minds will be employed fully. I will have no attention left to monitor and prevent Miss Winger's miscreances. Nor did it seem likely that invitations to your real friends would attract nearly so much attention.

"Which maybe tells you something about the crowd you hang with, Garrett."

"A crowd that includes you, old buddy. Speaking of hanging around. Keep him up there, Chuckles. Dean, see if you can find a stick. We'll let Morley be the piñata for this soiree."

Dean had just come in with a disreputable-looking pair of chairs he must have found in an alley. He considered Morley. "I believe I saw something suitable in the cellar while I was recovering these chairs." For once in his cranky old life he agreed with me.

Dean, our other guests will begin arriving shortly. Garrett, play along for the time being.

Morley turned over and drifted to the floor. "You should've let him have an extra gallon of beer last night. A hangover might help.

Even in this light he doesn't look like he's dying. Though any honest tailor would be overcome by grief after just one glance."

"What will I be going along with if I don't go upstairs? What do you hope to accomplish, anyway?"

I wish to locate Miss Montezuma. I believe she is still in the city. And I suspect that Pular Singe knows where she is hiding. I believe that because she has broken her ties with Reliance, Miss Pular has been unable to take advantage of her knowledge. I believe we can form an alliance beneficial to all of us if we can draw her close enough for me to initiate negotiations.

Now I knew just enough to feel completely at sea. And I got to ask no more questions because the Dead Man's guests began to arrive, very nearly in a rush. When Lieutenant Nagit came in, as starched as a parade-ground martinet, he was in animated conversation with the redheaded despair of my life. Tinnie scarcely spared me a glance and a feeble wave. Which was no way to treat a dying man.

Of course, she'd be in on the gag, somehow. She'd been to the house enough to know that my health crisis must be somewhat exaggerated. And since they weren't loading me into a hearse, I was fair game for torment. Which explained Lieutenant Nagit.

Manvil Gilbey managed a timely arrival, accompanied by the expected brace of lovelies. Alyx looked as tasty as ever. But Nicks . . . Miss Giorgi Nicholas had made an effort. Miss Giorgi Nicholas must have left a trail of broken hearts all the way to my humble shanty. Miss Giorgi Nicholas looked like what the devil was dreaming about when he invented Temptation. And she'd thrown an extra log on the flirtation fire.

Tinnie ditched Lieutenant Nagit so fast his hair streamed in the breeze as she headed my way.

I suggest this as an opportune time to exercise extreme caution, Garrett.

"Go teach granny to suck eggs, Old Bones." Tinnie arrived. "You look lovely tonight," I managed to croak with one of my last few hundred dying breaths.

"I don't want to see you even looking at that tramp."

"Which tramp would that be, my sweet? The lothario with the epaulets on his shoulders and the board strapped to his back?"

Exercise extreme caution, Garrett.

He did have a point. "Nicks does clean up surprisingly nice. But you'll still outshine her on your worst day."

Much better.

"I knew I should've worn my hip boots." Peace had been declared. For the moment. "What's this all about, anyway?"

"You'll have to take that up with the resident haunt. I just found out I'm dying and you all are here to help me through it."

"You look pretty healthy to me," Alyx said, striking a little pose meant to test her hypothesis. To my destruction.

"Ladies, please. I've only got a few thousand heartbeats left. Don't make me use them up in the next three minutes."

Tinnie scowled at Alyx. Alyx remained oblivious. Maybe that was how she was getting by these days, by just not seeing anything she didn't want to see.

Belinda made her appearance. She, too, had taken some trouble, though all that black still made her seem a gorgeous beast of prey. After a somewhat cool greeting for me she fell into conversation with Lieutenant Nagit, who had been worshipping Nicks from across the room. . . . Where had *she* gotten to?

Gilbey edged close enough to observe, "You don't appear to be in any immediate danger."

"I'm having one of my good spells. Check me again after the ladies go home and I have nothing more to live for."

That earned me a nail in the ribs from the handiest lady.

Once again I had to explain that I had no idea what was going on. Gilbey nodded but didn't understand. "Should you go into remission Max wants you to oversee our interviews for replacement staff."

"Huh?"

"He decided to fire everyone who had anything to do with the conspiracy. He wants to pick up some trustworthy replacements. To do that we're going to have to go outside and take on people we don't know. Max doesn't want to get stung again. You'll interview and you'll background some of the candidates."

All that time cruising on retainer was back to haunt me again. "How'd Skibber Kessel take it?" His nephew had been one of the villains in the stable, back at the start of it all.

"Thinks we let the boy off easy. Skibber is loyal and he hates politics. He hates anything that might interfere with his art."

"Good for Skibber." Most people should understand that brewmasters are genuine artists. The best brewmasters, anyway.

Dean showed Colonel Block into the room. At that point I discovered Morley missing. That made two of them, one of each persuasion, one of whom was a rake and a rogue and a ruffian. "Not in my house, you tailor's dummy!"

"What?" Block had come over to offer his greetings. "If you're as weak as rumor says, you shouldn't be getting excited."

I didn't need to, anyway. Nicks came through the doorway lugging the Goddamn Parrot. Morley was right behind her but seemed chagrined. Was it possible his charm had failed him? I need to live forever because the wonders never cease.

Nicks had the oversize magpie perched on her left wrist. The bird basked in her attention. He didn't say a thing. Was his behavior one of those projects that would preoccupy the Dead Man tonight?

I told Gilbey, "You tell Max to say when, I'll be there. I don't have anything else on my calendar."

Gilbey glanced at Tinnie, sighed a little sigh to tell me I was hopeless, turned to accept a glass of wine from Dean.

Colonel Block told me, "We could always use your talents. Should you recover."

"Righteousness don't put food on the table. How're my two favorite professional killers?"

"Not real good. They were in such bad shape we had to put them in the Bledsoe. Sadler died from his wounds. Crask passed, too, but he might have had some help." Block looked Belinda's way as he said that. "An interesting family. I'd like to get to know them better."

"No, you wouldn't."

Miss Contague and Lieutenant Nagit seemed to be hitting it off.

The Dead Man, I noted, was not a participant in anything. He seemed to be sleeping. But I'd been around him long enough to sense that he was anything but. Right now he was totally focused.

I said, "I'll be upstairs if anyone needs me. A dying man has to get his rest."

Once I reached my room I lay down on my back, tucked my hands behind my head, and began systematically reviewing every encounter I'd ever had with Marengo North English. And my memory is very good.

110

There are ratpeople in the neighborhood.

I jumped. I must have dozed off. I listened. His dinner party certainly hadn't gotten rowdy. Too many people with too many agendas for everybody to relax and have fun—especially since everybody down there assumed that I'd had some sinister purpose for inviting them here. I was confident that not even Morley really believed that the whole thing wasn't my idea.

I am unable to penetrate a rat mind with sufficient finesse to remain undetected but I do sense at least three such minds out there, all interested in this house. I assume them to belong to Pular Singe and her confederates in defying the ratkind Uncle.

Some ratfolk call bosses like Reliance Uncle, presumably because the bosses treat everyone like favorite nephews and nieces as long as they behave.

I did not ask the Dead Man why he figured Singe would have accomplices. That seemed self-evident. Somebody had to be helping her stay hidden, had to be bringing her food and news and warnings. Fenibro would head my initial list of suspects. But I suppose he would receive the same honor from Reliance and thus would never be trusted by anyone as smart as Singe.

It is time for you to stop sulking and rejoin our guests.

"Whose guests? This ain't my shindig, Chuckles."

Come down here, Garrett. Your presence is required.

Well, if he was going to get nasty about it.

I drifted into the Dead Man's room as unobtrusively as a servant who didn't consider himself one of the family. Things seemed to be going fine without me though the merrymaking hadn't turned into a rowdy kegger. On the way I had tested my office door and found it locked. Dean could do good work when he wanted. Following the meal Dean had broken down his makeshift table and left folks free to circulate around the ground floor.

The Dead Man must be a better entertainer than I thought. Nobody had pulled out. Yet.

I stood back and observed, not without company for long. Tinnie wriggled herself in under her arm. "You all right now?"

"I needed to figure something out."

"Did you?"

"No. But that's probably because of my personal prejudices."

Soon afterward Manvil Gilbey developed a strong need to get back to the Weider mansion, dragging two unhappy young women with him. Alyx and Nicks had flourished under the gallantries of Lieutenant Nagit and Morley Dotes. They weren't quite ready for the game to stop. Even Belinda had received some intriguing attention, cautiously from Colonel Block and, much less cautiously, from the amazing Mr. Gilbey, whose inhibitions may have gotten a little assistance looking the other way. So the evening was not a complete disaster despite poor sick old Garrett not having come floating belly up. It could've gone on indefinitely had not the Dead Man lost interest.

Next day the whole lot would be wondering what the hell it had been all about. And their confusion would be all my fault. Of course.

I offered Nicks another opportunity to take the wonder buzzard home but she passed. Again. "But you can bring him over to visit," she suggested with husking voice and smouldering eye and just a hint of a mocking smile because the good ship Tinnie Tate, away momentarily refreshing her teacup, was closing fast, under full-dress sail, cutlasses flashing like lightning.

Morley overheard the part where I offered the Goddamn Parrot. He took the opportunity to remind me that parrots often live longer than human beings do, a fact which amused him greatly.

"I can see it now," I said. "Me and the crow in the clown suit still together fifty years from now, living it up in Heaven's Gate." By then the bird and my so-called friends ought to have made me crankier than Medford Shale on his blackest day. "And a certain contentious old woman would come around every day to bang on the bars of the gate just in case I started to get comfortable or showed signs of beginning to enjoy myself."

"You'd better not be talking about me, Garrett," Tinnie declared. "I'm twenty-six, I like that just fine, and I'm never going to get any older."

I was surprised she confessed she was that long in the tooth. Generally she admitted only to a half decade less. And pulled it off pretty well. "I'm glad to hear it. Maybe you'll keep me young, too. Manvil, I need you to do something. Ask Max if he noticed anything unusual about North English when we saw him. Think about it yourself. Let me know right away if you think of anything."

"What? . . ." Gilbey frowned suspiciously.

"It's probably nothing. I've got a bee in my bonnet that's driving me crazy. I'm eighty percent sure I'm wrong. But I'm just as sure that I shouldn't be. I think that answer is in North English's behavior, but the most unusual thing I can come up with myself is that he paid my fees without complaining. Ever."

Still frowning, Gilbey nodded and resumed the difficult task of herding Alyx and Nicks toward the front door.

I turned to say good night to Lieutenant Nagit. "You overheard what I said. You're around your boss all the time. You notice anything unusual about him lately?"

"I know where you're going. And you're way wrong." But he frowned, a long way from convinced. There was something bothering him. He confessed, "He does seem to have developed a strong spiritual streak since he dodged the reaper."

"I can see how that might happen. Is he more social now that he doesn't have Montezuma to talk for him?"

"No. But I do see more of him because I have to."

"Did you find Tollie? Did you identify that dead man?"

"No. And no. And good night." Nagit went away not happy at all.

Then there was just Morley and Tinnie and Belinda. Belinda was surprised to find herself on the front stoop with me as her coach rolled up, almost as though someone had been reading minds. She offered me a darkly suspicious look.

I turned on the boyish charm. "You knew it would be dangerous when you came here. When you didn't have to come."

That touched her sense of humor. She flashed a quick smile, then swamped me in a brief, impulsive hug that left Tinnie tapping her toe.

"They go off together?" Morley asked as I closed the door.

"No. Nagit might be just smart enough not to swim with the sharks. I wouldn't be surprised if he didn't volunteer to make sure Gilbey gets home safely, though."

Garrett, it is time we moved to the final phase. To do so I must have Colonel Block removed from the premises.

"Damn! I almost forgot he was here." The good Guardsman had been making himself small, perhaps hoping to find out what everyone was up to now. And my brilliant associate would be interested in what the Guard was up to. What Block himself might not know directly he could infer from experience and reference to other sources.

A modicum of respect at last. The colonel?

"I'm on it. What about Morley and Tinnie?"

Mr. Dotes' special skills may prove useful. Pular Singe will not be the only observer in place though I have yet to detect any obvious watchers.

Of course. Brother Relway would have his eyes anywhere any pair of my guests crossed paths.

"Surely there'll be no need for excitement."

That will hinge upon how badly the interested parties wish to gain control of Pular Singe or Tama Montezuma. Ah. The ratgirl has summoned her courage and is approaching. I suggest you see her in the kitchen. I will ask Miss Tate and Mr. Dotes to remain out of sight here with me.

"What about Dean?"

He will have to answer the door. Singe might bolt if you do and she sees that your ill health has been exaggerated.

"You set this whole thing up just to pull her in?"

Not just. It was a tapestry. A work in progress. Pular Singe's arrival is the final thread.

"You learn anything while you were slithering around inside their heads?" I can figure things out. I'm a skilled detective.

Enough.

"Meaning you're not going to share."

Not unless it becomes necessary. Singe is standing in front of the stoop. She will find enough nerve to knock. Establish yourself in the kitchen.

"How about the other watchers? Her showing up will excite them."

Pular Singe is invisible. Go to the kitchen. Try to look sick. Dean! Answer the door.

Singe knocked as Dean and I passed one another in the hall, me wondering how much of that exchange Morley and Tinnie would recall later.

Not a word. They are enjoying a visit with Mister Big. Go to the kitchen.

111

I did my best to hunch over and look miserable as the sound of claws on wooden flooring rasped toward me. Dean was talking but the words coming out of his mouth definitely were not Deanish. Damn! That meant I would have to listen for a week while the old man pissed and moaned about the Dead Man taking control without asking.

I suggest you muster what charm you can, Garrett. This child is more difficult than I anticipated. I cannot examine her thoughts without alerting her to my interest.

I muttered, "I'm beginning to wonder just how much good you are. Seems everybody's opaque to you lately."

The kitchen door swung toward me. I sipped tea but thought about getting together with some beer. Dean said, "Here's Mr. Garrett. Mr. Garrett, it's long past time I retired. I'll see you in the morning. Please remember to lock up."

I grumbled something uncharitable, turned my head to look at Singe.

I did not see Singe. Not immediately. I saw a bent old woman bundled in layer upon layer of rags the way some street folk do. A huge, ugly hat that could only be of dwarfish provenance cast a shadow deep enough to leave her face indefinite. She must have bound her tail up behind her somehow because it wasn't out where it could be seen. She leaned on a heavy cane, which went a long way toward disguising the strange way ratpeople walk.

"Very good. You amaze me yet again. You're going to conquer the world. Tea? Something else? There's beer."

"You were expecting me?"

"I wasn't. Until a few minutes ago. Take a seat." Ratpeople can sit on their behinds although they find human furniture difficult. "Associates of mine wanted you to come see me."

"You're not dying? This is a trap?" Her Karentine seemed to be improving by the hour. She didn't have much more accent than Winger now, though her sibilants still gave her difficulty.

"I'm not dying. Sorry to disappoint you. On the other hand, this isn't a trap. You have my personal guarantee on that. Whatever anyone else might have had planned. That was a clever trick you pulled on us last week."

"Maybe. But foolish." Her "L" sounds still gave her trouble, too. "I did not think through the consequences. A common failing of my people."

"A common failing of everybody's people. Go ahead. Sit."

She sat. I patted her hand, then poured her a cup of tea, pushed across the pot of honey. She showed manners enough not to gobble the stuff straight from the container. Her hand was unsteady as she drank her tea, which she found difficult with a human cup.

I felt a little guilty even though this encounter was not of my manufacture. She was smart enough to understand that her emotions had been manipulated, which meant that they were no secret to those who had manipulated her. Which, of course, she would find embarrassing. "Why did you want me here?"

I reminded her that this was not of my doing but then admitted, "Tama Montezuma. My associates believe you know where she's hiding."

Singe sighed. "Of course."

I whispered, "Montezuma's money means nothing to me. Except that I don't want it to get back to the kind of people who would use it to finance cruelty toward those they hate."

"I am afraid, you know. Very much afraid. I did not foresee the interest others would show in finding that woman. I thought that once she disappeared they would forget about her."

"Human people have very long memories, Singe. Particularly in regard to grudges. Which is a thought to keep in mind if you're ever about to cross someone."

"That is a thought to keep in mind even if you are going to cross a nonhuman. Reliance, I am told, has been very bitter about my show of independence."

"I'll warn him not to be unreasonable. *Do* you know where Tama Montezuma is hiding?"

She had to think about her answer. It took her several minutes to decide to trust me and nod. I didn't become restless, waiting. Unlike other members of the household, I was willing to accept whatever decision Singe made.

I found it both amusing and a tad disturbing that the Dead Man couldn't snoop around inside her head—at least not subtly, undetected. Maybe she could teach me the trick.

"Yes. I know where she is, Garrett."

"Will you show me?"

"Am I wrong about you? Are you just after the money, too? Like your dark-elf friend up front?" She tapped her nose to tell me how she knew.

"Morley? He's my friend. But you're right. You have to keep an eye on him. He has his own agendas. He's interested in Tama mainly because of the money. I'm interested because the things she did caused a lot of people to die. Some of them were people I was supposed to protect. I can't let that go. Not even if I wanted to. Not even though I understand what made her do what she did."

"She is very unhappy. She has not moved since she entered the place where she is hiding now. It was prepared ahead. She can stay there a long time. She cries a lot."

"She sure can't wander the streets. Somebody would recognize her before she walked two blocks." I had trouble imagining Tama Montezuma in tears. They must be on her own behalf.

"She has disguises. But she is waiting for a time when she is mostly forgotten." My look caused her to add, "She talks to herself. Out loud. I found a way to get close enough to listen. That is where I have been hiding most of the time."

"Fenibro and Reliance himself came here looking for you. Several times. They've been at The Palms nagging Morley, too."

"Uncle will have to accept what he cannot change." She shuddered. "Yes. I will take you there."

"I want Morley to go along. I'll keep his greed under control."

"He will be disappointed, anyway. And the copper-haired woman?"

"Hunh?"

"She is in that room with the dark-elf and the bird and something else with an odor like death buried deep. She was at the mansion where the shapeshifters were caught. What is her part?"

A very neutral response was in order, I suspected. "A friend of long standing who heard the rumors you had and came here the same as the others tonight. She won't join us." I hoped. Tinnie made some strange choices when the mood took her and she was hard to dissuade. "She just hadn't left yet when you came to the door."

No telling what was going on inside Singe's head. She accepted my explanation. For the moment.

I suggest you be on your way before she changes her mind. Do not dawdle exiting the neighborhood. I will bewilder and confuse any watchers but I can manage that only for a few seconds. Certainly less than a minute.

I grunted grumpily. Any watchers would want to follow me, not the ragged crone.

Singe made an unhappy noise, too.

"What's the matter?"

"I was dizzy for a second. It was like there was a buzzing inside my head."

"Hunh." She had some slight psychic sense, too? Amazing.

112

"Quite a comedown from a manor in the country," Morley observed. The structure before us wasn't abandoned but certainly deserved to be. There was no charitable way to consider it fit for human occupation.

We stood in shadow, waiting while Singe shed her disguise. I mused, "But it's probably the kind of place she lived before she found out what she could do with what nature gave her and went to work on TunFaire."

"Where the streets are paved with gold."

Everyone comes to TunFaire to find their fortune. Mostly the survivors find despair. But there are just enough success stories to keep the gullible coming. "Fool's gold."

"Ready," Singe whispered. "Follow me." She darted from cover to cover, her true nature guiding her. The Goddamn Parrot fluttered across, high enough to be heard only, not seen, scouting from above. Morley and I followed the ratgirl. Dotes continued grumbling about not being allowed to bring along any of his friends from The Palms. I stopped listening.

We practically stumbled over a trio of ogre teenagers, one of each sex, who were way out of their territory and almost certainly up to no good themselves. They never saw Singe. They turned tail quickly once they glimpsed the equipment Morley and I were carrying. I decided I had yet another reason for wringing the Goddamn Parrot's neck. What the hell kind of scouting was he doing? He should've warned us.

The encounter did shut Morley up. Which would've happened

anyway. He shows no lack of concentration when the situation gets tight.

We took the rat route inside. No front door. We wriggled through a huge gap in a broken foundation That placed us inside a cluttered, stinking cellar so dark even Morley couldn't see and had to be guided to a rickety stair by Singe. She murmured, "Stay close to the wall. Especially you, Garrett. It might not take your weight otherwise." Sounded like she was trying to crack wise. She needed practice. Maybe I'd let her work with the Goddamn Parrot.

The stairs groaned in protest. I sneezed despite a struggle to avoid that. Morley was having trouble with the musty air, too. I wondered why we hadn't just come in using the people route. Maybe I'd ask later. Maybe the simple thing hadn't occurred to Singe. We're all creatures of habit.

Tama Montezuma was multitalented but being a light sleeper didn't appear to be amongst her skills. Moreover, she snored like a drunken boatswain. That seemed way out of character.

The memory of a cloying, sweetish odor hung on the air. As Singe struck a spark to light a lamp for my benefit, I recognized that smell. Burnt opium. Opium smoking is an uncommon vice in TunFaire. It's an expensive, dangerous indulgence in an area where far cheaper, safer substitutes will whack your brain just as far around sideways and leave you drooling and acting even more stupid.

I had seen nothing to suggest she was an addict. But many addicts do function quite well much of the time, if they have money.

The light revealed a woman who had fallen apart, not at all the Tama Montezuma I had encountered at The Pipes. This Tama had fled all the way back to her roots, and beyond, in almost no time. This wasn't the Tama everybody wanted to find. This was a Tama overcome by despair, a Tama who had no more reason to live. This was a Tama who couldn't possibly have a stolen fortune hidden.

"You could have taken her," Morley murmured to Singe. "You didn't need our help." He looked at me. I could see the same thoughts flaring behind his eyes as were exploding behind mine.

"Yes. But it did not seem there was anything to be gained."

Our talk roused Tama. She struggled to sit up. She hadn't been eating well or keeping herself clean. She managed to look up at me. "You finally got here."

"I'm a little slow. Singe had to come fetch me." I didn't tell her I hadn't been looking.

She reached for her pipe. Morley pushed it out of reach. If she was addicted, she would cooperate more fully if he kept that carrot dangling just out of reach.

Morley said, "Get a ring on Singe's finger before she gets any older or cleverer, Garrett. She played not just you but the Dead Man this time."

"Wouldn't have a coin on you, would you?"

"She's wearing a silver wristlet. So is the woman."

So was the woman. They weren't shapechangers. "Tama. You want to tell me something?"

"The fortune everyone thinks I got. I didn't. They knew. They found it. It wasn't where it was supposed to be when I got there." Tama's eyes wouldn't focus but her brain seemed sharp enough. "They only left the silver I took and the opium I bought as an investment. They expect me to destroy myself for them."

I had a mind like a razor tonight. I saw the answer she'd give me before I asked but I asked anyway. "And who might 'they' be?"

"The shapeshifters. The Dragons."

Maybe. But I didn't think so. More likely the Wolves hoping Tama would think Dragons and point a finger that way when she got caught.

Why would the Dragons leave opium behind? It has value even it it's not popular. It can be exported. There's a good market in Venageta.

"But you got all of the shifters, didn't you?" Morley asked me, in as close to a whine as I'd ever heard pass his lips.

"No. We missed at least one. For a while I thought that one might be North English. I figured he really did die the night he was attacked." It had taken only a slight adjustment of viewpoint, coupled with recollections of odd behavior, particularly at the Weider place when Marengo steadfastly avoided joining the rest of us on the main floor, to make me intensely suspicious. I'd decided he must've wanted to avoid running into Singe and her marvelous nose. There'd been other indicators, too, but once I cleared my head, lay back, considered nothing else, I'd been forced to conclude that the Marengo who had returned to The Pipes the morning after the aborted Cleansing could not have been a shapeshifter—much as I might want to stick him with something. But I was just as sure that he was supposed to have been killed. That he was supposed to have been replaced after he was attacked, that he was supposed to return home apparently badly injured as a means of covering and explaining the differences betrayed by the replacement as he took control of The Call. I had a feeling he might have gone into seclusion temporarily while Tama Montezuma relayed his orders to everyone exactly as she had done with the Brotherhood Of The Wolf. I had a strong suspicion that Marengo's bacon really did get saved by marauding dwarves, contemplation of which irony, ranged alongside various betrayals by supposed true believers, explained North English's newfound spirituality. Only I couldn't quite buy that, either. Maybe because it didn't satisfy my prejudices. Maybe because there were still loose ends.

I kept telling myself that there are always loose ends. Where there are people involved nothing ever wraps up neatly. Truth becomes more elusive than leprechauns. Hell, I've downed a few beers with leprechauns. Truth, when I run into it, often is dressed up in a cunning disguise.

"This is new," I told Tama, gesturing at her opium paraphernalia, pushing her pipe a little farther when she reached for it again. "Was Marengo supposed to be replaced the night he was attacked? You knew about the shapeshifters, didn't you? You were already working for Glory Mooncalled by then."

She tried to ignore my questions by focusing on her addiction. She continued to try for the pipe. I could almost hear it talking to her. She whined, "They forced me. They knew what I was planning. Gerris must have told them." She showed no contrition as she confirmed my suspicions by adding, "Gerris thought he was going to go with me when I went away."

"It was you outside the Weider front door the night Genord killed Lancelyn Mac." It struck me like a lightning bolt. Of course.

Tama nodded. "Gerris figured it out. He was extremely upset. We were arguing. Then the cripple and the other one appeared and Gerris made up a stupid story to cover himself but the one who came to the door saw me. . . . I didn't take them seriously enough. They did this to me. To get even."

"By 'they' you mean Genord's friends, right? The Brotherhood Of The Wolf?" I intended to take her confession with a twelve-pound grain of salt. The woman was a professional liar and now at that stage where she would try to lay the blame on anyone she could make fit.

"Marengo made up with them after he almost got killed. They were thrilled. They were ready to do anything—"

"Tama, don't bother. Your head's not clear enough. You can't make up believable stories. Marengo couldn't have made up with the Wolves. He was far too angry with them. What they'd done could destroy all his work. It could destroy The Call. He didn't know anything for sure until that last night at the Weider mansion but I'll bet he had some strong suspicions. Not exactly on the mark, because he was terrified by Perilous Spite, but close enough to worry you. When did Glory Mooncalled recruit you? I'm sure you didn't fight hard. Then you got your talons into him exactly the way you had Marengo and Gerris and your other accomplices. Didn't you?"

A spark of honesty. "Men are such idiots, Garrett. Especially older men."

A point. A good point. I propose the thesis that the span of time during which a man can be manipulated via his appreciation of a woman shrinks as he ages, because eventually—when he's been through it a few times—reality sets in ever more swiftly after the initial rush. "You say the Wolves did this to you?"

"Yes." Of course there were Wolves out there who hadn't been captured, who hadn't been sought, and more who had been released when the rest of the Hill turned on Perilous Spite.

"Just minutes ago you said the Dragons took everything."

"They did. Before things fell apart. The Wolves found me and did this to me and then hid me here so Marengo wouldn't find me until it was too late."

Could I believe this any more than her claim that North English and the Wolves had gotten back into bed?

Singe touched my arm lightly. "The opium is their revenge."

Tama began to weep. Her hands wouldn't stay still. "I made a mistake once. Long ago. When life was very cruel. I told Gerris about how'd I'd broken the habit afterward but I still craved it almost every day. When the Wolves came they knew. They forced me. In Gerris' name. It took them very little time to get me going again. But they left me only this much opium. And only this much money. So when the opium runs out and craving gets so bad I start throwing up and suffering cramps and screaming about things coming after me out of my memories, I'll have to go out looking for an opium seller. That time isn't far off now. And I don't know any opium sellers. It will take me a while to find one. It will take Marengo less time to find me. I don't expect him to be in a forgiving mood."

That rang true. But a lot of people were looking for Tama Montezuma, not just Marengo North English. And Tama Montezuma stood out. Somebody would get her.

Avengers try to be as cruel as their imaginations allow. Not many soft-hearted men survive to become the breed who make up groups like the Wolves.

"What about Glory Mooncalled and his friends?"

"I don't know. He must have run away. The Wolves. They're going to destroy Marengo. Because they think he betrayed them. Because the lying weasel really did keep them together and did send them underground. Then he never did anything with them. I was using them when I gave them orders. Singe thought you should know. I don't care anymore. TunFaire can burn to the ground. The world will end when I die anyway."

Morley muttered, "A solipsist in despair. Interesting."

"I still care," Singe told her.

I wondered how much of this the Dead Man knew or had reasoned out without bothering to tell me. I also wondered why so many people had been able to dodge around His Nibs. Was he starting to fail? Or was it just the way the dice had come up? The unlikely does happen.

My life is a testament to that possibility.

"How many of those changers were there?" Morley asked. "Do you have any idea how many are still running around loose?"

Tama shrugged. Her hands remained busy, crawling all over her, but her eyes had glazed over. We weren't going to get anything more from her until she'd smoked a pipe and then had had time to ease back out from behind a veil of dreams that were sweeter than life.

Dotes muttered, "We'll end up all having to wear silver amulets if this doesn't get wrapped up soon."

He had a point. I didn't have to invest much imagination to foresee a future in which—if the shifters reproduced successfully—a silver test would be part of every transaction. Every home that could afford them would have silver and spells worked into its doorways. The price of silver would soar. "We'll find out. I know who'll know." The Dead Man had been inside Glory Mooncalled's head. Mooncalled would've known exactly how many shapeshifters had come to TunFaire. We could work it out from there.

"What shall we do with her?" Morley asked. Singe watched me with big eyes, as though this was some kind of test. I had a feeling I would disappoint her.

"I still owe Max Weider. She chose the targets. She sent the killers."

I considered my first night at The Pines. That night visitor with the knife might have been Carter Stockwell thinking about settling up. Might have been. But it might have been Tama Montezuma with a special surprise for the troublesome fellow who turned up just as she was about to take over The Call completely.

Separate bedrooms, eh? I owed that little sneak Tinnie an extra kiss. No telling what I'd have gotten myself into if she hadn't been there.

Right now Miss Montezuma looked like the ideal gift for a friend in the secret policeman racket. Nor did Morley demur, she no longer having any fiscal capacity for arousing his sympathy. Singe did feel for her, as for a sister in despair, but even she wasn't prepared to excuse the evils Tama had wrought—of which those known to us were likely to be only a fraction.

113

I sent a note asking Lieutenant Nagit to visit me when next his duties brought him into the city. I received a polite, formal reply to the effect that he was under instructions to have nothing further to do with me. Insofar as Marengo North English and The Call were concerned we had nothing to say to one another anymore.

I didn't try again. I took it up with Max while I was helping interview prospective employees. Morley tagged along and stood around looking bored. Probably because what I was doing was as dull as watching rocks mate.

Nicks sent Lieutenant Nagit an invitation to dine with the Weiders. To no one's surprise but hers Nagit not only showed up, he arrived early, polished till he shone, reeking of rosewater, a bouquet of posies in hand. He was less than thrilled to discover that he'd share the dinner table with me and my feathered haunt but chose to endure the bad with the good.

The Goddamn Parrot attached himself to Nicks as soon as I went over to the mansion, early in the afternoon. They were made for each other, those two. Why couldn't they see it themselves?

Nagit never scowled once at Tinnie or Alyx. He didn't know what to make of Morley since they'd never been introduced. Morley paid him no attention. Dotes was charming to Alyx and all her male relatives. Nagit had no trouble with Max or Gilbey or Ty, either, so it had to be the way I parted my hair. Or something. But he was coldly courteous to me at best.

The servants brought dinner all at once, instead of in courses, then withdrew, except for Neersa Bintor, who made sure the kitchen door stayed closed. She kept her giant maul in hand.

There was little conversation while we ate, though the lovely ladies all tried to get something going, each in her own unique way.

Max growled, "Get on with it, Garrett." He'd barely nibbled his venison and had touched nothing else at all.

I made a small gesture. Morley excused himself from the table. He and Neersa Bintor left the room. With no apology for tricking him I said, "Mr. Nagit, we have one final problem. One more shapeshifter to expose." Now that he had demonstrated that *he* could eat using real silverware, off real silver plates. "Process of elimination says it's inside The Call now. For a while I thought it had replaced your boss. Then I decided it hadn't. You've just demonstrated that it couldn't be you. . . . Yes, boss." Max had begun to glower. He wanted me to get on with it.

I said, "If it wasn't Marengo, I wouldn't much care—except that having a shapechanger inside The Call means Glory Mooncalled still has a foothold there. A reliable witness tells me that Mooncalled has become an evil old man with terrible plans. This shifter could help Mooncalled do truly wicked things to TunFaire. *Then* I realized that even though Marengo hadn't been replaced by a shifter, the way I'd worked it out at first, back when he was attacked, he still could've been later, at The Pipes, in the last week or so. But why should I care? Marengo is Mr. Weider's friend. They went through the Cantard together. And Max is my friend. So I arranged to get you here so I could fill your head with my suspicions. You can deal with the threat to the friend of my friend. You can find the last shapeshifter. The one who left us wondering what happened to Tollie and the one-mitted thunder-lizard lover."

"Venable."

Morley and Neersa ushered Tama and Singe and a short, incredibly ugly little woman into the room. Montezuma was more frightened than the ratgirl was. She had been in the clutches of the Guard for twenty hours, with nary a whiff of opium. The short woman pretended to be a terrified servant of some sort. Nobody bothered to explain her presence. I stifled a grin.

Relway made one truly repulsive woman. But he'd insisted that he couldn't loan out his prisoner if he couldn't come along himself.

I hadn't had the nerve to disappoint the head of the secret police—particularly when I had no good reason to shut him out.

I do believe he nurtured some idea of making a connection and being invited to The Pipes with Lieutenant Nagit.

Nagit never noticed Relway. He blurted, "You found Montezuma. How? We never caught a trace."

"Somebody out your way sure did, Ed. Some of the Wolves. Who'd gotten a word or two from Gerris Genord. Remember, they weren't wiped out, either." Nobody had a big enough grudge. Hell, the Wolves were heroes to a lot of men whose minds followed the same paths theirs did. Good old Bondurant Altoona was publicly very vocal about the treachery of The Call. Altoona might have profited more had he not been blessed with the personality of a toad.

I told Nagit the whole story, the way I saw it now, and added, "Tama says she'll cooperate. Reluctantly." She was a survivor. The only way she might get out of the pit she was in now would be to help save a man who might then hunt her for the rest of his days. I asked Nagit, "How's your status with North English?"

"It's weak. I know too much. He's reminded of that every time he sees me. But he does still talk to me. He doesn't have a choice—until he finds somebody dumb enough to want my job. I don't believe he's been replaced."

"Figure out how we could be alone with him long enough to check his reaction to silver, if we have to. Meantime, tell him whatever he wants to know. And you could isolate your senior officers and check them one at a time. That shouldn't be difficult. The real trick will be dealing with the shifter if you find him."

Nagit shook his head. He didn't want to hear it.

"There is one out there, Ed. Has to be. Otherwise, Tollie would still be chasing sheep and Mr. Venable would only be short the one hand."

Nagit rose. He made appropriate remarks concerning his invitation and the quality of the meal. He bowed in Neersa's direction to let her know he knew who was responsible for the latter. Then he asked, "Can I take Montezuma?"

Weider said, "No." Like it was his call. He was grim. In his heart Max had convicted Marengo of being a changeling already. The wounded Max within was looking for somebody to share his pain.

Nagit didn't argue. He did remark, "The boss will be disappointed."

Max observed, "Mr. Nagit, should you find that your employment with Marengo has become too honorous for your conscience, don't hesitate to contact Manvil. We can find a place for a man of your caliber. Don't you think, Garrett?"

"I can't see any objection to that." Well, except for a sudden sparkle in Alyx's eye and a little smile Nicks failed to keep corralled. And a dig in the ribs, in the same old sore spot, that I got for noticing those responses and maybe turning just the faintest bit dour.

Nagit headed for the street door.

Relway went after him. I didn't hear anything he said, but I assumed he was selling himself somehow, while Nagit was distracted by a headful of horrible possibilities.

"Satisfactory?" I asked Weider.

"Satisfactory. I'm going to turn in now."

As Gilbey rose to help Max, he said, "We'll be continuing those interviews tomorrow, Garrett. You and Ty will need to make yourselves available directly after sunrise." He smirked. He knew well my feelings about that godsforsaken chunk of the day forced in before the sun is sensibly standing directly overhead.

The Goddamn Parrot laughed and laughed.

I just sighed. Nobody promised me the world would be fair. Or even a little sane.

114

I thought that would be the end of it, as dramatically unsatisfactory as it seemed. I judged Nagit to be the sort who would save me the trouble I'd set myself up for, just to keep everything inside The Call's goofball family. But life—mine, anyway—doesn't come stocked with a surplus of dramatic unity. I resigned myself to the boredom of posing trick questions to men interested in replacing workers dismissed from the brewery. Everybody in town wanted to work for Max Weider. But halfway through the third day of tedium following that dinner the gloom parted when Giorgi Nicholas stepped forth for no better reason than wanting to see me.

Or maybe just to visit my stylish shoulder accessory, I concluded, when her killer smile and sparking eyes seemed to be aimed off center of what I considered the appropriate target. She extended her hand. I started to take it.

"This came hidden inside a note I got from Ed Nagit. It's addressed to you. It might be important."

The Goddamn Parrot began charming her as she started scratching his head. I made a growling noise. She was getting letters from Nagit now? Brother Ed wasn't wasting any time.

Lieutenant Nagit wanted to meet. He offered suggestions as to how we could manage that without distressing Colonel Theverly, whose influence in The Call had swollen substantially lately. Theverly had strong ideas about how a freecorps should be run. Those included excluding contacts with outsiders as questionable as me, be those business or social. I might be dressed in human flesh but the True Believers could smell the Other hidden inside me.

"I assume you'll be answering your own mail. Tell him I'll meet him there."

It was a nice autumn day. Big hunks of cotton cruised around a deep blue sky. The birds and bees were extravagantly cheerful and the temperature was almost perfectly comfortable. It was almost possible to forget this was morning, that half of the day the gods laid on us as punishment for original sin.

Lieutenant Nagit awaited me in that same pasture where Tinnie and I had hidden from the centaurs—who had been, only yesterday, finally discovered by cavalry supported by several sorcerers off the Hill. Official TunFaire had a big hunt on for the Dead Man's onetime role model, Glory Mooncalled, too. I was sure nothing would come of it. That old man had been running his enemies in circles for decades.

"Thanks for coming," Nagit told me.

"How could I resist?" His note insisted he had identified the last shapeshifter but claimed he couldn't do anything about it without help. And he wouldn't name names. "Why not handle this in-house?" I had an overdressed dwarf turkey riding one shoulder and a full-grown shrike of paranoia nesting on the other.

"Colonel Theverly insists the matter is closed. *Very* pointedly. There's no one else I can ask for help. Out here they all want to believe it's over. They want to get on with the mission. And they especially don't want to catch Theverly's eye by doing something he's forbidden."

"What about you?"

"He's a pain in the ass, not a god." A declarative statement which seemed somehow evasive. Lieutenant Nagit had something on his mind. And didn't want to share.

Gee. I never ran into that phenomenon before. "Why me?"

"Because you could bring her." He indicated Tama Montezuma, whom I had borrowed back from the Guard by sweet-talking Colonel Block and making several promises I have no intention of keeping. "And with her along we can get to the changer before anybody reacts."

He was right about that. He definitely held back on me.

Nobody challenged us at the gateway to The Pipes even though an increase in security had been mounted. Nor did anyone prevent us from entering the house. There was a lot of gawking and whispering and finger pointing because of Tama, though.

Montezuma looked worse than she had when I found her. Winger would've said she looked like death on a stick, well warmed over. Her will had collapsed in the cruel torment of withdrawal. She had little reason to go on. But she'd been lucky, in a way. Relway hadn't been around to abuse her.

I didn't go in there with nerves of steel. I had only Tama and Nagit to count on and no faith that either would stand behind me. I was betting to an inside straight. And Moms Garrett had taught me better over twenty years ago.

Was Lieutenant Nagit conning me? Or worse? The man was a true believer in the raging lunacies of The Call. He shared a domicile with numerous gentlemen who bore me huge grudges. I'd seen several familiar Wolf faces already.

Then came a shock that flipped the old pump. We ran into the ugly little woman who looked so much like Deal Relway's twin sister, scrub scrub scrubbing the hallway floor.

Lieutenant Nagit considered her beneath notice even though it was his fault she was haunting the manor. Apparent inconsequence is Relway's great and frightening strength.

The man guarding Marengo's sanctum didn't quite know what to do when Lieutenant Nagit stomped past without bothering to ask to see North English. The fellow must have been a soldier in his earlier days. Marines are taught to think on their feet.

We were through the doorway before he reacted.

As Lieutenant Nagit had promised as we walked, there were several men cozied up with North English. One was my old skipper, Colonel Theverly, who still didn't remember me. Another was the gent who had spoken for the Wolves at Weider's. What was his name? Tilde? Evidently he was back in good odor. There were oth-

ers, all elderly. Great. I didn't see a spry bodyguard anywhere
around.

Our advent interrupted a heated discussion. A frustrated Theverly wanted North English to approve something operational.
North English seemed unable or unwilling to grasp the fact that
this was the perfect moment for whatever the colonel had in mind.
I did catch the Weider name, though.

There was a lot of anger in the air. It blistered in North English's
eyes. He surged out of his chair, about to vent that rage on whatever idiot had dared to enter his sanctum uninvited.

He saw Tama. He froze. There couldn't have been anyone he
less expected to see.

We kept moving. Lieutenant Nagit said, "See what Mr. Garrett
caught. I was sure you'd want to see her right away."

"Uh . . . Yes." Confused and puzzled as well as angry, North English finished rising. And fear began to drive earlier emotions off
his face. That seemed to shimmer momentarily as he gawked at
Tama. Maybe that was a trick of flickering bad candlelight. Or of
my imagination.

Theverly, Tilde, and the old men gawked, too. They hadn't expected to see Tama Montezuma again. Which effect was exactly
what Lieutenant Nagit wanted her to produce. Tilde seemed almost
distraught. Was it possible that Tama's hoard hadn't found its way
back into the loving embrace of the chieftain who had denied the
Wolves repeatedly?

I shoved Tama forward. She fell at North English's feet. He
would be target the first. Tama played her role flawlessly. She was
a superb actress, her skills honed in a harsh school. I couldn't have
pushed her around if she hadn't been willing to cooperate.

Tama lunged into Marengo's legs. He squawked, flung himself
backward. Colonel Theverly had an impulse to help North English
but he couldn't manage much on one leg. He would be target two,
chosen so because of his handicap. I kept an eye on him because,
the way I'd worked it out, he was more likely a villain than North
English, despite my prejudicial preferences.

Lieutenant Nagit surprised me by slipping a silver-chain noose
over Marengo's head. He got behind North English. I grabbed
Marengo's right arm. Tama caught his left and held on for dear life,
which was about all she could expect to get out of this.

Nagit had scammed me mildly. I hadn't thought he believed his
boss was the shifter. But he had started murmuring a mantra of a
prayer that he'd figured this correctly. If he hadn't, he was going to

wish he was doing his time in Hell already. With me right across
the dining pit saying, "Please pass the brimstone." When this was
over I was going to kick his scruffy butt. He could've given me a
little more to go on if I needed to change my mind again.

As Nagit had hoped North English's companions remained so
stunned they did nothing for the vital few seconds it took him to get
Marengo under control. A long moan escaped North English. He
shimmered, began to get soft, spongy, loose, and I knew for sure
now that Max Weider had yet another loss to mourn. And I had to
go back and tell him. And I had to go back and think all the evidence through yet again because I'd been ready to give North English a pass despite his odd behavior.

When did his replacement occur?

The old men began to babble in confusion as it became obvious
that their boss not only wasn't Mama North English's beloved son,
he was one of *them*. One of the Other Races.

North English gave one violent surge, then just lost control. He
strained to change but couldn't manage it in any useful way. Silver
poisoning caused his body to grow more and more limp. By the
time Tilde managed a lame effort to pull Tama away the arm she
held had stretched two feet. Marengo's face had wax-melted into
something not human at all. It looked like a giant slug's head.

I used a foot to push Tilde away, said, "Find more silver, soldier.
Anything silver." Theverly kept hopping and I kept watching him
closely. A glare was enough to control the old men. The paranoia
I'd brought with me began to whisper of the possibility that there
were still more shifters to be found. I was developing the suspicion
that I might spend the remainder of my life as worried about change-
lings as I was about horses. In a few strange years I could be one of
those street prophets who screech doom and despair and weird
conspiracy at the most embarrassing times. . . .

The Marengo changer didn't fight with the ferocity and vigor
we'd seen from others earlier. Maybe he was young, not yet at his
full strength and wickedness. Maybe he'd worn himself out passing as Marengo. Maybe it was because he was alone, the last of his
kind, lacking the psychic support of fellow changers. He had sunk
to the floor before Tilde and the old men began to jabber about the
implications this had for The Call. I held on, shaking, wondering
what insanity had put me here. I couldn't imagine myself commit-
ting deliberate murder even though that was the custom in these
situations. I felt the changer weakening, losing its plasticity. Soon
it just lay there shivering.

I kept that eye on Colonel Theverly every second. His gaze locked with mine. I let go the shifter with one hand, plucked my own silver chain from inside my shirt. I'd brought it just in case. I hadn't wanted to reveal it. Theverly's face changed, but only into a slight frown. "I should know you from somewhere, shouldn't I?"

"Yeah. You should. The islands campaign." I couldn't find a "sir" inside me anywhere.

"Ah. I was there only a few—Three Force. Black Pete's bunch. Sergeant Peters. You were the kid who could find a girl anywhere, even in the middle of an uninhabited swamp. Garrith? Garrett."

Shucks. He was embarrassing me.

"Did I pass, Garrett?"

No changer could've learned all that. I nodded.

The door opened. A butler type with a refreshments tray invited himself into the room. "Damn my eyes!" I muttered. What a clever pose for a mastermind.

"The tea you requested, sir. . . ." Mooncalled's eyes bugged as he took in the scene. The tea service crashed and splashed.

Through clenched teeth I told anyone who cared to listen, "Grab him! That's Glory Mooncalled. He's the one behind everything that's gone wrong."

Theverly responded instantly. Unfortunately, the race seldom goes to the one-legged man.

The old man was spry. He was out of there before anyone else made up his mind that I might be right. They were just getting their minds around the fact that Marengo North English wasn't Marengo North English anymore. And Tilde was handicapped by his opinion of Colonel Theverly, who tried to order him to get after Mooncalled.

That old man hit the hallway and vanished into thin air, never to be seen again. Even now I don't quite accept Relway's assurances that the man didn't change shape as soon as he was out of our sight. Relway isn't what I call an unimpeachable witness. But the Dead Man also insists Mooncalled was no shapechanger. However, it hasn't exactly been that long since the world proved that His Nibs can be fooled, too.

No matter. Like Tama Montezuma, Glory Mooncalled is a survivor. But he's definitely out of business now.

We didn't finish strangling the shapeshifter. Once Lieutenant Nagit got a good, controlling choke on the thing and had breath of his own left to gasp out a few words he started lobbying Tilde and Theverly alike. His chatter became a constant in the background, like a ringing in the ear. Eventually, he won his point. His mutiny was excused. But Theverly and the Wolf, having formed an alliance without a word being spoken, insisted on taking possession of the changer.

Both men looked like they had a score or two to settle. Both were wondering just how long this thing had been managing and manipulating the movement. I didn't tell them it couldn't have been more than a few days. Already it was their messiah of misfortune, assuming the blame for every screwup in the last three millennia.

Damn! If they were clever enough, they could gain back everything The Call had lost—and more—by playing the existence of the changer off against rightsist prejudice.

You could see Theverly and Tilde evolving, the way humans do when huge changes in their power ecology occur. I made a small sign to Tama. I let go of the shifter's now-rubbery, flaccid limb. "It's all yours now, Ed."

I grabbed Tama's hand. "Time we made ourselves scarce, darling. Let this family clean its own house. Next time you're in town, Ed, if you've got nothing better to do, come by the house. We'll round up Tinnie and Nicks and go out to this romantic little ethnic place I know." Maybe I could find a place that served stuffed, roast parrot.

"I'll look forward to it."

Tama and I hit the hallway. I pushed hard getting out of the house. Heading across that big pasture out front, I whispered, "Keep moving, woman. Get as big a head start as you can. Nobody else promised you anything." Actually, Nagit had but we'd all known that he was lying.

"You going to keep your promise?"

"I always try to, no matter what. Even if I'd rather not. Because my word is really the only thing I've got to sell." We were moving fast, headed toward the gate. All I'd ever really offered her was a running start. If our paths crossed again, I'd pick up my grudge on behalf of the Weiders instantly. I wouldn't have any overriding obligation to society, as the Dead Man had argued in our discussions of Marengo.

"I'm not much on remorse, Garrett. But I do regret that what happened happened. It wasn't planned. For what that's worth."

"It's not worth much. But I do understand. I'm going to have a regret or six when I look back on all this myself."

"Maybe we'll have better luck in the next life."

"Maybe. See you there."

Tama turned south after we left the estate, broke into a long-legged, ground-eating lope. I turned north. Never the twain to meet. But meet something I did, in just a quarter mile. It looked a whole lot like Deal Relway in drag. He must have been planning a party because he had a whole lot of friends with him. I observed, "I take it you've given up the day job." How had he gotten out here with all these secret police thugs? I hoped he didn't have some dumb idea about trying to raid The Pipes. Those people up there were confused, but they wouldn't be shy about burying a few nosy Guardsmen in the back pasture.

Then my paranoia returned. There were lots of secret policemen and only one Garrett. And I was handicapped by the weight of the world's premier talking chicken. But Relway just wanted to chat.

"Soon as you exposed North English as a changer I knew there wasn't much future in scrubbing his floors. Nobody else in The Call can hold that mob together. I got out and waited out here."

"I never did see what his followers saw."

"That's because you're a cynic and a pessimist functionally incapable of believing in anything bigger than yourself."

The Goddamn Parrot began to snicker like he'd just heard a potent off-color joke.

"Bird, you and me and a roasting pan got a three-way date when we get home."

Relway mused, "Now that it's happened I'm not so sure I'm happy with the outcome. Spared their racial theories The Call would've been good for TunFaire."

He would appreciate their interest in law and order and proper behavior. "Here's a challenge you still need to meet. Glory Mooncalled. He's weak now but he's still out there somewhere. If you don't get him now he'll try to put something back together someday. He can't help himself."

"It's still great day for TunFaire, Garrett. One of pure triumph."

I don't know if he meant that or was being sarcastic. You never quite know anything with Relway. And he wants it that way.

"I liked the way you put it, Garrett. Faded steel heat." I'd mentioned that to him the night he'd discovered the tanks in the old Lamp brewery.

"But the war goes on."

"The war never ends. Tell you what. Send me a note when you do decide to roast that pigeon. I've got dibs on a drumstick."

"Ha! You hear that, bird? Your time's almost up."

"Help! Please don't hurt me anymore. . . ."

Chuckling, Relway said, "Don't forget to pick up your rat friend on your way home."

"Huh?"

"The guys say she's hanging around in those trees over there. Lurking and skulking. General rodent stuff. Probably worrying about you. Would've been amazing to see her try to rescue you from all those thunder lizards and rat-haters."

The Goddamn Parrot had a good laugh at that. I couldn't think of a thing to say, then or when I did see Singe.

Life's a bitch. But it does go on.

Kara Dalkey

STEEL ROSE

☐ 0-451-45639-4/$5.99

"Dalkey's meticulous research pays off in ravishing atmospherics...."—*Publishers Weekly*

"Quirky and colorful enough to stand out from the crowd."—*Locus*

"A nice blend of humor and drama...an enjoyable light fantasy."—*Starlog*

CRYSTAL SAGE

☐ 0-451-45640-8/$5.99

"Dalkey's meticulous research pays off in ravishing atmosperics..."—*Publihsers Weekly*

S T A R G Å T E

SG · 1
The Price You Pay
by Ashley McConnell

SWORDS OF HAVEN

The Adventures of Hawk & Fisher
by Simon R. Green

THE BORDERS OF LIFE

by G.A. Kathryns

July 1999